The American Tyranny of 2020

By Dr. Patrick Johnston

The American Tyranny of 2020
by Dr. Patrick Johnston

Printed in the United States of America

ISBN 9781619043015

www.xulonpress.com

Acknowledgments

This novel is dedicated to all of the gentle Christian warriors who faithfully pray and labor to save children from death by abortion. You are God's remnant, who stays His gavel of judgment from falling against this nation for the shedding of innocent blood. In due season you will reap, if you faint not. Be faithful, and you will see your Promised Land.

I want to thank all of those who edited this second volume of the Trilogy: Cal Zastrow, Don and Carolyn Asbell, Tammy Johnston, Tenney and Shirley Fuller, Matt Byers, and my daughter Charity Johnston. May the Lord reward you for your service to Him.

Part I

The Remnant's Cup

Chapter 1

Austin, Texas

"You're under arrest."

A look of utter horror emanated from the abortionist's face as one of the irate police officers thrust him against the wall and began to frisk him. A second officer retrieved the physician's .38-caliber pistol from the bloodstained tile floor. The abortionist sniffed the blood that drained from his nose and began to sob. "I, I shot him in self-defense."

"What!?" The officer took offense at the doctor's justification of putting a slug in the sheriff's shoulder. "He didn't even have his gun drawn!" The officer pushed the suspect against the wall with more vigor, kicking his legs apart to frisk him more thoroughly. "It was the sheriff's mistake to trust a baby-killer."

Dr. E whined in a high-pitched squeal, "But the state Supreme Court ruled that the state's abortion ban was unconstitutional!"

The officer didn't show an ounce of sympathy, and spoke gruffly while squeezing the cuffs tightly around the abortionist's wrists. "Save it for the jury. You have the right to remain silent. Use it."

David Jameson stood in the doorway with his hands in his pockets, his muddy orange U.T. cap low on his brow. He prayed a final prayer for the hemorrhaging woman who was being wheeled down the aisle in a gurney, having suffered through half of an abortion procedure. "God, drench her in Your mercy. Save her…"

In the corner of the room the nurse set down her clipboard and tried to scoot by Jameson and dart for the exit. He put up a palm to stop her. She skidded to a halt, her forehead six inches from David's right hand. "And where do you think you're going, ma'am?"

One of the officers cast an angry glance at her. "You're under arrest as an accomplice! Stay!"

She nodded and began to cry as the officer led the abortionist from the room and another officer headed toward her.

David felt as light as air while he followed the officer down the hall over the well-trodden beige carpet of the last abortion clinic in Texas.

The abortionist regained his composure and waxed bold when his staff saw him being led down the hall in cuffs. "This is wrong!" he blurted out. The bloodied and hysterical abortionist continued to protest his arrest. "Texas' abortion ban is wrong!"

"You've got no business lecturing us on right and wrong," the officer rebutted, jerking on his cuffs.

"And neither do corrupt courts," the other officer spat. This physician had dared to test the resolve of Governor Henry Adams after the Texas State Supreme Court attempted to rule his Texas Life Bill as unconstitutional. In the eyes of these officers and most Texans, Dr. E was a mass murderer.

Behind David, the clinic nurses and secretaries were led out in cuffs. They were much more subdued than their angry boss, freely confessing the clinic's medical and legal violations, hoping to win leniency from the authorities.

David overheard the moans from the state investigators who combed through the patient rooms for evidence. Their gasps of disgust reminded him of what had been happening in this abortion mill for decades. As they dismantled the suction machines and sifted through the containers of bloody debris and little carcasses, David knew all too well what they were encountering.

He stopped to check on Sheriff Wellington, who lay on a gurney while paramedics applied a pressure bandage to the gunshot wound in his right shoulder.

"Are you going to be all right?"

The sheriff saw David and smiled. His speech was slurred, evidence of his second morphine injection. His gaze darted to his wounded shoulder, then back to David. "I've never been so proud of an injury in my whole life. Lord willing, this will be the last blood ever to be shed in this place."

David smiled back. "Praise the Lord."

"My boys said that you did an amazing job back there. You saved that abortionist's life."

"Thanks." He grinned sheepishly as if he were unaccustomed to praise. "That's one compliment I honestly never expected to receive."

When David stepped out the front door of the abortion clinic, camera flashes reminded him that he was still a wanted man. He nudged his muddy orange U.T. cap lower over his brow and brought his right hand up to massage his thin, light brown goatee.

The yellow school buses were emptied of all the pro-lifer protesters who'd been arrested. There was no evidence of the U.S. Army or the FBI SWAT teams, which were in full retreat. The Texas State Guard formed a perimeter around the pro-lifers who had trespassed onto the abortion clinic property. Some FBI agents filmed the event from the roofs of nearby buildings while two helicopters circled overhead. Some agents pointed sniper rifles at the crowd below. It was a potent reminder that the battle for justice was far from over.

David gazed in awe at the throng of gentle Christians rejoicing, clapping, cheering, and singing. The last abortion clinic in Texas was being shut down, and the church of Jesus Christ was ecstatic. Suddenly, an unfamiliar emotion welled up inside of him. It startled him as if he had been unexpectedly pricked in his chest with a needle. The joy drained from him and he turned his attention to his own heart, trying to discover exactly what so troubled his conscience. He made his way down the three stairs into the crowd of pro-lifers as the child-killers were being led away to squad cars.

He turned beside the stairway handrail and began to study the entrance of the clinic. Nausea welled up inside him. The words "Austin Women's Clinic" were tacked up in black wooden letters over the double doors. His heart grew heavy and his countenance drooped, contrasting sharply with the elation of those around him.

His mouth went dry and he swallowed hard. His lips mumbled the words, "Maybe this was the place."

He felt a heavy hand rest on his left shoulder and heard a familiar voice utter "Praise God." He turned to see the joyous grin of his friend, Elijah. Elijah's thick black lips thinned as they widened, but David couldn't find it in himself to smile back. He turned from Elijah back to the clinic and Elijah asked a question that pained David's heart. "This was the place for what?"

David's face reddened. Beads of sweat broke out on his brow. Elijah's smile faded when he saw that David appeared to swoon. "David?" Elijah moved in front of him and placed a hand on each of his shoulders. He tried to make eye contact with him, but David wouldn't distract his gaze from the clinic doors. "Are you all right, David?"

Suddenly, David began to weep. It wasn't just any cry, but a deep wail that erupted from David's bosom. It was as if a stream of volcanic lava had suddenly broken through the rock and shot out an ugly spray of ash, steam, and orange liquid stone into the cool blue sky. It was the kind of weeping that one would expect if someone has just learned that his whole family had been killed. It was unlike anything Elijah had ever heard. David appeared overcome with grief and horror. Elijah was at a loss to discover what had afflicted David so. "David, I'm here for you, man."

David ignored Elijah's pleas and fell to his knees in a mournful cry. Elijah knelt down beside him. "David! What is it?" David's bitter crying summoned the pity of those nearby, and they asked Elijah if his friend was okay. Elijah ignored them and leaned down close to David. He watched David heave great pitiful sobs over and over again until Elijah began to insist, "Tell me what's bothering you. Tell me what I can do for you?"

"Oh, I'm so sorry, Lord!"

"What is it, David?" Elijah dipped underneath David's cap and saw tears dripping down David's grimacing face. "How can I pray for you brother?"

Without making eye contact, he said, "Pray for Darlene. Pray for my family."

"About what?"

The question caused weeping to break out afresh. David wiped his tears with the back of his hands. Then he grabbed the sides of his U.T. cap and pulled it as low as he could over his head. He bowed his face so low to the ground that the front of the cap sunk an inch into the mulch of the trampled flowerbed.

Between heaving sobs, Elijah managed to hear David mumble, "I've got to tell her."

Colton, Texas

"What's she doing? I can't hear her well."

A gray-haired senior federal agent rolled his chair across the room till he was next to a bald-headed agent who wore a set of headphones tightly over his ears. They sat in front of two large computer screens.

The senior agent's gaze darted from the screen to the agent two decades his junior. "What's she doing?"

"My system records the kitchenette and bathroom. I can't hear whatever it is she's doing in the bedroom."

They sat in the room beside Darlene Jameson and her three young daughters, spying her every move in the hopes that her elusive husband - the most wanted man in the country - would contact her. A whole team of the FBI's best investigative agents had been assigned this duty, but because of what just happened outside of the Austin Women's Clinic that morning, the others were occupied with contacting their superiors and receiving new directives.

The senior agent donned a second headset over his ears, and without distracting his gaze from the computer screen, he blithely reported, "She's praying."

"Dear God, keep him safe." Darlene sat at the foot of the twin bed, holding the hands of her two oldest girls while the 1-year-old girl played with a Veggie Tale toy on the floor. Her prayer had dwindled to a whisper. After ten minutes her 3 and 4-year-old daughters became distracted and paid more attention to their sibling on the floor than to their mother's prayers. "Be the glory and the lifter of his head," she mumbled, her head bowed reverently. "Be his Savior and Deliverer. Exalt him to be a prophet to the nation, to stand before governors and leaders and show them the way to righteousness and blessing..."

The 4-year-old girl let go of her mother's hand and pointed excitedly at the muted television. "Look Mommy, Daddy's on TV."

Darlene raised her eyes to the screen and grabbed the remote control. She unmuted the station as the newscaster reported the breaking news story with the picture of David Jameson on the screen to the newscaster's right.

She caught the newscaster mid-sentence: "...who is the chief suspect in the terrorist attack in Ohio two months ago that killed President Raymond Fitzgerald and over 3,000 pro-choice activists and healthcare workers, including dozens of judges and congress-persons. This photograph was taken after David Jameson apparently assisted the sheriff of Austin, Matt Wellington, in the first arrest of a physician for the crime of committing an abortion since before the *Roe v. Wade* Supreme Court decision in 1973..."

Washington, D.C.

President Brighton was watching the same breaking news story on her desktop computer when her cell phone vibrated. She glanced at the caller ID, then with a "Humph" tossed the phone onto the desk in front of her and let the vibrations continue unanswered. She stared deep into the face of David Jameson on her screen. She knew he was innocent. She knew that the explosion in Columbus was an accident and that Jameson was an innocent bystander.

But the arrest and conviction of this man would save her administration, and her administration could save the country. The congressional calls for the details of the Bureau's investigation of the explosion would cease. The burly Texas governor's popularity would take a fatal plunge if his connections to a convicted terrorist, however sparse those connections were, could be exploited. The momentous calls for her impeachment from the floor of the House of Representatives would lose its teeth. If only they could convict David Jameson of the most deadly domestic terrorist attack ever committed by an American, then she would have a face that would exemplify the far-right extremism, the homophobic, anti-choice hatemongers. Fanatics like David Jameson would turn this country into a sexist, fascist theocracy if they had their way. They had to be stopped.

The phone vibrated again. She glanced at it and noticed that it was the same caller, but this time she answered it.

"Madam President, I have good news."

The president let a long uneasy moment pass before she answered. "I have a question, Mr. Hamilton."

The director of the FBI overheard the chatter of a newscaster in the background. He let out a heavy sigh, knowing what must be coming.

"How many billions of dollars, Mr. Hamilton, do we expend on domestic intelligence?" Her voice was cold and loud.

Todd Hamilton stuttered a response. "Uh, well, Madam President, I suppose you're asking this because—"

"How much do you make every year, Mr. Hamilton?"

Hamilton didn't answer the question, which he found quite irrelevant to remedy the day's tragedies. The president wanted to make a point, so he thought it best to be quiet and let her. She sat upright at her desk. "It's a lot of money, isn't it?"

"It's above average, Madam Pres—"

"Tell me then, Mr. Hamilton," she interrupted him, "how does a freelance photographer on welfare gain intelligence that we cannot?"

Todd Hamilton snickered. "I suppose he was in the right place at the right time."

A second call came through on the president's computer line. She glanced at the caller ID on the top of the screen and told Hamilton, "Find out where he is. I've got to go."

"Yes, Madame Presid—"

The president cut Hamilton off with the tap of a button and a woman on the other end of the line said, "Madame President, hold for General Tiller."

"No, I'm not holding for General Tiller! Tell him to—"

"Here he is, here he is." The anxious woman quickly handed the satellite phone to General Tiller and the live feed appeared on the bottom right hand corner of the president's computer screen. She tapped a button on her keyboard to maximize the image of the general and minimize the television news broadcast.

"Did I give you permission to turn tail and run, General Tiller?" The president's voice cracked and strained at an ear-piercing volume. The disgraced general's embarrassment was immediately evident on her monitor. "You backed down in front of the only functional reproductive health clinic in the state of Texas. You ran like a *coward*!"

"I fought next to some of those guardsmen in the Terrorist Wars," he piped up as much as he dared, leaning into the monitor. "I wasn't about to slaughter them, risk civilian casualties in the crossfire, all to keep an abortion clinic open."

President Brighton cursed him spitefully. "You incompetent fool! Don't you know how to follow orders? Why didn't you clear your decision through me first?"

"We didn't have time and might not have won the engagement. Would bright red American blood on Texas soil make you happy?"

The president flung the papers she held in her hand at the monitor. The general didn't appear startled by this outburst. "When I give an order," the president spoke in a commanding tone, "I expect you to put your life on the line to fulfill it! If you can't do that, then resign and I'll put a braver, more worthy man in your shoes. Those people were blockading a *legal* medical establishment and intimidating those women with criminalized hate speech. We had them outnumbered, General. The Texas Guard was bluffing. We let the religious fanatics win with the whole world watching. You, you humiliated me! You've emboldened our ideological enemies. The physician, nurses, and even some of the clients at that clinic have been in jail ever since we withdrew. They're actually going to try to prosecute them, General! We were there to protect their rights and we let them down. We threw them to the wolves."

The general hung his head for a moment and took a deep breath. It was time for humble pie. "I'm sorry, Madam President. It was an impulsive decision, and one that I regret. I promise you that it will not happen again."

"Now Governor Adams has dug his trenches, defended his actions, and he's encouraging other states to do the same. South Carolina's Abortion and Euthanasia Ban may pass this week!"

The general sighed and leaned back into his chair. "I'm not a politician, I'm a soldier, Madam President, and you need to comprehend the scope of the military's situation. I've been in contact with Hamilton and Erdman, and I think we're going to have to push back the deadline for turning in illegal firearms. The FBI and ATF aren't ready and there are too many battle lines to manage. This is a huge, daunting task."

The president wiped her forehead with both palms and sighed. "I already told Erdman that we're going to push it back to July the third. We'll activate the reserves at Camp Bullis and Fort Bliss. We were counting on the Texas Guard's assistance, but, with this turn of events..."

General Tiller bit his lip and his face flushed at the president's loss of words. They both were just coming to grips with the fact that unmanageable hordes of Texas guardsmen were supportive of or sympathetic with Governor Adams' attempt to resist the federal government. It was a tremendous humiliation to them both.

"The Adjutant General of the Texas National Guard, Alan MacIntosh, has been court-martialed this morning in absentee as you requested. We're calling the Texas Guard into active service under my authority. This is a minor setback, Madam President."

The president raised her eyes and appeared pleased with General Tiller's unexpected mischievous grin. He added, "Kooks like Henry Adams, Muslim terrorists, and anti-abortion vandals help us out, unbeknownst to them. We couldn't implement our agenda without them." He saw the corner of the president's mouth raise a bit and General Tiller knew that he was back in her good graces.

*****

After the United States Army retreated in the face of the Texas Guard's resistance at the Austin Women's Clinic, conservative governors and statehouses rushed to develop legislation akin to Texas' Life Bill. Many governors imitated Henry Adams' hard line stance and refused to sign any other bills that the legislature placed on their desks until their abortion and euthanasia bans passed.

Governors called for urgent meetings wherein Guard officers were grilled about their allegiance. Would they submit to the federal government supremely, or were they committed to state and divine law supremely? Would they enforce state statutes to outlaw abortion and physician-assisted suicide? Would they protect the First, Second, and Fourth Amendment from federal infringement, or would they bow down to Margaret Brighton and violate the constitutional rights of citizens? It was a time of weighing priorities, and many were proving that their allegiance to God, the Constitution, and their state transcended any obligation to the federal government.

The brushfires of revolution were kindled in Austin and the grass was dry. The fires of freedom were wildly contagious. Talk of resistance spread throughout living rooms, statehouses, and churches all across the nation. The pulpits began to thunder forth rebukes to government leaders for sin and lust and to their people for dependence upon government instead of God. The salt was beginning to sting again.

Helena, Montana

The governor of Montana, Benjamin Boswell, enthusiastically spoke to the overwhelmingly supportive state legislature one hour after the showdown between federal troops and the Texas State Guard.

"It's a new day in Montana!" The thick-limbed governor waxed bold and abrasive before the somber Montana State Legislature. Television and radio stations broadcast his sound-bite-laden words around the state and the nation. "We *gladly* defy Margaret Brighton's New World Order tyranny. The law of nature and of nature's God will reign supreme, not the law of God-hating feminist dictators. The Ten Commandments and the Constitution of the United States are the law of this land. Executive orders and Supreme Court manure that dares to try to usurp our God-given rights are hereby held in contempt. While the federal government becomes a moral and financial disaster that persecutes people of faith, a pathetic rotting corpse under the judgment of Almighty God," a rumble of applause caused him to pause, "Montana will be that shining city on the hill. As the federal government and other states bow down to their idols, Montana's statehouse will have the Ten Commandments restored to our halls and the spirit of liberty restored to our hearts." The applause that followed these proclamations was vigorous and prolonged.

"Your state leaders will be your servants, not your slave masters." His confidence increased with the cheers and his voice grew louder. "We will trust you," he pointed at the television camera in front of him, "to keep and bear arms to defend yourselves. Our judges will give you justice, even if we have to prosecute an agent of the federal government to do so. We will begin to put an end" - he slapped his podium - "to the holocaust of preborn babies in our state." He paused for a hail of affirmations all over the statehouse. "Montana will defy tyranny and secure the freedom of all of our people, including the preborn, the handicapped, and the elderly." Governor Boswell paused for another round of rigorous clapping. Many began to stand to their feet.

"I'm asking you to pass this bill that bans physician-assisted suicide and all chemical and surgical abortion in all cases," he said, waving a two-page bill in front of him. "For far too long, the medical community has exploited the life-of-the-mother exception to murder one and wound another. If an abortion must be employed to save a mother's life, then a jury will decide whether the mother's life was really at risk, just like they do in other cases wherein justifiable homicide is argued. In short, we're going to treat preborn children like people, because they are. Although Montana has many concerns about federal usurpation of our most fundamental God-given rights, this bill is our priority because it ends *our* state government's usurpation of those rights. We must remember that as we judge, we shall be judged. If we don't protect the right to life of the least of God's children among us, then we don't deserve liberty. Montana must stop the murder of innocent children if we're going to have the blessing of God." The applause quieted as they all considered their governor's somber words.

"We're not alone in this holy endeavor. States and communities all over this nation are beginning to resist the tyranny coming out of Washington, D.C. I am happy to announce that this very morning,

I've been on the phone with leaders from *every single state* that borders Montana, and *each* of them is in the process of passing similar legislation as this bill that I place before you now."

At hearing this news, the remainder of the Montana legislature clamored to their feet with thunderous applause. "We are cooperating as a loose coalition of free, Christian states to protect the life, the liberty, and the property of all who live here. God help us, because without Him we can do nothing."

Bozeman, Montana

"Mr. Harris, the communication inconvenience is rapidly becoming a crisis." The secretary updated her superior, senior FBI bureaucrat Ernie Harris, through the speaker on his desk.

Harris, who sat in Sheriff Woods' chair, ignored the secretary's complaint and spoke into his cell phone, "Please think about it, we could use your—" He stopped mid-sentence and looked angrily at his phone for a moment. He slammed the phone into its cradle and stomped out of his office.

The secretary sat surrounded by several phones whose lines were all blinking. "They've clogged the whole system. It's been nonsense calls all day. They're trying to shut our system down."

"Answer them," he ordered, pointing to the phones. "If they're full of hot air, tell them that we have their number and that they *will* be prosecuted for obstructing justice. Where's Marley?" When no one answered, he shouted louder, "Marley!"

A thin, redheaded woman rushed into the room from the back office. "Yes sir?"

"Where's the phone company?"

"Representatives from the phone company are on their way."

"They were on their way three hours ago," a nearby agent reminded them.

"Marley, I sent you to get new phones."

"There's no open place nearby where we can obtain the phones you requested. We'll have them tomorrow morning."

"Can we break into one of the stores in town?" Harris pointed out the window. "For goodness' sake, there's one right there." He motioned to a large department store down the road.

Marley shrugged and winced at the suggestion. "You want us to break in, sir?"

"Agent Harris!" The secretary's shrill tone turned all eyes toward her. She had the phone to her ear and her eyes were wide with fear. "We have a bomb threat!"

Harris sighed deeply and made his way to the secretary. "Calm down, calm down."

Rather than calm down, the lady grew even more frantic as she squealed, "He said the building is going to blow in 30 seconds and that we need to get out now if we want to live! Then he hung up!" She was crying and trembling as she bent down to grab her purse at her feet.

Harris rolled his eyes and cursed. "Not again. Everybody out!" He waved his arms toward the door. "No running, quick pace..." He rushed for the door and held it open so the swarm of federal agents could exit. Then he followed them out. In the middle of the parking lot, he turned and shouted at his subordinates, "Get those protesters behind that line!" He pointed at 150 chanting protesters on the sides of the street who were pressing against the yellow caution tape. "Let's get the dogs in here ASAP."

Harris opened his cell phone and hit the speed dial number for Todd Hamilton's personal line.

When Hamilton answered, Agent Harris sounded desperate. "Mr. Hamilton, I can't do this! We need more personnel. This morning's events in Austin have fanned the flames of fanaticism here."

Todd Hamilton grimaced at hearing the lack of confidence in Agent Harris's voice. He tapped his pen rhythmically on his desk as he listened to Harris' update via his Bluetooth connection. "Well, Harris, publicly and violently arrest those making the threats."

Harris had to raise his voice to be heard over the chaotic noise from the protesters' chanting and the evacuation of the Bozeman police station. "We're having technical difficulty identifying the perpetrators because the phones are antiques and the phone company won't cooperate with our request for phone logs." He paced in the field beside the parking lot as the bomb-sniffing dogs cleared the building. "I need you to send more men."

Hamilton grunted disapprovingly. "Men?"

"Personnel - please! Now's not the time for sensitivity training for sexist agents."

Hamilton grunted as he typed on his laptop. "Can you get the local authorities to help you apprehend the suspects?"

"They won't help, sir. We've begged and even ordered but they say they're busy enough. Arresting Sheriff Woods was supposed to make the others fall into line, but it's having the opposite effect."

The secretary tapped Harris on the arm. "We can go back in now."

"All right. Back inside." Harris waved the horde of bureaucrats back toward the building. "Mr. Hamilton, we need to adapt. We need a Plan B."

"We have a game-plan for incarcerating a massive number of people out west if it ever became necessary. We may have to resort to that."

"Our agents can't infiltrate well for some reason." Harris entered his office, shut the door behind him, and lit up a cigarette. "Montanans are naturally untrusting of new-comers right now."

"How about churches? We always had success at that. Have you infiltrated the churches?"

"Yes, some." Harris pulled the thin, vertical rope beside his window to part the blinds and get a better look at the long line of protesters in front of his office.

"Let the agents cry some tears and get 'born again.' Then when they put their ears to these church walls, they'll discover who the trouble-makers are."

"We did make inroads into some churches, but our agents got kicked out with the revival of religious fanaticism."

"Kicked out?"

"Yeah. They got caught in sin and wouldn't come clean. These are the excuses I'm getting from the agents anyway." He peeked through the blinds, suspicious of some increasing noise outside on the sidewalk. "I personally think they just got fed up with faking holiness and wanted breathing room." He put back his head and laughed heartily. "Looks like Christ-lovin' round these parts can be hard on the whore-mongering habits."

An unexpected blast pierced the cigarette-smoke-filled air. Shards from the shattered window sprayed into the room. Agent Harris' lack of regret for his whore-mongering habits was his last thought. A speeding .223 chunk of lead poked a hole in the glass between two strips of the vertical blinds, went through his mouth and out the back of his neck, sending matter and blood onto the desk.

"Hello? Harris! Are you there?"

At the sound of the gunshot and shattering glass, two agents rushed into the office with their guns drawn. They found Harris flat on his back, breathless in a pool of his own blood.

"Mr. Harris!"

"I'll call 911."

The other agent knelt at Mr. Harris' side. "It's no use." The agent tapped a button on the communication device over his right ear. "I want all units on the southwest side of the building. Agent Harris has been shot. I repeat, Harris has been shot. Identify and pursue suspects."

The other agent picked up the phone that was still in Harris' pale, lifeless grip. "Anybody there?"

"This is Todd Hamilton. Harris has been shot? Is he dead?"

"Yes." The agent slowly stood to his feet.

"Has the perpetrator been caught?"

The agent glanced through the window, and saw that the crowd of protesters had scattered.

"Suspects have been engaged in pursuit."

Bull Seibert laid his .223 bolt-action rifle beside him. The barrel was still warm from the friction of the speeding bullet. He thumped the floor to let Jeremiah, his driver, know that it was time to make their get-away.

Jeremiah Woods was Randy's youngest son, 18 years of age. They both were stunned at how easy their plan had materialized. The shot was from 150 yards as Jeremiah's metallic gray Lincoln sedan came to a halt at a stop sign. They had passed this way about

15 times in the past three hours before the target became visible through the blinds.

When Bull first presented the idea to Jeremiah, he was very skeptical about resorting to violence. But once the president refused the release of his father, even after Governor Boswell and the state legislature passed a resolution declaring his incarceration to be unconstitutional and unlawful, he knew that it was time to resort to the force of arms in defense of his dad.

"If not now," Bull reasoned, "when?"

Bull could hit a deer in full stride from that distance, but shooting from inside the trunk of a car through a hole the size of a softball was tricky. He practiced for days, shooting targets from the closed trunk through the round opening, where the gas was usually pumped in the side of the car. He was careful to stuff a rag into the pipe that led to the fuel tank to prevent igniting gasoline fumes. To a passer-by, it just looked like they were driving with their gasoline lid left open and with the flash-guard on Bull's gun, hardly a spark was noticeable. Furthermore, since the shot was from inside the trunk, the sound of the blast was muffled considerably. They had given all of this much thought and they knew that video cameras were carefully watching all of the areas surrounding the sheriff's office. Bull hoped that this plan would keep Jeremiah from becoming a suspect. He might be questioned once the vehicle was identified as belonging to the family of the incarcerated sheriff, but both of Jeremiah's hands were on the wheel. The plan was flawless.

Jeremiah Woods turned right at the stop sign and breathed a sigh of relief. "That was for you, dad," he whispered audibly.

With his gloved hand, he reached over in the seat beside him and picked up an envelope. He drove toward the downtown post-office where he intended to drop the letter in the mail. The letter informed the Bureau that one trespassing agent would be executed every month until Sheriff Randy Woods was released.

Austin, Texas

It had been eight hours since David's emotional breakdown in front of the Austin Women's Clinic. They spent the day with the

Christians in front of the clinic and at a nearby church that offered meals to all pro-lifers involved in the sit-in. It was a long day filled with joy and encouragement, but Elijah noticed that David hardly smiled.

David sat in the passenger's seat of Elijah's van in the downtown civic center parking lot, gazing out the window at the setting sun.

Elijah sat in the driver's seat and extended a warm McDonald's Big Mac toward him.

"I told you I wasn't hungry."

"You ready to tell me what's going on with you?"

David sighed and ignored Elijah's question. "Where's Jared? We've got to find him and go get my family."

"He's probably inside." Elijah motioned toward the civic center over the thousands of cars that had filled the parking lot. "Let's go."

"What's going on here tonight?"

"I told you. Dozens of pastors and political leaders had planned a gathering to pray for God's blessing on Texas."

When they walked into the civic center, what they saw and heard stunned them. They immediately heard a roar of prayers from thousands of Christians. Throughout the building there were small groups of 20 to 80 Christians huddled up praying together. Some were on their knees, some were standing, and others were lying prostrate on the ground.

David tapped the shoulder of a man wearing ostrich leather cowboy boots who was coming out of the bathroom. He pointed to the cell phone affixed to his belt. "Hey, can I borrow your cell to make a quick call?" The man nodded and handed David the phone. "Thanks."

"I'm going to go look for Jared," Elijah told David. "Stay around here." Elijah took off as David dialed the number he had memorized.

Colton, Texas

"A call's coming in. Who is it?" The senior federal agent in the room next to Darlene Jameson's room called the other agents to attention. Darlene had taken the kids for a walk and the room was

25

empty, but the agents immediately went to work to try to discover who was calling her.

When no one answered the phone, the front desk operator picked up the call. "May I help you?"

"Yes, can I leave a message for Darlene Jameson?"

"Yes. Begin your recording at the blink."

"Will she be able to know that she has a message when she returns?"

"Yes. A light on her phone will beep. You have 60 seconds."

"Okay."

Beep.

"Hello Darlene. I miss you and the girls so much. I have something I really need to talk with you about, but I don't have a way that you can call me…"

"It's him! It's David Jameson!"

The four federal agents holed up in the next room scurried about, flipping on high-tech recording equipment, typing on computers, and adjusting homing devices to try to determine the exact location of her husband, the terrorist suspected of killing the former president of the United States.

"The cell phone belongs to Riley Peters, a mechanic from Austin."

"Connections," the senior agent barked as he pressed his headset tight against his ears to listen in on the conversation. "How does he know Jameson?"

"I'm on it," chirped an agent whose fingers tapped hurriedly on a laptop.

"It looks like he's in Austin." One agent leaned close to his computer screen as his software triangulated the GPS location of the suspect. "About 20 seconds…"

"What's happening right now is unlike anything I've ever seen in my life, Darlene. Thousands of saints are on their faces before God in the Austin Civic Center, praying. Oh, I wish you were here…"

"Ah ha! He gave up his location." The senior agent gave a double thumbs-up to the agent who was studying the computer screen to determine the suspect's location. "Activate the nearest SWAT. He's at the civic center."

"Hold up," another agent interjected with his palms raised. "There are thousands of people at that civic center right now. We need to stay incognito or they'll scatter and Jameson will get away."

The senior agent scratched his temple, deep in thought. "All right. We'll notify our inside personnel at those meetings and get them busy trying to locate and arrest him."

"Please pray, Darlene. I feel like we're on the edge of the wilderness and the spies are about to give their report. Our faith is going to be tested. I have an uneasy feeling in my gut, the same kind of feeling I'd experience if I were to see the ocean get sucked out past the horizon, knowing a tsunami must be speeding my way. That's the same sensation I've got right now down deep in my spirit." Jameson patted his chest. "We can't give up, but we've got to realize that faithfulness in the desert is the key to conquering the Promised Land. It is very important that I talk to you soon. I've got something personal I need to talk to you about. I'll call tomorrow."

David shut the cell phone and handed it back to the man with the ostrich cowboy boots. "Thanks."

"Uh, sir, sir?" A junior agent handed the senior agent a fax he had just perused. "It's from Durango."

"Can it wait?"

"No. You need to read this now."

The senior agent grunted and grabbed the fax that was deemed so urgent. He read the fax and blurted out, "What!? They've already got an inside man close to David Jameson? Why haven't they brought him in? I thought that this man was a priority. And why is this the first time that I'm learning about this?"

"That can't be!" someone exclaimed.

The senior agent set down the fax and picked up the phone to speed-dial Mick Durango, the director of the Midwest Division of the FBI. "This doesn't make sense."

"Well, what do we do?"

"Our mission doesn't change. Find and apprehend David Jameson."

"But why haven't they done it already?"

"Wires get crossed and missions conflict all the time in this Bureau," the senior agent responded. Someone picked up on the other end of his phone line. "Let me speak to Durango."

Chapter 2

Columbia, South Carolina

For decades, South Carolina had grown into a haven for Christian re-constructionists and secessionists. Thousands of Bible-believers and libertarian patriots relocated to the first state to secede in America's Civil War, hoping to intensify their influence on state government to resist the gradual demise of their culture and erosion of their liberties. Since the election of Raymond Fitzgerald in 2016, their numbers tripled. Secession was a platform plank for several third parties that actually had representatives in the statehouse. Minority parties were no longer the "red-headed stepchildren" of politics. United, they were a formidable force. Many Christian leaders across the state publicly called for secession from the godless central government, risking their church's 501c3 IRS status and their freedom in the process. The chains were loosening.

The various Christian and libertarian factions historically disagreed with each other just as vehemently as they disagreed with the federal government, but the actions of the feds were unifying them. Although they couldn't agree on what the state government should look like with regard to economics, the use of the military, criminal justice, public education, the legalization of drugs, or the reliance on religious principles in governing, they could set aside their disagreements to come to a consensus on what the government should *not* look like.

With the federal government's usurpations snowballing, the consensus in South Carolina's Christian communities was that it was time for the legislature to begin to separate from the federal government. Fighting the federal beast on one front, such as abortion, was insufficient. The entire federal government was corrupt to the core. God's Word asks, *When the foundations are destroyed, what can the righteous do?* What's the use in rebuilding on the same corrupt foundation? What's the use repairing damaged structure on a cracked and crumbling foundation? They must rebuild on a new foundation, the law of God, that eternal standard without which man cannot long remain free.

The resolution the statehouse debated the day after the Austin conflict was a sovereignty resolution with teeth. It pressured the executive branch of the federal government to redress a long list of grievances and laid down an ultimatum. If the federal government would not constrain itself to the limited powers and obligations set forth in the Constitution, then it had violated the contract that created it and was unworthy of the submission of a free people. Secession was formally on the table as a viable last resort.[1]

Austin, Texas

"Ow!" complained Terry Markison.

"Hold on, I'll fix it." The female FBI agent adjusted the wiring on Markison's lean torso. He stood shirtless with his arms horizontal as she affixed the mic to his chest.

It had only been 20 hours since the confrontation at the Austin Women's Clinic, but the feds were wasting no time in their attempt to subjugate Texas' seditious government. Markison could sense their impatience and it frightened him. He was smart enough to know that they desperately needed his help and also that he was expendable to them.

"What do you want me to do?"

A dark-haired senior agent stood across from Mr. Markison, leaning against the wall. "Just lure him into admitting that he wants to make war on the federal government."

"He does *not* want to make war. He just wants to outlaw what he considers to be murder. He's made it plain that force is a last resort. Listen, why do we have to do it this way? You've got him on the hate-crime statutes."

The senior agent shook his head, stepped closer to Markison, and put a hand on his shoulder. "It's not enough. Not for a governor. We need to convince not just a judge but also the general public that the arrest was justified. In order to do that, the president wants you to try to get him to admit that he wants to secede with violence. Get him to admit that he'd be willing to fire on American soldiers."

Markison nodded. "Then what?"

"Then we'll arrest him."

"Then what?" A nervous tic showed above Terry Markison's right eyelid.

The agent studied Terry's countenance for a moment. "Are you okay?"

"I'm fine!" Markison snapped, visibly upset at the delayed answer to his question. "What happens to Texas after you arrest him?"

"That's up to the president, Mr. Markison. She'll probably instill martial law until..."

Terry winced as if he had just been slapped. "Martial law?"

"Just until we can get some leadership that we can trust. Secession is almost as popular in the statehouse as it is in Henry Adams' administration, so we can't just hand over leadership to your representatives. Not right away."

Terry sighed nervously as he buttoned up his outer shirt.

"You're not developing any sympathy for Henry Adams, are you?"

"No. I just..." He paused, sighed, and cast his gaze sheepishly at the ground. "I hope he doesn't have to do hard time. He's nuts, but *sincerely* nuts."

The senior agent laughed. "If he only gets hard time, he'd be getting it easy."

The female agent tried some humor to calm the nerves of their inside man. "The freak should be shipped out on the first flight to

31

Mecca, where he'd be more at home. Don't be nervous. You're doing a great service to your nation."

"Especially the gay community," the senior agent added, patting him on the shoulder again.

Terry's lover, Brie, swung open the door from the bedroom, took one look at Terry, put one hand on his hip and flapped his other wrist in his characteristic flamboyant fashion. "Oh, you look nice, sweetie." There was excitement in his eyes and enthusiasm in his voice. "I can't believe my boy's going to work undercover for the FBI."

The male agent tried not to appear uncomfortable with Brie's boisterous public display of affection. He turned to Markison and saw him wince, appearing embarrassed at his lover's stereotypical gayness. He turned back to Brie, discerning that this fellow might say something impulsively without thinking about the consequences. "This must be kept secret, do you understand?"

Colton, Texas

"Hello Darlene. You must be having a lot of fun with our lovely girls at that park." David was leaving a message on her hotel room answering machine again. "Can't blame you. I wouldn't want to be cooped up in a hotel all day either. I just want you to know that I love you and I'll try to call you tomorrow on a borrowed cell. Elijah and I have spent the night at the Austin Civic Center in prayer with thousands of others. This is an awesome, just awesome move of God. Haven't found Jared though, or else we'd come and get you. Elijah doesn't feel right about leaving Jared, not with how volatile things are right now. Gotta go. Call you tomorrow. I've got to talk to you about something important."

Darlene walked into the room just as the message concluded and the light began to blink on the phone. "No!" She rushed to pick up the phone and listen to the message.

"Is it Daddy?"

"Yeah, we missed him again."

"Is he all right?"

"Shhh. I want to hear the message." Darlene was curt. She couldn't hide her worry. Her insides had trembled ever since David reported in his last phone message that he had something personal to talk about with her.

Austin, Texas

"I'm shocked." Robert Boniface walked into the room just a minute before the Texas governor's cabinet meeting. He cast four local newspapers directly in front of the Adjutant General of the Texas Guard. The newspapers hit the long wooden table with a "slap" and slid off each other until they were side by side. "Polls show half the people in Texas *favor* your actions. *Half!* That's a miracle."

"Half?" General MacIntosh blew out a sigh and smiled. "That's hard to believe." He leaned closer to the newspapers to peruse the headlines.

"That's hard evidence of a major revival, brother."

"Reading my hate mail, you'd think the half that hates me would shoot me and the half that loves me would take the bullet."

When Governor Adams walked through the door, he immediately blurted out the most pressing question on his mind at the time. "Any lead on David Jameson?" The video of David Jameson speaking to him on the sidewalk in front of the statehouse had hurt him in the press and the legislature. Now, the media had not stopped showing the images of this mysterious suspected terrorist in the crowd outside of the Austin Women's Clinic, interspersed with images of him outside of the Columbus Civic Center before it blew up. However, once Adams recalled the wisdom in the stranger's words and studied the claims in Josh Davis' article, which indicted the president for conspiracy and treason, he became suspicious of the federal government's reasons to pursue David Jameson.

The director of the Highway Patrol Department had just filled his mug from the coffee machine sitting on the office's corner table. He settled into his seat beside Boniface, a steaming cup in his hands. "The feds had already scoured the apartment for evidence and the owner, Natalie Slate, is in their custody for hate crimes." He took an airy sip from his cup. "Don't even know where they're keeping her. Her brother Elijah Slate and David Jameson must have gone into hiding." His countenance grew grave. "Probably," he added. "The feds may have—"

"Hold that thought." The governor raised an index finger to pause the Highway Patrol director mid-sentence. "We'll get back to Jameson later." The rest of the cabinet trickled in. "Come on, take a seat." When everybody was seated, Governor Adams invited the stern-faced Robert Boniface to open in prayer.

"I have invited Representative Franklin here," Governor Adams said, nodding at the rep across from him, "to share the consensus of the legislators on what happened yesterday." All eyes fixed on the new man at the table whose face was familiar to all of them. He was a bald gentleman in his fifties with a reddish-blond mustache.

Representative Franklin, the highest ranking conservative in the Texas legislature, returned the governor's nod and thanked him. "Todd Hamilton, speaking on behalf of the president, is pressuring us hard to impeach you for calling out the Guard to resist federal authorities. They may file charges from treason to FACE Act violations. The AG, Victor Meyers, has written a letter to assure us that your arrest for those crimes is imminent. Thousands of Texans have flooded our lines calling for us to impeach you."

Some of the cabinet members appeared disturbed at the announcement, but not Adams. "Oh, this was expected." Adams waved his thick, calloused hand in front of him as if he were swatting away a sluggish fly. "We've counted the cost and we're willing to pay it."

"It may cost you your re-election. The Republican Party has already been busy recruiting candidates in the House and the Senate to compete with you in the general election."

"No way," someone commented. "How can the Republican Party drum up independent candidates to compete against *their* candidate? That can't be."

"The word is that you'll be imprisoned before November," Franklin said, nodding at the governor. "The Party wants a strong candidate on the ground that can move into your slot on the ballot. Sending the Guard out to stop the Army was *very bad* for your administration and for the pro-life movement. Shutting down the clinic and arresting—"

"*Bad* for the pro-life movement?" Adams interrupted the representative, his voice raised in irritation. Robert Boniface appeared equally stunned. "Did you just say that shutting down abortion in Texas was *bad* for the pro-life movement?"

"Uh, I didn't expect that to be a controversial statement." He glanced around the room, his eyebrows raised as if he expected others to come to his defense.

"Was it bad for the babies scheduled to die?" Boniface inquired.

"And who are alive today because we intervened to protect them?" Governor Adams added.

The Texas rep shrugged. "How do you know that a life was saved? They could have just gone to another abortion clinic."

"We shut those down too," Adams responded, raising his voice even louder. "For the first time since 1973, the preborn are protected in state law. If that's bad for the pro-life movement, I can't imagine anything good."

"Hey, it's me. You know me. I'm pro-life," Miles Franklin contended with his arms outstretched. "Many of us trust you, sir, but those who distrust you have momentum and the backing of the federal government. Many states are following your lead and so the feds are investing a lot into taking you down. I've heard Governor Boswell from Montana even refer to a block of northwestern states called the 'Confederacy of Free Christian States' that are trying to outlaw abortion."

"That's the president's misquote," Governor Adams informed them. "Ben Boswell called it the *Coalition* of Free Christian States."

"Why *Christian* states?" Franklin wondered.

"Why, because they're Christian, Miles! That's a whole lot better than non-Christian." Adams appeared frustrated that even principled Christian politicians like Miles Franklin were skeptical of establishing a government on the word of God, as if a secular, godless government was preferred over a Christian one.

Franklin rolled his eyes at the governor's apparent ignorance of the separation of church and state and thought that he would come quicker to his point rather than debate with him. "The legislature needs you to come and answer some questions to help us discover how far you're willing to take this. Pointing a gun at the Army is one thing, but pulling the trigger is another."

"We're willing to go as far as we must to protect innocent lives," said Robert Boniface, answering the question for the governor.

"As far as seceding from the Union?" Terry Markison asked. "As far as firing on American troops?"

"As far as necessary to protect the innocent," the governor reiterated. "If you saw an American soldier stomping a toddler in the street, wouldn't you intervene? Come on! Physician-assisted suicide and abortion are murder and Texas is banning it and protecting the innocent. It's that simple."

Markison shook his head as he studied the faces of the leaders around the table, his eyes wide with anticipation. "So you're seriously considering armed secession?"

The governor sighed deeply and clasped his hands in front of him. "We will take a defensive posture to protect the innocent within our jurisdiction. If the federal government insists on a conflict of arms, then we will act defensively."

"Will you secede?" Franklin asked directly.

A pregnant pause followed. The entire cabinet was on the edge of its seat.

"We entered the Union voluntarily, and if a voluntary departure ever becomes necessary to act defensively," Governor Adams paused to glance at Boniface, who gave him a confident wink, "then, yes."

"*Secede with violence from the United States?*" Terry Markison squealed in vehement disapproval. "I can't believe this!" One-third of the cabinet members present echoed Markison's sentiment with their depressed countenances, wagging heads, and furrowed brows.

The governor expected this response. He allowed tempers to cool for a few moments. "Let's get past the emotional trauma and try to think intelligently about this. It's not the end of the world."

"Not the end of the world?" the director of the Texas Board of Education responded. "It's definitely the end of public education."

"It'd *fix* education by restoring local control," Boniface remarked. "Hasn't federal control been your biggest complaint about the public education system?"

"And what about federal funds for transportation?" asked the transportation commissioner.

"And funds for state parks," added the parks commissioner.

"Hold on," the governor pleaded. "If profit were our motive, then we'd gladly submit to tyranny, for we'd probably make more money in the short term if we submitted. But should we let fellow Texans be disarmed, murdered, and enslaved for our profit? We can't just think about our own budgets for the next four years. We need to think about the preborn, the elderly, the handicapped, and our posterity. I mean, would you kill a man, Jamie, if it'd help you keep your big budget for state parks?"

The park commissioner shook her head. "No. But secession?" She tapped her silver pen rhythmically against the table. "I understand that you have an obligation to your constituents and I know that Texans are fed up with federal tyranny, but have you really thought this through?"

Governor Adams looked the park commissioner in the eyes. "Texas has seceded before when we were under lesser tyrannies."

"That's right," said Rob Boniface, nodding. "Texas seceded from Mexico. The United States seceded from Great Britain. State law plainly allows us to secede from the United States. We're on firm legal ground here. The Declaration of Independence said that the consent of the people is sufficient for secession."

State Attorney Stratton had grown sympathetic with resisting the feds in banning abortion and physician-assisted suicide, but secession was a frightening prospect. He didn't think that Governor Adams would ever take it this far. "Governor Adams, didn't the civil war settle the issue? Discontented states don't have the right to secede."

"Might does not make right, Mr. Stratton," the governor responded. "The war proved who won the war, not who was lawful and right."

Boniface interjected with a pearl from the Civil War: "When the President of the Confederacy, Jefferson Davis, was arrested after the

Union's victory, federal prosecutors refused to take the case against him because they feared that a jury would rule that state secession was constitutionally justified. They actually *freed* Jefferson Davis rather than risk a jury trial."

From the pained distortion of Stratton's grimace, Adams judged him immovable. "If stopping the slaughter of hundreds of Texans every day isn't reason enough to secede, Mr. Stratton, there ain't any reason that'll suit ya."

"But Texas, not being a part of the United States anymore? Are you serious?" Stratton and Representative Franklin shook their heads in disbelief. Conservative leaders in the Texas statehouse were vastly more sympathetic with resisting federal tyranny than the other state legislatures, but this was all too surreal and they were having a difficult time processing what was at stake.

"Article One, Section Eight of the U.S. Constitution," Stratton zealously objected, "gives Congress the power to provide for the calling forth of the militia to execute the laws of the Union in suppressing insurrections."

"A peaceful secession is not a violent insurrection," Boniface argued. "Trying to peacefully govern your own jurisdiction in accordance with the U.S. and state constitutions is not the same thing as violently trying to overthrow the federal government. The Constitution says that the federal government may *aid* a state in suppressing domestic violence if" – he paused, tapped his index finger on the table, and repeated – "*if* a state requests its help."

"Secession," Governor Adams assured them, "would be a last resort. Even if we do secede, force of arms would be a last resort, appealed to only in self-defense."

"If the federal government were killing thousands of already-born Texans every single day," Boniface added emphatically, "none of you would protest Texas' right to defend itself. The only reason you're so shocked about talk of secession now is because you're impervious to the plight of preborn Texans, hundreds of whom were killed every day for the past 40 years. You must join us in repenting for our apathy. As long as you prefer the slaughter of the innocent to secession, you'll be more of a liability to freedom than an asset. Doing justice and obtaining the blessing of God on our state is our aim, and if nuclear-armed secession is a means to that end, then God be praised."

"God be praised for nuclear-armed secession?" Markison wagged his head disapprovingly. "I can't believe what I'm hearing."

"If a husband is beating his wife and committing adultery, a divorce is justifiable according to Scripture," said Adams. "This proves that even the most sacred of contracts is conditional. If I'm trying to protect thousands of Texans from a blood-thirsty tyrannical power, I'll use a pole on the ground or a missile in the ground, if I must."

"Don't you know how the federal government will respond?" Markison asked.

Boniface leaned forward in his chair and put his elbows on the table. "Brighton would probably do as Lincoln did, call us traitors and rebels and declare war on us. But I don't think that she can afford to wage war. The federal debt is—"

"Wage war?" Stratton's eyes were wide and his voice cracked as he spoke. He glanced at Markison. *"Wage war!"* His eyes roamed to the reclusive and shy lieutenant governor, who appeared equally troubled. Thoughts of satellite-guided smart bombs, 20-ton tanks, and explosion-tipped .50 caliber machine guns on Apache helicopters made their heads spin.

"They're going to bomb us to smithereens," said Markison, "until we come to our senses, tie our little Texas Life Bill on a pole and throw it up into the air like the white flag of surrender!"

General Alan MacIntosh puffed his cheeks and furrowed his heavy brow at the scrawny youngster's disrespect for the austere Henry Adams and his courageous pastor Rob Boniface. He turned to Markison and reproved him as sternly as a Guard general could. "Don't talk so confidently and arrogantly of that about which you have no knowledge whatsoever, Mr. Markison! History is full of examples of small, dedicated militias defeating much larger forces. The American colonies, the Viet Cong, Afghanistan, the P.L.O., the Irish Republican Army - these all defeated superpowers against all odds."

"Add to that the Finnish and the Swiss militias in the Second World War," Boniface added.

General MacIntosh nodded. "Texas has more guns per capita than any other state besides Montana. Texas'll join the ranks of victorious underdogs in the blink of an eye if we're called upon to do so."

"Hopefully our numbers and our willingness to resist invasion with force will keep the feds from invading," Boniface speculated. "Texas has one-fourth of the nation's oil wells, one of the largest state economies, and the most significant import border in the country. Our threats are probably sufficient to keep the federal forces at bay. They'll try to choke us economically and socially, but not militarily. We need to be proactive to get our people off of the federal handouts and prevent the kind of strife which will tend to anarchy should the federal government begin to withhold funds."

"Yep. A fat man's got to skinny up," Adams said with a charming smile, "before he runs a marathon." They discerned a hint of pride in their governor's comment for his loss of 50 pounds in the past several months.

"And we must act *before* we're disarmed," Boniface counseled. "We don't have a lot of time."

Terry Markison sat back and crossed his arms over his chest, comforted in knowing that this fly-by-the-seat-of-your-pants insanity would soon be humbled when it collided with the impenetrable brick wall of reality.

"The deadline for surrendering your now-illegal weapons has been postponed until July the third," the governor reminded them.

"Texas is buying more guns than they're getting rid of, Governor," the director of Highway Patrol informed them.

"I can't 'be-lieeeeve' that we are having this conservation," complained an exasperated Terry Markison with an effeminate lisp.

"You guys already have this all figured out, don't you?" spat Stratton disrespectfully.

Boniface's face reddened at the opposition at the table. "Stopping the Abortion Holocaust and winning God's blessing on Texas is more important than our peace, wealth, comfort, jobs, our sentimental attraction to Old Glory or even our very lives. This is not Texas versus the United States. It's the baby-killers versus the baby-defenders. It's the big city, communist, globalist elite versus your average church-going, gun-totin,' over-taxed American. Governments are created to protect God-given rights; the Declaration of Independence says that whenever a government becomes destructive to these ends, it is the right of the people to alter or abolish it."

"You know this is treason, Governor." Terry Markison squirmed in his chair, quite aware at that moment of the itchiness of the tape that strapped the miniature microphone to his chest.

"If this is treason," Henry Adams barked sarcastically, "then killing babies on the government dole must be the epitome of patriotism for you, huh?"

"Wait," said Representative Franklin, sensing the reluctance of Boniface and Adams to own up to the implications of their position. "Let's be honest with ourselves. This *is* treason against the United States." He put a palm up to keep Boniface from interrupting. "You're just calling it *good* treason, *justifiable* treason, treason against tyranny, but let's not kid ourselves. This *is* treason."

"You got that right, Miles Franklin." One of the FBI agents listening in on Markison's concealed microphone was downright giddy. "He's given us all that we need." They were listening to the conversation from a black windowless van in the parking lot.

The senior FBI agent next to him picked up the phone. "I'll call the president." He dialed the president's direct line for the final approval.

"You're begging the question, Miles," Adams rebutted. "It's *stopping* treason." The governor's gaze shifted from Terry Markison to Representative Franklin and then to his somber state attorney. "If you define treason as betraying a sacred obligation, then they're the ones committing treason against our people, against our faith, against our Constitution, and against God Almighty."

Markison leaned toward the governor with his elbows on the elegant oval table. "Do you know what's going to happen to you? Do you know what the president's going to do?"

"It's irrelevant. Right and wrong doesn't fluctuate with our prejudice for self-comfort."

"Even though," said Markison, raising his voice as he stood and walked behind his chair, "it might cost you your career, your freedom, and even though you might very well be charged and shot as a traitor to the United States, you still insist on pursuing this treasonous course of action?" He gripped the back of his chair as he leaned in toward the governor. "Are you insane?!"

"I've surrendered myself to God's Will. You should do the same or resign, Mr. Markison. If you're so worried about personal repercussions, then I think the best thing for you to do would be to resign." He glanced at his AG and Representative Franklin, hoping their tone would soften as they witnessed their governor urging his youngest and smartest member to quit his cabinet.

Terry smiled in response to the governor's proposal. It was a conniving grin that Henry Adams did not expect, and it troubled him.

There was a buzz on the phone from Henry Adams' secretary. "Governor, there is a—"

"I'm having a very important meeting right now, Melissa," he interrupted her. "I asked not to be disturbed."

"There's an important phone call from Governor Cropp in South Carolina. He asked to speak with you immediately. He wants your thoughts on a secession resolution that his legislature has just placed on his desk."

"A secession resolution?" wondered Boniface. "That was quick."

Governor Adams smiled. *This couldn't come at a better time,* he thought. His gaze shifted back and forth between Markison, Franklin, and Stratton. He knew that he wasn't alone. There were many who haven't bowed the knee to tyranny.

"Ask him if he can wait five minutes."

"Yes sir. I—" Suddenly, the secretary paused and screamed a high-pitched scream that chilled them all to the bone.

Everyone stared at the phone in fear - everyone except Terry Markison. The governor's eyes met his resolute countenance and the governor's heart skipped a beat. Henry Adams stood up just as the doorknob turned. Terry backed away from the door just as Adams reached for it. Suddenly, without warning, the door splintered into five or six pieces with a loud "crash". Rather than simply open it, the feds decided to kick it in. The fractured door struck the governor and thrust him over the table, heels over head.

Into the room rushed a stream of screaming FBI agents in casual clothes. "Hands in the air! Place your hands in the air!" They barked out orders as they ran around the table to where Governor Adams was lying, cradling a wounded forearm and a bruised forehead. Everybody else slowly complied with the FBI agent's orders, everybody except General MacIntosh, who appeared indecisive.

Robert Boniface, whose face turned red as he absorbed the gravity of the moment, grabbed his cell phone out of his briefcase and ducked underneath the table.

"Hey! Come here!" The agent nearest him threw the chair in which Boniface had been sitting up against the wall. He knelt down and placed his M16 to Boniface's scalp. Boniface speed-dialed the Austin Sheriff's Department, presuming the governor's security team to be either infiltrated or held at bay by the feds.

"Put it down! Hands on your head!"

Boniface grabbed the leg of the table and refused to succumb to the agent's persuasion. The agent was forced to grab him by his belt and pull him out from underneath the table. Boniface rolled over onto his back, holding his cell phone close to his side. The agent saw that he was still holding tightly to his cell, so he stepped on the wrist that held the phone and Boniface groaned in pain.

"What are you trying to do?" The armed federal agent lowered the barrel of his gun to the upper lip of Robert Boniface.

Hello, Sheriff Wellington's office. May I help you? Boniface could hear the faint sound of the greeting of the sheriff's secretary.

"**The governor's under attack by the—!**" Boniface's frantic attempt to shout to the phone he held at arm's length ended abruptly with the butt of a rifle against his forehead. A two-inch gash first blanched and then began to gush blood. Boniface drifted into unconsciousness briefly as the Bureau agent stepping on his wrist lifted his foot and smashed the cell phone to bits with two stomps and a string of foul words.

"Did he get through?" an agent near the door asked worriedly.

"We need to get out of here just in case."

The secretary who answered the phone at the sheriff's office pulled the phone away from her ear and glanced at the caller ID. *Robert Boniface?* She hit redial and her call went directly to Boniface's voicemail. She put the phone back in its base and rubbed her chin for a moment. She looked up the phone number for the governor's office on her computer and called two different numbers. No one picked up. She put the phone in the cradle and hit the intercom button on the phone.

"Sheriff Wellington?"

He looked up from his desk, his shoulder cradled in a sling. "Yes?"

"I just received a strange, urgent-sounding phone call from Robert Boniface, Governor Adam's media correspondent. He said the governor's under attack and then we got disconnected and I can't reconnect. Now no one's answering at Governor Adams office."

"No one's answering?"

"And I called two numbers. We should probably have someone investigate."

Sheriff Wellington was shot during the resistance at the last Texas abortion clinic, but was already back in his office. His forehead wrinkles lengthened at the secretary's report. "Keep trying his line. I'll send some squads immediately."

As the members of the Texas cabinet were being frisked and handcuffed, Governor Henry Adams looked through the door and saw the secretary in her chair, her nose three inches from the barrel of a federal agent's weapon. One of his security officers was unconscious in the hallway just outside his office with a dart in his neck. Black-clothed SWAT agents soon stepped over him to join the plain-clothed agents that frisked them.

When an agent prepared to handcuff the lean, gray-headed General MacIntosh, the feisty general suddenly thrust the agent hard against the wall.

"Hey!" one of the agents shouted at him.

General MacIntosh opened the door beside his chair and jumped through the doorway into the darkness.

44

One of the agents near the door had a Taser at the ready and got a shot off at the general just as he slammed the door shut.

"Ahhh!" The voltage threw General MacIntosh to the floor in the dark room. Fortunately, the Taser wires had been slammed in the door and the current shorted out. MacIntosh pulled the Taser darts out of his shoulder with a painful grunt.

He reached up to twist the lock on the knob just as the agent on the other side of the door reached for it. They both received a shock from the live Taser that was in contact with the metal frame of the door.

"Ow! Turn it off!" the agent at the door shouted at the agent with the Taser gun.

Once the Taser was flicked off, MacIntosh tried to bolt the door but in the dark room, he was unable to do it quickly enough. The agent opened the door and saw the silhouette of the general standing inside the doorway. He aimed his rifle at the general's chest and ordered him, "General MacIntosh, come out!"

Without warning, the general kicked the door as hard as he could. It swung open and slammed against the left side of the agent's forehead. The agent screamed in pain and cursed as he reached for the door with his left hand. Then MacIntosh grabbed the inside doorknob and slammed it shut as hard as he could, crushing the agent's fingers in the door.

"Oww!" the agent screamed a curse and then removed his hand. Two agents grabbed the doorknob this time and there was a tug of war, until Robert Boniface awoke from his unconscious state and saw what was happening. As blood dribbled down his forehead, he lunged for the agents at the door. One of the agents lost his grip on the doorknob, turned and delivered a swift kick into Boniface's stomach. He gasped and curled up into a ball on the floor.

The other agent who grabbed the doorknob was winning the tug of war, until Representative Miles Franklin, who had already been cuffed, threw himself between the federal agent and the door. The other agents nearby were ready, and fired their Tasers at Franklin. He cringed at the shock and fell to the floor, his body writhing in spasm. This gave General MacIntosh enough time to slam the door shut and twist the lock button. Breathing heavily with adrenaline, he felt for and turned on the light. When he saw that he had entered a closet, he shouted, "No!"

Terry Markison intervened when the agent looked as if he were going to shoot at the doorknob. "It's just a closet."

"We need to keep this as discreet as possible." A senior agent walked over and tried to calm the fury of the injured agent. "Don't shoot the doorknob. He can't call anyone on his cell. Tech should be blocking all cell calls in and out by now."

"He broke my hand!" The injured agent raised his left hand above his shoulder to ease the throbbing pain as he aimed his assault rifle at the center of the door with his right hand. Blood began to trickle down his nose from a laceration on his forehead received from his collision with the door. "I'm gonna kill him!"

"He probably didn't know that it was a closet," Markison speculated. "There's nowhere for him to go in there."

The senior agent near the door twisted the doorknob and when it wouldn't budge, he kicked the heavy wooden door several times, but to no avail. Then he smashed the doorknob with the butt of his gun, but it still wouldn't open. "Open it now, General MacIntosh! Or I'm going to open it with bullets!"

"Knowing General MacIntosh," Markison speculated, "he's probably carrying a concealed weapon."

The senior agent moved to the right of the door and unsheathed a silenced handgun. "You have three seconds, General. Three, two, one." The agent aimed at the doorknob. Two shots through the doorknob jarred it open.

The door swung open and the agent got just the glimpse of the general's foot heading into the spacing between the floors through one of the ceiling tiles. The senior agent cursed as he tried to climb the same shelves that the general so aptly ascended. One of the wooden shelves broke and he crashed to the ground.

"Ow! I'm gonna kill him!" he screamed in agony and anger.

The agent leading the handcuffed Henry Adams from the room turned and yelled at the furious agent in the closet, "We gotta go, now. We'll have our insiders scour the place for General MacIntosh."

The governor's hands were violently jerked in response to his reluctance to passively be guided out of his room. He had one last glimpse at Terry Markison, who had taken refuge next to the agent giving all the orders to the others. Adams recalled the words of David Jameson on the sidewalk in front of the statehouse and mourned his lack of discernment. Jameson warned him that someone close to him would betray him, someone he had installed into a position of leadership through his own moral compromise. All failures are leadership failures. Henry Adams was reaping what he had sown. It's the little foxes that spoil the vines. His administration was only as strong as its weakest link. The leaven he tolerated within it had become his downfall.

Columbia, South Carolina

Governor Cropp placed the phone on speaker after Henry Adams' secretary saw the dart in the neck of the security guard and screamed. She dropped the cordless phone into her lap when she raised her hands as ordered. Governor Cropp and his cabinet heard it all. They listened in amazed disbelief as the federal agents arrested the Texas governor and the members of his cabinet.

Austin, Texas

After Governor Adams had been escorted out, a SWAT trooper saw the phone in the secretary's lap. He pointed his M16 at her. "Is someone on that phone?"

"I, I don't know."

He moved the gun closer to her temple. "Check and see."

She anxiously picked up the phone with one hand while her other hand was still raised high. With trembling voice, she said, "Hello? Are you still there?"

"Yes ma'am. Are you all right?"

She held the phone aloft toward the federal agent. "He's still on the line."

"Who?"

"South Carolina, uh, the governor of South Carolina was calling for Governor Adams."

The federal agent grabbed the phone and shouted into it, "Who is this?"

"This is Gary Cropp, the governor of South Carolina. Who is this? What happened?"

The federal agent cursed and threw the phone against the wall. He then slammed the butt of his rifle against the phone's cradle several times, causing debris to fly and causing the secretary to flinch with each swing of the rifle.

A fellow Bureau agent hollered from the hallway, "Come on."

The agent rushed from the room as the secretary burst into tears.

Columbia, South Carolina

Governor Cropp and his entire cabinet trembled with shock and anger. They all just stared at the speakerphone in silence, unable to articulate the rage they felt with what they just heard. The temperature seemed to rise in the room as seconds of reflection turned into minutes.

Governor Cropp broke the uneasy silence. "We called to get Governor Adams' advice about seceding from the United States and I think the sovereign Lord has answered our prayers and confirmed the right path for South Carolina."

When the dial tone resounded throughout the room through the speakerphone, he added, "God's also warned us to count the cost." Someone pushed a button on the speakerphone and the dial tone ceased.

Washington, D.C.

"At a time when America is still healing from the worst acts of terrorism ever on American soil, we have discovered treason among us." The president's urgent press conference was teeming with anxious reporters and well-aimed camera flashes. "Henry Adams, the right-wing governor of Texas, sent armed guardsmen to interfere with a cooperative attempt by the FBI and United States Armed Forces to arrest about 400 violent anti-abortionists who trespassed onto the property of the Austin Women's Clinic. The governor ordered guardsmen to point their guns at *your* Army," the president stated emphatically, "an act of war against the United States. According to members of the governor's cabinet who have cooperated with federal authorities, Governor Adams admitted his willingness to fire on American soldiers and even *steal nuclear weapons!*" Her words evoked gasps of disbelief and disgust from the congregation of admiring journalists.

"We're working with the Texas Legislature to restore sensible leadership to Austin's executive branch as soon as possible. I do hope and pray that other governors and state legislatures will take note. A traitorous confederacy inside the United States stands zero chance of success at overthrowing our laws and dividing us. We will not tolerate hate speech in the name of religion. We will neutralize any threat to the peace and unity of the United States of America.

"Ernest Harris, a decorated FBI agent with 20 years of unsurpassed service, was tragically shot yesterday afternoon as he sat behind his desk in Bozeman, Montana, doing his duty, fighting crime and hate. The suspect, who we believe is a member of the Militia of Montana, is still at large. Anti-abortion violence is at an all-time high and many local authorities throughout the United States are refusing to help our investigators bring these criminals to justice.

"We *must*" - she pounded her glass podium with her fist for emphasis - "eliminate the threat of dangerous firearms in the hands of our citizens. I implore you to be sure that all of the illegal firearms your friends and neighbors own will be turned in before the deadline of July third. If your family or friends violate the law with your knowledge, you may be found culpable in a court of law unless you report them to the proper authorities. We intend to enforce these anti-terrorism statutes to the fullest extent that the law allows."

Part II

The Bible Belt Buckles

Chapter 3

Auburn, Alabama

"Sin! That's the problem with America, not President Brighton, not gun control, not Congress, not the Supreme Court. It's sin! And it's the sin in the church that brings the boot of tyranny to our necks." Pastor Anthony Henderson waxed bold before his congregation of 500 in the suburbs of Auburn. The entire rear of the building was lined with standing observers due to a lack of seats. It was the seventh straight night of a three-night revival. The past week they needed to have two meetings a day to accommodate the crowds. As the participants have said, the Spirit moved on day three and the altars have been filled ever since.

"We are a nation under judgment because we have abandoned God's law for man's. We have worshiped and served the created rather than the Creator. We deserve the wrath of God as much as Sodom and Gomorrah. America is doomed without Jesus Christ."

Some shouted "Amen!" but a few gasped at this relatively abusive rhetoric by Pastor Henderson. One tall elder, with a round face and a boyish haircut, sat in the third row with a smile from ear to ear. This was Cal Manning's dream – revival!

"Preach it!" Cal hailed his beloved pastor with shouts of encouragement interspersed throughout his sermons. He was thrilled to see such a breakthrough in his church and his community. He'd never witnessed such conviction. His pastor's speech offended many, but only the unrepentant. As Jesus said, "Wisdom is justified of her children," or as the truth is more commonly articulated, "the proof is in the pudding." Every night, weeping souls flocked to the altar to confess and forsake their sins, to pray and weep for the lost, or just to worship the One who saved them from sin and hell. The whole congregation was aflame with a holy desire to know God and make Him known. Prayer meetings were packed and lasted for hours. The Spirit of God was filling willing vessels. If there ever was a revival, this was it. The pastor spent hours behind the pulpit every day passionately pleading for holy living, patiently demolishing every secular and religious excuse for sin.

When the public confessions began, the depravity and depth of hypocrisy was shocking. Elders confessed pedophilia and pornography addiction, local politicians confessed hiring prostitutes, youth confessed homosexuality, and elders' wives confessed slander and prescription drug abuse. The greatest temptation Cal Manning faced was a reluctance to forgive the vilest of hypocrites in the congregation, but with God's help, he found the strength to embrace them as brothers and sisters. He must, lest he be like the elder brother of the prodigal son. The words of Christ rang fresh in His mind, "For if you forgive not men their trespasses, neither will your Father in heaven forgive your trespasses." *There, but for the grace of God, go I,* he constantly reminded himself. The whole city of Auburn, in the very buckle of the Bible belt, was shaken to the core with the mighty power of God.

"Jesus is coming for a bride without spot or wrinkle, but how some of us love our spots and wrinkles. We rest contently with being mostly clean. Oh, the typical Auburn hypocrite doesn't mind singing hymns on Sunday morning, putting some change in the offering plate, but it's like Judas Iscariot's kiss. Judas said, 'Hail, master' and then betrayed Him for 30 shiny coins. God wants obedience, not sacrifice. Like Saul, you may do *most* of God's will. You sup with King Agag to the baah-ing of the sheep and think that just a *little bit* of sin won't hurt."

He paced back and forth on the platform as he preached, occasionally pointing at the congregation for emphasis. "But as the prophet Samuel told King Saul, a little bit of rebellion is like the sin of witchcraft. A little bit of sin is like idolatry – it's like worshipping another god. Saul lost his kingdom and perished a backslider, alienated from God's blessing." He paused as he returned to the pulpit and glanced at his notes.

"Are you a Judas Iscariot or a King Saul? As you sit in your pew, wide smile, chest out, thinking that you're all right because you have *mostly* obeyed God: you've quit most of your pornography, you flirt with your co-workers less, or you honor your parents more often than not." He glanced at a block of youth who sat in the front left of the congregation. "Have you, like Saul, allowed yourself to keep peace with sin? James said that friendship with the world makes you the enemy of God. Do you have faith without works, which the Apostle James tells us cannot save? Have you betrayed your master with a kiss? Have you cherished the glittering jingle of the trinkets and treasures of this ole' world more than the reproach of the cross?" He took a deep breath and paced back and forth on the platform, praying silently as a heavy conviction began to settle across the congregation.

"Every place in which Paul the Apostle rebuked sin in the churches, he warned them, 'those who do such things shall not inherit the Kingdom of God.' The cross provides victory over sin and the devil, but the hypocrites prefer the devil's candy. Jesus said, 'No man can serve two masters.' God would rather you be hot or cold; the lukewarm, He'll spew you out of His mouth." At hearing these words, a young man in the front row rushed to the altar, trembling with the fear of God, tears of repentance streaming down his face. His remorse was the crack in the dam as the altars began to fill with mourners.

How much more can I take of this? thought the undercover FBI agent in the back row. He was ordered to follow this preacher's sermons ever since the Bureau received a complaint about hate speech and threatening words about the president and abortionists. *This guy's a kook. Probably beats his wife after he's done with the congregation. But he hasn't spoken against abortion, homosexuality, nor uttered a critical word of the federal government.*

He looked to the right side of the building at the plain-clothed police officer that accompanied him. Their eyes met and the FBI agent shook his head to express disgust at having to endure this verbal abuse. His cell phone vibrated and he glanced down at it. *You're needed at Christ Church in Montgomery*, it read.

He texted back, *Ratcher's team has that under control.*

Seconds later, it vibrated again. *No they don't. Conclude your investigation and assist Ratcher.*

The agent sighed and decided that he would leave in two minutes.

"When God sent Israel into the Promised Land, He told them to not make peace treaties with the wicked in that land. Intolerance was the rule. Israel was commanded to destroy the inhabitants of the Promised Land because of the wickedness of those nations." Pastor Henderson walked down the stairs and wandered past the 30 repentant mourners who were kneeling at the altar. "God warned Israel that if they made peace pacts with the wicked, then they'd face defeat at the hands of their enemies. Instead of God using Israel to judge the wicked nations in the Promised Land, He used the wicked nations in the Promised Land to judge Israel instead."

Pastor Henderson paused and crossed his arms over his chest. "The American church has made peace pacts with the wicked," he said soberly. "We tolerate sin in our churches. Rather than rebuke the hypocrite and demand repentance, rather than excommunicate the impenitent brother as First Corinthians 5 instructs, the church calls for a treaty. 'Peace,' we cry, 'Peace!' – at the cost of our purity. The Aachans we tolerate in our midst rob us of our victory. Rather than conquer sin in our Promised Land, sin conquers us. The salt has lost its savor. The church has tolerated the evil in the world around us, and now evil is no longer tolerating us. For decades, we've kept the sword comfortably in its sheath, retired from the battlefield, and sent our children into the pagan classrooms of the Canaanites. Our government's open defiance of God and our publicly-condoned, taxpayer-funded national sins have not brought the rebuke of the church, but rather our caressing silence."

The federal agent leaned forward in his pew. The preacher's transition into the political arena peaked his interest.

"Oh, the tinkle of the 30 pieces of silver in our 501c3 pockets'" Pastor Henderson said, jostling the keys in his pockets. "Oh, that we would realize that our freedoms are only as secure as the righteousness of God's remnant. We'd rather be the sugar of the world than the salt. So, as Jesus warned, we are going to be trodden under the foot of wicked men. If we don't repent, He'll remove our candlestick, just as He threatened to do to many of the churches addressed in Revelation chapters two and three." He paused to let the gravity of those words sink in. "God has been longsuffering with the church in America, but now, judgment begins at the house of God."

The agent received another text, *Call en route to Montgomery.* When he stood to leave, the undercover police officer saw it and sighed in relief. The officer didn't agree with the harsh tone of Pastor Henderson, but he heard nothing that merited the cost of an extensive investigation managed by a meddling federal bureaucracy.

"We must judge ourselves or we will be judged by God," Pastor Henderson said, lifting his open Bible again, pages facing heaven. "We must long for the God-blessed remnant, rather than the sin-stained majority. When God has his pure remnant, then we will take His Word in the mountain-moving power of His Spirit to this wicked and perverse generation and God will give us victory. We might not live to see our land turn back to God – our children or grandchildren might be the ones to reap the fruit of our labors. But if we have victory in our hearts, we'll have victory in our land. If professing Christians repent, humble themselves, and pray, God *will* heal our land…"

The agent burst through the doors in the rear of the church and entered the foyer. He was fed up with Anthony Henderson's fire and brimstone preaching, but the moron was not a political dissenter.

Pastor Henderson's preaching could be heard through the speakers in the hallway and the foyer. "The United States of America has long ago forgotten God, and as Psalm 9:17 says, 'Every nation that forgets God shall be turned into hell.' Any nation that murders millions upon millions of its offspring, uses tax-payers money to fund it, employs U.S. Marshals to protect the murderers, is *not* blessed by God. No way! God's Word says these murderers are headed for hell."

"Amen!" shouted some.

"Preach it!"

Others glanced nervously at each other, aware of how many who have made such stances publicly on that particular issue are now behind bars or prodded out of church leadership by federal bureaucrats threatening to revoke the church's 501c3 status.

Cal Manning had a smile across his face from ear to ear. "That's right, Pastor!" He was glad that his pastor was not going to be intimidated by the federal hate crimes laws. *The devil's bark is worse than his bite,* he thought.

The FBI agent had his hand on the doorknob that led out of the church when he heard the pastor touch on the forbidden subject. "Amen," he mumbled mockingly.

The agent texted his superior, *Henderson violated the hate crimes statute. I'm arresting him after the service.*

When the pastor uttered those forbidden words, the police officer that was with the agent sunk down into his chair. He had counseled the pastor to avoid political issues like abortion, but the pastor couldn't take a hint. *At least the Bureau agent had left,* he recalled with a taint of hope.

"God is doing in America right now what He often did to nations that forsook Him. He set tyrants over them…"

A moment later the Bureau agent received a text message. *Apprehend him tomorrow. Your team is needed in Montgomery.*

"We've preferred human rulers over God," Pastor Henderson continued, "and now we're going to suffer under human rulers. When I read the Bible, I see that the two sins that bring destruction on a nation more than any others are sodomy and child sacrifice. Of this, America is guilty. Now, even the few godly rulers we do have, like Henry Adams, are being forced from office. If the wrath of Almighty God does not fall upon us, he will owe Sodom and Gomorrah an apology. The United States of America *was* one nation under God, but now we are one nation under God's curse – thanks to watered down, diluted, pathetic salt."

"Now, he's going to belittle gay people?" thought the agent out loud. *I'm not going to stand for this. I'll arrest him now and then go to Montgomery.* He stepped into the church auditorium, paused, and when his gaze met the eyes of the undercover police officer, he gave him a smile and a nod.

What? the officer thought to himself. *He surely doesn't mean to arrest him now, does he? In front of everybody?* He frowned and shook his head.

The agent reached up to his right ear, tapped on his wireless microphone and whispered, "The line's been crossed. I'm apprehending the subject now and then we're heading to Montgomery. Requesting back-up." His voice notified the leader at an Austin office full of armed federal agents on standby. He reached under his jacket and unholstered his stainless steel Smith and Wesson .45 semi-automatic.

The pastor's tone was growing in intensity as he concluded his sermon. "God's eyes roam to and fro throughout America, looking to show Himself strong on behalf of a pure people. Will you come out from among them and be separate? Will you—" Pastor Henderson thought the man was headed for the altar, but then he saw the semi-automatic pistol in his right hand. Row by row of people let out gasps of disbelief as they saw the tall, armed man in a black suit walking down the center aisle toward the pastor.

"Stop preaching." The agent unfolded his identification with his left hand and pointed his gun at the floor in front of Pastor Henderson with his other. "Anthony Henderson, you are under arrest. Spread your legs and put your hands on top of the pulpit."

The church was stunned. A few men even started making their way to the front to reason with the agent. Those at the altar paused their praying to give their attention to the commotion in the center aisle behind them. The federal agent walked up the stairs to the pastor, frisked him, and handcuffed him behind his back.

Cal Manning stood and boldly shouted, "Get away from him! You had better back down!"

The undercover police officer in the back of the church now stood up and began to counsel the congregation. "Everybody calm down. We're just going to question him. Calm down."

Manning walked toward the pulpit as the federal agent led Pastor Henderson down the stairs. "Don't you fear God? You have no right to—"

The FBI agent suddenly pointed his gun at Manning's chest and stopped him in his tracks. "Who are you to say what I have a right to do and not do? Keep your distance," the agent ordered, raising the gun to Manning's forehead.

As he spoke, several SWAT police officers and FBI agents in full tactical gear with automatic weapons made their way into the rear of the building. Screams and gasps from those in the rear of the church caused all to turn and watch the helmeted, black-clad agents make their way to pre-planned positions. They shifted nervously, almost as upset at this public display of force as the church members.

"Listen to me," said the agent loudly to the entire congregation. "This man is being arrested for hate crimes against abortion-providers and gays. The United States' government will no longer tolerate such inflammatory speech. Unless you also want to wind up in jail, you had best keep your hate to yourself and learn to be tolerant."

Pastor Henderson looked down at his wife who sat in the first row, her jaw agape as tears gushed from her eyes.

"Keep the faith," Pastor Henderson urged his congregants as he was led down the aisle toward the rear of the church. "Grieve all men but God."

The plain-clothed officer stood up on the back row and assured them, "We are just going to question him. Don't do anything rash."

"Mr. Manning, I can't give you any more information than that," the tight-lipped secretary at the Auburn Police Station replied.

Cal tried to keep himself calm in front of this obese woman in a tight blouse. The church had been in round-the-clock prayer meetings for their pastor the past two days. The church elders were having a difficult time managing nightly meetings, a presence in front of a courthouse, and a sprouting church full of new converts. He leaned forward and tapped his finger against the counter that was between them. "All he did was preach the Bible."

"The defendant knew the law and should've known the consequences of speaking about gays in derogatory terms."

"Derogatory terms?" Cal couldn't believe his ears. "You gotta be kidding me! Why can't his family see him? How come the rapists and murderers can see their families but a Bible-believing pastor is locked away in solitude?"

"If you are chosen to testify at his hearing, you can tell that to the judge. That's all I can tell you." She leaned back into her chair and pretended like she was answering a phone call.

Cal sighed deeply and marched out of the police station back to his post on the sidewalk beside the other members of his church. He looked at the gentleman who stood next to him. "Your turn."

A hundred Christians – men, women, and children – lined the sidewalk praying quietly as the arraignment proceeded inside. Cal Manning wore a blue sports coat, a baby blue dress shirt, and a blue striped tie, which was the standard deacon's dress at the church. He sat in the second to the last row in the almost packed courtroom. He looked over his left shoulder and glanced at Mrs. Henderson, his pastor's wife. Her eyes were bloodshot and pink hives had erupted on her face and neck. Her face paled when she saw her husband enter the courtroom in an orange prisoner outfit, taking small steps because of leg irons. His hands were cuffed in front of him. His hair was disheveled and his eyes appeared glossy.

Pastor Henderson appeared to lag behind the officer that led him and was prodded along by the officer behind him. He staggered as if he was drunk. Manning was stunned. He looked back at Mrs. Henderson, who had a look of fright on her tired face.

Pastor Henderson looked back and his eyes caught Manning's. Henderson opened his mouth to speak but no words came out. The officer behind him put a hand on his shoulder to direct him to his seat.

Henderson sat down, looked back, and finally spit the words out in a slurred growl, "They drugged me." The officer scolded Henderson and told him to be quiet.

A roar of whispers erupted in the courtroom and Cal felt a surge of righteous indignation burn within him. He leapt to his feet and his eyes wandered aimlessly around the room, as if looking for equally infuriated friends and neighbors. He was aghast at what was transpiring before his eyes in the U.S.A. He didn't know what to do with this surge of adrenaline he felt rise within him, but he felt like he had to do something.

An officer stepped into the room and announced, "All rise for the Honorable Judge Smith." Everybody rose to their feet as one, joining Manning who was already standing.

A woman in a black robe with short, black hair stepped through the large wooden back door. Her voice was cold and stern. "Be seated." She took her own seat, elevated above the on-lookers.

Manning remained standing for a moment as everyone else sat down. He was still in a state of shock at the thought that his beloved pastor was being drugged during his incarceration. Everybody stared at him for a brief moment before he slowly sat down, shaking his head. He caught the disapproving glare of the judge as he settled into his seat.

"Anthony Henderson," the judge announced, "please stand."

Pastor Henderson didn't move. She repeated the command and the officer who sat next to him nudged him to his feet. He stood and looked around as the judge read the indictment against him. "You have been charged with violating Federal Statute 19230: hateful public speech intended to intimidate or threaten protected minority people groups, a third degree felony."

The fiery indignation in Manning's gut erupted. Cal Manning jumped to his feet. "That is absurd!" he shouted from the rear of the courtroom. The judge lifted her eyes and slammed her gavel against the table as the courtroom erupted in whispers.

"Quiet!" she ordered, slamming her gavel twice. "Order!"

"He preached God's Word!"

"Another outburst like that, mister, and you'll find yourself in jail for contempt of court."

Manning would have continued, oblivious to consequence, if it were not for the pleading of Mrs. Henderson in the row behind him, who urged him to sit down.

"Quiet!" The irate judge slammed her gavel against the table once more to silence the murmuring that filled the courtroom. "Officer Yablonsky." She motioned to the officer in front of the podium. "Please go back there and stand next to that fellow in the blue sports coat. Even a whisper from him, you take him to jail."

The tall officer with a crew cut and sharp facial features nodded and marched to Manning's aisle. He stood and turned to face the judge, but kept his head cocked so as to keep an eye on the rude church deacon. Cal prayed silently and tried to keep his impulses under control.

The judge turned her attention back to the accused hatemonger. "The second charge against you is violation of Executive Order 19229: hateful public speech intended to intimidate and threaten abortion providers and those who have obtained such services. A third degree felony. How do you plead?"

Henderson didn't answer the question, but rather stood silently with a blank look on his face.

The judge repeated the question and, again, no answer was forthcoming. Whispers rose throughout the courtroom.

Judge Smith grabbed the gavel, slammed it on the table again, and repeated the question. "Anthony Henderson, how do you plead?"

The officer nudged Pastor Henderson while a short, clean-cut man behind him stood up. "Your Honor, I've been chosen to represent Anthony Henderson. He wished to give his own pleading, but seeing that he is presently unwilling, I am prepared to speak on his behalf."

"What did you do to my husband?" Mrs. Henderson exclaimed through a pitiful flurry of tears.

The judge slammed her gavel down several times. "Order! There will be no talking in the..."

"What's the matter, Tony?" Mrs. Henderson called out to her husband.

"Order!" the judge shouted before slamming her gavel again. "Be quiet or I'll empty the courtroom. How does he plead, Mr. Wilson?"

"Innocent," the attorney proclaimed. "My client hereby waives the right to a jury trial."

"What?" Manning was livid. *Why would he do that?* He turned to see the puzzled look on Mrs. Henderson's face. At least a jury trial would give Pastor Henderson a chance.

"Very well," said the judge with an approving nod and a grin. "The trial of Anthony Henderson for the aforementioned charges will commence tomorrow morning at nine a.m."

She grabbed her gavel, slammed it once on the table, and gathered her things to depart. The officer at the front of the courtroom coldly stated, "You are dismissed."

Cal Manning stood to his feet, disturbed at the sight of the police officer prodding Pastor Henderson out of his seat and toward the door adjacent to the judge's bench. Judge Smith had her back turned and was heading for the door, which another officer held open. The soft rumble of whispers and murmuring began to fill the room.

"This ain't right!" shouted Manning with a critical finger pointed at the judge. "You drugged the man and set him up for an immoral judgment based upon immoral law! He has the constitutional right to a jury trial!"

She stopped, turned in the open doorway, and shouted an order, which was inaudible because of the roar of conversation that filled the room.

"I demand," Manning raised his trembling voice, "I demand that you release Pastor Tony Henderson! The only crime here is the one you are committing against our pastor!" The officer to his left at the edge of the aisle was unable to reach Manning quickly because the two ladies between them were incidentally obstructing his way. The officer waved the ladies back to a sitting position as he struggled to reach Manning.

Judge Smith rushed to the microphone and reiterated the order that she had spoken seconds earlier that no one heard. "Arrest him! Contempt of court." She picked up the gavel and slammed it hard against the table. "We'll see if a night in jail will teach you some manners." She turned and rushed from the room as Manning continued his rebuke.

"Thus saith the Lord," Cal Manning bellowed authoritatively, "those who justify the wicked and those who condemn the just are both an abomination to God!" Judge Smith had left the room at the end of that sentence and Manning had a captive audience. The room full of supporters and journalists held their breath as the tall, thin officer struggled to move down the aisle to apprehend this courtroom rebel.

"Keep the faith, Pastor Henderson," Manning addressed his beloved pastor with passionate inflection. "We are praying for you!"

Suddenly, the officer jerked Manning's left arm and twisted it. He pulled him over the laps of two ladies and down the aisle toward the back of the room, where a handful of angry officers were anxious to get their hands on him.

"Please, listen to me," Manning pleaded to the officers as they roughly frisked him for weapons. "I know you guys are just doing your job, but you took an oath to defend the Constitution and—"

"Shut up!" The officer squeezed the cuffs extra tight over his wrists. Manning gritted his teeth as the metal edge of the cuffs pressed into his flesh.

"Open up your eyes." Manning searched the eyes of the officers. "Can't you see that our law is under attack? Where's your fear of God?"

The senior officer jerked him toward the back door. He was led down a hallway toward another door. "You fellows are under no obligation to enforce immoral laws and judgments..." Manning pleaded with them as he was pushed through several doors into a foyer where an officer sat behind a thick glass window. The officer nodded and pushed a button. A heavy door made of steel bars opened and they walked through. A cell door was unlocked and he was pushed into it with five other criminals without a word from the officer who led him there.

"Aren't you going to take my cuffs off? Hey!"

The officers disappeared down the hall, leaving Cal Manning handcuffed in a jail cell full of criminals.

Chapter 4

Cal missed dinner and his stomach growled as furiously as his imagination. He was a floppy-framed, middle-class Caucasian who had never been in a fistfight in his life, and he felt helpless locked up in a cell with five steroid-fertilized criminals, whose muscular bodies were covered with tattoos and metal piercings. The worst part of it all was that he had to go to the bathroom and the handcuffs were still on his wrists. He tapped his feet to try to control his urge, but that drew attention from the others. He was so desperate that he would have asked someone in the deepest masculine voice he could muster to undo his drawers so he could relieve himself in that filthy urinal in the corner. But with a 250-pound drug dealer on one side and a serial rapist sitting on the other, he knew he would probably just stand there unable to overcome the spasm in his groin. That would draw even more attention to him, which was even worse than the full bladder he couldn't relieve.

He always thought that if he were ever locked up in jail for doing right, he'd just witness to everybody in the cell with him. Reality, however, seemed to put that notion far out of his mind. He screamed down the empty hallway for several minutes to have the cuffs removed or to be re-cuffed with his hands in front of him, but that upset his roommates.

A few hours passed and the sky, barely visible through a barred window down the hall, grew dark. Finally, he heard footsteps coming down the concrete hall.

"Hey! Please! I need these cuffs taken off."

"What's the matter, pip-squeak?" asked the African-American with braided hair. He chuckled at Cal's anxiety. "Get a load of this virgin," he said to the others as they laughed at the blushing handcuffed stranger. They continued making wise cracks at Cal's expense as the doors to the cell creaked open.

"Come on," one of the two officers waved the criminals down the hall toward another part of the jail. They followed him down the concrete hallway, their laughs and chatter echoing incoherently off the cold brick walls.

"As for the cuffs," said a second, cranky-looking guard who gazed at Manning, "they can come off. You must have really upset that judge for them to leave the cuffs on you like that." He put a key into the cuffs and opened them. Cal immediately rubbed his wrists and stretched his arms. "But you ain't going anywhere for 24 hours, pal."

"Hasn't anybody posted bail for me yet?"

"Not for contempt of court. You got a day and a night at the most expensive hotel in Alabama." He pointed down the hall. "That way. Let's go."

*****

The director of Children's Services in Auburn answered the phone on the second ring. She set down her half-eaten Snickers, swallowed the bolus hard, and said, "Hello" before washing it down with a gulp of her Mountain Dew.

"Mrs. Rhonda Dolan please."

"This is she."

"This is Shirley Wheeling, National Director of the Human Resources Department."

Rhonda's eyes opened wide. She coughed and patted her stiff perm as if the director could see her. "Oh, hello. I'm just finishing a snack." Her heavy southern, small-town accent relayed her sudden anxiety to her superior. She sat upright in her chair, well, as upright as a 250-pound pendulous woman can in a desk chair designed for a skinny secretary.

"I'm calling the local offices per presidential request. Have you received the packet from the national office?"

"Um, I think I remember seeing it around here somewhere." She shifted the papers around on her cluttered desk.

"It's a questionnaire about the make-up of your child abuse cases in the past year. The president wants that information immediately. In that same packet is a memo regarding the president's recent executive order pertaining to Homeland Security measures."

"Yes, I think this is it." Rhonda found the manila envelope under the most recent edition of *Southern Cooking* magazine.

"It reviews some of the high-risk factors the president's EO established. The EO mandates your immediate intervention in these high-risk cases. Protecting these children is a priority for the president. She believes our abilities to operate as a watchdog for these high-risk children is under-utilized…"

"Of course." She was excited at the thought of obtaining more authority against the child abusers in her community.

She took out the packet of papers and glanced at the highlighted items on the sheet that identified the department directives relating to the president's Executive Orders.

High-risk families:
　Involvement in an extreme amount of religious activity,
　Intolerance of alternative lifestyles and cultures,

Involved in anti-abortion activities or donations to anti-abortion causes,
　Home-schooling,
　Have firearms present in the home,
　Practice spanking…

"You have in your files information on the at-risk children, particularly those who are spanked as a method of behavior modification."

Rhonda grunted in agreement. Formal disapproval of all violence as a means of child discipline was a prerequisite to her candidacy for employment at Children's Services. Of course, she, like all competent parents, spanked her children once in a while, but she would never admit that.

"Now that we have this legislation, we need to start picking up these children before they wind up in an E.R. with shaken-baby-syndrome, missing, or worse. They'll eventually embrace the same extremist ideology as their parents, perpetuating the same cycle of fanaticism and violence in the next generation."

"But we're overloaded dealing with the *real* child abuse cases already."

"Just read the memo, Mrs. Dolan," the HRS director snapped, irritated at the implications in the subordinate's comments. She'd been through this conversation 30 times already today, and she could just about predict the responses from the rural Children's Services offices. "The president's financial plan accounts for the increased funding needed by the local Children's Service organizations all over the country."

"Wonderful!" Rhonda exclaimed in her slurred southern drawl.

"In addition and more importantly, I've just faxed to your office a list of high-risk families compiled through the cooperation of the FBI, ATF, NEA, and other groups."

"Yes. I have the fax right here." She picked up the four-sheet document from the D.C. office.

"These children are at an *extremely* high-risk level and require your field workers to actively pursue evidence against the parents and begin removing the kids from their homes as soon as possible."

"You want them to remove the children even if there is no evidence of abuse?"

The director smirked as if expecting the inferior to already know the answer to that question. "This list *is* your evidence. But if you visit the homes and interview the children, you'll find more evidence of a high-risk nature. The success of your activities in the coming months will have a direct relationship on the amount of federal money your local department is granted in next year's budget. The only way to avoid deep cuts is to remove these children until their parents pass the NEA-directed course on tolerance and parenthood. Is that understood?"

"I understand, Mrs. Wheeling," she said, fantasizing about the Bahamas vacation she could afford with her raise. *Maybe she could get back on those diet pills that Dr. Willow prescribed.*

"Protecting these children is a priority for President Brighton."

"I understand. I received a complaint just this morning from a neighbor who heard screams coming from one of the children living next door to her, the child of a well known religious extremist whose name I see on your list." She thumped the fax that she held in her hand. "He's an elder of a popular homophobic church whose pastor's on trial right now for hate speech."

The secretary could practically hear the HRS director's grin over the phone line. "You've got the idea, Mrs. Dolan."

*****

When the guard pushed the button and the barred door swung open, Cal was the only one remaining in the cell.

"Have you heard about the trial of Pastor Henderson?" Cal asked him. "It was supposed to start this morning."

"Yep. It's done. Twelve weeks at the Alabama State Psychiatric Prison in Montgomery."

"*Psychiatric* prison?"

"The judge said that he needs some sensitivity training so he'll learn to like gays and abortionists or something like that."

Cal gasped in disbelief.

"Your wife's in the waiting room. Follow me."

Cal's heart sped up as he looked through the door and saw his wife's warm smile. She carried their five-month-old son toward the door as her other children followed her. When the door opened, Cal rushed through it to embrace his wife. "Sabina!"

He kissed her tenderly as his baby boy cooed and smiled, excited to see his daddy. The baby reached for him and Cal took him. He knelt down as his two little girls walked up to him and grabbed each thigh, hugging it and squealing, "Daddy! Daddy!"

"Oh, I love you guys so much," he said as he bent down and kissed them. His wife dressed them up in matching clothes, their cherry blond hair pulled to the side in pigtails.

When he stood back up, Sabina smiled and wrapped her thin, firm arms around him for a hug. "I'm proud of you. You did the right thing."

They were all on their knees or lying prostrate in prayer. Every square foot of Manning's small living room was covered with the 20 fellow church members in fervent prayer. Some had their hands clasped, praying silently. Others wept and cried out to the Lord loudly, pleading for deliverance of their pastor. Others took turns praying more formally for the church, the new converts, the community, and the government leaders. One of the teenagers watched the children upstairs in a bedroom, where they played with green, plastic army men in a makeshift battle trying to free the pastor from the bad guys.

"Oh God," Manning prayed out loud from his knees in front of the couch. "Your Spirit moved mightily through our pastor, convicting of sin and transforming many lives..."

Sincere lips mumbled "Amen" and "Yes, Lord" as he prayed.

"Now, dear God, as you used Joseph in prison, use our pastor. It was your will to let Joseph suffer in Pharaoh's dungeon, to refine him and prepare him to rule in Egypt. May Pastor Henderson find such grace in Your sight. Keep his mind safe from the medicines and humanistic counseling. We believe, God, that his best days are yet to come." Sabina, who was kneeling beside her husband, reached over and grabbed his hand.

"We pray the same for Governor Henry Adams and all the other righteous men and women who have been persecuted lately," Sabina added.

"Amen," Cal nodded.

"Lord, help our country." Sabina let go of her husband's hand, put her face in her palms, and let out a troubled sob.

Cal looked up to see her weeping. He placed his hand gently on her shoulder. "Lord, we pray for America." He paused. *How shall I pray for America? Should I pray for mercy? Or shall I agree with what surely must be your judgments against us for our sins?* "Lord, help." His voice cracked with a heart-wrenching grief.

Manning's mind raced when he paused, as one does when unsure of what to do or say in a moment of stress. The mind considers dozens of alternative routes, the consequences, and subjects all to a list of priorities. Manning thought about the abrupt interruption of the awe-inspiring move of God in his church, the arrest of their pastor in the middle of service, and the sentence the judge pronounced against him. He thought about the evolution of the federal government the past several decades into a more tyrannical, unconstitutional government with more taxpayer-subsidized abortion, more promotion of homosexuality, expanding federal hate speech laws, and more state control over schools, religion, business, and families.

Anger rose within him as each image flashed across his mind. He knew that the actions of the present administration were simply the culmination of many years of systematic dismantling of the foundation upon which those freedoms were based. He felt a *holy fury* rise up even more within him. It was a fierce emotion that surprised him with its energizing power, and yet felt refreshing. It was the kind of righteous indignation that you would feel if you were forced to witness an assault, and then were given an opportunity to intervene to protect the victim. It was the kind of anger that fuels the pursuit of justice and tempts common men to take up the sword of vengeance on their own when the magistrates become the violators and usurpers. It was not the kind of fury for which he felt guilt – not at all. This was a holy anger. A fierce, yet pure fury, the kind the saints will feel when they reign with Christ over the nations with a rod of iron. He recalled a Scripture in Psalm 7, verse 11: *God is angry with the wicked every day.* He felt the fury become white-hot within him, boiling, stirring, strengthening him, and he thought to himself, *I'm angry with the wicked, too, God. Just like You.* Then the Scripture came to his mind, "The wrath of man worketh not the righteousness of God," and his emotions were checked.

He whispered his prayer, "Let your Word rule us, let your Spirit move us, not the carnal desire for vengeance or self-promotion. We lay down our lives, if need be, for Your Kingdom." Several in the room agreed with his prayer by their verbal affirmations and nods.

"Oh Lord," he prayed through clenched teeth, "we believe that we shall be victorious against the enemy and that we will trample Satan under our feet shortly. Lord, help us to be faithful, no matter what..."

Knock, knock, knock, knock, knock.

It startled everybody in the room. It was not the kind of knock from a latecomer to their prayer meeting. It was an intrusive knock, intentionally loud and arrogant. Cal glanced at Sabina, who shrugged. *Who could that be at 9 p.m.?*

A church elder near the door got up on his knees and twisted the doorknob as he rose to his feet.

On the other side of the screen door stood a middle-aged brunette with short, straight hair, dressed in a black pants suit. Two police officers stood behind her, muscular arms crossed over their chests, golden badges shining on well-pressed black shirts, and their handguns dangling from wide black leather belts.

"Is Mr. Calvin Manning here?"

Cal stood to his feet and made eye contact with her. Her eyes were piercing and her countenance pitiless. She was on a mission. Cal's heart dropped into his gut. For a moment, he wished that he weren't wearing his black NRA polo shirt, as that surely was a mark against him.

He stood and walked to the door. Those kneeling and lying prostrate around him looked up at him, puzzled at the unwelcomed interruption. "Can I help you? We're in the middle of a prayer meeting."

"I am a child abuse investigator from Children's Services."

Cal nodded, his face flushing as he imagined what they were conspiring to do. "What can I do for you?"

"Mr. Manning, who else lives here?"

"Why?"

"We've received a complaint."

"What complaint?" He was curt.

So was she. "Does anyone else live here besides you, your wife, Sabina, your son, Tim, and two daughters, Naomi, and Rachel?"

"Why?"

"We have received reports that your children have been beaten." Cal's jaw hung low and he grew nauseous. "We have multiple reports of neighbors hearing their screams."

Cal took a deep breath. "What neighbors?"

The social worker calmly smiled and glanced at one of the officers. "You know those reports have to be confidential, Mr. Manning. We can't have child abusers knowing who filed complaints to the authorities. People wouldn't report abuse for fear of retaliation."

"They wouldn't *falsely* report abuse either." Cal raised his voice as he moved closer to the door to face the intrusive social worker. "That's one of the benefits of being able to face your accuser."

"Calm down, dear." Sabina pleaded with her husband in a soft voice. "It'll be all right."

Cal glanced back at Sabina and then walked to his living room window where he saw his neighbor staring at them from her porch. A college-aged girl with a buzz cut was reclining in a hammock with a book in her hands, watching the commotion out of the corner of her eye as she pretended to read. Manning raised his voice at her, "What did you tell them?"

She stood up and stared at Cal Manning with her hands on her hips. "I told them the truth! You beat your kids and it's not right!" She turned and stomped back into her house.

He returned to the front door in shock and disbelief and glared at the social worker. She just scowled at him disapprovingly, as if to say, *I told you so*. The officers shifted uneasily as Manning's face flushed red.

"She's lying. Our kids are the best kids anywhere."

"I'm sure they are. It's their parents we're worried about. Do you hit your kids, Mr. Manning?"

"What? Of course not!" He raised his voice, exasperated and trembling with both fear and rage. His conscience was pricked when he realized that the social worker probably considered spanking "hitting" and so he re-worded his answer. "It's none of your business!" He glanced down at the lock on the screen door and noticed that it was unbolted.

"I'm afraid it *is* my business, Mr. Manning." The officers shared an anxious glance with each other as voices rose, fingers pointed, and grimaces tensed.

"Where do they go to school?"

"They're home-schooled."

The social worker's lips tightened as she glanced back at one of the officers. "Of course. Well, we're going to have to take your kids for a—"

"No, you are not!" When he screamed, Sabina jolted and her face contorted to reveal an indescribable horror, as if a childhood nightmare was finally coming to pass. She stood up and began to race toward the stairs.

The Children's Services worker reached to open the screen door just as Cal twisted the bolt shut.

"Mr. Manning! Open the door!"

He shut and locked the wooden door and motioned for someone to go lock the back door as well. The police officers took a deep breath. This was not going as easily as they hoped.

"We have a court order, Mr. Manning," the social worker calmly announced.

Cal looked through the small diamond-shaped window in the door and the social worker pressed the white piece of paper with the county's seal on it against the screen door. "If you cooperate, you'll get a court hearing and you may get your children back."

"*May* get them back?"

"You have no choice. The court has decided that this is in the best interests of your kids. I have two law officers with me who will break this door down to protect the children." The two police officers nodded. They were just as fearful of the children's safety as they were of their own. This was not an easy job. But they were especially motivated – the only thing they hated more than "cop killers" were "child molesters."

"This court order is not based upon the opinion of just one of your neighbors, Mr. Manning. A federal risk assessment also labeled your children as high risk."

"What?!" He put his eye up to the diamond-shaped window again. "High-risk for what? Loving God? They're happy and they love us as much as we love—"

"With your behavior tonight, Mr. Manning, you're confirming the risk assessment."

"We don't beat them. We gently spank them, lovingly." When Cal admitted that, he could hear the gasps of the fellow church members behind them, as if they were disappointed with his naivety. Cal looked back at them and shrugged.

"You can tell that to the judge. I'm sorry, Mr. Manning, but you have no choice." **Knock, knock.** "Open the door!"

"Should we call for back-up?" one of the officers asked. "Cover the rear of the home?"

"No, no. They'll come around." The social service worker had plenty of experience in these situations. "They always come around."

"Oh, God, help us." Cal began to look around the living room frantically, looking for a place to hide his children. He received no comfort from those around him, many still kneeling, some beginning to pray again.

Oh God, what do I do? His mind raced. *If I flee, I'm an outlaw. Where will we go? It'll just be a matter of time, and then, then I won't get to raise my kids at all. If I let them kidnap my children…* His heart raced at the thought. *The Bible says that I'm worse than an infidel if I don't care for my family.*

It was as if a light bulb lit up in Cal's mind. He rushed across the living room to the fireplace mantle. He had a secret compartment installed on the side of the mantle with a special door that could be pushed open. That's where he kept the only weapon he owned, a nine millimeter handgun. It was the federal paperwork that he filled out to get this handgun that contributed to his name being put on the government's high-risk list. He kept it there in the center of the house so his wife could reach it easily if someone broke into either the front or rear of the home.

Cal tried to be discreet as he removed the handgun, but some fellow church members saw it and gasped. Cal chambered a round, and then placed it in the small of his back under his belt as he walked toward the front door.

"If you don't cooperate, you'll go to jail and then you might *never* see your children again. There is counseling available for people who have your problem." **Knock, knock, knock, knock.** "Mr. Manning!"

Cal placed his eye to the diamond-shaped window in the door to make eye contact with the social service worker. "Let's be reasonable. I'm not going to let you kidnap my kids, so give me some other alternatives." He studied the two police officers. They looked resolute. Both of them had their right hands resting on their holstered handguns.

"There are no other legal alternatives for you, Mr. Manning. You have no choice."

"I'll compromise. Come back tomorrow and we'll try to have our attorney present."

"I can't do that, Mr. Manning. You've no choice but to comply. We have reason to believe your children are at risk of bodily and mental harm, and we cannot—"

"You're the one that has no choice!" Manning interrupted. "You can give up trying to convince me that it's in my kids' best interests for you to kidnap them. That will terrorize them! I'm a loving father. I know what's better for my kids than you or those God-hating lesbians next door!"

Sabina had brought the kids, wide-eyed with fear and confusion, downstairs and they stood in the middle of the room. *Why is Daddy screaming?* Their mother carried the diaper bag over her shoulder. Sabina began to cry when she saw the gun inside her husband's belt.

"No, Cal," she whispered frantically.

He whisked his head around and put his finger over his lips. "Shhh!"

"Ask them if I can go wherever she takes the kids."

Cal looked back, cringing at the thought of trusting the secular Children Service's Department with their kids, putting their livelihood at the mercy of pagan judges. He whispered back to Sabina, "No way. They would lie to you to get the kids out of the house. We're both suspected of child abuse, dear. When they ask Naomi who put those wooden-spoon-shaped red marks on her legs, she's going to tell them 'Mommy did it.'"

Sabina began to cry as her two oldest children hugged her waist. "Tell them that they can bring someone to live here for a while," she proposed.

"Give 'em your kids," one of their fellow church members recommended. "It happens every day, Cal. Take your anger management classes, and then you get a lawyer and get 'em back. That's the way it happened with me and my sister."

"Well, the times are a-changing," Manning snapped. "Even after they take our kids, I'd still be going to jail for hate crimes."

"It's just a class, man. Not jail, not for most people anyway."

Cal turned his gaze to Sabina. "We are church leaders and have a long paper trail of violating their so-called hate crime laws. We'd probably wind up in a psychiatric prison like Pastor Henderson. Who will raise our kids then? The lesbians next door?"

"We'll have legal recourse, Cal." Tears streamed down Sabina's cheeks. "But not if you do this."

"Oh yes we will!"

"Shhh," she urged him to keep his voice down.

He leaned toward her and whispered, "Lethal force to stop a kidnapping is justified, if we ever have a godly government. Short of godly government, we're probably going to end up in jail anyway. Why not pick up Samson's jawbone and wield away? Why not aim the slingshot and see if God defends us? Grab Jael's hammer and swing?"

"We *can* still fight it in court." Sabina wiped her tears and tried to be strong. Her husband was beginning to worry her as much as those policemen on the front porch.

Cal shook his head and looked back out the window. "There'll be no justice for us under this government, not for us." He turned back to his wife as his eldest child began to weep. "Are you telling me that you could just give our kids to these sinners standing on our front porch? How could we do that? I'm telling you, if we turn our children over to the Children's Services, we're sinning against them."

"Please, not in front of the kids." Sabina was much better at concealing their disagreements from their children whereas Cal was more impulsive. He said what was on his mind when it was on his mind with much less concern about what people thought about it.

"Not in front of the kids? What? Do you realize what's about to happen in front of our kids?"

This time, the knocking was so vigorous that it shook the whole doorframe. **Knock! Knock! Knock!**

"Mr. Henderson!" an officer shouted. "We're going to kick this door down if you don't comply!" **Knock! Knock!** "Open the door now!"

Cal told Sabina, "Our children may be raised by atheists, sodomites, or some divorced, authentic child molester." All three of his children began to cry and grab tighter onto their mother. "No way!" He shook his head vigorously back and forth as he bit his trembling lip. "I can't do it."

Knock, knock. "Mr. Manning, you have ten seconds, and then we're calling for back-up and breaking in. You'll go to jail for obstructing justice, resisting arrest, as well as a possible child abuse charge and any federal charges that may be filed. We have a judge's warrant."

Sabina tried to comfort their sobbing children, but the tears in her own eyes invited theirs. Her gaze darted to her husband. "What else can we do, Cal?"

He didn't answer, though he was seriously considering the unthinkable. The same anger that he had felt in his prayer, the same pure, passionate fury, was raging in him now. *They're the intruders. They're the violators of our God-given rights. They're trying to kidnap my kids. God protects His sheep from the wolves. So can I!* Cal's handgun was cold against his bare, sweaty skin under his belt in the small of his back.

The social worker overheard a woman inside encouraging Mr. Manning to open the door and she knew that he would give in any minute now. They always won.

"Mommy!" cried the eldest child, who was beginning to comprehend the gravity of the confrontation. "I don't want to leave." She began to weep bitterly, hugging tightly to her mother's leg. "Please don't let them take me."

This broke Sabina's heart. Sabina bent down and told her, "Stay here for a minute." She walked to the front door and handed her infant to her husband. "Let me speak to her."

Cal sighed and backed away from the door, one of his hands covering his mouth as he tried to hold back a waterfall of tears and sobs that rose to the surface. He held his son close. "It's okay, buddy." He looked down at the two little girls, who were now crying and clinging to his legs. "We're not going to let them take you, girls. If God be for us, who can be against us, right?" he said to them, reminding them of a Bible passage they had recently memorized. "The Lord is my helper." He paused to let them finish the passage.

His oldest daughter concluded it, "I will not fear what man can do unto me."

"It's going to be all right. Trust Jesus."

Sabina walked to the door and, much to Cal's dismay, she unlocked the deadbolt and twisted the doorknob.

"Don't open—" Cal tried to stop her but the door was already swinging open. All that stood between their foyer and those who threatened to steal their kids was a locked screen door.

"Please, ma'am," pleaded Sabina, crying. "I promise you. We don't hurt our children." The tears were generous and sincere. She put her hands together and pleaded with the social worker. "How would you feel if someone tried to take your kids when you never mistreated them and loved them so much?"

The social worker looked away, fighting the urge to pity the poor woman. "Ma'am, you'll have to tell that to the judge. As for now, we have a court order to take your children into our custody. I can be culpable if I don't obey it." She waved the piece of paper in front of her.

"Please, ma'am, please!" Sabina began to sob and beg. "We'll take any classes you require. You can send social workers to our home regularly. We'll even cook them meals when they're here."

"I'm sorry, Mrs. Manning, but—"

"Please!" Sabina fell onto her knees as the tears swam down her cheek in rivers. "Please don't take my babies!"

The officer pulled on the door, looked up, and his eyes met Cal's. With one well-trained move, the officer punched through the screen and reached in to unlock the screen door.

"No!" Cal handed his youngest to another church member as the officer unlocked the screen door and began to open it.

Cal Manning took a deep breath and then screamed at the top of his voice, startling everyone, "Nooo!"

The officer took one step into the house. He saw Cal Manning reach around to his back with his right arm, pull the handgun out, and raise it to the chest of the officer. The officer gasped, let go of the doorknob, and instinctively reached for his own gun.

"No, NO, **NO!**" Cal shouted louder and louder as the officer unholstered and began to raise his weapon towards Cal.

Blam!

The world stopped for a second. Everyone in the room cried out in shock. The line had been crossed. There was no turning back. Cal just couldn't let them take his kids, not as long as there was breath in him. He didn't trust corrupt government officials with his children. He was responsible for his babies and he couldn't abandon them. But now, they were outlaws. Now they were to be hunted. Now, sirens would be approaching, and APBs and "Wanted" posters would carry their names and photographs. Now, they would have to run.

The bullet went through the officer's upper chest and out of his back. Blood splattered through the screen onto Sabina, who was on her knees in front of him, weeping. The officer fell like a pile of bricks, crumpling in a pool of his own blood that flowed freely onto their "Welcome to Our Home" rug.

The second officer instinctively reached for his holstered handgun, but Cal shouted, "Stop!" and the officer froze with his gun in his grasp. They stared each other down for a moment. The officer's mind buzzed through possible contingencies. Without a bullet in the barrel, he would have to chamber a round before he could even fire. He studied Cal's weapon. He could see the index fingernail against the trigger was paler than the thumbnail. He could see that the assailant's legs were spread as one who was accustomed to shooting and his right eye was lined up along the sights toward his torso. The assailant's hands gripped the weapon perfectly; his gaze was firm, and his brow void of the sweat that he'd expect of a novice criminal. This isn't someone who would miss if he pulled the trigger at this distance.

"Put it down, now," Cal calmly insisted, resolved that he'd pull the trigger again before he would let them steal his children. "I have nothing to lose." The officer dropped his gun and raised his hands high.

The social worker's confident grimace instantly evolved to a wide-eyed look of absolute terror. She unleashed a blood-curdling, ear-piercing squeal.

Cal heard gasps of disbelief from behind him as his church friends looked on with trepidation. He pointed his gun at the social worker's head. "Told you I wasn't going to let you take my kids." His calmness in the situation even surprised his wife. Sabina found her lower legs drenched with the dying police officer's blood, as she knelt in front of her screen door. She couldn't take her eyes off of his body as his breathing rate quickened and the pool of blood underneath him continued to grow, spreading across the foyer's tile floor. His perishing body pressed against the screen door.

Sabina was in shock. Their perfect life was coming to an end. The officer breathed his last while Sabina slowly stood to her feet. She backed away from his carcass and wiped her bloody palms on her dress. She grabbed the screaming child that a friend tried futilely to comfort and she held her close.

The surviving officer started pleading with Manning to calm down and drop his weapon but Manning interrupted him, "No talking. Both of you get on the floor."

The social worker and the officer immediately started to get down on their bellies on the front porch. "No, pull the officer away from the screen door and step inside the house." They entered and lay on the floor with their hands on their heads. Cal flipped off the switch to the front porch light.

"Please don't kill me, don't kill me. I don't wanna die." The social worker was overcome with dread. She began to hyperventilate from the anxiety. She watched as the pool of blood gradually extended towards Cal's shoes. "I was following the government's orders."

"The government doesn't have a right to break God's law any more than you do." Cal's voice was relaxed with his gun firm in his confident grasp.

Cal saw curtains part across the street as his neighbors carefully peeked out of their windows. It isn't every day that gunshots are heard in this middle-class neighborhood.

"Sabina." Cal pointed at the door. "Get the kids in the van, now."

She looked up at him with pitiful, tear-filled eyes and whimpered, "Where are we going to go?"

He leaned into her and whispered something in her ear. She nodded, picked up the two youngest children, and stepped past the officers and the terrified social worker. Their oldest child followed close behind. "Meet me where we spent our first anniversary," Cal told her.

"Yes sir."

"Dan." Cal called out to a young man close to the kitchen. "In the third drawer under the left kitchen cabinet, there's some rope. Bring it, quickly. Everybody else, leave now. Drive off in different directions." The church folks stood up, confused, many crying, grabbing their purses and Bibles and heading for the front door. "Hurry. Please hurry." As they made their way out the front door, Cal urged them, "Tell them the truth, brothers and sisters. Don't get in trouble for us. You'll have to fight the beast in due time."

Dan tied the officer's hands and legs as everyone rushed to the cars that were parallel-parked in front of the house.

The police officer looked up and began to plead with the assailant. "Surrender, Mr. Manning. With a good attorney you can still turn this around."

"Don't you know that the federal government doesn't even have to give me an attorney anymore? The government can hold us without charges, without bail or trial. It was bound to happen someday, officer. If you keep pushing the envelope against good people, one day they're going to defend themselves."

"I'm against the president's executive orders," the officer informed him. "My brother home schools his kids."

Cal was taken aback. "Oh really? Well then why are you enforcing ungodly law if you're against it?"

The officer was stumped. "It's my job."

Cal grimaced. "And of course you have to do evil if your employer demands it…"

"Do evil?" The officer boldly reproved the assailant, "You just shot a police officer!"

"Who was trying to violently kidnap my kids!"

"What are you going to do to us?" the social worker wondered.

"You." Cal pointed his weapon to the back of the social worker's head. "You come with me." He took the guns from both officers, ejected the magazines, threw them down the dark street, and tossed the empty guns onto his lawn. Then he helped the social worker to her feet.

She began to cry and plead for her life. "Please don't kill me, please don't kill me!" He led her at gunpoint to his white Ford Escort in the driveway.

"Get in," he ordered. She reluctantly complied.

He walked around to the driver's side and pointed the gun at his terrified guest through the window. He stepped into the car, started the engine, and locked the doors. "Sit on your hands and look straight ahead." She quickly obeyed.

Sirens rapidly approached as he drove away. He took one last glimpse of his house in the rearview mirror and realized it would never be home again. All of their things, clothes, photo albums, paintings, computer files, the rough draft of a book on family that he was writing – everything was gone for good. He gulped hard and squinted away the salty moisture that burned in his eyes. *At least my family's safe.*

"What are you going to do to me?" His guest wailed frantically, fearful for her life.

"You and me? We're going to have a talk," he said, his voice distorted by his grief. "Keep your eyes faced directly ahead."

"Okay."

"Do you have any kids?" She nodded. "What are their ages?"

"Two girls, four and six."

"Same age as my little girls. What a coincidence. Do you spank your kids?"

She hesitated, her lip trembling. He raised his voice, "Answer the question."

"Uh, no, I don't."

"You know what the Bible says about you?"

She shook her head side to side.

"The Bible says if you don't chasten your children with a rod when they behave badly, then you *hate* your kids. You *hate* your kids. Did you know that?"

She sat there speechless.

"You know what else the Bible says? It says that if you will spank your children and not let yourself spare the rod for their crying, then you'll save their souls from hell. Just a swat or two most of the time does the trick. According to these passages, who's the one that abuses their kids, me or you?"

She paused. "Well, uh, I don't know."

"And now, your kids are brats, aren't they? They throw temper tantrums when they don't get their way. You probably don't like to go out into public with them because of the way they behave. You probably take them to a doctor for mood-altering drugs. Am I right?"

"Actually, I do pop them on the hand when they do something wrong."

Cal was aghast. "So you hit your kids too? Does your employer know that?"

There was no answer from the social worker. Her weeping escalated along with the harshness of Cal's tone. "You were going to kidnap my kids from me, torment us and my children, for doing something that *you also do!*"

"We were told that you beat them."

"On the hand or the leg, a couple of times maybe. Like you."

The social worker gained control of her emotions and looked down at her twiddling thumbs.

"I said to sit on your hands!" Cal took a deep breath. "You know, the most prevalent form of child abuse in America today is *not* spanking your kids. People are scared to obey God's command to discipline their kids for fear of you knocking on their door and stealing their kids."

When she saw that he was leaving the city limits, she trembled afresh. "Where are you taking me?"

"I'm dropping you off in a few miles."

"How could you kill that police officer?"

"How *couldn't* I? I pulled the gun in defense of my family and pulled the trigger in self-defense when that officer aimed his weapon at me. I have the right to defend my family from an unlawful kidnapping."

"It wasn't unlawful."

"It was according to God's law, which is the law that's going to scrutinize us on Judgment Day."

"He was a police officer and I work for the government."

"An elected government has *no right* to do what those who elected them don't have a right to do. Those lesbians next door don't have a right to kidnap my kids, and neither do they have a right to get you to do it for them. You don't punish a suspect until he's been convicted of a crime. Innocent until proven guilty, right?"

"Sir," she said cautiously, "we were honestly concerned about the welfare of your children."

"Well, now maybe you'll be concerned enough about your own welfare that you won't try to kidnap the kids of any more Christians."

Cal pulled off the main highway down a dark, curvy two-lane road and drove west. The social worker looked around and saw no cars within sight. Cal drove silently for a few miles, pulled over on the side of the road, and unlocked the doors. "You can get out now."

She opened the door, stepped out, and he skidded back onto the road without even giving her a chance to shut the door. He did a 180-degree turn and sped back the way he came, leaving her alone with her thoughts and fears in a moonless sky.

Cal wept as he drove away, wondering if he made the right decision. He didn't regret what he did to save his children from being taken away. No, his conscience was clean in that. But he worried that he would now be relegated to hiding from the government for the rest of his life. How could God use him now?

"Oh God," he prayed with tears streaming down his cheeks, "make my life count for something."

"Meet me in the parking lot behind the laundry mat at Jackson's Gap," Cal had whispered in his wife's ear. "In a second I'm gonna give you another location in front of everybody else to throw them off, but you're gonna meet me behind the laundry mat."

Jackson's Gap was close to Auburn and she could get there through back roads without ever getting on a highway.

"When are we gonna be there?" her eldest asked from the backseat of the minivan.

"Soon, baby, soon."

"Are the police gonna arrest Daddy for shootin' that man?"

"No, baby." A sob rose in Sabina's throat and her heart throbbed with pain as she recalled the horrifying image of that slain officer, whose blood still soaked her below the knees. For the sake of the children, she held back her weeping. "Those bad people were gonna take you all away from us, but your daddy stopped them."

Little did Sabina know that another reason Cal picked Jackson's Gap was that it was on the way to Birmingham, where he planned to get on I-20 and head west towards Texas. It was an impulsive decision, but one which would lead him on an adventure he could never imagine.

Chapter 5

Colton, Texas

"Ah! Daddy's calling!" Darlene flung open the door of the hotel room that she had left cracked while she was sitting and watching the children play outside in the grass. She ran to where the phone sat in the corner of the room and picked it up just in time. "David! Thank God."

"Hey baby." She could hear his smile in his voice. "I miss you so much."

She took a deep breath of relief. "You've been leaving messages for three days."

"I'm so sorry."

The three girls entered the room with their arms full of toys. "Daddy!" they squealed.

David heard their little voices in the background. "Oh, tell my girls that I miss them so much. There aren't payphones at these civic centers, Darlene. I've had to borrow cell phones to call."

"Are you still having revival services there?"

"Oh, you wouldn't believe it! Hundreds won't leave, the power of God is so strong. After Henry Adams and his cabinet were arrested, it's been 24 hour prayer meetings and worship services for three days."

"Are you staying out of the public's eye? You know that they identified you on the news. They even have a reward for anyone that turns you in."

"I know. I've been careful. I shaved and changed my hat, and have been at smaller meetings with a bunch of Holy-Ghost-filled, fasting pastors." He nudged the well-worn John Deere cap he purchased at a local Goodwill. "Elijah has been one of the leaders preaching and teaching. But let's talk about that later. I've got something else I need to speak with you about."

"Where are you sleeping?"

"Elijah and I have a room in the corner of the civic center. We're crashing in sleeping bags."

"Why don't you pick us up?"

"Oh, we haven't found Jared yet." She could hear the frustration in her husband's voice. "We have no idea where he is, Darlene. We lost him at the sit-in. He's probably around here somewhere. I hate to leave him."

"I hope he wasn't arrested."

"I don't know. Besides, if I picked you up, I couldn't conceal my identity as well here, and I hate to leave this place now."

"I can't believe you were there at the closing of the last abortion clinic in Texas. How did it feel?"

"Um, Darlene, there's something personal I need to talk to you about." David couldn't stand the small talk anymore. There was something he just had to get off his chest.

At that moment, the 4-year-old daughter tripped over the legs of the toddler and her forehead came against the corner of the dresser, lacerating her brow. She screamed and Darlene turned to her. "Oh no!"

"What is it?"

"Charlotte fell." Darlene intended to carry the phone with her to tend to the screaming child, but the cord wouldn't stretch. "I'm sorry David, but Charlotte's hurt."

"Is she all right?"

"I'll set the phone down and be back in a minute."

"Darlene? Darlene!"

David's eyes darted toward the man beside him who tapped his foot as if waiting to get his cell phone back. "Sorry man, but I've got my wife and kids waiting in the car."

David spoke into the phone once more, "Darlene?"

He could hear Charlotte still crying in the background and Darlene comforting her, telling her that it was "Just a scratch."

David sighed, slapped the cell phone shut, and handed it back to the man. "Thanks."

The man smiled warmly at him. "You're welcome, bro."

David headed back into the civic center, more troubled in his spirit than ever. He was going to find Elijah and beg to borrow his van to drive to Colton to pick up his family. He couldn't stand one more day apart from them.

"What's that?"

"I don't hear anything."

"I heard gunshots." Elijah rolled down his window and turned the radio down as they waited in line at a fuel pump in a gas station near the civic center. They had given up trying to find Jared, and were heading to Colton to pick up David's family when they heard on the news that looting and firefights had erupted in Dallas, Ft. Worth, and San Antonio. It was rumored that the feds may step up their gun confiscation plan for known gun enthusiasts and patriots in Texas. Many Texans, furious about the arrest of Governor Adams, were planning to resist with force. Elijah suspected that fuel prices might begin to skyrocket and shortages were imminent. He thought it wise to fill up and stock up on groceries before hitting the highway.

Elijah rolled his window back up and shook his head. "It was nothing."

David sighed. "Thanks so much, Elijah, for going with me to get my family."

Elijah sighed and cast an uneasy glance at David. "We haven't got them yet, bro. There are cops and federal agents everywhere." He eyed with suspicion a black SUV with tinted windows that sped past them on the two-lane road. "Pray that no one recognizes my license plate."

"I know, I know. My family is only 25 miles and 25 minutes away in good traffic."

"It may wind up being 25 miles of federal roadblocks."

"You don't know that."

Elijah started the van when an unexpected loud voice from the open passenger window startled them.

"Somebody say something about fighting the feds?"

David jolted in his seat and his hair stood on end. "Jared!"

"Surprise!"

"Where've you been?" Jared entered through the van's side door and sat down in the back seat.

"Making connections, hanging out with activists, instigating open revolution, as usual. What an amazing few days, huh?"

"How'd you find us?"

"I figured y'all had to be helping out in the revival services at the civic center. I was there this morning and someone told me that you two were out to get fuel and food. Did you hear the president's speech?"

"Heard excerpts on the radio," Elijah responded, glancing at Jared in the rearview mirror.

Jared took a deep breath. "It's time for war, boys. It's time to dig the trenches and make the revolution happen before the guns are gone."

Blue and red lights suddenly flashed in Elijah's rear view mirror. "Down!" David and Jared speedily ducked out of view.

A police officer parked his car directly behind them. He stepped out with his hand on his holster.

"Did they follow you, Jared?" asked David.

"No way."

"Quiet down." Elijah peeked at the officer through the side mirror and was relieved to see him walk perpendicular to their vehicle. He walked up to the driver of a red, convertible Mustang and apparently started writing a ticket for the driver's expired tag.

"He's writing someone a ticket," whispered Elijah. "We'll leave in a minute and get fuel elsewhere."

The news station that they were listening to suddenly turned into static. Elijah turned it up and then tried to change stations. "That's strange. They're all static. Radio must have busted."

In the next several minutes, the lines at the fuel pumps grew ten cars long. Suddenly, traffic on Austin's downtown streets quadrupled. "What's going on?" Elijah watched a traffic jam begin right in front of his eyes. Automobiles backed up as far as he could see in every direction of the intersection.

"What?" David kept his head low in the back seat.

"Traffic's getting thick real quick." Elijah tried in vain to search for a radio station. He saw the officer in his rear view mirror respond to a radio call, rush back to his squad car, and speed off.

"I don't think we'll be able to go through Austin, David. Sit up and look at this."

David and Jared sat up and were stunned at the traffic jam going both ways on the busy two-lane intersection. Horns were honking and nerves were on edge. "Something must have happened."

Elijah lowered his window and poked his head out to ask a passer-by, "Sir, excuse me. What happened? Where's everybody going?"

"You haven't heard?" The bearded, obese man in the U.T. football jersey breathed heavily as if he had just jogged a quarter mile. "The president just declared martial law in Texas. She's shipped in federal bureaucrats to govern us. Our constitutional freedoms have been suspended indefinitely."

David began to pray fervently in the back seat.

"Thanks, man." Elijah waved at the man and then glanced at the map that lay in his lap. "We're on the north side of Austin. We need to go further north and try to find a way around Austin on back roads. Your family's in Colton, right?"

"Yeah, south of Austin."

Elijah studied the map carefully. "The feds are probably setting up roadblocks on all roads leading out of Austin in preparation for the gun confiscation."

Elijah thought he heard gunfire again in the distance. He saw that the store was quickly filling with hordes of anxious customers who were emptying the shelves of groceries. "We could have crazy looters stripping that store in a few minutes." He opened the door and stepped out. "I'm going to get some food and drink while we still can. Come on, Jared." Jared followed Elijah out of the car. "David, you fill up when our time comes, and don't let anybody butt in front of you." David got into the driver's seat. There were two cars ahead of them.

"I can't believe this is happening," Jared exclaimed in disbelief as they jogged into the store.

"Wear your sunglasses and don't look suspicious," Elijah reminded Jared. Jared exacerbated his characteristic disheveled look as he ran his fingers haphazardly through his bleached hair.

Crash!

A thunderous collision of the front bumper of a large pickup truck and the rear of a van took place right beside them. "Look at that!" Jared pointed to two drivers who began to argue over who was at fault.

"If you think this is bad," said Elijah as he entered the store, "wait until the Army and Marines are policing the streets."

David stuck his head out of the open window and yelled, "Hurry!" Elijah turned and gave David a thumbs-up.

David pulled his John Deere cap down low on his brow and began to adjust the knob on the radio, hoping to find something besides static. A sudden knock on his half-rolled-down window startled him. A well-dressed businessman in a white shirt and a purple striped tie smiled at him. "Sir, do you have the time?"

David glanced at the digital clock on the dash. "Noon."

"Appreciate it," he said as he darted for the store.

David pulled the car forward. He was next in line. He closed his eyes and began to pray for his family when some loud shouting startled him, bringing him back to reality.

"Troops are coming! Troops are coming!"

David began to look around him for the source of the shouting. He turned his attention to a camouflage-painted pick-up truck in line on the other side of the gas pump. A middle-aged hunter in cams sat in the driver's seat listening to a short-wave radio. David got out of the vehicle and made his way over to the anxious Texan.

"They're coming. They're already in San Antonio, Lubbock and San Angelo." David noticed the man was trembling. He also saw a 30-06 rifle setting next to him on the passenger seat.

"Partner, you'd best get rid of that." David motioned toward the gun and wondered if it was loaded.

"I'll *never* get rid of my guns."

"Hide it, I mean." David nodded agreeably. "Don't keep it out in the open like that."

"I'll keep it where I wish!"

"Fine, friend. That's fine with me." David backed away from him with his palms out as if to try to calm the nervous fellow down. "I'm on your side."

The hunter turned his attention back to his short-wave dial. "They'd better not knock on my door. They try to take my guns, I'll kill 'em all." An irritated blasphemy punctuated his hasty threats.

David winced at his foul language, and thought, *Maybe I'm not on his side after all.*

David stared wide-eyed at the interstate beside them. The hunter saw David's fear-stricken countenance, turned, and was also gripped by a frightening sight. A caravan of dozens of Army green trucks, personnel carriers, and semi-trucks carrying tanks were coming off the interstate exit ramp right beside them and driving toward them on the shoulder of the road. The cars that were waiting in line at the fuel pumps began to drive off. David jumped into the van and saw that the fuel gauge neared empty. He drove forward and hastily began to pump fuel. He took two 20-dollar bills out of his wallet and put them into the crease of the LCD display, knowing that he may not be able to go into the store and pay the cashier under these circumstances.

The Army caravan turned down the road that led to the truck stop. David began to panic. He honked his horn, wondering where Jared and Elijah were. One of the Humvees sped up to the line of cars that was trying to leave the parking lot and blocked the exit. The military vehicles began to stop traffic all around the store.

Two intelligence officers in Army-green slacks and ties walked over to the hunter in the camouflage-painted pickup truck. As the fuel pumped into the van, David got back in the driver's seat and ducked.

"I.D., please." The intelligence officer's hand rested comfortably on his holstered sidearm as he stood beside the camo-clad hunter. Other military personnel approached the occupants of vehicles closest to the road, and asked for identification.

"You want *my* I.D.?" The hunter fearlessly balked at the soldier's order.

"No. I want your mama's," he responded sarcastically. "Of course, I want *your* I.D." The military officer's gaze darted to the gun case in the backseat where the hunter stashed his 30-06 when the caravan neared.

"Yeah, it's a semi-automatic and yeah, it holds more than four rounds of ammo, and no, I'm not going to give it to you."

"Juke," the intelligence officer closest to the pick-up said to the other. "Just my luck. First time's a charm." The other unsnapped the holster, wrapped his fist around the stock of his .45 caliber Beretta, and slowly approached the vehicle.

David watched it all, wondering if there was any possible way out of this parking lot that wouldn't provoke a chase. He glanced at the gas tank gauge. The needle was barely up above the *E*. "Where are Jared and Elijah? Oh God, help us!"

"Turn off your car and show me your I.D.," the former drill-sergeant shouted at the hunter in his loud, hoarse, boot camp voice that had as welcoming a tone as fingernails on a chalkboard.

"This is still America, punk! If I'm not under arrest, then I don't need to show you my I.D. Besides you're not a police officer and can't arrest me anyway."

"I said, ***turn the truck off!***" The military intelligence officer leaned into the open window to grab the ignition key and turn off the pickup when the hunter grabbed the soldier's wrist, pressed it against the dash, and slammed the gear into drive. He stomped on the gas and spun the tires. The truck lunged forward, snapping the soldier's forearm with an audible crack. The unfortunate soldier let out a gut-wrenching scream. The second soldier shouted and aimed his handgun.

The hunter accelerated toward the store and turned sharply to the right, still pressing the soldier's wrist firm against the dash. Then he slammed on the brakes, sending the soldier forward onto the hood of his truck while the wrist remained firm against the dash. This shattered his upper arm and shoulder. Sharp edges of fractured bone broke through the green camouflage sleeve and drenched the side of the pickup with blood. The tormented soldier let out another terrifying scream as the truck spun sideways onto the elevated walkway in front of the store and shattered the front glass windows.

Elijah and Jared watched the mayhem in awe from the rear of the store. Soldiers rushed from their armored vehicles past Elijah's van toward the camouflaged pickup truck.

Elijah and Jared ran into the kitchen of the restaurant, frantically searching for a rear exit. Jared collided with a cook carrying a pan of noodles that sent the hot noodles sliding across the floor. "How do we get out?" Elijah hollered. They sprinted in the direction that the cook pointed, through the rear exit.

"Follow me." Elijah started running away from the truck stop.

"Where are you going?" Jared followed Elijah into a ditch next to the road that led away from the truck stop toward the interstate. Civilians who were able had begun to drive away on the side of the road, allowing the traffic to clear. "Get down. If David is gonna leave, he's gotta leave this way." They were situated 50 yards away from the truck stop and 100 yards from the on-ramp to the interstate.

"If?" Jared repeated, panting from his adrenaline rush as he squatted in the ditch, heel deep in smelly brown water. "What if he's arrested? What if your van's impounded?"

Elijah peeked over the edge of the ditch toward the truck stop. "The feds are distracted. Let's hope he can scoot away without attracting attention."

"Get out of the truck!" A soldier shouted at the driver of the pickup truck as he moved closer to get a clean shot without hitting his partner. The unfortunate intelligence officer covered with shattered glass from the storefront window was still sprawled out on the pickup's hood and screaming in excruciating pain. Twenty other soldiers closed in around the pickup and searched through the smoke of the spinning tires for a target with their M16 rifles.

With his foot flooring the gas pedal, the hunter ducked down, turned his truck toward the store and accelerated through the wall as the soldier on his hood continued to writhe in pain, trying in vain to grab the holster on his right hip with his left hand. The truck burst completely through the shallow brick and glass wall and into the store, sending glass, brick, chips, and candy bars flying in all different directions. Shoppers and customers recoiled in horror as the truck continued to press through the aisles of goods to the rear of the store. The hunter released his grip on the soldier's forearm when his car struck the counter of the restaurant on the far end of the store. The force of the final collision against the counter flung the semi-conscious, blood-drenched soldier over the counter onto a lit gas stove. The driver tried to drive his truck through the counter, but it was reinforced with concrete and so his tires spun futilely, filling the air with the black smoke of burned rubber.

The soldiers moved into the store as the terrified cooks tried to put out the fire on the semi-conscious soldier. The troopers carefully approached the side of the vehicle, shouting orders with guns at the ready. Confident now that their unfortunate comrade was no longer on the truck's hood and that customers and employees behind the counter were not in the line of fire, one soldier began to shoot. The others followed suit, filling the vehicle with holes until the tires stopped squealing and the roar of the engine subsided.

"Cease fire," a short, cranky Captain Willis, ordered. "I said, cease fire! Hit that gas tank and we're all dead!"

Juke slid forward along the side of the car, and pointed his gun into the front seat. "Where is he?"

The hunter was gone. Under the cover of the smoke billowing from his tires, the hunter had crawled through the broken windshield and through the hole his truck had punched in the counter. He suddenly jumped up from behind the cashier's register, where the fearful cashier lay prostrate on the floor, and started firing at the soldiers with his 30-06 rifle. He got off three shots before he was filled with bullets from automatic weapons fire.

"Got him!"

"Juke! Juke!" shouted one of the soldiers when he saw his friend motionless face down on the ground. There was a tennis-ball-sized bullet exit hole in the unfortunate soldier's back. Blood and torn tissue was splattered a dozen feet down an aisle littered with snacks.

"He's dead." Captain Willis turned from the slain soldier and pointed to the severely burned one being tended to by a cook behind the restaurant counter. "Stop his bleeding. Call a medevac copter to come pick him up, and I want you men to search this place now! Check I.D.s, search bodies and vehicles and confiscate all weapons and… Hey!" He pointed through the broken windows in the front of the store. "Stop the driver of that gray van!"

Elijah and Jared hugged the ground of the damp ditch, fearful that David had been shot in the flurry of automatic gunfire in front of the gas station.

A tall, plump fellow in a black NRA polo shirt jumped into the ditch in between Elijah and Jared, carrying a half-filled, red gasoline jug. "Hey. Do you guys have a car? Are you going north by any chance?"

The uninvited guest startled Elijah and Jared. "Who are you?"

"A patriot who doesn't want to be disarmed, like you guys, I guess." It was Cal Manning, who had just arrived in Texas from Alabama with his family. "I ran out of gas on the interstate," he said as he pointed north.

Elijah ignored the stranger and pointed in the direction of the fuel station. "There he is." Jared looked and saw the van skidding around the rear of the store, through a shallow ditch, over the curb and into the street. Tires were squealing loudly and dust flew as the van made the turn, the fuel pump and hose still protruding from the side of the van. One side of the rear bumper broke off and began to drag against the ground, throwing sparks into the air.

Elijah jumped out of the ditch and waved down the van. David was relieved to see Elijah and Jared on the side of the road. He looked into his rearview mirror and his heart dropped as he saw a Humvee pull out of the parking lot in their direction, giving chase. David slowed and pulled to the side of the road. As he coasted, Elijah opened the door of the van for Jared and then jumped in himself. Before he could shut the door, the stranger with the gasoline canister grabbed the door.

"I need a ride!"

"Sorry pal." Elijah tried to shut the door but the fellow wasn't taking "No" for an answer. The stranger was halfway in the vehicle, holding onto the side door as David tried to speed up.

"My family! We're out of gas. Please!"

Elijah started to pry the stranger's fingers from the door, but David had already floored the pedal to escape the Humvee. The stranger was being dragged with one of his hands on the side of the door and the other hand gripping a gasoline container with barely a pint of fuel in it. "Please! I'll pay ya!" the man hollered. "Please!"

Elijah chuckled at the stranger's gentlemanly tenacity. His thought went to the biblical story of the Canaanite woman who asked Jesus to heal her daughter and wouldn't take "No" for an answer. Jesus succumbed to the Gentile woman's persuasion and Elijah was feeling similarly sympathetic for this fellow.

David gained speed and looked back at Elijah, his eyes wide with adrenaline. "Get him in or out!"

Elijah finally helped him in. Cal Manning plopped into the nearest seat, breathing heavily.

"Go, go, go!" Jared urged David.

"What do I do?" David was dodging traffic, coming up quickly to the interstate on-ramp.

"North!" Cal Manning pleaded. "Please!"

"North! Go north!" Elijah thought it best to go the opposite direction of the caravan of Army vehicles heading south. He wanted to make it as inconvenient as possible to be pursued.

David turned the wheel sharply right to take the on-ramp to the interstate. "This thing won't accelerate. It's making a loud noise..."

"It's the bumper," said Jared. "It didn't survive the ditch."

"Floor it!" Elijah looked back and noticed the camouflage-painted Humvee closing ground. He saw the passenger of the Humvee sticking his rifle out of the open window.

"This isn't everybody," shouted Captain Willis as he sifted through a stack of confiscated driver's licenses. He glanced at 40 shoppers and drivers who stood against the wall in the refrigerator aisle with their hands up. One mother held a child who was crying, yet she still held one hand up in deference to a soldier with an automatic rifle pointed at them.

"Where are our suspects? We had a witness. Which of you made the call?"

"I made the call." A well-dressed young man in a white dress shirt with a purple striped tie stepped out of the crowd toward the Army captain. "I saw him. It was David Jameson, I'm sure of it. He was with an African-American and another white guy. I remember them from their pictures on the news."

"Are you sure?"

"I knocked on the door of the van and asked for the time and David Jameson rolled down the window and told me. I got a good look at his face."

Sergeant Harvey was at the wheel of the wide-framed, camouflaged Humvee, while his partner, a skilled sniper, was looking down his sights for a clean shot at the driver of the fleeing metallic gray van.

"No shots, Daschle! No shots. Too much pedestrian traffic. We'll pull them over."

"This *could* be our suspect, Sergeant." Daschle kept his right eye fixed to the van through his rifle's scope. "He was last seen in a van. This could be the fellow who killed the president."

"It was a black van, not light gray." Harvey accelerated and began to close on the van.

"It's a new paint job..."

"He may have just washed it!" When he saw that Daschle appeared ready to discharge his weapon, Harvey put his palm on his shoulder, "Daschle! You're starting to worry me."

"Why are they runnin' then?"

"Maybe because we're chasin' them?" Harvey swerved through a narrow space between a Volvo and a pickup truck. "This ain't Afghanistan. We don't shoot Americans because they *could* be terrorists."

"They trained me to be a killing machine, and that's what I do best." Harvey continued to search for target through the van's windows, startling the driver of a red Volkswagen bug as they passed.

"What do you want me to do?" David asked Elijah anxiously as the green and brown desert-cam Humvee weaved in and out of traffic, continuing to gain on them.

"Lose him! Come on!"

David came close to a Camry's bumper and then he darted to the roadside to go around the Camry, but the Humvee was right on their tail.

"He's pointing a gun at us!" shouted Cal Manning.

Blam!

"He shot at us!" Jared ducked down in the front passenger seat, his eyes wide with fright.

"Into the air," said Elijah. "I saw him. He shot into the air. It was a warning shot."

David had enough of this. "I'm pulling over."

"No! Keep going!" Elijah crawled into the back seat, lifted a strip of carpet on the floor, and opened a small door to a compartment he had built into the van. It held a shotgun and 100 rounds of ammunition, but was large enough to hide a person. He reached into it and pulled out his pump shotgun with an extended magazine.

David saw the barrel of Elijah's shotgun in the rearview mirror. He half turned to look at him briefly. "No Elijah."

"They're going to take it anyway," Elijah contended. "Might as well give them the ammo first."

"Those are Army soldiers with automatic weapons. You're going to get us all killed."

"Not if you lose 'em, David." Elijah peeked through the rear window and saw the passenger in the Humvee level his large caliber rifle at their van again. "I'm not going to just sit here and watch him shoot us down, David." Elijah loaded several three-inch magnum shells into the chamber. "I *will* defend myself."

"Don't do it!" Cal Manning looked back at Elijah and grabbed his forearm. "We should pull over. I've walked that road and you may live to regret it."

"Living is the deciding factor in that equation." Elijah shook loose of Cal's grasp on his forearm. "Dying for freedom's better than living in jail under Texas' new military dictatorship."

A sharp swerve in front of a semi-truck caused Elijah to loose his balance and lurch against the side of the van. They lost sight of the Humvee for a few seconds, but the semi-truck beside them braked quickly and the Humvee pulled in front of the semi and came up right next to them on their left.

"Pull over!" The driver of the Humvee spoke into a microphone that amplified his voice through speakers on top of their vehicle. The passenger aimed his rifle at the van's driver. "Pull over now!"

David slammed on the brakes and pulled in behind the Humvee momentarily, and then behind a semi-truck beside them. He then drove onto the shoulder of the road and accelerated past the semi, bypassing the Humvee.

"Are you positively sure it was Jameson?" Captain Willis asked the informant with the purple tie in the convenience store.

"Yes sir."

"Where's the vehicle?" Captain Willis motioned to the parking lot.

"It was right there, a gray van." He pointed to the fuel pump on the far right.

"That's the van Harvey's chasing," another soldier informed Captain Willis. The captain let out a vile curse that characterized his casual conversation but was exaggerated when he was giving orders under stress. He tapped his headset and shouted, "Harvey! Harvey! Respond! You..."

Sergeant Harvey tapped the microphone on the Humvee's receiver and braced for the extreme decibel level of Captain Willis' vulgar communication. "Do you have those suspects in custody, Sergeant Harvey? You pathetic..." The captain's voice bellowed so loudly that even Daschle overheard it.

"We're in pursuit on the interstate, Captain."

"*You're following our suspects*, Sergeant!" Sergeant Harvey swerved to miss a Cadillac, pulled behind a semi, then over to the shoulder to try to catch up to the van that continued to out-maneuver them. "Do not, I repeat, do **not** let them get away under any circum-stances. Understand?"

Harvey glanced over at Daschle, and saw a sly smile creep over Daschle's face. Private Daschle winked and leaned out of his window slightly, his short, bristled haircut immobile in the stiff 65-mile-per-hour breeze. "Aye, aye, sir," he mumbled.

"We're sending reinforcements. We need David Jameson alive!"

Harvey tapped Daschle on his shoulder. "Did you hear that? We need Jameson alive."

"I'm pulling over, Elijah!" David observed in his side mirror that the passenger of the Humvee was still aiming his rifle at the van. "He's gonna kill us!"

"That soldier in the passenger seat has got his finger on the trigger, man," complained Jared, ducking his head low.

"Don't stop, David!" Elijah shook his head back and forth as he firmly grasped his shotgun. "I don't think that he's going to shoot at us if we're in thick traffic like this. The risk of hitting others is too high."

Blam!

The gunshot blast provided the exclamation point to Elijah's sentence. This was not a warning shot. The bullet penetrated the side of the van with a sharp metallic smack, whizzed past Jared's head and shattered the front right passenger window beside him. A ray of sunshine pierced the van through the bullet hole in the windowless rear left side.

Jared screamed, "That almost blew my brains out!" He pushed the glass shards off his lap and onto the floor and put his head between his legs. "Pull over, David!"

"I'm doing it, Elijah. It's over." David slowed down and pulled to the right of the road.

"I can't get caught." Cal Manning anxiously blurted out. "My family needs me. My Christian beliefs have got me in trouble with the government."

"Welcome to the club." Elijah slumped to his knees, grasping his pump shotgun as if his life depended on it.

"Take the van down through that ditch and crash it through that fence." Cal pointed to a fence that separated the shallow ditch and a neighborhood. "Then we'll make a run for it."

"You're crazy." David slowed the van to a stop and put it in park. "That hill's too steep."

Elijah's vision evolved into that narrow tunnel vision that one gets when the adrenaline begins to take over the intellect. He had struggled with this sensation as a police office for many years, though he never had to kill a man. All those years of perfecting skeet shooting with his shotgun had filled him with daydreams about opportunities to save his or another's life with it. But now he felt like the Benelli shotgun he grasped would get him killed before it would save him. His palms were sweaty and his mind grew as numb as his fingers. As David flipped the transmission into park, Elijah fought the strange sensation that he wouldn't be alive in five minutes. He breathed deeply and tried to calm his senses. His lips whispered a prayer of faith, for bravery, for his sister.

"No, you don't understand!" Cal frantically objected when David turned off the ignition. "My family needs me!" Cal flung open the van's side door and made a break for the woods.

Private Daschle came around the front of the van, his sniper rifle slung over his shoulder, his hands grasping his handgun. He saw the tall fellow in the black NRA shirt running for the woods and instinc-tively fired several rounds at the man's feet. Three steps into Cal's sprint, bullets at his heels threw clumps of dirt up onto his pants. He stopped in his tracks and raised his trembling hands toward the blue, cloudless sky, more from fear of what would become of his wife and kids than for fear of dying.

"Hands up or you're all dead!" Private Daschle stood directly in front of the van's windshield. His aim with his .45 caliber handgun shifted from Cal to the van's driver. "Get out of the van!"

As David stepped out of the van with his hands raised, he glanced into the rear of the van and briefly saw the whites of Elijah's eyes in the shadows between the rear passenger seats. Elijah quietly lifted the carpeted, hinged plywood door on the floor between the row of rear passenger seats, where he kept his gun and the ammunition, and he dropped down into the small compartment.

"On your knees! Hands behind your head! Move!" David moved past the front of the van at Daschle's urging to the right side of the vehicle, away from the traffic. He saw the soldier's finger on the trigger and his heart began to thump rapidly.

"Out of the car!" Sergeant Harvey shouted from his right, pointing his M16 at Jared.

Jared shuffled out of the right side of the van and got on his knees next to David and Cal.

Harvey looked inside through the side door of the van, and not seeing anyone else, he kicked the door shut.

"Mind telling me what we did wrong?" David asked.

"You left the parking lot without permission." Harvey's voice was roughened from two decades of screaming orders at subordinates and three decades of two packs a day.

"And you didn't have your seat belt on." Daschle tried to add humor to the scenario that he found absolutely delightful.

Cal spoke up, his voice trembling, "I just hitched a ride with—"

"Shut up!" Daschle ordered.

"Search 'em." Harvey motioned to the trigger-happy private.

Cars continued to whiz past them on the busy highway and David briefly wondered what those passengers were thinking about their situation.

Daschle began to roughly frisk David, who protested, "Ever heard of the phrase, 'unreasonable search and seizure'?"

"How's a bullet between the eyes sound for reasonable?" Daschle quickly unholstered his handgun and pointed it at David's forehead. David looked past the black handgun into the soldier's stern eyes and thought that the young man would actually enjoy killing him.

"Daschle!" Harvey shouted.

Daschle grinned, re-holstered his weapon, and continued to frisk the suspect. "Americans who kill presidents don't have constitutional rights," Daschle mumbled.

"How about 'innocent till proven guilty' for people who *don't* kill presidents?"

"Don't go lecturing me about constitutional rights!" Without warning, Private Daschle slapped David on the right ear.

David's head whipped to the side, his ear ringing from the smack over his eardrum. His John Deere hat fell off his head and tumbled to the ground.

David turned and gazed into the soldier's eyes as Daschle pulled his fist back, preparing to unleash another blow at David's face. David wondered for a moment if this is what Jesus felt like after the Roman soldiers stripped him, tied him to a post, and prepared to crack their whips against his flesh.

"That's enough, Daschle." Harvey could sense the tension between Daschle and the man they recognized as David Jameson, and he was about ready to order Daschle to stand guard so he could frisk them instead.

Daschle bent over in front of David and spoke right into his sweating face. "How'd you like 15 seconds to make a run for it."

"Just frisk him, Daschle."

"Why not?" Daschle looked up at Harvey with a wide grin. "Let's give him a chance."

Harvey's countenance changed and he chuckled at Daschle's creativity. "All right. Go ahead."

"David Jameson, make a break for freedom." Daschle helped David to his feet and pointed at the tree line. "Head for the woods."

David looked fearfully at the two soldiers, wondering if they were serious.

"I'll even turn my back and close my eyes," said Daschle, surprising everyone as he turned his back to David. "Now I won't even see what direction you're heading."

Cal dared to raise a hand and ask, "Can I go?"

"No!" Harvey and Daschle simultaneously responded.

Harvey stepped forward and began to frisk Jared as he laughed at the ambitious private's spontaneous intimidation of the suspects.

David Jameson didn't say a word or move a muscle. He continued to stand, clasping his hands tightly behind his head. He glanced at Cal Manning, who was still on his knees between him and Jared.

Cal's mind was on his wife and children. He wondered what Sabina would do, where she would live. He had almost all of their cash in his wallet. How would she get to an ATM to pull out money? Would the ATM even give her anything? Passers-by on the highway slowed to observe the conflict on the side of the road.

"You're a United States soldier," David said. "You think your parents or your children are going to think well of you if you go and kill innocent Americans?"

"Oh, please." Daschle turned around to enjoy the fret that emanated from David's countenance. "You ain't gonna' psychologically intimidate a trained assassin like me. I'll eat your heart rare with Heinz 57 for Sunday mornin' breakfast and still be on time for mass." He turned his back to them again. "Don't you want to get to your wife and three girls?" he said, laughing. "They're waiting for you at a hotel in Colton, aren't they? Run for it, David Jameson!"

David's heart sunk when he heard those words. *How did they know my family's in Colton?*

"You didn't think you could hide from American justice, did you, Mr. Jameson?" Sergeant Harvey was getting a kick out of the way Daschle's head games were affecting the terrorist suspect. "Do you know how many millions of dollars we allocate to capturing domestic terrorists like you?"

"Go ahead and make a break for the tree line, David," Daschle urged with a sadistic laugh. "Here's your chance to stay free and avoid the Army's water-boarding treatment for your schizophrenia." Daschle turned his head to the right and winked at Harvey with his back still facing away from the van and away from David, Jared, and Cal.

David began to plead with the soldiers, "What did you do to my family? Did you arrest my wife? Where are my kids?" His voice strained with sincerity as his breathing quickened. "Please!"

"Maybe we haven't done anything to them," said Harvey, "*yet.*" The cruel laughs of the two soldiers harmoniously punctuated the tension in the air. The heat fell down on them like a blanket, soaking their clothes with sweat. Horseflies descended upon them from out of the trees. David imagined the breeze blowing past his arms and face as he fled toward the tree line. Could he make it?

Daschle turned back around to face the three terrorist suspects. "Go save your wife and kids from the mean, ol' federal government. Come on, your family needs you."

Harvey's radio buzzed. "This is Captain Willis. Have you got 'em?"

Harvey lifted his two-way radio to his lips. "We have all three of them on the east side of the interstate northbound, about five miles north of your junction. Over." Then he tapped the button on his two-way radio that de-activated the microphone and he acted as if he was still speaking to Captain Willis. "One man escaped into the woods, but I'm holding the others. Daschle's in pursuit, but the suspect got a good head start."

A second later Captain Willis responded, "Very well. We'll be there in a few minutes."

Private Daschle smiled at Sergeant Harvey's trick. "There you go, Mr. Jameson. Better take off." He pointed in the direction of the woods away from the road. "Time's running out."

"Anything I can do for you gentlemen?" This was the voice of a sizable highway patrolman who stepped out from behind the van, startling the two soldiers. He had quietly parked his unmarked patrol car 40 yards behind the Humvee.

Harvey's smile quickly eroded and he turned to the highway patrol officer. "No thank you. We've apprehended a federal suspect. This is the fellow who killed President Fitzgerald and all those others in the Ohio bombing."

"Oh, really? The infamous David Jameson." The officer rested one hand on his unsnapped holster and the other on his hip. "Why were you trying to get him to run for the tree line?"

David, who still stood with his hands clasped tightly behind his head, blurted out, "They're trying to kill—"

"Shut up!" Harvey shouted.

"They're trying to kill me, officer."

The officer appeared unmoved by David's accusation of the two soldiers. He grinned and calmly said, "Every law enforcement officer this side of Canada's looking for you, Mr. Jameson."

"I just hitched a ride with them," whined Cal Manning, still on his knees between David and Jared. "Can I leave?"

Cal acted as if he was about to stand to his feet when Daschle and Harvey simultaneously shouted, "No!"

The patrolman studied the soldiers' demeanor for a moment. "In law enforcement, we don't consider suspects guilty till a jury does."

"Thank the Lord that's the case," commented David. "I'm just as innocent of bombing that Reproductive Right's Convention as you are, officer. I was there as a peaceful preacher of God's law and the Gospel."

"We'll see." The officer reached to the rear of his belt and withdrew a set of handcuffs. "I'll take it from here soldiers." He walked over to David Jameson and put a hand on his shoulder.

"Whoa!" Daschle moved closer to the patrolman. "Not so fast."

"I can fit all three of these guys into my car. Thanks for your help." The patrol officer ignored the soldiers as he moved David against the van and briefly frisked him.

"What do you think you're doing?" Daschle was indignant that the officer was ignoring them and that his superior Sergeant Harvey was not preventing him.

The patrolman handcuffed David's hands in the front and not the rear. It was then that David suspected that this highway patrolman was friendly. "Thank you, sir."

"We can't let you take him." Sergeant Harvey glanced uneasily over at Daschle once he saw that the patrolman's holster was unsnapped. "We have orders to keep him until reinforcements arrive."

"And these are orders we intend to keep." Daschle raised his handgun at the officer and then quickly lowered it again.

"I heard you tell your superior officer that Mr. Jameson was running for the tree line. So why would you get in trouble if he weren't here?"

Sergeant Harvey and Daschle were stumped and the patrolman grinned. "It was a lie that I'm sure you'd prefer that he not know about, right?"

Sergeant Harvey shook his head violently from side to side. "No, you can't take him." He raised his rifle until he was aiming at the patrolman's feet.

The officer ignored the soldiers' attempt to intimidate him. "You fellows have your hands full with firefights at your checkpoints all over Texas. Thank you for apprehending the suspect, but now he'll be tried in a civilian court."

David had never wanted to be arrested more by a police officer in his whole life! He glanced over at Jared, who was wide-eyed with apprehension.

Sergeant Harvey stepped in close to the officer and put his left hand on the highway patrol officer's forearm. "Can't let you take him, sir."

"You don't have a choice." The officer shook off the soldier's grasp. "He's in my custody. You see, the commander-in-chief has suspended *habeas corpus* for her political prisoners. Well, I took an oath to uphold the Constitution and the law of the land. So since Mr. Jameson here has been brought up on state charges, I'm arresting him and taking him downtown. Mr. Jameson," he said, looking at David, "you have the right to remain silent. You have the right to an attorney..."

When the officer turned to usher David Jameson to his squad car, Sergeant Harvey grabbed his arm again, tighter this time. "I'm sorry, officer, he ain't going anywhere."

The officer responded calmly. "Follow me if you like, but he'll be at the station. Excuse me." He stared at the tight grip of the soldier on his left forearm. "I could have you arrested for obstruction of justice. Let go of my arm." He paused to give the soldier a moment to comply, but Sergeant Harvey held firm. "Do you want to let a Texas jury comprised of citizens you've been disarming all day to decide the matter?" He stared into the cold, blue eyes of Sergeant Harvey, each trying to convince the other that there was no budging on their missions. For a long moment, nobody moved.

The highway patrol officer had the momentum. "I won't be dissuaded by your stare, boy. I know the law and I know the bounds of your jurisdiction. Local law enforcement is going to uphold the Constitution. It's what makes this country great. Mr. Jameson here could sue you personally under Title 42 and win, mind you, in a state jury trial."

"The U.S. Army is what makes this country great, you little peon," Daschle taunted the officer.

"You're talking to a Green Beret veteran, sir, who suffered two bullet wounds in my gut in the Terrorist Wars." The officer turned and sent his own intimidating stare at the young Army private. "I've tortured my share of enemy combatants behind enemy lines, but you don't treat citizens the same way you treat foreign enemy combatants."

"If you're a vet, you know I have got to obey my orders." Harvey glanced over his shoulder down the interstate hoping to see Captain Willis' line of camouflaged Humvees and armored personnel carriers racing toward them. The highway patrolman also peeked over his shoulder at traffic, wondering why his backup had not yet arrived. Traffic was bumper to bumper as far as he could see, yet still moving along at a good pace.

"If our orders conflict," the officer argued, "then we should obey the lawful, constitutional order, and disregard the other. I'm in my jurisdiction, sir, whereas your superiors violated the *Posse Comitatus Act* in ordering you to apprehend criminals in Texas. You can remove your claw from my arm and follow me to the police station, or you can let go and ride with me in handcuffs next to Mr. Jameson here in the backseat of the squad car. Or you can shoot me in the back. The choice is yours."

"You, you, uh," Sergeant Harvey stumbled over his words as he glanced at Daschle, who looked just as indecisive. Harvey lifted his two-way radio and tapped the receiver. "Captain Willis, we have a situation here."

The officer tried to pull free of Harvey's grasp but the Army sergeant wouldn't let go. "In just a minute or two our superior will arrive. Can I ask you to wait until then?"

"I've already arrested the suspect and you're obstructing justice." The highway patrolman spoke forcefully as he glanced down at Harvey's tight grip on his forearm. "Your superior can come down to the office and file a complaint like every other citizen in the state of Texas if he's got a problem with the way we do justice around here."

Daschle heard something coming from the van that attracted his attention. "Hey!" Daschle slowly moved across the front of the van to the side facing traffic. From the shadow the afternoon sun was casting, he thought he saw the back door of the van open and close again. "Hey! Stop! Show yourself!" Daschle tensed his trigger finger against his handgun.

Sergeant Harvey, who held three suspects at bay with his M16 in his right hand and gripped the patrolman's arm with his left hand, didn't see what had so excited Daschle. The patrolman and Jameson were obstructing his view of the rear of the van. He released his rifle and let the sling over his shoulder hold the weight of the gun for a moment while he tapped the button on his two-way radio. "Captain Willis?"

"We're one minute away on the other side of an MVA, Sergeant."

Harvey blinked hard as sweat dripped down his brow into his eyes. There were too many variables for his comfort. There were just too many things that could go wrong. "Come lively," he told Captain Willis, who winced at the tremor in Harvey's voice. "We've got a highway patrolman who is trying to take Jameson into his custody."

"You've got bigger guns, Sergeant."

Without distracting his gaze from Sergeant Harvey, the highway patrolman tapped his own radio and asked for the ETA of his backup. His gaze darted to the Army sergeant. "Let go of my arm!" he ordered forcefully. He stared into Sergeant Harvey's shifting eyes. "Now!"

"We're occupied with firefights all over Austin, Officer Kline," the patrolman's dispatcher responded. "You're going to have to handle it on your own."

"Freeze!" Private Daschle shouted to an unidentified suspect who'd opened the rear door of the gray windowless van. Daschle tensed, his back hugging the hot metal of the van about halfway down the side facing the traffic. He squatted and looked underneath the van and didn't see any legs. He banged the van with his left elbow. "Show yourself, hands up or you'll be shot!" The fear that someone inside could shoot him through the van paralyzed him. Traffic slowed as it passed him while he tried to wave them on. His indecisive mind wrestled with various contingencies.

David glanced at the van. *Don't do it, Elijah.*

Harvey yelled out to Daschle. "Daschle, what are you doing? Is there someone in the van?" Daschle didn't hear the question because of the noise of passing semis.

Private Daschle yelped the order again to the unidentified suspect he figured had stepped out of the van's rear door. "Show yourself or you'll be shot!" With his back to the van, he continued to slowly inch his way toward the rear. The shadows at the van's rear were a mystery to him, and the fear of being shot made him break out in a sweat. His breathing quickened and his hands began to tingle. He loosed his grip on the handgun and tried to relax.

"Do you see somebody, Sergeant?" Daschle yelled. Sergeant Harvey was occupied with his own crisis and didn't respond.

Harvey witnessed Cal Manning momentarily unclasp his hands and let them hang at his side. "Put your hands on your head!"

Cal immediately complied. "Take it easy, buddy."

The officer grew angry at the soldier's reluctance to let go of his arm. So he changed his tactics. "All right," the patrolman said, relaxing his grip on David's handcuffs. "You can have him." The officer pretended that he would be complicit with Harvey's persistent grip on his arm. Then suddenly, without warning, he lunged away from the soldier, breaking free, grabbing and jerking David by the cuffs in the process.

David let out a yell from the sudden pain in his wrists that twisted him sideways. The soldier sternly objected to the patrolman's burst of aggression. "Stop! I can't let you take him!" He reached for the officer and fastened his hand around the officer's wrist.

"Yes, you can." The calm voice came from beside the van. Sergeant Harvey looked to see the civilian wearing the black NRA shirt point a cocked nine-millimeter handgun at his chest. Cal Manning's right pants' leg was wrinkled above his calf holster where the compact handgun had been concealed.

"Ah, Daschle, I told you to frisk 'em," he said in a voice too soft for Daschle to hear on the other side of the van.

"Not a sound," Cal said softly, carefully trying to disarm the sergeant before the private on the other side of the van caught wind of what was going on. "Throw your gun on the ground in front of you." Fortunately, another flurry of passing semis obscured their conversation from Private Daschle's ears.

Daschle appeared frozen on the other side of the van. He was uncomfortable at the closeness of the thick, passing traffic, but also unable to force himself to move any further toward the rear of the van. Daschle decided that it was best to guard this side of the van until Captain Willis and his fellow troopers arrived, to keep the suspects from fleeing across traffic and jumping the median to the other side of the road. He figured that would be the suspects' best path of escape, and he thought it wise to plug it.

"Put your finger on your trigger and you're dead," Cal Manning warned Harvey in a soft voice. "Throw down your gun." Cal rose to his feet and backed up tightly against the van to better see out of his peripheral vision should the other soldier come around and intervene.

"That's not necessary, citizen," said the patrolman, his voice stern as he turned to face Manning. "There's no reason to risk your life." The officer stealthily reached for his own handgun as he spoke, careful not to provoke the ire of the irate soldier beside him. The highway patrolman was well aware that the civilian's gun was pointed in his direction and it would be very easy for the soldier to step behind him and his prisoner to use them as a shield behind which to shoot at the civilian in the NRA shirt. Harvey reluctantly let go of the officer's arm and placed both palms up toward the armed civilian.

Jared appeared frightened at what was transpiring and let out a blasphemous curse that startled David.

"Jared!" David glared at Jared in disapproval. Jared appeared unashamed of his curse and with his hands behind his head kept his gaze fixed on Sergeant Harvey and the highway patrolman, without blinking or acknowledging David's reproof.

"You must be wanting to turn that *illegal* gun in, sir," said Harvey to Cal, his palms facing outward, careful to keep his hands away from the rifle that the sling held to his chest. He only had to stall until Captain Willis arrived or until Private Daschle came back around from the other side of the van.

"Nope." Manning's gaze darted uneasily from the sides of the van to Harvey as he shifted his double-handed grip on his gun. "I'm taking yours."

Harvey's eyes searched for Daschle but he only saw Daschle's feet frozen to the ground on the far side of the van.

Daschle's fear was authentic, but Elijah's hands were getting fatigued. He was standing on the van's rear bumper, holding onto the roof with his right hand and grasping his loaded, cocked shotgun with the left, careful to stay out of the view of both soldiers.

A passing driver, aware of what was happening, slowed down to assist the soldier between the gray van and the lane of traffic. The driver pulled over just ahead of the van and poked his head out of the driver's side and shouted at Daschle, "He's on the back bumper!"

Daschle turned to glance at the citizen yelling at him. "What?"

"He's on the back bumper!"

Daschle turned back toward the rear of the van and was stunned to see a shotgun pointed along the side of the van at his head.

"Drop your weapon," Elijah calmly insisted. But the soldier reacted.

Blam!

One shot from his .45 handgun preceded a louder, more obnoxious blast from a shotgun.

Blam!

Everyone on the far side of the van ducked except Sergeant Harvey, whose jaw dropped and eyes widened as he turned his attention to his fellow soldier whom he couldn't see. "Daschle!" he called out, still keenly aware of the handgun that was pointed at him.

"Now! Drop it or I'll kill you!" Manning increased the confidence and volume of his order but the stubborn soldier still didn't comply. Manning tensed the pressure against the trigger. He shot a police officer a day earlier, and here he was again, finding very appropriate what just a month ago he would have considered unthinkable.

Harvey glanced under the van and saw Daschle fall down into the road amidst sprays of blood. ***Blam! Blam!*** sounded two more rounds from Daschle's handgun.

A passing vehicle was hit with the second round of the semi-conscious private's erratic trigger pulls. The car swerved and smashed into the three-foot-high cement divider in the middle of the highway. Another vehicle collided with that vehicle, spinning them both alongside the median for 30 yards, littering the highway with glass and chunks of metal and rubber, sending billows of black smoke heavenward. Cal stepped away from the van, still pointing his handgun at the stubborn Army sergeant, yet glancing worriedly in the direction of traffic, concerned that a speeding car might strike the van.

"Daschle!" Harvey called out again, giving only temporary heed to the multi-vehicle accident beside them.

Suddenly, the side of Elijah's van was sideswiped by a black Jeep Cherokee as the driver attempted to avoid the wreck. Elijah's van lurched forward and further off the road by several feet, almost smacking Cal's back. Elijah jumped out of the way just as the Cherokee nicked the tip of his shotgun and sent it flying into the air. The Cherokee ran over Daschle's pelvis, squishing his body flat against the road. The sedan that had stopped in front of the van was struck by the spinning Jeep Cherokee. The collision ignited the fuel in the gas tank and caused the vehicle to explode in a 20-foot high ball of fire, thrusting the patrolman, Sergeant Harvey, and David and company to the ground with a thick wave of heat.

While Cal Manning was off balance from the force of the explosion, Sergeant Harvey made his move. He dropped to his knees and fired a three-round burst from his M16 at Cal Manning.

Tat-tat-tat!

Manning was leveling his sights at the soldier when he let out a painful yelp. One of the M16 rounds struck his handgun, sending sparks and droplets of blood spraying into the air. He heard the bullet whiz past his left ear, deafening him. He fell onto his back and his head struck the van's tire. He shook his head to arouse himself, grabbed his right wrist and gasped when he saw the bullet hole between his thumb and index finger beginning to hemorrhage. His wound looked more painful than it felt and the fear prompted him to scream.

"Oh God!" David called out, the right side of his face flat against the hot gravel.

Elijah rushed into the road between erratically swerving vehicles to quickly retrieve his damaged shotgun, hoping that it would still function.

Sergeant Harvey saw the patrolman reach for his handgun. Exhilarated at his initial success against the suspect in the black NRA shirt, he turned and fired a three-round burst at the patrolman.

Tat-tat-tat!

His gun sounded simultaneously with two rapid shots from the patrolman but only one bullet hit its intended target.

The police officer was struck in the shoulder and in the throat. He involuntarily dropped his gun and fell hard to the ground onto his back beside David, clutching his hemorrhaging throat, the gargle of death in his breath. David half expected the Army sergeant to shoot him dead, but when he looked up, he saw that the sergeant was aiming another shot at Cal Manning, who was recovering and reaching for his handgun. Cal saw the soldier aim his weapon at him, so he stopped and raised his hands in surrender.

When the sergeant saw Elijah at the rear of the van pointing his shotgun at him, he turned and aimed his M16 at Elijah instead. Elijah had pulled the trigger before the sergeant even saw him, but when his damaged Benelli wouldn't fire, he hoped that simply aiming his weapon at the soldier would force him to drop his weapon. But now that the M16 was being aimed at him, he quickly dropped his shotgun and urged the soldier not to shoot. When the soldier sent a three-round burst at him, Elijah dove to the ground behind the van into traffic, his backside barely brushing against the rearview mirror of a passing car. Cal reached for his handgun with his good hand and Harvey aimed the gun at him again.

Before the soldier could shoot Cal, David grabbed the fallen patrolman's gun, aimed, and pulled the trigger. ***Blam! Blam! Blam! Blam! Blam! Blam!*** David emptied the magazine full of hollow points into the Army sergeant's chest and abdomen before the soldier could fire his weapon. Sergeant Harvey collapsed onto his back like a felled tree, his body ripped to shreds by the bullets, his glazed eyes wide with horror and his throat gaping in a silent scream as his wounds dragged him into eternity.

Passers-by on the highway were stopping their cars and rushing to help the injured people in the wrecked and smoking vehicles. At the sound of the gunfire, many ducked behind their vehicles and watched the gunfight on the other side of the highway.

David, breathing heavily, crawled over to the patrolman, his hands still cuffed. The officer wasn't breathing, his lifeblood drained through a coronary artery onto the sandy gravel next to the road.

David looked at the name on the officer's identification badge. "Sam Kline, rest in peace. The Lord receive you."

"Is everyone all right?" Manning shouted as he picked up the dead soldier's M16.

"You?" Jared asked, rising to his feet.

"It's nothing," Manning replied. "Barely hurts."

"Elijah!" David shouted.

"I'm all right." Elijah stepped out from behind the van and picked up his damaged Benelli.

"Your leg's bleeding." Jared pointed at Elijah's right thigh.

Elijah glanced at it briefly. "It's just a graze."

Jared examined the smashed side of the van while Elijah studied the bullet hole above the right front tire.

"It'll still ride," said Jared.

Elijah set Cal Manning with his bleeding hand into the passenger's side. David reached down and picked up his John Deere hate, and then Jared and David got into the backseat. Elijah thrust the vehicle into drive and left the small crowd of those involved in the motor vehicle pile-up wondering what was going on, aghast at the bloody corpses on the side of the road.

Chapter 6

Elijah drove 90 miles per hour northward on the interstate, his dragging bumper sending sparks in his wake. Jared carefully monitored the skies for helicopters as the gravity of their predicament began to sink in. David was in his favorite position in times of duress, on his knees in fervent prayer for their safety and for the safety of his family.

Cal pressed napkins retrieved from the glove compartment against his bleeding wound. He was struck by the passion of David's strong praying. He also turned and knelt to pray for his wife and kids. What did he have to lose?

Suddenly, the van began to shake. Elijah realized that the van was more damaged in the collision than they initially thought. "That bullet must have nicked the steering column."

Cal looked up at Elijah. "Are we gonna make it?"

"I'm gonna have to slow down."

Jared put his hand on David's shoulder as David looked up at him. "You shot somebody!" Jared studied David with amazement. "With cuffs on! I can't believe it."

"Leave him alone and let him pray, Jared!" Elijah passed a semi at an uncomfortable speed in the trembling van. "We're not out of the woods yet."

"Take the next exit, a half mile ahead." Cal read the reflective green sign to his right. "I don't see anybody following us yet."

Jared turned to look out the back window. "Looks like the pile-up blocked the Army's chase."

"You know we're going to get blamed for that dead patrolman, too." Jared pointed at the highway patrol cars and the fire trucks, lights flashing and sirens blaring, that raced toward the accident in the opposite direction.

Elijah called out to the stranger with the NRA shirt beside him, "Hey, dude, what's your name again?"

Cal looked up from his prayer. "Cal."

"Where's your family?"

"I ran out of gas next to a Wendy's at this next exit and I coasted into a parking space. Fuel gauge must have been stuck at a quarter of a tank."

"You said you're a wanted man for your Christian beliefs, huh?"

"Yeah." Cal answered the question with a thin smile, pleased to be in like-minded company. He cast a curious glance at David. "Hey, man." David stopped praying and looked up at him. "What's this about you killing the president? Is Margaret Brighton dead?" All three of them laughed at the question.

"They were referring to President Fitzgerald," Jared informed him, "and no, we didn't kill him. A lot of pro-life activists were investigated and our names rose to the top of the list when we fled. Where are you from?"

"Alabama. Children's Services was persecuting us for our faith and trying to remove my kids. I resisted. That's how I ended up here."

"I know what you're going through." David's thoughts immediately went to his own family. He finally was able to give some thought to the words of the soldiers and his heart became very troubled. *They know where my family's hiding out in Colton. I hope they're okay.*

Elijah followed Cal's instructions, turned right at the exit, and into the Wendy's parking lot. He parked the car in the rear of the restaurant behind the dumpster and they all rushed into Cal's maroon mini-van as Jared poured the quarter-gallon of gas from Cal's red plastic container into the vehicle. Cal tossed the keys to Elijah and ran into the restaurant to get his family. "You drive while I brief my wife on what's going on."

"Be quick," Elijah responded. David followed Cal into the store. "Now's not the time for a potty break, David."

Elijah started the mini-van and drove it up to the door. Momentarily, Cal rushed back with his two girls in his arms. They grew frightened when their daddy wouldn't answer their questions. Then their father handed them to a scruffy looking stranger with bleached, spiked hair and silver loop earrings. Their eyes began to well up with tears and their bottom lips quivered.

"It'll be all right," Jared told them unconvincingly.

Cal's wife, Sabina, was right behind him, with the diaper bag over one of her shoulders and the infant boy over the other. "What do you mean? How'd you get shot by a soldier?"

"Details later. In the car," he ordered.

"We need to get you to a hospital. Did you get hurt anywhere else?"

"I'll tell you in a minute. Get in." He helped her in, and then jumped in and slammed the door.

"Where's David?"

"We're closing early, sir," the African-American cashier addressed David. "I'm sorry."

"Let me speak to the manager?"

"I'll get her for you."

"No, no. You give this to her. Please." He extended a folded white paper toward her. "Tell her to get this to the Highway Patrol office. It's very important."

"Okay." She took the hand-written note from the stranger, who then rushed out of the restaurant.

The restaurant manager came out of her office momentarily and was handed the note. She read it: *Patrolman Sam Kline died bravely defending the Constitution, trying to protect the innocent. God grant his family peace. I'm sorry I couldn't take a bullet for him. He took a bullet for me. David Jameson.*

David hopped into the van just as Elijah hollered, "Duck!" Two police cars whizzed past them, sirens screaming, blue and red lights flashing. Elijah was glad that he had parked his gray van behind the dumpster, out of the view of the road.

When they were 15 minutes away from the restaurant traveling back roads, they all began to feel much better about their situation. Elijah began to search for a fuel station. Nerves calmed and they began to process David's dilemma.

Jared was the first to bring it up. "What are you going to do about your family in Colton, David?"

"I was thinkin' the same thing." Elijah glanced at David in the rearview mirror. "You can't go get them. The feds will be waiting for you. You can't call them. They're surely bugged. The feds are stakin' them out, trying to catch you."

David shook his head and sighed. "I've got to protect them."

"How?" Elijah wondered.

"Maybe I should turn myself in."

"And how's that going to help them?" Elijah shrugged his shoulders. "You know they'll just arrest her too. Then who's gonna be there for your kids?"

"We could sneak in concealed," Jared proposed, "and try to whisk them away in the middle of the night."

David shook his head. "No. If the Army knows about it, then surely the FBI has a massive stakeout on her. We can't risk going to get them." He sniffed back his tears. "I'm not going to put you all at risk. Besides, they couldn't fit in this van anyway."

"You've got to at least call them and tell them something." Cal held his cell phone aloft with one hand. "It's one of those rent-a-cells, purchased with cash without using my name."

"Cool," said Jared. "You've got a gun on your calf and an untraceable cell phone in your pocket. I'm half expecting you to pull a microwave out of your wallet." Jared's lightheartedness didn't fit the somber mood.

"Oh, it's traceable," Elijah remarked. "If you call her, they'll know that David's speaking on that phone and they'll triangulate us. If it's GPS-equipped, they'll track us."

"You've got to call them, David." Cal extended the phone to him. "Do it. We'll destroy it when we're done."

David thanked Cal and began to dial the phone number he'd committed to memory.

"Wait." Elijah put up his palm. "Don't call yet." He retrieved the atlas on the ground beside him and laid it up over the steering wheel. "What we want to do is make the call north of the route we actually want to take so that they think that we're further north than we really are. Let's use the call as counter-intelligence to throw them off."

He studied the map of their location for a moment, his gaze darting back and forth from the road to the map. "We'll call about 20 minutes north of Lampasas, next to Killeen. I'm sure the tower will be in one of those two cities. They'll think we'd be going north, headed for the border away from San Antonio. But instead, we'll be heading southwest back to Stonewall, then west on the back roads all the way to the New Mexico border."

"Sounds like a good plan." Cal was impressed with Elijah's forethought.

David's tone was sorrowful as he held the phone to his chest with both hands. "I know what I have to do. I can't live with myself if I don't."

Colton, Texas

"Where's Daddy?"

Darlene looked up from her newspaper as the eldest, Charlotte, turned from *Nickelodeon's Blue's Clues* to ask the daily question. Her mother proceeded to give the daily answer, "He's preaching God's Word, honey." That was a statement of faith more than fact, for she feared that, at best, David was hiding from the 50,000 troops and dozens of roadblocks between Austin and their little motel. At worst, he'd been captured. She was running out of money, just buying time, staying out of the public's eye as much as possible, and waiting for directions from her husband or from the Lord. Her mind was haunted with fears. David had an atypical melancholy tone in his voice the last time they talked on the phone, and it was keeping her awake at night. He also said that he had something personal to talk to her about that he never got around to; she hadn't stopped wondering about what that could be. She fought her anxiety with continuous praise to God. All day long, she made her requests known to God and the peace of God filled her heart and mind, at least until she stopped praying and praising. It was a constant struggle to have faith. She was growing weary of fighting the doubt and anxiety.

"When is he going to *stop* preaching God's Word?"

Darlene laughed at Charlotte's lack of pretense. "He'll *never* stop serving God because he loves God. He'll be coming home soon."

"When?"

"One day soon, dear, he'll walk up to us and we'll all run up to him, hug him, and tell him how much we missed him." Darlene grinned when she saw a smile light up the face of her oldest, whose grief was magnified by the fact that it was her fifth birthday. Yet underneath the warmth of Darlene's comforting smile, there was an ache of fear and despair that only prayer and praise could temporarily quench.

"Why can't he stop preachin' to be with me on my birthday?"

At this, Darlene laid down her newspaper, sat on the floor beside the bed, and embraced her oldest daughter. They had sung "Happy Birthday" upon waking and gave her a cupcake with five candles on it after breakfast, but the absence of her father left an emptiness in the annual rituals. Darlene kissed Charlotte on the forehead. "I'm sure Daddy would be here if he could." She combed her daughter's curly blond hair with her fingers. "But God sent your daddy on a very important mission. He's trying to help save the babies and the sinners."

"Am I his baby too?" Her sincerity almost brought Darlene to tears.

"Of course you are. He loves you so much, Charlotte. I'm sure he wishes he were here on your birthday. Maybe he'll call. I pray so."

The middle daughter, Mary, saw the attention that mother was giving to big sister and became envious. She affectionately grabbed onto her mother's arm.

"Is Daddy comin' for Char's birf-day?" The child cocked her head to one side and raised her reddish eyebrows slightly.

"I hope so."

The hotel phone rang and Char squealed with glee. "It's Daddy! It's Daddy!"

"Shh." Darlene tried to hush the girls, yet was unable to calm her own throbbing anticipation.

She pulled the phone to her ear. "Hello?"

"Hello, Darlene." Darlene's heart leaped upon hearing her husband's voice.

"Are you all right? I've been so worried about you since I learned about the fighting all around Austin." The girls cheered upon seeing their mother's smile, knowing only the voice of their daddy could cause that.

"I'm fine. How are the girls?"

"They're great. They sure miss you."

"And my birthday girl?"

She breathed a sigh of relief. *He remembered!*

"Hold on, I'll let you speak to her."

Darlene handed the phone to Charlotte, who smiled broadly as she greeted her father. "Hello, Daddy."

"How's my 5-year-old big girl?"

"I'm growin' up, Daddy. Mommy said I'm growin' up fast."

"Yes." He grinned at her enthusiasm. "That you are. I wish I could be there for your birthday today."

"Can you stop serving God for just a minute to come and eat a piece of birthday cupcake we saved for you?"

That comment broke the dam of tears in her mother's eyes and David took a deep breath to fight back the waves of sadness that threatened his composure. "I, I wish I could, dear. I hope you have the happiest birthday ever."

"It can't be the happiest birthday *ever*, because *you're* not here."

"Well, then the second happiest birthday ever. I love you very much, my 5-year-old princess. Lord willing, I'll see you again very soon. You pray so, okay?"

"Okay."

"I love you."

"Love you too, Daddy."

Charlotte handed the phone back to her mother, who wiped her tears and cradled the phone close to her round cheek.

"Darlene. I need you to be quiet and listen to me for a second."

"Okay." Fear gripped her and her smile faded to a frown upon hearing the serious tone of her husband's voice.

"Listen very carefully. Do you remember the second year of our marriage when I confessed to you that I had a problem with pornography and we decided to beef up the parental controls on our computer to help protect me from temptation?"

Darlene's heart dropped to her stomach. "I remember."

"I made a comment to you that I had struggled with lust on and off for a couple of years. Then you forgave me and that was that. I've been living free ever since."

"Yes?"

"I never did come clean to you with what I did."

Her face turned pale and she turned her gaze away from the children toward the wall. "What?"

There was a moment of silence and Darlene thought that they had been disconnected. Then David whispered, "I cheated on you, Darlene."

She gasped as she put her hand over her mouth. She pulled the phone down to her chest and her body went numb. "Jesus, Jesus, help me," she prayed softly. "Help me." This had always been her nightmare and it was coming true. Her heart raced, her palms began to sweat, and she felt as if she was about to pass out.

"Darlene? Are you there?" she overheard David say over the phone.

She put the phone back to her ear and took a deep breath. "I'm here."

"It was the main reason I resigned the pastorate. It was Melinda."

"What!" Darlene squealed in horror. The children turned from their toys and watched their mother begin to grow hysterical. "What? You committed adultery with Tom's wife?!"

Jared, overhearing the conversation, snapped his head around and glared at David critically. "Tom's wife? No!"

"Shh," Elijah urged him.

The federal agents recording the conversation from the hotel room next door glanced at each with their eyebrows raised in surprise. This was a turn of events that they didn't suspect. The room bustled with anxious orders and hasty phone calls as they carefully planned responses to the discovery of the location of the suspect they were staking out.

"Hypocrite," one of the agents listening in to the phone call mumbled.

"It was only once. I confessed to Brother Samuels."

"Oh God! Oh God!" Darlene dropped the phone to the floor and fled to the bathroom.

"Hello? Darlene? Darlene?" Tears dribbled down David's cheeks. "Darlene?" When he heard his wife slam the bathroom door shut and his three girls rush toward the door to find out what was wrong with their mother, he began to sob.

Cal and Elijah began to pray as they overheard David's confession. Elijah knew that this was the Lord's will and would bless their marriage in the long run. Jared, on the other hand, was furious. He couldn't believe what he was hearing. He was close to the Jameson family and couldn't imagine how much Darlene must be suffering right at that moment.

Five-year-old Charlotte picked up the phone. David could hear the weepiness in her voice. "Hello?"

"Charlotte? Where's Mommy?"

"She's in the bathroom. What happened, Daddy?"

"I need you to do something for me. I want you to set the phone down on the bed, go to the bathroom door, and tell Mommy that Daddy's not done talking with her yet. Will you do that for me?"

"Okay."

As David waited, Elijah glanced at him in the rearview mirror. "You're doing the right thing, David. Everything's going to be all right."

David shrugged and furrowed his brow, giving Elijah a sharp glance as if to say, *That was nothing, wait and see what I say next.*

A moment later, Darlene gained control over her emotions and returned to the phone. "I'm here."

"I'm so sorry, Darlene. I've been faithful to you ever since."

"You've been living a lie ever since! How can God forgive you if the person you sinned against hasn't forgiven you? That's like stealing from somebody and trying to repent without returning what you stole, or lying to somebody and trying to repent without telling the truth! You sinned against *me*, David!" She slapped herself in the chest. "Me!"

"I'm sorry. I should've told you. I didn't want to hurt you."

"You didn't want to hurt me?" Darlene sobbed for a few seconds, and then repeated the words in a more shrill tone, "You didn't want to hurt me?"

"There's more." David took a deep breath and forced out the words, "Melinda conceived."

Darlene gasped again as David continued, "She went home to Texas after she and Tom separated and I never learned what became of the baby, but I saw her at a fuel station in Austin soon after we arrived. I was fueling up my lawn mower. I only spoke with her briefly, but she told me something, something that was very difficult for me to hear."

After a moment of suspenseful silence, Darlene inquired, "She told you what?"

David began to sob openly. "Oh Darlene, she got an abortion."

Darlene's jaw dropped open and she lifted her weeping eyes to heaven. David began to sob and weep so strongly that she began to pity him, similar to the way a driver of a car would pity an injured raccoon on the side of the road. For a brief moment, she began to entertain the thought of telling him that she never wanted to see him again. He was the scum of the earth, the embodiment of everything that was wrong with this church and country. Men like David Jameson were bringing God's judgment upon the whole nation, and here he was, trying to be used by God to turn the tide and win God's grace for his children. What a Judas! What a hypocrite!

But then she turned her gaze to the children. The two oldest had tears in their eyes as they knelt beside the bed, listening to every word that their mother spoke. They had never heard their parents speak to each other in such a way and were horrified. If it wasn't for them, Darlene may just have shut the door forever on the marriage right then.

"No way!" one of the federal agents listening in the hotel room next door exclaimed. "The president's going to love this."

"I've killed one of my own babies!" David cried between sobs.

"No, no you didn't. Adultery, yes, but murder?" She sighed deeply. "Not murder."

"If any man doesn't care for his own, he's worse than an infidel. That's me, Darlene. I've preached it so many times, and I've had a huge beam in my own eye."

"Oh, quit your pity party." Darlene gritted her teeth, feeling stronger in the atmosphere of her husband's humility.

"Please forgive me, Darlene. Please."

Elijah looked in the rearview mirror at David. David dropped his head toward the floor and Elijah could only see the top of his John Deere cap. But he could see David's hands were shaking. "I've wanted to confess to you ever since I walked out of the Austin Women's Clinic and realized that this was probably where my baby was killed. Please, pray for me."

Darlene could sense her husband's brokenness and realized that God had David right where He wanted him. At that moment, she didn't think that things could ever be the same between them. The wound was too painful to even think about the future. But she knew that God had broken her husband in the wilderness.

"You did a horrible thing, David, but I have, too. I was a sinner, too. And the Bible says that if I don't forgive you for sinning against me…" She paused to take a deep breath. She didn't feel the words, but she knew that they were true, so she spoke them anyway, "If I don't forgive you, then God won't forgive me."

"Oh, Darlene!" David's words tapered off to a pitiful, mournful cry.

Darlene's sigh was audible. "David, Jesus said that those who have been forgiven much love much, and those that have been forgiven little love little. The greater sinner has the greater grace.

You're the prodigal come home, and the Father rejoices more at the one stray sheep that gets found than the 99 that never got lost." She paused. The words were coming to her mind but she hesitated to speak them. There was some shelter in bitterness, but if she forgave him, she would have to give up the right to punish him. "If you think I'm going to cut and run," she said, "you've got another thing coming. I forgive you. I'll never leave you, David. Never." With those words, Darlene knew she was picking a fight with the devil. The fiery darts of doubt and bitterness were sure to come, but Darlene knew that the shield of faith could quench every one.

To David, those words were like water to a man minutes away from perishing of thirst. He drank them in desperately and mumbled the words under his breath, "Jesus, have mercy."

Cal, sitting in the rear of the van with his family, reached his hand forward and placed it on David's shoulder. He had a smile on his face, ear to ear. He had witnessed so much contrition and humility with the recent revival in his church, that it thrilled his soul when he witnessed the Spirit's cleansing work. He loved to see hearts break under the power of conviction and mourn their way to mercy. David had just scaled the peak of the mountain of repentance. The hardest part was over for David. He had confessed his way to the full glory of the Father's countenance. But the suffering of David's wife, Cal knew, was just beginning. Cal began to whisper a prayer for David's wife and family.

"I want to apologize for deceiving you, Darlene. I want to apologize to you for dragging you and the girls through so much poverty."

"Oh, if poverty's the heaviest cross I have to carry—"

"Just listen, Darlene. Don't say another word until I'm done." Darlene swallowed hard and braced for what she suspected would be even more tragic news. "You've been a very humble and submissive wife and I'm sorry for taking advantage of that." Those words sent a fresh wave of numbness through her body and nausea into her stomach. She closed her eyes and turned away from the children as he continued. His words were slow and deliberate. "I want your last act of obedience to me to be to *disassociate* from me. FBI agents are probably going to question you about me and I want you to tell them *everything* you know. Don't tell them my views on abortion, tell them *your own...*"

Now she was confused. She squinted her eyes shut. *My own?*

"Tell them that abortion isn't a big deal to you." He paused. "Do you understand what I'm saying?"

Momentarily, she responded with a weepy voice. "I understand what you're saying, David, but it doesn't make any sense."

"I don't expect it to, Darlene. Just trust me and do what I say. I'm a wanted man, and it's just a matter of time, Darlene." He paused to conceal his weeping. Darlene could hear his bitter gasps of grief over the phone. "I want you to be free, Darlene. I want the kids to stay with their mother. And don't defend me – that's an order, non-negotiable. Hold no secrets."

"What?"

"I love you with all my heart, Darlene. I know you don't understand and I'm sorry. You're free, Darlene. Bob and Lisa have a place where you can stay," he mumbled, his voice faltering as he spoke. "You've got enough cash to get there."

"I'm not leaving, David."

"I won't be calling or coming around. Just, just pray for me." David's voice trailed off until all was silent.

"David? David?" A click and a dial tone reminded her that this was no nightmare.

Char stood at her mother's knees, tears in her eyes, troubled by the fear and grief in her mother's countenance. "What's the matter with you and Daddy?"

Darlene dropped to her knees beside the bed, placed her head in her arms and wept as her heart began to break in two.

"Who would have expected that?" The senior federal agent listening in on the conversation held one earphone tightly to his ear as the other hung loosely against his jaw.

The second agent couldn't believe his ears. This was unlike anything they had ever heard about David Jameson. "He's leaving her? This piece doesn't fit the puzzle."

"It was an easy trace. He's heading north out of Austin. We've GPS'd their location." A third agent with pepper gray hair set down his earphones and tapped a few keys on the laptop computer that was hooked up to Jameson's line.

"He's leaving his wife and kids? I know this man like the back of my hand," the senior agent responded. "He would never do that."

"He's a psychotic freak," the gray-headed federal agent reminded them. "Unpredictability is the only predictable characteristic. I'm activating the SWAT teams and police in the area to converge on him."

"Something's not right. He's leading us on. We need to tear apart every bit of that conversation. Let's locate and interrogate these Tom and Melinda characters. Find out who Bob and Lisa are."

"I'm already on it." An agent on a computer in the back of the room had already begun to search the computer file on David and Darlene.

A junior agent listened through his headset as the two oldest Jameson children questioned their mother's sadness. He glanced at the senior agent. "What do we do now?"

"We notify Durango. Hopefully the inside man close to Jameson when he was at the Civic Center is still with him. I don't know why they didn't just pick him up if they knew where he was."

The senior agent picked up the phone to notify the director of the Midwest Division of the FBI. "Ours is not to reason why. There are factors of which we must be unaware. You just keep listening and recording."

"What do we do about Darlene? Should we move on her?"

"Patience. We're not going to lose her."

The agent looking at Jameson's list of contacts on his computer cleared his throat. "Bob and Lisa Messer are a couple that used to go to their church before they moved. They live in Pataskala, 30 miles from the Jameson home in Columbus."

The two oldest Jameson children gathered around their weeping mother, tears flowing down their cheeks. The baby started to cry and Char picked her up and was trying to sing to her. They were all filled with confusion. Darlene's mind wandered to all of the possible scenarios. *Maybe David's having a nervous breakdown. Maybe he's been kidnapped and was forced to say those things at gunpoint.*

Maybe he thinks our phone's bugged and wants to try to fool anyone listening in. Maybe he did blow up the civic center...

"What's the matter, Mommy?" Charlotte gently scratched her mother's back, trying to comfort her.

"Why you crying?" moaned the middle child, Mary, her bottom lip trembling as she bravely dried her tears.

Darlene dabbed her eyes with a tissue. She must be strong for her children, even if their father isn't. "We just need to pray for Daddy."

The two oldest children knelt beside their mother as she began to pray. "Dear Lord." She paused for the children to repeat the phrase, which they did with much enthusiasm. "Help Daddy" – the children repeated again – "to trust in God. Keep him safe. Help him to come home." The children repeated her words with such passion that their mother began to weep afresh.

Charlotte rose from her knees and placed her hand on her mother's head. "Help Mommy, dear God, to trust in You."

Little 2-year-old Mary, who always tried to imitate her bigger sister, stood and did likewise, repeating the same words as solemnly as she could with her hand on her mother's head. Darlene's head collapsed onto her arms as she knelt by her bed and wept. "Help me, dear Jesus. Help us."

"What did you do that for?" Jared was perturbed at David's final words to Darlene. "Now she thinks you're leaving her for good."

David didn't respond but gazed out of the window. Elijah pulled off the interstate and tossed the cell phone in the cabin of a pick-up truck that was about to get on the interstate heading north. He pulled back on the interstate, heading south, and angled the rearview mirror so he could better study David's countenance. He saw the fear and doubt in David's eyes.

"I did what I had to do." David's voice cracked with emotion, his red eyes welling with tears.

"You just emotionally murdered her!" Jared blurted out.

David's head snapped around to Jared, his teeth clenched in anger. "It's the only way Darlene will stay out of jail and my girls will be able to stay with their mother!"

Jared's temper matched David's. "You mixed a heart-breaking, painful confession with a ruse that you were leaving her! How's she supposed to make sense of that?"

"You'll see them again." Elijah spoke with a confidence that was more of a statement of faith than a matter of fact. "Mixing that confession and that ruse is probably the best thing you could have done. The government will confirm the facts behind the confession and that will add authenticity to your ruse."

"I hope so." David's words protruded from his lips in the form of a crackling moan and he couldn't hold back his sob.

Elijah looked at David through the rearview mirror. "David, look at me. Look at me." Elijah's voice was commanding and insistent. David held his peace and made eye contact with Elijah. "It is through much tribulation that we'll enter the kingdom of God, David. Just as the suffering of Texas now will be the tithe for justice for the pre-born later, so your suffering will be the tithe for nationwide revival. We've got to be willing to drink from the cup if we want to sit on the thrones Jesus wants to give us." Elijah was prophesying and he had David's attention. "At the moment of your greatest exploit in the Austin Women's Clinic, you were made to face your most shameful sin, and now it's all washed away, as far as the east is from the west. Cast your care on Jesus, for He cares for you. Your humility will exalt you to greatness in due time. Your emotional suffering, and that of Darlene, will be your thorn in the flesh lest you should be exalted above measure. Cling to Jesus with all your heart. Where He's going to take you, you'll need Him more than you know."

David nodded soberly, his eyes wet with tears. "Oh Elijah, my family's suffering."

"God won't give you or them more than you are able to bear. His grace is sufficient. His strength will be perfected in your weakness." David nodded, dropped his head into his hands and wept until he ran out of tears.

Please, Darlene. Remember. God help her remember.

Suddenly Darlene stopped her weeping. "Oh!" She startled her children as she sat up. "What a fool I am!" She jumped off the bed, grabbed her purse beside the television, and ran into the bathroom.

"Are you okay, Mommy?"

"Yes. Char, I want you to entertain the children for a moment." There was renewed hope in her voice and the two oldest perked up upon hearing it.

Char picked the Veggie Tale book off the ground, wiped off her youngest sibling's slobber, and sat beside her younger sisters on the floor. She began to make up words to the story as she turned the colorful pages.

Darlene turned the bath water on full blast and then sat on the tiled floor with her back to the wall. She rummaged through her purse. *Where is it, where is it?*

She pulled a small five by seven card from the bottom of the make-up bag in her purse. *Bob and Lisa, Bob and Lisa, Bob and Lisa...*

She ran her fingers down a list of code words her husband had given her when they fled their home for Texas. In the planning stages of their flight from the authorities, David made some phone calls and planned for various contingencies. She trembled as she read the message beside the code words "Bee & Elle." Suddenly, she smiled and quietly wept tears of gratitude. *Thank you Jesus,* she passionately whispered her gratitude to God, and brought the five-by-seven card to her mouth to kiss it. She realized now that since David used his code words, he must have only pretended not to care about her anymore; he must suspect that the phone at the hotel was tapped. She rejoiced in the soothing realization, but then was struck with the harsh reality that the federal authorities were probably watching her every move.

She opened the door so she could hear the children and then she took a bath. She tried to memorize the code words and their respective messages on the card that she initially mocked when her husband gave it to her. When she got out of the bath, she ripped up the paper into little pieces and flushed it down the toilet.

She got dressed and called the children together to sing several praise songs and dance before the Lord. She even let the girls jump between the two beds in the hotel room, a special treat. If the federal authorities were spying on her, she wanted them to hear her sing and shout praise to her Savior.

Chapter 7

Columbia, South Carolina

"We're not going to let you do it." The senior FBI agent stood before Governor Gary Cropp and was insistent. "It's not happening." He wagged his index finger over the governor's desk as he towered above him.

"I don't need your permission." Governor Gary Cropp's classic southern drawl fit his stubbornness perfectly. "You tell your president that she must respond to our list of grievances in a satisfactory manner or I will urge the legislature to vote for secession. Our 'States' Rights Resolution' passed overwhelmingly. You know that we have the votes."

"Do you want to be held for treason?"

The governor stood up so that he was eye to eye with the senior FBI agent. "For a vote to acknowledge our constitutional rights and restrain the federal government to the Constitution's limitations? You've got to be crazy. You go ahead and try it," he dared him, glancing to his right at a former Clemson lineman and an ex-Special Forces Navy vet, who were now his chief bodyguards. "You're imposing tyranny on us in defiance of the laws of our land. If anyone should be worried about committing treason, it's you and that godless dictator you worship."

"Work to change it legally," the agent urged him, softening his tone.

"We *are* working to change it legally. If the federal government will not abide by the Constitution and if they continue to persecute and kill our people, secession is a valid, legal option."

"That's, that's absurd!"

The governor sat down and raised his palm toward the agent, who took a deep breath and settled back into his seat. "Hold on, hold on. Stop right there. We wouldn't exist as a nation if we didn't have the right to secede from tyranny. Even without the abuses of Margaret Brighton, the federal government has become a monster of usurpation and evil. South Carolina entered into this country voluntarily and the covenant has been grievously violated. We have the God-given right to withdraw from voluntary associations. We should have done it years ago, like in 1973 when you started murderin' babies."

"If there's violence at this rally," the senior agent said as he pointed out the window, "we'll use force to quell it."

"There will be no violence on our part or from anybody associated with this movement. This is a move of peace-loving South Carolinians."

"Yeah, right." The agent mocked him with a roll of his eyes.

"You have received our signed pledges of non-violence."

"Yeah." The agent nodded. "I've got the 15 boxes cluttering my office in Charleston. And I'm sure every domestic terrorist in South Carolina has signed one."

"You've got no business lecturing me on violence, sir." The governor smacked the table with his palm and then raised a critical index finger at the senior FBI agent. "I was on the phone with Governor Adams when your people burst into his office with guns a-blazing and kidnapped him and his—"

"Don't speculate on what you have no knowledge," the agent interrupted him in a harsh tone. "Henry Adams was a criminal and a traitor. He was guilty of treason and conspiracy to commit acts of terror."

Cropp shook his head back and forth. "I don't believe your president's spin. If someone's willing to murder preborn babies and the elderly handicapped, how can you believe a thing that they say?"

The agent raised his voice and stood to his feet again, his hands firmly pressed against his hips. "Henry Adams was planning to capture nuclear weapons, Governor!"

Gary Cropp took a deep breath. "If there's violence in South Carolina as a result of our secession, it will be because the federal government was violent. We intend to divorce peacefully. And we will not make Governor Adams mistake of having a lesser force for our defense than you can muster against us. You go tell your president: if she sends any agents to attack us, make sure they've finalized their wills."

Outside, thousands of South Carolinians were gathering for a prepared speech from the governor and several Christian and conservative leaders. The mood was cheerful and light. Women pushed strollers, men chatted as they sat on lawn chairs, and merchants sold hot dogs and memorabilia. Confederate flags and yellow "Don't Tread on Me" pins were hot items. A large screen had been erected in front of the capital building in downtown Columbia and a projector cast the images of a video on the screen, *The Patriot* with Mel Gibson, which told the story of a South Carolina Revolutionary War hero. Loud speakers boomed the sound all over downtown Columbia.

Greenville, South Carolina

At the largest predominantly African-American church in downtown Greenville, three senior federal agents of African-American descent sat down with the leadership of this and several other predominantly black churches. The president of the local chapter of the NAACP was also present. Similar meetings were taking place at community centers and offices of black churches all over South Carolina.

"Are you sure this is absolutely necessary?" The NAACP president had a worried look on his face.

The federal agent with the blackest skin and the grayest hair fretted as he turned his attention to the NAACP president in the room full of the most influential black leaders in the area. "*Please* tell me that you have our people ready."

"Oh, they're ready, but, well," he paused, glanced at the pastor of the church where they were meeting, and then down to the carpet.

"We're having second thoughts," the senior pastor interjected with a worrisome countenance.

"What? Why?" The senior agent raised his voice, dumbfounded, trying to resist the urge to lash out in anger. "You know what's going to happen if South Carolina secedes, don't you? *All* federal funds for Medicaid will be gone. South Carolina gets more in federal funding than it gives in taxes. *All* the social programs that our people enjoy will die. Medicare checks will disappear. Schools in poor districts will go bankrupt. No more help with housing, infant formula, or medical care. Do you think that the state of South Carolina and its Caucasian governor, which cannot afford to take care of us even *with* federal funding, are going to take care of us when South Carolina is an independent nation? The same white people urging secession are also planning on cutting our social programs, our food banks, our welfare..."

"I know, I know. It's just that..."

"I'm not even bringing up the sanctions that are going to be placed on South Carolina if you all secede and the federal government has to intervene with force."

"We *are* on board with you but we want guarantees." The senior pastor spoke with passion as he glanced back and forth from the NAACP president to the federal agents. "You need to guarantee us that our people won't get hard time for doing this."

"Oh, please!" The agent waved his hand at the pastor as if he was swatting a pesky gnat. "You should have asked for guarantees weeks ago when we first had this conversation. We need at least 5,000 on the streets in Columbia in two hours! You'd *better* have done your job! We ordered judges to extend early parole to 2,483 young black men to help you get the numbers you need. You'd better have them."

"They're in Columbia right now," the NAACP chapter president assured him.

"Well, what's the fuss about? You're giving me a heart attack here." The gray-haired agent leaned back in his chair and sighed deeply.

"I just have this Tuskegee feel about this whole thing," the pastor asserted, "like y'all are using us to get what you want without regard to what our people sacrifice to help you or what we need."

"Come on!" the agent exclaimed with his hands outstretched. "What's the color of my skin, man? Would I do that to you?"

Columbia, South Carolina

Mitch Paine, the popular professor from the University of Texas, stood on an elevated platform in the gymnasium, surrounded by a crowd of 1,500 hippies, gothic head-bangers, and university students from the gay, feminist, and atheist student groups from nearby public universities. He wore his colorful flowery shirt, unbuttoned halfway to show off his hairy chest and fake tan. His light brown hair was pulled back into a ponytail. Sweat dripped down his brow from the heat of the powerful spotlights focused on him. He rallied his diverse congregation into a frenzy with his passionate rebukes of the religious fanatics in South Carolina's leadership. With one fist clasped around a cordless microphone and another thrust into the air, he bellowed, "How many of you are fed up with their hate-mongering?"

The horde of students and dropouts thrust their fists into the air as one. "Yeah!"

Professor Paine pushed the microphone stand toward the ground and then stepped on the base to thrust it back up to him. He grabbed the mic stand and screamed into it like a rock star, thrusting his hips with the rhythm of their cheers. "How many of you are fed up with their anti-choice sexism?"

"Yeah!" The students were growing more inebriated by the minute, thanks to freely distributed bottles of vodka in water bottles and local drug peddlers selling marijuana and narcotics dirt-cheap.

"How many of you are fed up with their homophobia?"
"Yeah!"

Paine's profanity-laden speech was concluding and it was time for his altar call. As if on cue, student leaders took their places at the exits with directions and instructions for their army of activists. These student leaders had no formal association with the professor in order to provide him with the necessary plausible deniability. Paine would be in the airport boarding his private jet back to Austin before these leftists would see any action.

Paine put his lips up to the microphone and screamed, "How many of you are ready to do something about it?"

*****

Governor Cropp asked his chief-of-staff the question one final time before deciding which version of his speech he was going to give: "Has the president responded?"

"Not a peep."

The governor shook his head in disbelief. "The audacity!"

The majority leader in the statehouse put his hand on the governor's shoulder. "We're behind you, Governor."

They stood up and walked quietly to a glass double door, watching as the governor's pastor concluded his passionate opening prayer. Then security guards opened the glass doors and Governor Gary Cropp marched out of the capital building foyer, followed by a dozen D.C. congressional leaders, two state Supreme Court judges, 55 state representatives and senators, and over 100 sheriffs and law enforcement officers.

The applause was deafening!

Twenty thousand South Carolinians roared and cheered in the square that sprawled out in front of the platform. As far as the eye could see, swarms of people packed in tightly for the historic speech. People even crowded into the alleys between the buildings that surrounded the square. In front of the platform, police held back the crowds that pressed in.

"Thank you so much." Governor Cropp tried to wave the mass of people to be quiet. "Thank you." When the applause finally subsided, he announced, "I am here to proclaim that from this day forward, South Carolina will serve the Lord Jesus Christ!" The applause erupted again for several minutes. The governor remained silent until the cheering quieted back down to a low murmur.

He spoke with great passion: "South Carolina *refuses* to remain apathetic as tyrants trample our rights underfoot, steal our wealth, and prosecute us for our faith. South Carolina *refuses* to remain silent as tyrants abort our children and grandchildren, and exterminate our elderly and handicapped family members. We *refuse* the evil judges who, in the name of free speech, force us to allow porn shops and crack houses to prosper in our inner cities, yet prosecute us for proclaiming the Word of God from our pulpits and our public schools. We will *not* consent to the federal government as it sends our soldiers and our jobs overseas and refuses to protect our borders and our economy from illegal immigration in the pursuit of their 'New World Order.' We will *not* consent to the federal government with its mandated gay marriage and no-fault divorce. We will *not* sit idly by while they shove atheism and contraception down the throats of our children through the federal mandates of the public educational system." He shouted to be heard over the vigorous applause and shouts of "Amen," "Right on," and the occasional "Huzzah!"

"We will *not* let them get away with it anymore!"

Behind the governor, the image of the top of the Declaration of Independence flashed up on the large, white screen and gradually zoomed out. "When in the course of human events," the governor recited from the Declaration, "it becomes necessary for one people to dissolve the political bands which have connected them with another, and to assume among the powers of the earth the separate and equal station to which the laws of nature and nature's God entitle them, a decent respect to the opinions of mankind requires that they should declare the causes which impel them to the separation. We hold these truths to be self-evident, that all men are created equal, that they are endowed by their Creator with certain unalienable rights..."

As he read this, a video began to play on the large screen. The opening frames were of an elderly woman holding a Bible sitting in a rocking chair.

"...That among these are life, liberty, and the pursuit of happiness..." The screen flashed a video of a human fetus sucking its thumb, and then switched to show some pro-life protesters being arrested and put in a black van with the white words "SWAT" painted on its side.

"...That to secure these rights, governments are instituted among men, deriving their just powers from the consent of the governed..." The video showed a live panoramic view of South Carolina's state capital building, surrounded by tens of thousands of listeners. The live video was taken from a helicopter overhead. On the edge of the video, you could barely see several hundred black clothed agents bunched together about a block away from the square. This was the first view that most of the governor's listeners had of the FBI's tactical response to their governor's courageous speech, although most of the viewers hadn't made the connection yet.

"...That whenever any form of government becomes destructive of these ends..." Here the video began to show clips of various arrests of prominent Christians, pastors, and local politicians who resisted the federal government, including a clip of Department of Justice Director Vic Meyers arresting Bozeman Sheriff Randy Woods. The video transitioned to clips of aggression against unarmed crowds in Bozeman, of federal government employees screening passengers at a security line at an airport, and of Americans lined up at gun shops with their gun cases in hand, preparing to turn in their banned weapons. "...It is the right of the people to alter or to abolish it, and to institute new government, laying its foundation on such principles and organizing its powers in such form as to them shall seem most likely to affect their safety and happiness.

"But when a long train of abuses and usurpations..." – here the video transitioned to clips of the president speaking at a cabinet meeting and then signing her gun control executive order –"pursuing invariably the same object reveals a design to reduce them under absolute despotism or tyranny, it is their right, it is their duty to throw off such government and to provide new guards for their future security..."

As he read the text of the Declaration, first dozens, then hundreds of young people gradually emerged from the walkways between buildings and from the basements of several government buildings until they almost surrounded the large crowd that was pressed into the courtyard, listening intently to Governor Cropp's speech.

"...The history of the present federal government is a history of repeated injuries and usurpations, all having in direct object the establishment of an absolute tyranny over these states..."

Two blocks away from the capital building in every direction, hundreds of FBI agents congregated at intersections and reviewed the rules of engagement. Intermittently, the videographers who interspersed live clips with the footage that coincided with the governor's speech moved from the planned footage to live clips of the SWAT officers gathering and conspiring.

"...She has erected a multitude of new offices, and sent hither swarms of officers to harass our people and eat out their substance. She has quartered large bodies of armed troops among us. She has protected them from punishment for any murders that they should commit on the inhabitants of these states. She has cooperated with others to subject us to a jurisdiction foreign to our Constitution and unacknowledged by our laws..." Here the screen showed a clip of UN soldiers training in Georgia, soldiers at a roadblock in downtown Austin, and a still shot of the monument in front of the UN building in New York, which is a statue of a large gun with a knot in the barrel.

"She has given her assent to the UN's acts of pretended legislation. She has imposed taxes on us without our consent. She has deprived us of the benefit of trial by jury. She has excited domestic insurrections amongst us..." Here the video transitioned to show images of the crowds of hippies, gothic dropouts, college students, and paroled criminals that gathered tightly on the outer edge of the massive crowd. "...In every stage of these oppressions, we have petitioned for redress in the most humble terms. Our repeated petitions have been answered only with repeated injury. A president and a Congress, whose character is thus marked with every act which may define tyranny, are unfit to rule a free people.

"We, therefore, the representatives of the state of South Carolina, appealing to the Supreme Judge of the world for the rectitude of our intentions, do, in the name of Jesus and by the authority of the good people of this state, solemnly publish and declare that the state of

South Carolina of right ought to be free and independent. We hereby are absolved from all allegiance to the federal government..."

The senior agent in charge of the force of 200 federal agents two blocks east of the capital building received a call from Todd Hamilton. They spoke through the radio receiver in his riot helmet.

"Agent Bowers, we've got the final approval from the president. Commence your operation."

"Yes sir."

"...And for the support of this Declaration, with a firm reliance on the protection of Divine Providence, we mutually pledge to each other our lives, our fortunes, and our sacred honor..."

As if on cue, those young paroled criminals, hippies, and gothic young people that had gathered on the crowd's edge, reached into wheeled coolers and nearby trashcans and began to heave fist-sized rocks into the crowd!

"Captain Dunfee!" The governor shouted at one of the chief law enforcement officers on stage beside him, pointing at the melee that was starting at the edge of the crowd in the courtyard. "Get that under control, immediately." Suddenly, the governor's microphone was turned off. The governor tapped the microphone but to no avail. The electricity had been disconnected. Soundboard operators became frantic trying to fix the problem.

Violent brawls erupted in the crowd. Some of the young men began to steal purses and wallets as they threatened their victims with knives or guns. Anyone who attempted to protect personal property was beaten with clubs or stabbed.

Two young men began to lob Molotov cocktails into the crowd from an alley, setting many people on fire and inducing a panic. People nearby began to scream, terrified mothers clung to their children as fist sized rocks flew all around them. The crowd began to press against the narrow exits. Armed citizens began to shoot those that assaulted them, but they soon ran out of ammo and the violence escalated.

The governor was desperately trying to direct the officers in front of the balcony to the area where the fights were breaking out.

However, they were prevented from moving by the sheer mass of those who tried to back away and flee from the assailants. A state representative behind the governor got his attention and motioned toward the white screen behind them. The camera had zoomed closer to the force of federal agents that began to trot toward them in two single lines two blocks away. For the first time, Governor Cropp realized what was happening.

The scuffles on the crowd's edge gradually turned into huge riots. The screaming, kicking, and punching were vicious and relentless. Men wielded sticks and rocks at each other as if they were on a battlefield. Two 20-year-old Bob Jones University students on the edge of the courtyard tried to intervene and six hippies beat and kicked them into unconsciousness. As one man's wife tried to protect her husband with an umbrella, screaming at others for help, the young men dragged her and the stroller with her 4-year-old daughter in it into an alley between two buildings.

The governor looked up and saw that on the top of every building around them were dozens of black-clothed federal agents.

"Get every officer in the city out here, now! Call the Guard out here!"

Without warning, gunfire filled the air, causing many to fall to the ground in fear. Rubber bullets poured down upon them from the building tops. Many tried to flee from the violence into walkways between buildings, into nearby parking lots and adjacent roads, but ran into a gauntlet of federal agents who wielded electric shock sticks and shot rubber bullets haphazardly into the panicking crowd. The weakest and most helpless were trampled.

Police officers surrounded the governor to protect him from the rooftop snipers. They tried to escort him quickly off the balcony and back into the safety of the capital building behind them. Dozens of officers began to shoot their pistols at the black-clothed federal agents on building tops, but speeding bullets from snipers with lethal ammunition quickly took those officers out. The statesmen followed Governor Cropp off the balcony, carrying or dragging the injured along.

When they entered the foyer of the capital building, they walked directly into a wall of 100 federal agents.

One of the agents shouted at them through a megaphone, "Get on the ground, now, and spread your hands out in front of you."

"We have a breaking news story coming to you from Columbia, South Carolina, where Governor Gary Cropp has unbelievably just publicly declared war on the United States." The CNN news correspondent reported from the rooftop of the tallest building beside the courtyard where the governor gave his speech. In her backdrop were several armed FBI gunmen who stood at the edges of the roof watching the melee below.

"A group of anti-government, white racists in the crowd picked a fight with some African-Americans and a riot broke out that local police were unable to control. Fortunately, federal agents were on hand to put an end to the riot. The governor and most of his inside circle has been taken into custody. An emergency session of the State Assembly has been called to re-establish order in the state."

Chapter 8

Ft. Worth, Texas

"Be careful. From this guy's belt buckle to his King James Version, this fanatic fits our profile for a violent dissenter in every conceivable way."

Under the light of a desk lamp in the middle of a huge room with hundreds of desks, the Army staff sergeant studied an FBI profile report and several Federal Firearm License forms obtained through the President's executive order. He pushed a button and spoke into the microphone, transmitting to four vehicles 45 miles away. "A neighbor has confirmed that he's home now. He's got a wife and three teenage boys, each known to be avid shooters, 12 licensed guns and two big German Shepherds. He home-churches, home-schools, um, there's a note here that he also frequents gun shows, so he could have more unlicensed ones than we know."

"Kids or more guns?" One of the ATF agents in the Hummer attempted to ease the fragile tempers with his humor.

It was 4:14 a.m. and the men were anxious after a night of raids. Two camouflaged Army vehicles parked behind two police cars in front of a home in a middle class neighborhood. The homeowner hadn't turned in his guns by the appointed date. The federalized local police force had the help of the ATF SWAT teams and Army specialists in repossessing illegal weapons throughout Texas and arresting the criminals. This team was one of hundreds that were combing Texas neighborhoods, knocking on doors with writs of firearms confiscation, handcuffs for the owners, and bullets for resisters. An ATF-manned Hummer and an armored personnel carrier full of Army troops waited patiently just in case their services were needed. Several social service workers were on call just a few miles away in case it became necessary to take possession of any children.

The Army staff sergeant at headquarters nodded at an assistant beside him, who proceeded to phone the home number of the residence Officer Bailey and company were preparing to raid. The assistant's job was to calmly inform the gun owners that they were surrounded and should submit so that things would go easier on them.

The Army staff sergeant spoke into the microphone, "Officer Bailey, commence."

The police officer turned his blue and red flashing lights on, but kept his siren off. Police officers were a rare breed for a couple of weeks after martial law had been declared in Texas. It seemed half of the officers left the force when Henry Adams was arrested. Most of them packed up and fled north. However, Officer Bailey, two years out of the police academy, was a new breed of police officer. He could adapt to any circumstance and anybody's law. Earlier in the night, he actually shot a citizen who tried to run out the backdoor of a house they were raiding. With the silhouette of a rifle cast upon the wall, Officer Bailey was quick to pull the trigger. Three shots and a 25-year-old man and a 2-year-old toddler lay dead on the floor beside a legal muzzleloader. *If they don't survive,* Officer Bailey reasoned, *then they can't sue.* Besides, with an Army sergeant giving you orders under a military occupation, who has the courage to sue? The young officer's malleable conscience easily adapted. He was, after all, just obeying the law.

"Let's do it." Officer Bailey opened the squad car door and headed for the house with his characteristic wild-west swagger. His partner was right behind him. The two policemen in the squad car in front of them headed for the backdoor of the house. From the front porch, Bailey noticed a light in what appeared to be the kitchen. Bailey looked carefully through the shades and thought he saw some movement on the stairwell. He could hear the phone ringing inside the home. He heard the answering machine pick up. Momentarily, headquarters called the home again, and again no one answered. He stepped to the door and rapped his knuckles against it.

Knock, knock, knock, knock.

The stillness of the cool evening came to an abrupt end with the thunderous announcement from the gravelly voice of Officer Bailey: "Mr. William Johnson! It's the police! Open up!"

The crickets in the bushes beside the porch hushed their chirping. The moist breeze appeared to suddenly drop five degrees and stiffen against their faces, as if the very weather of Texas resisted them. After the pause of a few seconds without any sound from inside, he repeated the order: "Mr. William Johnson, it's the police and the U.S. Army! Open the door! We know you're there and we're prepared to take possession of your illegal weapons. Resistance is futile. Your cooperation will be taken into consideration at your hearing."

After the third knock, they drew their weapons. Bailey's partner, who was heavier by 50 pounds, lifted his right leg and tried to kick the door open, but it didn't budge. Apparently a heavy piece of furniture had been pushed next to the front door. Bailey and his partner shared a troubled glance. Bailey's partner prepared to kick again when Bailey stopped him. Bailey punched through the pane of glass nearest the doorknob with his gloved hand and attempted to unlock the door when he saw some unexpected movement out of the corner of his right eye. Someone on the right side of the driveway threw something at the nearest Hummer idling in the street next to the mailbox.

In the dimly lit street, Officer Bailey could make out a burning fuse directly under the Hummer that was between his police car and the armored personnel carrier behind it.

He shouted at those in the Hummer's front seats just as they began to quickly scurry out of the vehicle. "Get out! Take cover!"

Bailey then commenced pursuit of the shadowy figure who threw the object. "Freeze!" He raised his state-of-the-art military rifle and his right eye searched through his night-vision EO-Tech scope, his index finger tight against the cold metal of the sensitive trigger.

The Army personnel carrier filled with several infantrymen reversed away from the Hummer, but not fast enough. A deafening explosion, made all the more extreme by the quiet stillness of the night, slammed Officer Bailey's head and back against the garage. He fell painfully to the driveway. From the whistling sound in the aftermath of this explosion, Officer Bailey knew that bullets were implanted in this homemade bomb. The bright ball of orange flame that billowed from the explosion temporarily impaired his night vision.

Bailey pulled himself to his feet, reached for his weapon, and hugged the side of the garage, knowing that fleeing from the house would make him an easy target for the shooters who could possibly take aim at him from the second-story windows. Some of the soldiers in the damaged armored personnel carrier behind the Hummer jumped from the vehicle and met a wave of speeding bullets from outlawed semi-automatics aimed from the six windows facing the driveway. Bailey was stunned. These were loud shots from large caliber weapons. They had walked into a trap.

The first four soldiers instantly dropped to the ground, clutching their chests and abdomens. The others tried to make their way behind the vehicle for cover. But they found themselves pelted with a hailstorm of bullets from the windows of the house behind them. Officer Bailey heard the booming blasts of shotguns in the back of the home and presumed that his partners in the rear were in a firefight. It seemed that the whole neighborhood was ambushing them! Surviving agents and soldiers hugged the swale in front of the home, hoping to camouflage with the grass and the dark night. When shots were aimed down on Bailey from a neighboring house, he made a break for the swale in the front yard.

One of the ATF agents managed to flee from the disabled and burning Hummer, his back and arms aflame. Officer Bailey pushed him to the ground and patted out the flames as gunfire blazed all around him. A bullet grazed his face and he fell to the ground in a daze. Hostiles were now firing at them from all sides. There was nowhere to flee.

The surviving soldiers returned fire but the civilians were moving from window to window and shooting from elevated firing positions inside the first and second-story rooms. The soldiers shot blindly into the windows, seeing nothing but the muzzle flashes that had fired at them. The armed citizens could exploit the darkness and take the time to aim at their targets. After half of the men that survived the initial explosion were either injured or dead on the ground, they quit firing at the windows, which just made them targets, and they hugged the dirt waiting for reinforcements, praying to survive.

"Discharge your weapons!" The senior ATF agent screamed out orders, but was barely audible so close to the burning Hummer and with the barrage of bullets that whizzed past his head.

"We gotta get out of the road." Officer Bailey crawled for the cover of the curb. "We need to get between those houses."

The ATF agent nodded, and then glanced at a veteran Army intelligence agent who laid flat against the ground next to him. "Come on. We gotta make a break for the space between those houses."

"We shouldn't be here," the intelligence agent screamed back at him. "We shouldn't be here."

The senior ATF agent, if he weren't busy ducking for his life behind a bush beside the mailbox, would have cursed out the cowardly trooper. He unsnapped his sat phone from his belt and pushed a button to make an urgent call to headquarters, but before they could pick up, a bullet from the neighboring house pierced his forehead and calmed his temper.

"It worked." Billy Johnson shouted, slapping the high five of a neighbor who joined him and six of his friends repelling the federals. "They want your guns, boys. Make 'em earn 'em."

"Hello? Agent Thomas? Hello?" The Army staff sergeant laid the FFL form on his desk and cupped the headphones more tightly to his ears. "Agent Thomas?" He paused and listened intently to the chaotic chatter of gunfire and the screams of the wounded at the other end of the line.

He pushed a button to put the line on speakerphone and called out across the room. "General Tiller? We've got another one."

The famed general turned away from the five other generals who were gathered around a map of the sister-cities of Ft. Worth and Dallas on a square table, where they stood, pointing, and conspiring.

"Agent Thomas from Nineteen called and is not responding on the other end. There's gunfire."

General Tiller exhaled a foul curse as he hastened toward the phone. He picked it up and listened for a moment when Officer Bailey, as he was checking the pulse of ATF agent Thomas, grabbed the phone and spoke into it, "Anybody there?"

"This is General Tiller."

"Team one-nine is under heavy fire. Several dead and several more injured. It was an ambush."

General Tiller turned to the five generals in brass-covered military uniforms whose faces were drawn and shoulders slumped, as if their multi-colored bars pulled their shoulders toward the map on the table.

Tiller gave the order without turning his gaze from his fellow generals: "Send Daniel's Ninth to back up Nineteen." One of the subordinates beside him picked up the phone and relayed the order. "Tell them to bring the Blackhawks."

"The Blackhawks are all occupied," a general reminded him.

"Well, bring up the reserves then!" Tiller screamed. Momentarily, he appeared apologetic for raising his voice. He set down the phone, put his palms on the desk and sighed heavily. "Gentlemen, if there's a worse place than hell, I'm there." General Tiller stomped back to the table and placed his 21st red pin on the map just south of Ft. Worth. "Expending the lives of my men in the suburbs of Texas in order to confiscate semi-autos from American citizens is not why I joined the Army and it's not the way I want to be remembered."

A senior ATF agent beside the general grunted disapprovingly at the unwelcomed commentary from the military commander presiding over the president's gun confiscation plans in Texas. The ATF agent inconspicuously clicked an icon on his laptop and began to type a complaint to Homeland Security. General Tiller should have known that publicly verbalizing what almost everyone in the room was thinking was very bad for morale. Perhaps ratting on his superior would earn him favors with the administration and he'd find a way out of this tedious exercise of futile violence.

Washington, D.C.

Todd Hamilton glanced curiously at the caller ID on his cell phone from his kitchen. He sighed with relief when he saw from the area code that it was not the Midwestern Division of the Bureau. All the reports he'd received from Texas recently were dismal. Their gun confiscation scheme was turning into a Bureau joke. This call was coming from the Montana office. He put his Bluetooth device in his ear and tapped the button.

"This is Hamilton."

"Chief Investigator Ian Gibson here."

"G'morning, Ian." He poured his first cup of morning brew as he spoke, hopeful that Ian had made some headway on his priorities. "Calling at this hour, I'm assuming your night shift finally identified our man in the Bozeman shooting of Agent Harris."

"In all three of the Bozeman shootings. The shooter of the two agents at the Bozeman riot also shot Ernie Harris."

Hamilton set down his coffee and stood erect. "Oh?"

"Yes sir. Evidence is strong."

"Took you long enough."

"Well, like I said, we had a lot of interference from locals. We finally got our hands on an un-cut security video from the raid of one of the storeowners' homes, sir, and the suspect is Ed Seibert, a member of the Militia of Montana. The clue to the Ernie Harris murder case came from interrogating the driver of a car that was seen on video surveillance nearby. He is the son of the former Sheriff Randy Woods."

Hamilton was surprised. "Randy Woods' son murdered Harris?"

"Under interrogation, he confessed that Ed Seibert, whom he called Bull, shot Harris."

Hamilton grinned, took a sip of his steaming brew, and laughed. "A little water-boarding goes a long way, doesn't it?"

"Yes, it does."

"In our attempt to pinpoint his exact location, Madam President, I discovered some interesting intelligence." Hamilton was at the end of his first cup of coffee as he informed the president of Gibson's findings. "Very interesting."

The president leaned back in her chair, her eyes affixed to Hamilton's image on her computer screen. "Enlighten me."

"You know how the militia movement has been booming since Fitzgerald's election."

"Of course," she snapped spitefully. "It's like a contagious plague."

"Well, a vaccine against this plague has just been handed to us on a silver platter. The entire Militia of Montana is getting together for a barbecue at a farm north of Garrison tomorrow. The host is an aging, right-wing pastor named Barry Friar. He directed the militia for many years and retired before a disillusioned conspiracy theorist and former Marine named Jack Handel took over. The whole civilian militia will all be together for plinking and horseshoes."

"Plinking and horseshoes?" There was disgust in the president's voice as she thought of the horde of rednecks shooting guns at targets with barbeque sauce on the sleeves of their camouflaged shirts. "Why don't we insist on a license before we let these pathetic morons breed?"

"Those 'plinking' guns will probably be illegal semi-automatic assault rifles, Madam President. With this evidence, we could certainly justify arresting the whole lot of them."

Brighton appeared deep in thought as she rocked in her swivel chair for a moment, and then crossed her arms. "You know that semi-automatics won't be illegal in the Coalition states until 7 p.m. on July the third," she was reluctant to admit. "Can we wait a week?"

"If it weren't for the likely presence of the primary suspect in the Bozeman slaying of the three agents, I'd say 'Yes.' However, this suspect's a hazard, off the grid, and therefore difficult for us to track. Now we have the grand opportunity to arrest all the militia and put them away for a long time. Or at the least, disarm them. The most positive aspect of the raid will be the positive publicity it will provide for your Initiative and your gun control plan. This might even pressure Congress to get on board and add some more teeth to your EO. With the civilian resistance you're facing in Texas, I don't think that your reputation can wait a week for the relief this raid will give you. This is just what you need."

The president smiled at the thought. "Do you have enough men on the ground to pull it off that quickly?"

"Absolutely."

Part III

Montana Aflame

Chapter 9

Garrison, Montana

"Jack!" Barry stood up from his lawn chair at the edge of a dying fire that was slowly evolving to black and white ashes. "Praise be to God, Jack." His beard had grayed since Jack saw him last and his standard blue-jean overalls were well worn. Barry extended a hand to him. "Good to see you." The handshake turned into a backslapping bear hug. Four inches shorter and 60 pounds lighter, Jack grunted in Barry's strong clutch.

"It's been too long, bro." Jack sat down on a stump next to his old mentor. He wore a camouflaged hunting cap, a camouflaged XL T-shirt over his medium size frame, black jeans, and decade-old Ariat cowboy boots. He looked around to soak in the serenity of Barry Friar's beautiful farm just north of Garrison. Sprawling hay fields over rolling hills were back-dropped by the snow-capped Rocky Mountains to the north and the west. Some horses grazed peacefully in the distance. A small, rocky creek, the width of which one could jump with a running start, criss-crossed the beautiful property. Large, symmetrical pine trees stood on each side of the front entrance to the three-story, six-bedroom white house with four large white pillars in the front. Children in the over-head balcony waved their plastic wands and sent huge bubbles into the air that slowly descended upon their parents and grandparents, who chatted cheerfully below.

Barry made himself comfortable in his lawn chair around the small fire. "You've met my adopted son?" Barry pointed to a 16-year-old, tan-skinned young man who sat cross-legged on the ground, wearing a light camouflage jacket.

"Good to see you, Marion. The last time my eyes fastened on you, you were just pushing through puberty."

Lonny, a thin, lanky fellow with unkempt hair, sat on the ground munching on pork ribs. He patted Marion on the back and laughed. "T'was an ugly sight, wasn't it?" Marion backhanded Lonny on the shoulder, and Lonny responded in kind.

Marion nodded at Jack and said, "S'up, Mr. Handel?"

"Call me Jack." Jack massaged the fuzz on his chin. "I'm not as old as I look."

Marion turned his attention to a plump, reddish-colored mutt who stretched out on the grass a stone's throw away. "Grits!" The dog turned from watching four young men play horseshoes. "Grits, here boy." The dog saw Marion hoist a pork rib into the air and ran to him salivating.

Marion turned back to Jack. "We got horseshoes over there, and some .22s over there." He pointed at a group of people who stood in front of some gun targets in the distance. "I'm warning you though, the competition's stiff."

Jack laughed. "Now you're tempting me."

"We got horses if you want to ride." Marion pointed and Jack looked over in the direction of the red barn where two fellows were strapping saddles onto some brown and white horses.

Vicki, Barry's wife, walked up and handed her husband his frozen cup in which he liked to drink his sodas. "Oh, hey Jack." Vicki greeted him with a wide smile. She was a thin, small lady with her dark brown hair in a bun. She wore a humble hand-made Mennonite-style dress. "It's so good to see you. In the back of the house, we got some of the best barbecue pork you ever had."

"Thanks, Vicki."

"Bought it yesterday and killed it myself," Barry added as he reached into the cooler beside him and poured a diet root beer into his frozen cup with a University of Montana insignia on it. "Grilled it whole over an open pit of mesquite and charcoal, just like we used to do it."

The dog begged and leapt for the bone that Marion held just out of reach. "Go get it, boy!" Marion tossed the bone across the yard and the dog fetched.

"How's Dixie?" Vicki asked Jack.

The question was like a dagger through Jack's heart, but he managed to keep his smile. "She's well, I suppose. We've been separated for a little while."

"Oh." Vicki's warm smile faded to a troubled frown. She was clearly pained by the news. "I'm so sorry."

"Mama!" A young teenage girl called out to Vicki from the front porch of the home. "The oven timer went off. Do you want me to take it out?"

"I'd like to talk to you some more about it later," Vicki said to Jack, "but right now I'm needed in the kitchen. We'll be praying for you two."

"Thanks." He waved at Vicki as she headed for the house. "Say, Barry, why don't you come back and help me train? We've got some good boys in the M.O.M. this year. It's been about four years since you've been gone and the whole country's going to pot. You're needed now more than ever."

"No, no, no," Barry shook his head vigorously. "God and family are priorities for me now. I'm pastoring Crossroads Church, you know. We got about 40 members, which ain't too bad in a small town like this." Jack nodded. "I put God's call on my life on the back burner too long while over-extending myself in the M.O.M., getting neck deep in all this paranoid conspiracy nonsense."

Jack looked at him as if he'd just been slapped in the face for no reason at all.

"Don't get me wrong," Barry added when he saw the disappointment in Jack's countenance. "I don't want to demean your work, Jack. You know I think we need to keep our guns and teach young 'uns how to use them, but it got to where we were protecting small-time criminal enterprises, risking clashes with the feds over stupid stuff like parole violations, delinquent taxes, and marijuana farms. We were paranoid about UN detention centers and black helicopters while ignoring our wives and kids. We're no better than they are if we aren't right with God." Jack opened his mouth to protest and Barry added, "I know the militia's better now that they've cleaned house. It's just a matter of priorities." He paused and stared off into the sky. "I wasn't there for my wife when she needed me and if a man ain't a godly leader in his own home then he ain't fit to lead anybody. I was letting my family suffer while I was out crawling through the woods, preparing for some phantom world government which never came."

"It's coming now! Look what's going on in Bozeman, in Texas, and now in South Carolina."

Barry closed his eyes and nodded. "I know."

"They locked up Randy Woods without a charge or trial. They're killin' unarmed civilians down there and sendin' a lot of good folk to the hospital or to jail."

"I gotta visit from some suits just the other day."

That comment took Jack by surprise. "You? You got a visit from the feds?"

Marion, hearing his dad confess this for the first time, was awed. "Is that who those guys were, dad? Were they federal agents?"

Barry nodded.

"I thought you said they were discussing a business proposition or something."

"They were." Barry took a swig of his root beer and wiped the suds off his chin with the back of his wrist. "They asked me to spy on the fellows. They asked me to tell 'em who had illegal guns and stuff. You know, semi-automatics, the ones banned by the President's executive order."

"They're still legal."

"They're getting ready to make them illegal and they want to know who will buck 'em when they do. They asked me to let 'em know if anybody was planning anything dangerous."

"You have got to be kidding me!" Jack exclaimed. He and Marion were equally infuriated.

"What did you tell them?" asked Lonny, who scooted a little closer on the ground to get in on the conversation.

"At first, I told them that I couldn't do that. I refused to betray my buddies to make their investigations easier. They told me that they knew I had gun-smithed a shotgun shorter than federal law allows and if I didn't help them, then I might find myself arrested."

"What are you talking about?" Marion asked.

"Some guy I did some custom gun-smithing for several years ago was probably a snitch. I did the shotgun barrel length specifications just like he told me and he said he'd investigated the legal limits. The suits said it was a quarter of an inch too short. They told me that if I didn't snitch for 'em, then they'd press charges against me. Can you believe that?"

"They might come get us all anyway, Barry."

"They also asked me some questions about my views on abortion and abortion-related violence, too," Barry recalled. "I don't think they were very happy with my answer." He smiled a crooked grin and Jack's curiosity grew.

"What did you say to them?"

"I told them that I was pro-choice in, uh," he paused to comb his pepper-colored beard with his fingers, "in certain situations."

"Certain situations?"

Barry chuckled at his own sense of humor. "I didn't clarify when they asked me to. But I do think it's okay to abort abortionists and dictators."

Jack and the others laughed at that comment. "Sounds to me like your wife and mine have a lot in common. You got out because Vicki couldn't hack it and Dixie got out because she couldn't hack it."

"Family's got to come first, Jack. When you get old, your priorities change. Know what I mean?"

Jack didn't respond.

"When you're a kid," Barry explained, "your family's everything. But then you become a teenager, and your mom and dad don't know too much. You'd rather be with your buddies. When you're 20, you leave home and don't visit too often. But when you're 30," he paused for a lazy sigh, "when you're 30, you start coming back around some more. You got a wife and a couple kids of your own. You sympathize with mom and dad now." He picked up a small wrist-thick log in the bundle of logs that lay beside his lawn chair. "Then you get old" – he tossed the log into the fire - "and your family's everything."

Family. Just the thought of his family aroused nauseating guilt and heartsick disappointment within Jack. He just stared into the embers with a blank look on his face, trying to forget.

Lonny, Marion, and the other young men sitting around the fire left to indulge in a game of horseshoes. Barry found it a good time to get personal with the director of the Militia of Montana. "So, Jack, tell me what happened with Dixie?"

Jack remained silent. Barry asked again and Jack turned toward him. When their eyes met, he shrugged and looked away. "She left a couple years ago. Took the kids. The kids are all out on their own now. Can you believe that?"

"You tryin' to reconcile?"

Jack kept his gaze fixed on the embers. "It's over." Barry grunted and then Jack looked up at him. "It's over, Barry." Jack rubbed his hands on his thighs, warming his slightly chilled fingers in cool breeze that descended upon them from the snow-capped mountains in the west. "I blew it. Dixie thinks I didn't spend enough time with 'em. She's right, I reckon." The admission was a painful one and he had to concentrate to lift his voice above the lump in his throat.

"You're not going to let her divorce you, are ya?"

"I don't have a choice, Barry."

"Sure you do. Chase her, Jack. Romance her, like you did when you first pursued her when y'all were kids." Jack looked like he didn't know what Barry was talking about.

Barry stoked the fire with a small stick, and then pointed the smoking stick at Jack. "According to the Bible, Jack, the man's in charge. You're the head of the home. You are responsible."

Jack interrupted, "She's got another man, Barry." Barry shook his head in disbelief, and Jack fixed his gaze on the embers. "I told you, it's over."

Barry pursed his lips and rubbed his beard, deep in thought. "It's not over."

"What are you talking about?"

"Jack, listen. It says in the Bible that the husband is supposed to love his wife as Christ loved the church and gave Himself for it. Didn't Jesus love you when you were unlovable, Jack? When you were a-whoring around in sin, didn't Christ pursue you, convict you, and try His best to rescue you from your sin and save you?"

"Yeah."

"That's how the Lord loves us. He chases us out of our hiding places and invites even the worst of us into His family. The goodness of God leads us to repentance."

Jack gazed into the fire as Barry spoke, finding his words strangely warm and penetrating. "You're trying to tell me I should try to pursue her even though she insists on a divorce and has another man?"

"You're the love of her life, Jack. If you pursued her, she'd find in you what she's wanted in you all along and what this counterfeit can't match. You just love her. You have to go the extra mile, wash her feet, and even be willing to die for her to win back her love. You already admitted that the divorce would be your fault."

"Yeah." Jack nodded.

"Well, don't let it be. Go get her, Jack. You're accepting defeat at the devil's hands too easily. The Bible says, 'What God has put together, let not man put asunder.' You both vowed - I was there, Jack - dressed up in your tux, with her lookin' all fancy and pretty in that long white dress, big smiles on both your faces. I remember it like it was yesterday. You vowed to love and be faithful to each other till death parts ya." He was preaching now and his tone of voice was confident and unbending. "Lavish her with apologies, flowers, and love notes, whatever it takes. You got to romance her, Jack. Serenade her. You've gotta win her back."

Jack's eyes were now fixed on Barry's deep green eyes. *Could it be possible? Can Dixie and I still get back together? Maybe I did give up too soon. I've never really apologized to her.* He swallowed hard. "Feelings change, Barry."

"Feelings, feelings, feelings," said Barry, mockingly. "Listen, Jack. God doesn't care as much about your feelings as he does about your vows. Love's a choice. You need to keep your promises even when you don't feel like it. Feelings are like this fire here. If it was running out of fuel and I didn't tend to it, it'd just off and die. But I stir the embers" - he put his stick into the fire and gave it a whirl - "and the fire grows. I toss in another stick" - he tossed the stick into the fire - "and it lasts longer. You gotta make the choice to rekindle that love and the heat will follow. But even if you never have another romantic feeling for the rest of your sex-less life, you should still love her as Christ loved the church and gave Himself for it..." As Barry continued his sermon, Jack looked across the field and saw Bull and Stein walking up.

"There he is." Jack was glad to change the uncomfortable topic.

"What? Who?" Barry looked over his shoulder at the direction in which Jack's gaze was firmly fixed.

"Bull." Jack stared at Bull and stood to his feet. "Sorry, Barry," he mumbled to him as he patted him on the shoulder. "Thanks for the advice, but it ain't happening. It's over."

Jack stomped toward Bull with a snarl on his face. Bull saw him coming and slowed his pace. "Hey, boy."

Bull tensed his muscular jaw and stopped in front of Jack. "What's up?" Next to Bull was his smaller twin brother Stein. Bull's hands were in his pockets and his thick shoulders and arms, streaked with bulging veins, slumped forward.

"Stein, take off. Bull and I need to have a little talk." Stein wiggled his black beret down lower onto his forehead and made his way toward the horses.

Bull and Jack started walking in the direction of the plinking competition across the field while Bull's shifty gaze wandered across the field, searching for familiar faces. They were quiet for a moment when Jack finally broke the silence. "You are a skilled militiaman, Bull. Real good. But you worry me."

Bull played dumb. "How so?"

"If you really want to take up arms against the feds, that's fine. I can certainly sympathize with all that's going on. But listen to me." He stopped and turned toward him. "You're going to get us all in a heap of trouble if you go saying it on nationwide television. What you said into a TV camera outside of the Bozeman sheriff's office was foolish. I know you think you're cool and your friends praise you for being so brave and all, but you can't show all your cards when you're playing poker." Bull just shook his head and looked away as Jack continued, "Don't open that trap of yours and say something that's going to get all of us arrested."

"You're going to be just fine," he snapped.

"Not when you talk into a TV camera about a violent revolution with *this* on your head!" Jack reached up and snatched the MOM hat off Bull's buzz cut. "When you say things about killing government bureaucrats with *this* hat on your fat head" - he threw the hat at Bull's chest - "you represent us!" The hat fell on the ground as Jack continued his heart-felt rebuke. Bull slouched his wide frame at the shoulders and looked only intermittently at the hat at Jack's feet as if he couldn't care less at what he said. "That's the way the feds and everybody else in America sees it. They're looking for a good reason to come out here, lock us all up in the slammer, and throw away the key. You just gave them a knockdown fantastic reason! You just rolled out the red carpet for 'em!"

"Good!" Bull returned Jack's critical tone. "Maybe if they come out here and do that, then you'll stop taking the path of least resistance and fight back."

"Bull, who shot those federal agents in Bozeman?"

The question took Bull by surprise, but he quickly regained his composure and feigned ignorance. "Whoever did it, I don't blame 'em. I'm glad it happened!"

"Listen to me, boy." Jack stuck his index finger in Bull's face and stepped in close to look him in the eye.

Bull disrespectfully swatted Jack's hand away. "No! You listen to me." Bull reached down to pick up his hat. "When the feds do try and lock you up, at least then you'll have a good reason to shoot the enemy. Or would you still hide behind your Bible and your little black book of quotes of American forefathers to try to coerce Him" - he pointed to the sky - "to protect you and your nation, something you won't do for yourself?"

Jack was taken aback by the audacity of Bull to dishonor him like this. Before he could respond, Bull turned and stomped away, leaving Jack alone with his red face and his burning stomach ulcer.

Chapter 10

Marion held his horseshoe forward, preparing for his throw, as his mutt barked and ran back and forth behind his heels. "Leave me alone, Grits."

"He just said that so he can blame it on the dog when his horseshoe lands five feet away from the stake." His competitor and lifelong friend, Denton, laughed at Marion's dilemma. Marion had to knock down a leaner and score a ringer in order to edge out his competition.

Marion didn't take his eyes off the stake, "Shhh. I need to concentrate."

"Yeah, quiet," another friend, Brad, reiterated.

Marion stepped into the swing when Brad exclaimed, "I said Shhh! Stop whispering while he's trying to throw."

Marion stopped in the middle of his swing and glared with irritation at his two snickering friends. "Y'all better cut it out. Act your age." He settled back into his horseshoe-throwing stance again.

Just then, Marion's elder brother Matt walked up carrying a plate of ribs and beans. Matt wore a two-decades-old, black, long sleeved Oakridge Mountain Boys T-shirt, the tattered threads stretched thin from his 30 extra pounds around the waist. He wore a bright orange hunting cap backwards on his head.

"Tell these bums to keep quiet, Matt, or they'll regret it." The beige mutt began to jump and bark at the smell of Matt's food.

"Get, ya mutt." Matt waved the dog away. Marion took a deep breath and prepared for his horseshoe toss.

Denton tapped Matt on the arm. "Marion here can't concentrate with all your talk, Matt."

Marion brought his throwing arm back up, lined up the horse-shoe tips with his eyes in the direction of the stake, swung his arm back, stepped into the swing, and let it release into the air as the dog backed up into his hind foot. The horseshoe spun crookedly through the air, and Marion shouted and acted as if he was about to kick his dog. "Dumb dog!" The dog sensed his master's displeasure and fell onto the ground, whimpering. Marion, frustrated at the interruption his pet had become, reached onto his brother's plate and grabbed a fresh rib.

"Hey!" Matt protested.

Marion leaned down and put the rib in the dog's nose. He pulled it away just as the dog snapped at it. "Here boy. Go get it." He tossed the rib as far as he could in the direction of the woods and the dog followed frantically, tail wagging and tongue salivating.

Marion wiped his sauce-covered hand on his blue jeans as his brother criticized him for taking food off his plate without his permission. "That was mine."

"You'll survive," Marion told him, glancing at Matt's mid-waist baggage.

A moment later, the dog began to bark vigorously, as if he would at a bear, a snake, or an intruder. Marion looked in the direction in which his dog ran. "Grits! Hey, Grits!" When the dog didn't return to him, he grew concerned. He stood on a lawn chair to search for his dog in the shin-high grass down the hill.

"That dog's going to blow our cover," a mustached federal agent at the edge of the tree line communicated to his superior. The whispered words were transferred through the headset in his Kevlar helmet to the commander of five squads of camouflage-clad FBI agents who were spread out at five strategic points around the property. Their camouflage was a perfect match to the grassy and leafy ground on which they hid. The body-length outfits had randomly placed yellow and brown grass-like protrusions.

"We cannot make our move yet." The captain of one of the five squads, sitting behind a tree on the edge of the field, grew nervous with the unexpected hurdle. "The suspects are still target shooting."

The captain of the squad closest to the target shooting was confident. "We can take them out with no problem, Mr. Hammel. There are only three of them holding guns."

FBI Sergeant Roger Hammel, who was in a well-concealed van a half-a-mile away, was the commander of this critical mission. He responded into his headset, "We don't want to take *anybody* out if we can prevent it, Rawls." Hammel began to pace inside the van, nervously twiddling a pen in between his index and middle fingersAgent Rawls responded with a wince of confusion, "But, sir, the rules of engagement—"

"The rules of engagement do not preclude measures to minimize the casualties, Rawls." Hammel took a deep breath, stopped pacing, and placed his palms on the counter as he studied the satellite image layout of the Friar's property. "Take out the shooters *only* as a last resort."

"The dog is coming closer," the captain of the first squad whispered. "He's going to give away our position. I'm going to shoot him."

"Don't you think *that's* gonna give away your position?" Hammel rebutted. "Not yet."

An African-American agent named Lex near the captain at the edge of the property shook his head and spoke into his helmet mic. "Sergeant Hammel, they're only shootin' .22s."

"Semi-automatic .22s," Hammel responded. "They've been banned by the president's E.O."

"They're kids, Sergeant Hammel. Some of them are girls."

Hammel's gut twisted at the unease in the voice of the subordinate. "They're militia, Lex! They're fanatics who'll make war on our country rather than give up their guns."

The troubled young agent shook his head and cleared his throat. "This isn't what I thought it'd be. I don't like this."

"Now's not the time to let your conscience play head-trips on you, Agent Lex. Get your head in the game. We have the president's orders, got that?"

The agent sighed heavily. "Yes sir."

"Grits!" shouted Marion. He looked back at Matt. "That's unlike him."

"Probably on the trail of a raccoon or something."

"No, he wouldn't be barking like that at a raccoon and he'd come if I called him. Maybe he got hurt or something." Marion started walking in the direction of the barking, and his walk turned into a slow jog. "Grits!" He jogged for about ten seconds and then caught a glimpse of his dog's head, barking and growling viciously in the direction of the tree line.

"I'm taking out the dog." The mustached agent reached down and unholstered a camouflage-painted .45 semi-automatic. He twisted on the silencer and then quietly exclaimed, "Oh no. Someone's coming."

"One of the militia?" asked Sergeant Hammel from his van. "Is he armed?"

"He's not armed."

"What's the matter, boy?" Marion's jog slowed to a walk as he came up slowly behind the dog 50 feet from the tree line. Grits didn't even look back but continued barking viciously.

Marion put his hand on his dog's head. "What is it, Grits?" The dog stopped barking but continued to growl, showing his teeth.

The sniper raised his silenced handgun to put the dog in his sights. When Grits saw the movement his anxious barking commenced afresh.

Marion didn't know what to think of his pet's strange behavior. "What is it, boy? Mountain lion? Bear?" He searched the forest shadows for the mysterious beast that infuriated his dog.

"All right boy. Go get him." Marion smacked the dog on the rear, releasing him to race off in the direction of whatever it was that fascinated him.

"What's up with Grits?" Matt asked Denton, who shrugged as he sat next to him in a lawn chair. Matt laid his plate down and began walking in the direction of the barking. "Betcha' he got bit by a rattlesnake or something."

The agent with his handgun's sights on the dog tried to make his case. "Sergeant Hammel, if I can take out the dog with a silenced handgun and apprehend the unarmed individual nearby without a struggle, we may still be able to maintain secrecy."

"All right." Hammel noisily inhaled and exhaled, and began to pace back and forth in the unmarked van. "All squads prepare for possible charge. Rawls, if the militia is alerted, you must try to subdue those target-shooters without lethal force."

"There's a second suspect coming toward the dog," Agent Lex added.

"Neither is armed as far as I can tell," his captain assured Hammel. "I'm taking out the dog."

The dog was mid-stride when it suddenly squealed and tumbled to the grass motionless. Matt stopped in his tracks about ten feet behind Marion, his hair on end. "Grits?" The dog didn't so much as whimper. "Grits!" At first, he thought it was a trigger-happy hunter on their property without permission, but he would have heard the gunshot. He and Matt froze in their tracks as they studied the tree line, looking for any sign of intruders. Marion looked back at Matt, and what he saw in Matt's eyes terrified him. Matt saw the assailant, rising suddenly from his concealment like a cloud of grass and soil, heading right towards him. Matt couldn't believe his eyes.

"What in the world!" Matt reached into the small of his back and pulled out a .357 magnum pistol. Marion snapped his head back around to see what had so startled his brother. Matt aimed a shot at the intruder's feet and pulled the trigger. **Blam!** The collision of the bullet with the ground sprayed dirt onto the camouflaged FBI sniper.

The agent raised his weapon in an instant and let off a round that almost tore Matt's arm off at the right elbow! Matt, in a state of shock, feeling more numbness than pain, looked down at his dangling arm as blood spurted onto the bluegrass. A dozen similarly concealed federal agents rose and headed toward them.

Marion turned and picked up Matt's .357 magnum. He fired the five remaining bullets as fast as he could at the intruders. The bullets shot at Marion missed, but one of the hollow-point projectiles found its way into the chest of the agent who shot Matt. It pierced his bulletproof vest as if it were made of cardboard and dropped him hard.

Marion turned and sprinted toward the house in a zigzag pattern, shouting for help. Matt's disabling arm wound didn't hurt, but filled him with dread. His arm dangled erratically at his side as he tried to keep up with Marion. Marion screamed as he sprinted, "Help! Help!"

"Freeze!" The captain of the squad nearest the two suspects shouted at them as they sprinted toward the house. He saw that his point man was down from a lethal wound, so he fired in retaliation toward the two fleeing militiamen. His squad followed close behind him like birds flocking behind their leader. He cut the still Montana air with his shrill orders for the suspects to stop. If they alerted the rest of the militia, the raid would suffer heavier casualties. Three rounds of his rifle dropped the young man closest to him.

Sergeant Hammel let out a muffled curse. "All squads close in," he ordered into his headset microphone. "Move quickly."

Three of the teenage sons of the militia members were finishing up a contest of 20 rounds each aimed at R.C. Cola cans while their fathers and friends stood behind them, praising their sons' sharpshooting skills. They were startled when they heard shouting coming from the tree line.

One of the fathers saw that it was the figure of a camouflaged man, running at them shouting something. He thought it was a joke at first, but then was sprayed with the blood from his son's face and chest wounds. The flurry of rounds from the automatic weapon ripped through his son's body and his son dropped into a contorted position on the ground. To his horror, he realized that his son was dying as he lay with his extremities jerking under the spray of a hundred spurting arteries. Before the father could even look up and scream in rage at the intruder, he felt a pounding of heat in his right thigh and then his upper abdomen. He collapsed next to his son in incredible pain and panic, still unsure of what was happening. The thought of his acutely injured son kept him from the brink of unconsciousness. He reached for his son and saw that a rising pool of blood filled the place where his face once was. His son was dead and once he realized that, unconsciousness was a welcomed escape from his pain and grief.

"Freeze!" The agent who fired the first round fired again, dropping another one of the fleeing civilians. The third teenager returned fire and struck the first agent in the stomach but the agent's vest easily stopped the .22 from penetrating. The agents behind him returned fire as they chased the crowd of ten toward the house. Other civilians fled parallel to the tree line away from the house and the charging troops. Men dropped one-by-one by the gunfire from behind them. Only a few of the young men made it to the house uninjured.

The shouting coming from the direction of the target shooters startled Jack Handel. He set down his plate of beans and ribs and stood up from his stump beside the small campfire. He heard shouting from several directions. It was incoherent. Confusion reigned. The soft blasts of .22 rifles from the range were interrupted by the frightful whisper of silenced automatic gunfire, a sound that few have heard except in the movies. But it was a sound with which the ex-Marine was familiar, and it chilled him to the bone. Jack's face paled and his mouth went as dry as cotton. He looked in the direction of the blasts, as did Barry next to him. They saw the boys begin to shoot their .22 rifles in the direction of the woods. One of them fell to the ground and another's skull exploded in a cloud of blood

Jack began to trot in the direction of the fallen men, assuming that there had been a tragic accident. He stopped when he caught sight of their attackers. Like bales of hay galloping through the field, the brown and green camouflaged troops rushed toward him with erratic shouts of, "Freeze!" – "You're under arrest!" – "Drop your weapon!" Their orders were barely discernible through facemasks and heavy breathing as the men rushed up the gentle slope. Jack gasped in disbelief and things appeared to move in slow motion as he turned and looked to his left to see another group of camouflaged soldiers charging up the hillside. Those federal agents suddenly ducked toward the ground as gunshots started coming at them from the barn and the second story of the Friar's home.

"To the house!" Barry pointed to his home. "To the house!" A half a dozen young men around the fire pit followed him as he began to sprint toward the home, keeping his head as low as he could.

Jack froze. He couldn't move. He couldn't run. His brain was anesthetized with a mixture of fear and disbelief. He'd been through this in his mind hundreds of times. Now he was living it and his stubborn body wouldn't move. *Go!* he told himself. *Go!* But he was indecisive as to which direction he should take, so he just stood there. He looked in the direction of the target shooters and saw a young man running with a .22 caliber rifle receive a bullet in the back. The boy fell hard to the ground with a gargled scream. Jack quickly looked toward the house; getting pinned up in the home with enraged federal agents outside was like a recurring nightmare. Death from federal sniper fire or from a lethal injection was imminent if he made it to the house. He glanced to his right and saw a clump of trees toward the tree line about 50 feet away, where no enemy troops appeared to be.

Suddenly, a burst of adrenaline flooded his senses. He at first leaned in the direction of the clump of trees and then his instincts took over. In a second, he was in a full sprint away from the house. He felt as if he was out of breath within the first five seconds; his legs felt numb, his head was clouded with dizziness, and his vision tunneled. When he saw the dirt spray up at his feet from the shots aimed at him, his pace quickened even more. He kept his head low and ignored the muffled shouts in the distance ordering him to "Freeze!" Every time he heard one of the intermittent gun blasts, he thought for sure he'd feel an explosion in his side and he'd look down with dimming eyes to see a softball-size, gaping hole in his chest or abdomen.

He dove over a shrub into a grassy clearing in the center of a clump of ten small trees, erratically shaped bushes, and tall grasses, and was smacked in the face with a low branch. He landed on his back, breathing heavily, his jaw and nose stinging from the branch.

The exhaustion of the 15 seconds of running seemed to cripple his senses. He looked up and saw the bark of the pine next to him shatter in different directions as a speeding bullet pierced it. Several bullets sprayed the trees around him. He reached for his right pants-leg and pulled it up, exposing a Taurus .38 special with six rounds. He unsnapped the fastener and grabbed tightly onto the revolver as he rolled over onto his belly. The gunfire from the camouflaged attackers was only intermittently halted, thanks to well-aimed gunfire from the first and second-story windows of the house.

More bullets whizzed over his head and into the trees beside him, making dirt, grass, and bark spray into the air. The debris landed on his body, camouflaging him even more with the ground. His wife had always been so critical of his sole choice of wardrobe - his camouflage-colored cap and shirt - but now he was so glad that he had it on. If she could only see him now, she just might retract some of her accusations of his paranoia. He dug his palms into the dirt and then rubbed the soil over the back of his hands and face to camouflage himself further. The gunfire ceased and Jack's eyes frantically searched for his pursuers as they crouched closer and closer to him. From the volume of the gun blasts, they weren't that far away. From the size of the hole in the side of the pine tree next to him, he would much rather see them before they saw him. He crawled backwards, staying as low to the ground as he could. He looked to his left, then right, and caught a glimpse of some attackers through the grass.

Two camouflaged troopers about 20 yards away stood next to Denton, one of Marion's friends. Denton knelt on all fours, blood drooling from his mouth. His face grimaced in pain as one of the soldiers kicked him in his side. Denton crumpled to the ground, disappearing into the thick layer of bluegrass.

Toward the barn, Jack could barely make out a dozen young men with their hands raised in the air as the federal agents ominously surrounded them. One of the boys held a small log over his head that he thought to use as a weapon. He threw it on the ground and raised his hands. "We surrender. Don't shoot."

Jack's eyes refocused just to the left of the two camouflaged troopers and saw a clump of haze and grass move nearby. It was one of them, crouching toward him, about ten yards away. Jack froze.

He doesn't see me. Sweat stung his eyes, which he refused to close as he looked for the eyes of the approaching intruder, the whites of which were barely visible under a camouflage-colored mask. The intruder's eyes looked to the left of him, then toward him, and then drifted to the right of him. He moved forward in a deep squat another step nearer.

Jack hugged the ground as tightly as he could, and tried to slow his breathing so as to minimize his movement. His right hand gripped tightly to his .38 revolver. Part of him wanted to echo what the fellow with the small log had said - "I surrender!" - and toss his gun on the ground, place his hands over his head, and plead for mercy. But that thought was abruptly interrupted with a gun blast and a shout in Denton's direction, followed by a final scream. Unbeknownst to Jack, Denton, even with two bullet wounds in his torso, managed to raise his nine millimeter Karr concealed-carry pistol at the nearest agent and received a lethal wound in the forehead for it.

Jack swallowed hard, keeping his eyes on the advancing intruder. Neither of them flinched at the sound of the gun blast that killed Denton. Jack thought to make for the tree line, using the clump of trees as his cover, but it was too far away. He wouldn't make it. *Don't move,* his warrior instincts told him. *He doesn't see you. But he knows you're here. You're going to have to kill or be killed.*

Barry stared helplessly at the ground as he knelt, breathing heavily, behind the pick-up truck closest to the front door. Two of the young men beside him had side arms on them and were returning fire. This temporarily kept the intruders at a safe distance. Crossfire on the front porch prevented many from successfully ascending the stairs and making it into the house. Three corpses were sprawled across the stairway, with a coalescing river of blood draining into the well-trodden sod at the foot of the stairs. The right hand of one of the dead young men still clasped a .22 rifle. Several other corpses were scattered between the vehicles that were haphazardly parked in front of the stairs.

Marion was frantic as he tried to explain to his father what happened down the hill. "They shot Grits! Then they shot Matt in the arm! We were running when they shot him in the back. Right in the back! I looked back and Matt's face down on the ground, dad! Matt's dead. He, he..."

Barry showed no emotion. Fear gripped his heart. Matt, his son, was dead. "Where?"

"Over on the northern field, down the hill."

Barry peeked over the red Ford Ranger and his lips mouthed the name of his son, *Matthew*. A sniper with a glimpse of Barry's forehead pointed and shot. The bullet grazed the front hood of the pickup truck, spraying flakes of paint onto Barry's face and into his left eye.

"Ah!" Barry fell to his knees and rubbed his eye to dislodge the foreign body.

"Dad? You okay?" Marion tugged his father's arm.

Barry tried to calm his senses as he collected his thoughts. His squinting eyes searched the dirt between his knees, as if examining a dozen different scenarios scribbled on the ground in front of him. Several of the young men beside him continued to alternate ducking and shooting: one would duck while the other would briefly raise his head above the car hood to fire a round, and then quickly duck down again. Several agents had been shot, mostly from the gunfire coming from the second floor of the house. Barry considered ordering his defenders to lay down their weapons so that they could surrender without any more bloodshed. But they probably would just be shot down like varmints lamed by passing cars on the highway.

"Mom!" Marion pointed at the front door. Barry turned to see the front door cracked. His wife was holding it open and waving him toward her. *That's it,* he thought. *Make for the house. Things will settle down and then wait for the media. This'll work out.* He looked at her and then to his son. "On the count of three, bolt for the door."

"But—"

"We stay here and we're dead." This was not the pastor in him, the political grassroots activist, or the former militia leader speaking - it was just a father and a husband who wanted his wife and children to be okay.

Jack was as still as death. The intruder was now 15 feet away and closing. Jack breathed shallow breaths slowly, and tried to still his trembling.

He could see the agent's lips moving, speaking to an unseen ally through an unseen microphone.

"I saw somebody run into this small group of trees and bushes."

"Was he armed?" Sergeant Hammel asked.

"Possibly."

"Well, it's not your problem then! Get up to that house and get your boys in order. You've got a firefight in front of the house. If anybody else dies I'll put you in front of Congress to explain it."

The trooper slowly stood up and turned toward the house as if he were about to leave for the sake of more vulnerable prey. Jack eased the grip on his pistol and squinted away the stinging sweat in his eyes. Suddenly, he saw the federal agent turn back toward him, look just past him, and mumble something. Then Jack heard sudden movement behind him - felt it more than heard it. One of the agents was directly behind him!

Jack rolled and shot his gun in the direction of a borderless haze of leaves and straw.

Blam! Blam!

He panted and a dying federal agent collapsed to the ground ten feet away from him. The other soldier had his head turned when his partner was struck. He turned back toward the clump of trees and bushes and began to frantically fire his gun back and forth into it, careful to avoid the area where his friend fell. The vegetation disintegrated all around Jack in a hurricane of noise, bark, dust, and fear. Jack got as low as he could to the ground, held his breath and aimed his gun in the direction of the intruder. **Blam! Blam!**

He paused to assess his target; the soldier was still coming at him, intermittently firing his automatic weapon. **Tat-tat-tat...**

Grass and dirt filled the air around his head. Jack couldn't see from the dirt in his eyes, so he aimed at where he thought the agent was. **Blam! Blam!** *Click...*

Jack would have panicked when he ran out of ammo if it hadn't been for the sudden silence. Through the settling dust, Jack could vaguely see the soldier fall face first into the grass. Then he rolled over on his side in a fetal position, moaned, and laid still.

Jack raised his head slowly to look around. Blood dripped down his brow and cheek from a graze he received from one of the bullets fired at him. His foot pained him; he looked down to see that one of the bullets had ripped the heel off of his boot. Toward the house, 50 yards away, he could see four or five camouflaged agents leaving the firefight near the cars and racing toward him. Jack crawled to the dead agent at his feet and fumbled around for the rifle in his lifeless grip. Jack pried it loose and pointed the gun into the direction of the rapidly approaching troops. He took careful aim, squeezed the trigger, and was surprised at the smooth *dat-dat-dat-dat* of the well-oiled high-tech machine, which hardly kicked in his hands. Two of the charging agents fell wounded and the other three fell to the ground for cover and began to unload their own magazines in Jack's direction.

Jack ducked from their fire and glanced at the tree line 50 yards in the opposite direction. The tree line was covered with piled fallen branches and briars, collected and undisposed of since the last winter ice storm sprayed tree branches over Friar's field. The brush pile stood about five feet high. He saw no deer path through the pile in either direction, and wondered if he could hurdle it without slowing down. A verse from Psalm 18 came to his mind and he mumbled it under his breath, "By You I can run against a troop and by my God I can leap over a wall."

He fancied himself making it to the tree line under the cover of the dust that the camouflaged troopers' gunfire had kicked up. However, the thought of getting shot in the back as he tried to climb the brush pile quenched his enthusiasm. He shuddered at the thought of dying in the next 30 seconds. *Not yet. Not yet, Dixie.* His thoughts mysteriously went to his estranged wife. He was suddenly haunted by the thought of her attending his funeral and having nothing good to say about him. Would she even cry? Would she miss him? Would she or the kids even care?

"I'm sorry," he whispered out loud. The words were like a warm blanket of velvet to a man chilled from the winter's bitterest cold. It felt so good to say it. As terrifying as his present circumstances were, he never felt two words come out of his mouth so smoothly, so sweetly. Those words felt so refreshing that he uttered them again, "I'm so sorry, Dixie." He never wanted reconciliation with his wife so bad until this moment, when it was so far out of reach. Even if he couldn't win her love again, he didn't want to die knowing that he hadn't tried as hard as he could. He wished he could hold her sweet, round, freckled cheeks in the palms of his hands again and kiss her lips gently just one more time. It had been so long since he'd seen her smile.

He gave up on the thought of running for the trees; he mentally tossed that notion into the graveyard of bad ideas. "God help me." He turned and squatted behind the broadest of the trees. Three soldiers shot their guns in three-shot bursts into the clump of bushes and trees as they slowly made their way toward him.

"One," shouted Barry, to be heard over the rattle of the bullets against the sides of the cars behind which he, Marion, and the other young men were hiding. Marion grabbed his elbow, waiting for the dreaded, "Three!" when they would dash through a maze of high speed bullets through the smoky air, up six bloody steps and into the front door that his mother would hold open for them.

"Two!" Barry looked back over his shoulder into the eyes of his son. He then glanced at his wife, whose face he could barely see through the front door that was cracked open slightly.

"We'll cover ya to the house," said one of the young militiamen with a .22 semi-automatic behind one of the cars, "then you cover us from the house." Barry nodded.

"Three!" Barry and Marion jumped up and sprinted in the direction of the house, careful to keep their heads low. They both expected a flurry of gunshots to come from behind them, but on the contrary, the gunshots came from the second-story window and the window next to the front door of their home. They raced over the gravel driveway, over the pool of blood in the dirt in front of the stairs, and up the stairs three at a time. Barry reached down and grabbed the .22 caliber rifle from the hands of the dead young man on the stairs, and then jumped through the open front door as gunfire penetrated it. His wife slammed the door shut as soon as they passed the threshold.

He and Marion ran behind the couch as the bullets whizzed around them.

Barry turned around toward the door in time to see the gunfire cause his wife's silhouette to crumple up against the wall and go limp. Blood and matter sprayed from her skull in their direction. Simultaneously, Marion screamed in pain and was thrown onto his back as if punched in the chest by an unseen force. Barry gazed in horror as the love of his life collapsed onto her knees and dropped her forehead against the ground with a nauseating thud. Then he heard the shrill cry of the baby. He saw cradled in Vicki's arms his wiggling infant son, Timothy, held tight against his wife's chest as her lifeblood soaked him. The door was partially ajar, kept open by a splinter of wood on the ground. His wife of 33 years lied motionless, hemorrhaging from a .223 round that tore off half of her jaw and exited above the left ear.

Horror and grief overcame Barry Friar's senses, and he began to hyperventilate. The room spun and he felt as if he would pass out. The trauma was too much for his mind to bear. He glanced at Marion, who rolled over closer to the couch, holding his left shoulder. Blood flowed down in erratic rivers past Marion's elbow-length sleeves down his arm.

"Mom?" Marion managed to call out between his cries of pain. "Mom?" The hailstorm of bullets smashed windows, powdered sheet rock, splintered wood and furniture, and sent shards of glass in all directions.

More groans were heard from the corner of the room. Barry's teenage daughter, Teresa, who was the shooter covering for them in the first floor window, had her forearm grazed by a bullet. She crawled in their direction with a .357 Glock semi-automatic handgun held tightly in her left hand and a half-used box of bullets squeezed between her arm and her chest. The barrel was still smoking as she tried to reload the empty mag with her bad arm. Barry looked at her, stunned, not knowing whether to hug the little girl for what could be one last time, or chastise her for risking her life to cover them as they rushed the front door.

She looked up at him and when their eyes met, Barry could see that she was quite proud of herself for her aim under fire. When she saw the lifeless body of her beloved mother kneeling on the ground as if in one last prayer, Teresa's moment of glory turned to awkward silence, then a blood-curdling scream: "Momma? Momma!"

Barry rolled over on his elbows as bullets again whizzed intermittently over his head. The ground was covered with remnants of his wife's knick-knacks that she had collected and displayed throughout their home. Their well-read family Bible exploded when a bullet blazed into the center of it as it rested on a bookshelf. Bits and pieces of thin pages and fractured Bible verses expanded into the air and slowly settled to the ground as if they were gentle snowflakes falling to the frozen earth.

"Oh Vicki!" Barry began to mourn pitifully. When his children imitated his cry, he held his peace and tried to regain his composure.

"Get a hold of yourselves," he told his two children sternly. "Stay here." He crawled forward on his belly toward his wife, over scraps of Scripture, hoping beyond hope that her wound was not fatal. The shooting outside slowed. He plainly saw that his wife was dead. All her blood had already pooled beneath her. An eerie silence filled the home, punctuated with the thumping of the debris that intermittently fell from the ceiling against the floor.

Barry tried with all his might to fight off the unbearable sobs that swelled in his chest. He wiped his tears and took several deep breaths. When he saw the struggling infant in Vicki's arms, he couldn't hold back the torrent of tears any longer. "Oh, Timothy," he wept, "I'm so sorry."

Barry tried not to look at the gaping hole in the back of Vicki's head as he loosened her clutches and pulled his son, soaked with the warm blood of his mother, out from underneath her chest. The baby cried hard and his little arms moved and kicked in short, energetic bursts. Barry pulled the anxious child close. He rolled onto his back to kick the door shut and with the indication of fresh movement, a single bullet blazed once again just above his head, followed by a furious barrage of gunfire. The sounds of whistling bullets, shattering glass, and splitting boards were the only interruptions to the pitiful sobs of the children and baby Timothy's screams for his mother.

Jack could feel his heart throbbing in his head as he knelt motionless behind a tree, out of the line of sight of the three soldiers who inched slowly toward him. *Don't freeze, Jack. Relax,* he thought. *One side of the tree, then the other. Shoot straight. Head shots. They may be wearing bulletproof vests. You've trained for this.*

The approaching troopers stopped shooting their weapons and for a short moment that appeared to last an eternity, he thought that they might have retreated. Then he saw something out of the corner of his right eye, something coming up the driveway. It was an armored vehicle with a dozen or so troops running behind it. Six of the agents started running toward him from about 100 yards away. The three agents nearest him briefly turned their attention to the approaching reinforcements.

No more time! he thought. *It's now or never.* He jumped to his feet, restraining his instinctive holler, and pointed the assault weapon at the camouflaged agent that was standing to his right 20 yards away. *Tat-tat-tat-tat!* sounded the hushed, powerful weapon in his hands. A pair of speeding bullets struck the head and neck of one of the soldiers, beheading him. Another soldier received a bullet in the pelvis, and fell to the ground moaning.

Jack ducked behind the tree as the third agent started shooting in his direction. When the agent paused to reload, Jack returned fire. Three bullets sped from Jack's weapon and then his magazine was empty; Jack was out of ammo. He ducked back behind the largest tree. His opponent stepped beyond the brush into full view with his gun pointed toward him and Jack thought this was the end. Jack threw down his gun and put his hands up in the air. It was over. He could hear the shouts of the agents who were running toward him from the driveway. Any moment, he expected to feel a breath-stealing punch of lead in his chest. He said nothing as he held his hands in the air. The camouflaged soldier walked toward him two more steps, hesitated, and then stumbled sideways and fell to the ground. The injured soldier began to breathe heavily through a gurgled rattle of blood in his throat. Jack's last bullet had penetrated his brain.

Jack's attention turned to the angry shouts of six men racing toward him with their rifles at the ready. Jack darted to the fallen soldier he had just shot just as the six charging him began to fire in his direction. He pried the gun out of the dying agent's hands and sprinted for the tree line 50 yards away. The clump of trees in the middle of the field temporarily concealed his retreat from the charging soldiers.

"Mom?" cried Marion through teeth gritted in pain. "Mom?" From where he lay bleeding, he could not get a clear view of his mother, but her silence was telling. Through his father's and sister's weeping, and his baby brother's unconsoled screams, he knew she had been hit.

Barry laid on his back beside his wife, trying to bottle up his grief with deep breaths, sucking the dusty, gunpowder-scented air into his lungs. There will be time to mourn his wife later. Right now, the living demanded that he be strong. "She's gone, Marion." He pulled his infant son close to his chest and tried futilely to quiet his cries.

"Oh, Mom," Teresa called out in vain through pitiful sobs of anguish as she gripped her handgun tightly in her good hand. She turned toward the nearest shattered window and screamed, "You killed my mom!"

Barry saw Teresa peek over the couch to get a glimpse of her mother. "Get down, Teresa! Keep your head down!" He crawled back to Marion and Teresa behind the couch while holding his infant son close to his chest with one arm.

"Matt's dead, too, Teresa," Marion informed her. "He's dead."

Teresa wiped her tears away when she saw that her father held her little baby brother in his arms. She laid the large handgun and the box of ammunition down on the ground and reached for Timmy. "It's okay," she said, her voice a pitiful whimper. Her baby brother needed her and that responsibility would help her cope with the waves of grief that rolled up and down her body like a black ocean's cold tide.

"I'm so sorry." Barry handed his screaming infant son to Teresa. She looked up and nodded at her father, trying to be brave.

"It's okay, Timmy." She comforted the child with gentle rocking. "It's okay. Mommy's in heaven, now."

Barry could overhear the cries of "We give up!" and "Don't shoot!" from the surviving young men in front of the house as they ran out of ammo and were forced to surrender. Following orders, the young men sprawled out flat on the ground with their legs spread and hands clasped behind their heads.

Barry looked over at Marion, who was shedding pitiful tears for the adopted mother he so deeply loved. Barry's heart broke for his children and he wished he could protect them from the fearful sight of their mother's dead body kneeling over a pool of blood that encircled her on the wooden floor. Marion leaned over to see around the couch. The sight of his mother's motionless body enraged him. Her clothes had begun to soak up some of the blood beneath her. The image burned hatred into his mind. The bullet that painlessly pierced his mother's skull found its way into his right shoulder and fragments of her mandible lodged in his upper chest, partially collapsing his lung. He was bleeding profusely from the shoulder wound. Marion began to curse and swear, but Barry prevented him.

"Shut your mouth! Your mother would weep in heaven for you if she heard you say things like that."

"Oh, Mom." He wept as he held his shoulder with his good hand.

Barry realized the severity of the bleeding from Marion's shoulder. "We've got to stop that bleeding."

Wincing from the pain in his foot, Jack sprinted as fast as he could in a zigzag pattern to the tree line as bullets sprayed the grass all around him. He decided he would try to dive over the shallowest edge head first. He dove and his shirt snagged on a branch, ripping his sleeve and sending him spinning sideways onto some briars that softened his fall, yet scraped his flesh. He leapt to his feet and rushed into the inviting cover of the untempered woods. He sprinted through the woods for about ten seconds when he twisted his ankle on a stone. He fell to the ground, and then rolled to duck behind a bush about 30 yards away from the tree line. He tried to control his heavy breathing. He listened intently for the footsteps and shouts of those who were following him. A long minute passed and Jack finally heard the men attempting to climb over the piles of branches and logs.

He looked down at his gun, felt the weight of the magazine half-full of ammunition and flipped the trigger to "full-auto." If he was on his way to certain death, he wanted to fire all of the bullets in the weapon en route. He jumped out from behind the tree and sprayed a wave of bullets at the men who were climbing the brush pile in pursuit. Three or four of the soldiers nearest him instantly hit the ground. Jack suddenly felt an electrical-shooting pain in his left thigh from a round shot by one of the men concealed in the woods to his right. Jack's left leg buckled and he fell back. He heard shouts and other soldiers began to run from the edge of the forest toward him. He leaned against a tree and pointed his weapon in the direction of the shouts. Tunnel vision and dizziness were settling in like a fog around him. He tried to fight it off by controlling his breathing and ignoring the incredible pain in his upper leg.

He saw some movement over a fallen log that was held aloft three or four feet from the ground by its thick branches. He could barely see the heads of the two camouflaged intruders. He shot under the log and heard one of the men scream. The mortally wounded agent emptied his magazine in Jack's direction, and then crumpled motionless to the ground. Jack took cover for a moment, and then shot another burst just under the log toward the men.

All was surprisingly still for a few minutes, save for the groans of the injured and dying agents. He tried futilely to slow the throbbing of his heart and the rapid breathing in his chest. He could feel his right sock getting wet from the blood that streamed down his leg. He heard the faint sound of more footsteps behind him. He turned into the face of sudden oncoming gunfire, and shot indiscriminately into the woods in the direction of the gunfire. Leaves and bark sprayed all around him and the camouflaged soldier at whom he was firing. Then the dreaded click of an empty magazine prompted him to duck back behind the tree. He quietly rested the rifle against the tree and instinctively reached for a six inch hunting knife sheathed on the right side of his belt. It had an engraving of Robert E. Lee on it and a colorful depiction of the Confederate flag. He held it tight and listened carefully for any sounds. Although his hands and feet were growing numb and he was dizzy from the loss of blood, his senses were elevated as he looked carefully from side to side. A strange euphoria came over him as he waited. He knew the sensation was probably from his rapid loss of blood and that death was near.

A soldier jumped out from behind the tree directly in front of him and pulled his trigger. One bullet grazed Jack's neck and then the soldier's gun clicked as the magazine emptied. The soldier let out a muffled curse through his camouflaged mask. He quickly pulled a fresh magazine out of his jacket pocket and prepared to reload when Jack lunged at him with as much strength as his one good leg could provide.

Jack's leg sent extremely intense pains up to his hip and he discovered that he didn't have the strength he thought he had. The soldier swung his gun at Jack and he blocked it with his left forearm. The fist that gripped the handle of his knife caught the soldier in the crease of his neck and jaw. The soldier reeled backwards and his rifle flipped to the ground. The federal agent quickly regained his composure and pulled a sidearm from his hip. He fired a shot that went just to the left of Jack's torso as Jack lunged again with his knife and knocked the agent back to the ground.

Falling on top of him, Jack brought the knife up instantly to the agent's throat and plunged it deep through the airway, esophagus, and carotid arteries to the very front of his cervical spine in a single sweeping motion. This caused the man to instantly go limp as his blood sprayed in all directions, covering Jack's face and neck.

Jack sat up next to the soldier and regained his bearings. The woods were momentarily silent. He reached for the dead soldier's rifle and the full magazine that had fallen on the ground. Then his thigh pain grew more terrible; he dropped the full magazine and grabbed his thigh with his own bloody hand. He noticed blood spurting out rhythmically from his leg between his fingers. Blood also drained out of his superficial neck wound, but he hadn't even noticed that injury. He knew he had to stop the bleeding in his thigh fast or he'd soon lose consciousness.

Suddenly, he heard a bone-chilling shout to "Freeze!" from behind him. He slowly looked over his shoulder and next to the tree stood a black-clad agent with FBI printed in white letters on his cap. The gun in Jack's hand had an empty magazine and the full magazine lay at his side. He set down the gun and slowly put his hands into the air. The steaming barrel of an M16 was aimed at his head and he knew that this was the end. The trees appeared to spin around his head; he was about to lose consciousness.

His thoughts were on his estranged wife when the agent threatened, "Move a muscle and I'll waste you." Jack took a deep breath, surprised that the agent didn't just shoot him. This black-clothed agent must be operating under different rules of engagement than the camouflaged agents. The agent tilted his head to the side to speak into a shoulder microphone when suddenly, a gun blast sounded: *Blam!*

The gun blast jolted Jack, who blinked just at that moment. For a heart-throbbing split second, he thought he'd been shot. Then he saw a familiar frame ten feet away aiming a rifle right into the federal agent's forehead. The sound of Bull's voice brought him to his senses.

"Jack! Jack!" Jack didn't respond, but simply stared at his comrade, who had a .22 magnum rifle in his hand. The world was spinning around as his arterial blood continued to drain out of his thigh wound. The federal agent received a shot to the temple and collapsed onto his side, his eyes wide open as his brain hemorrhaged.

"Come on, Jack." Bull helped him to his feet and Jack momentarily lost consciousness because of the pain from his wound and the escalating blood loss. Bull took off his belt and tied a tourniquet around Jack's thigh.

"You did it, Jack. You beat 'em." Bull grabbed the sling of Jack's rifle and slung it over his shoulder. He picked up the two rifles of the fallen FBI agents nearby and slung them over his shoulder as well. He then picked Jack up like he was a sack of horse feed and tossed him over his shoulder. Bull carried him quickly through the trees down the hill and away from the chatter of gunfire above.

Barry Friar's home was being surrounded with angry federal agents craving swift vengeance, with many more on the way.

Agent Lex ducked behind a pick-up directly in front of the front door of the home. He tapped the button on his helmet that relayed his words to the mission commander. "Sergeant Hammel! That was a disaster of our making!"

Hammel swore at the subordinate and ordered him, "Shut your mouth, you fool!"

Lex was furious at how at how many died as they rushed the home. "Most of these boys died defending themselves against our excessive and unnecessary force!"

The captain of Lex's squad marched over to him and grabbed him by the scruff of his camouflage jacket. "Look around, Lex! We've got dead men on the field, too!" He pushed him back two feet and leveled an index finger at his pained grimace. "They had it comin', Lex! Don't you dare indict your Bureau! You keep it inside, got that?"

"Captain, get Agent Lex out of there, and get him to my office ASAP."

Chapter 11

B arry crawled to the gun safe in a closet on the first floor and pulled out an AR15, a large caliber handgun, and a few hundred rounds of ammo. Marion had taken Teresa's .357 Glock and laid it in his lap as he pressed his left hand against the bullet entrance wound in his right shoulder to give greater pressure to the bandage his father tied around his arm. The bullet lodged within the bone, fracturing it. He was somewhat short of breath from the injury to his chest, but that pain paled in comparison to his shoulder. Barry didn't risk going to the medicine cabinet where a couple of hydrocodone tablets were stored, left over from a broken wrist injury over a year ago. The entrance to the restroom was in clear view of a tree close to the house. From the trajectory of the bullets that penetrated their wooden floor, he knew that the feds stationed a sniper in that tree.

Barry expected the worst and Marion's pessimism was matching his father's. Marion just knew that soon they'd all be killed, so he clenched his teeth and prepared himself mentally for the end. His pain made him wish for it. He tried not to moan too loudly, so as not to alarm his sister and baby brother more than necessary. He leaned against a chair just behind the couch, in clear view of his mother, whom Barry covered with a knit-blanket. His mother gave Marion that red, white, and blue blanket for him two Christmases ago. It read, "The fight for freedom never ends."

Teresa held baby Timmy tightly to her chest with her good arm and spoke softly to him to try to hush his crying. The infant was fatigued with hard crying from not being able to nurse his mother.

"What's that?" Teresa winced as she looked at the ceiling above the foyer. A circle of pink wetness had soaked the white drywall. Pink drops were rhythmically dripping to the ground like drumbeats of a retreating, defeated army. The stain of blood was about as large as a door.

"Anybody alive up there?" Barry shouted.

Marion mumbled with a contorted grimace through grinding teeth, "There's another body at the top of the stairs."

Barry could see halfway up the stairwell from where he was sitting. Blood had stained the beige carpet.

Teresa shuddered at the sight of the bloodstained ceilings as she tried to calm Timothy down by putting her pinkie into his mouth.

Hopelessness crept over Barry's mind and body like a cold chill. This was a nightmare from which he could not wake. *We're next.*

The ATF and FBI agents, who had cooperated in the raid, occupied themselves with rounding up the injured and carrying off the dead while counting their losses through the foulest of curses. The battle was thrilling while it lasted, but now as they bandaged wounds and the body count rose, the shame of it all hit them. The high body count and the stalemate would be an extreme embarrassment to both bureaus. These weren't Mexican drug lords or Arab hijackers. These weren't escaped convicts holding hostage a department store full of shoppers – these were American civilians having a barbecue. They were told to avoid casualties at all cost and their superiors would assuredly accuse them of utter failure. But they were fired upon, they would rebut. All of the logic of the attorneys' seamless arguments would shut its mouth as the body bags of federal agents were lined up side by side. At that sight, hate overwhelmed every criticism and justified every drop of the Montana bloodbath in the minds of those who charged the Friar "compound" in Garrison that dreadful day.

A perimeter was set up to keep the media at bay at the bottom of the mountain, away from any clear view of the house. This was done in spite of the strongest of protests from the major news stations, which fought and clamored for a better view of the compound, the more emotional interview, or the more heart-touching testimony of bravery and loss. The pundits introduced the story with the cameras focused on the distant image of the house only barely visible through the thick pine trees and foggy mist.

"We are here at the foot of the mountain on which Barry Friar, former director of the Militia of Montana, had a shoot-out with federal law enforcement agents this afternoon at his compound in Garrison, Montana." The camera zoomed in on the stoic FBI agents who guarded the gravel path that led to the militia fortress. "Dozens have been killed and the FBI and ATF are refusing to let anybody closer to the compound because of the threat of those well-armed militia fighters trapped inside." The whole nation tuned into the breaking news story on radio, television, or internet to follow the crisis, flipping from station to station for the most heart-throbbing story and images.

The commander of the mission, FBI Sergeant Roger Hammel, had soundly cursed out every one of the captains of each of the five squads. He leaned against the armored vehicle, wringing his hands at the thought of having to personally communicate the details of the failed raid to his superiors.

The captured militiamen were held in chains in black vans with bars on the windows. Their hands were cuffed to chains around their waists. Their ankles were shackled to a bar under the seat. Two armed agents kept guard and disallowed them from speaking. Tears trickled down the faces of those young men as they looked out the windows at the carnage, the shock ebbing as reality set it. They would probably never marry and have children. The married men would probably never see their wives and kids again without an armed guard present. They would never walk a mountain trail, never shoot a deer, never ride a horse, and never eat a Thanksgiving meal with cousins, parents, grandparents or grandchildren. They knew that they'd never be free again. Some of the men, who watched their dead friends stuffed in body bags and laid side by side, considered themselves to have received the greater cup of suffering. The older men looked more angry than sad, and they snarled bitterly at the federal agents who guarded them. The few young women that were in bonds in the van could not stop their weeping. The federal agents militantly paced outside the vans with assault rifles at the ready.

The troops carefully and systematically scoured the property and the woods, looking for any injured or dead, especially for the elusive terrorist Frederick Seibert, known as "Bull" by his comrades in treason. Bull was, after all, the primary excuse given for the raid on the Friar's farm. Bull would be their trophy fish, to be mounted on the wall of the Bureau. These other guys, well, they're just small fry, bait to be hung out on a hook to attract the bigger trophies: the planners, the leaders, the arms-sellers, and the crazed homegrown terrorists like Fred "Bull" Seibert.

Sharpshooters were given the responsibility to surround the house and look for clean shots of the rebels inside. With their friends' deaths and with the sight of black plastic body bags impressed deeply into their minds, they were very enthusiastic about this mission. They moved quickly into position knowing that soon the politicians might search for peaceful solutions and any chance of getting bloody vengeance against the traitors would be gone. Any movement at all inside the house was to be fired upon, in order to protect the agents outside who busied themselves tending to the wounded and piling up the dead. Snipers climbed the trees around the home to gain a better look inside.

The Friar's calico cat came rushing down the stairs and jumped on the deep blue armchair in the family room and was cut in half by a sniper's bullet. The cat meowed pitifully as her claws pulled the upper body away from its detached lower legs for a moment until she died. Teresa gasped in horror, turned her gaze away, and wept afresh.

Barry gained the courage to venture the long distance into the kitchen to retrieve the phone. He crawled slowly on his belly to where the phone was set on a corner table. He knew the snipers in the trees outside were scouring every nook and cranny of this old house with their high-powered, light-gathering military scopes, and he didn't want to give them a target. Almost all of the bullet holes were above the knees in the house. *Thank God for the stone base I put around this house,* Barry thought to himself.

He reached up for the cordless phone, quickly falling back down and hugging the floor, bracing for the expected gunshot at him. When no shot was fired, he brought the phone to his ear, fully expecting it to be dead. It was. Their lines had been cut prior to the raid. Marion's cell phone was also dead.

Suddenly, they heard the sound of another cell phone ring. "Whose phone is that?"

"I dunno," said Teresa. "Maybe it's in that jacket." She pointed at a leather jacket in the corner of the room beside a chair.

Barry retrieved the phone just as it stopped ringing. "Pray this works." Barry quickly crawled back into the kitchen and removed a phone book from the bottom shelf of a small bookcase. He opened the phone book and dialed a number from the blue pages, which had the numbers for government offices.

"Who are you calling?"

"Quiet! The feds will probably turn it off any minute." As the phone rang, Barry mumbled, "Answer, come on, answer."

"Governor Boswell's office. May I—"

"Yes! Thank God!" whispered Barry excitedly. "Marianne, I need to speak to Ben. It's urgent."

"Who's this?"

"It's Barry Friar. I need to speak to Ben."

Marianne had just learned about the raid at the militia stronghold in Garrison, but she hadn't yet discovered that it was Barry Friar's home. "Um, he's in a meeting right now. He's not available. Can I take a—"

"No, it's very important, a matter of life and death! Interrupt him, Marianne, now! He's probably in a meeting about me. He's probably on the phone with the FBI."

He was trying to keep his voice down, but his whisper carried the passion of a man in an emergency and Marianne was worried.

"Just a second. I'm going to put you on hold."

Barry whispered a passionate prayer for divine aid as a bluegrass song played in the background on the phone.

Come on, Marianne, come on. A minute passed, and then a second long minute. Then the line suddenly went dead, dragging his hopes along with it.

"Oh no!" Barry cried out loud. He tried to call the number again, but could not get through. "They blocked the line!"

"There are some more jackets over there." Teresa pointed at the dining room table. Barry, hoping against hope, crawled over, pulled the jackets off the table, and checked each pocket. They were empty of anything helpful. He saw a purse resting on the floor in the corner of the room. He grabbed it and checked for a phone. He found one, opened it, and quickly dialed the number for the governor's office. "Yes!" he exclaimed when it began to ring. "You two keep your guns at the ready. Feds could be charging into this room any second. Pray that I can contact the governor."

"Yes sir." Marion's painful grimace developed into a more serious, solemn squint. His acute pain and grief made him wish that the feds would just raid the place and get it over with. Maybe he could shoot a few of them before the end.

Barry dialed the number and the governor's secretary answered on the first ring. "This is the governor's office. May I—"

"Marianne! Get me Ben, quick!"

"Hold on."

A familiar voice spoke hastily on the phone, "Barry, is that you?"

"Ben!"

"What in the name of Moses is going on up there? I got the director of the FBI on-line here telling me that you have been harboring a murderer and a domestic terrorist, a Mr. Fred Seibert, and that you have holed up in your house holding your children hostage."

"What?"

"They tell me that they have evidence that you have physically abused your children and have violated federal gun laws making illegal weapons. Do you mind clarifying for me what is going on?"

"Lies! Ben, those are all lies! We were having a barbecue with the boys from the civilian militia, a friendly barbecue around the campfire, when we were attacked, I'm telling you Ben, attacked! Without provocation! Camouflaged soldiers, dozens of them, came out of the woods from every direction. They were shooting at us, Ben. They killed my wife!" His voice cracked in a restrained sob. "She's lying there dead about 20 feet away from me right now!"

"Vicki's dead?"

"Matt, remember my son Matt? Shot in the back and killed."

"What?"

"Marion's been shot in the chest and shoulder and is in a lot of pain. My daughter's injured."

"Are you saying you had no knowledge of harboring a murder suspect by the name of Fred Seibert?"

"No way! Do you think I would do that? I had no idea he was a suspect in any criminal investigation, but yes, he was out here today."

"Did you shoot some of the federal agents?"

"I didn't. If you mean to ask if some of us shot back, yes, some of us did, but what do you expect?"

"Lord, have mercy!"

"They were butchering us, Ben! I'd have shot back if I had a gun."

"The FBI just informed me that you shot a dozen federal agents, Barry! What can I do now? You should have surrendered and fought it out in the courts."

"They..." Barry hesitated, sympathizing with the governor's dilemma. "We defended ourselves, Ben. You gotta help. They're still shootin' at us."

"Is that your baby I hear crying there?"

"Yes."

"You need to let your kids out of there, Barry. Just let them walk out the front door. You could die in there."

"No kidding, Ben!" he said mockingly. "They're shooting at us through the door and the walls. They're in the trees. They'll probably shoot my kids dead and claim I did it. They're already lying and sayin' that I abuse 'em..."

Just at that moment, the FBI's hostage negotiator began to call out to Barry through a megaphone from inside an armored vehicle, which was parked just beyond the civilian vehicles in front of the house.

"Barry Friar, you are surrounded. Come out with your hands up!"

"Who's that?" Governor Ben Boswell asked Barry.

"They're asking me to surrender."

"For God's sake, do it, man!"

"Let your children go, Mr. Friar," the hostage negotiator pleaded, **"and it will go better for you."**

"I don't trust 'em! They'll give me the death penalty, Ben. Even if they don't shoot my kids, they're going to take them away and give them to some sinners and—"

Blam! A bullet shattered a window and caused everyone in the room to jump. The baby started crying hard again.

"Are you shootin' at them? What was that?" inquired Boswell.

Barry closed his eyes as shards of glass sprayed all around him. He looked up and saw a bullet hole in the forehead of his image in a family portrait that hung, crooked now, on the wall above him.

"Somebody shot me in the head," Barry muttered.

"What? Barry, you okay?"

"Not for long."

"Get out of there! Stick something white in the air on a stick or something."

"I don't trust them, Ben. They..." He heard a buzz on the line. "Hello?"

"Your service has been discontinued. Message 213."

Barry dropped the phone, put his head in his palms, and wept.

Helena, Montana

Ben Boswell stomped out of his office and ordered his secretary, "Try to get him back on the phone."

"Todd Hamilton's waiting online, sir." Boswell walked back into his office, slammed the door, and then sat behind his desk. His computer monitor showed Todd Hamilton, impatiently tapping his fingers against his desk as he perused some intelligence updates.

Their eyes met and Ben Boswell unmuted the microphone and caught the last half of Hamilton's angry reproof, "...the compound of the former director of the Militia of Montana! A dozen federal agents have been shot. Have the sense enough to prioritize your obligations!"

Governor Boswell swallowed hard and tried to hide his mixed emotions. "I'm sorry for the interruption."

"Like I was saying, we have evidence that Barry Friar has sexually molested his children and that he may kill them before surrendering. We have evidence that he has manufactured illegal weapons.

We have convincing evidence that they were knowingly harboring the murder suspect, Fred Seibert, and possibly even aiding him in planning and implementing multiple terrorist attacks on federal buildings within the northwestern United—-"

Governor Boswell interrupted, "I don't believe you."

Hamilton frowned and hoped he had misunderstood the governor. "Excuse me?"

"I don't believe that Barry Friar knowingly harbored a murder suspect and I don't believe for a second that he's holding his children against their will. I certainly don't believe anyone else outside your agency is a threat to those kids. My sources tell me that his—"

"*Your* sources? What sources?"

"My sources tell me that his wife has been killed, one of his sons killed, two of his other three children shot and injured. All they were doing is running for their lives from your trigger-happy agents who went on a murderous rampage."

Hamilton's face reddened as fury kindled within him. "What sources?" When the governor's answer wasn't forthcoming, Hamilton snapped critically, "Are you withholding information that may be helpful in our investigation? That would be a federal crime, Governor Boswell. Whoever is supplying you information is working against your country."

"Your men, Mr. Hamilton, are working against my country." Governor Boswell clenched his fists and raised his voice. "You attacked a lawful assembly of citizens that were eating barbecue pork and roasting marshmallows over a campfire!""Do you think those dozen agents shot themselves, Governor? Those militia fanatics fired on my men first with *illegal* weapons."

Governor Boswell blushed, but held his peace. He had major problems with President Brighton's executive order, but what could he do about it?

"We've got the body bags to prove it!" Hamilton slapped the desk, enraged. "Nine dead agents, plus several that are in critical condition." An agent pushed a fax across the desk where Hamilton could see it. He glanced at it. "No, make that ten dead Americans. How do you think that will look on the evening news, Governor Boswell? Ten dead federal agents, killed in the line of duty by right-wing extremists with illegal weapons who were harboring a terrorist suspect and who, by the way, has the sympathy of Montana Governor Benjamin Boswell."

"I think we're done with this conversation, Mr. Hamilton. I may not have all of the facts yet, but I intend to get them."

He reached for the button to end the call as Hamilton made another plea, "We need your help, Governor Boswell. We think Fred Seibert escaped. He's armed and dangerous. He may be the culprit that killed a few of our men on the outskirts of the property. We need your help in apprehending him in a statewide manhunt. Your Guard forces would be of service in—"

"How do you know he escaped? What makes you think he's not dead inside the house along with all the other civilians shot in the cross-fire?"

Hamilton's face was beet-red and beads of sweat swelled on his brow as his frustration over the governor's stubbornness climaxed. "I can't believe what I'm hearing!" he shouted. "This borders on aiding and abetting, Governor, treason if you ask me!"

"Well, I'm not asking you, I'm telling you," he responded calmly. "I will be speaking to the president personally about your troops in my state, but if I were you, I'd start thinking about ways to end this conflict without any more fatalities."

Hamilton swallowed his anger and forced a diplomatic smile. He relaxed his fists and raised his palms toward the camera. "Do you think we would prefer it any other way?" His politician smile suddenly turned to the grim frown that more aptly matched his sweaty face. "But I have reports that gunshots have been heard coming from inside the house. Friar's children may already be dead. You're wasting time we don't have."

Governor Boswell looked down and shook his head back and forth as he bit his bottom lip. *Stinking liar!* he thought but didn't say. "Those gunshots are coming from your snipers outside, Mr. Hamilton! You are in charge of this investigation, right? The FBI has jurisdiction, right?"

"Yes sir, the ATF was assisting because of the illegal weapons on the scene."

"But you're in charge, right?" Hamilton nodded. "Then I will hold you," Boswell pointed at the small webcam affixed to the top of his monitor, "wholly responsible if one more person dies on Barry Friar's property, got that? Anybody else winds up dead and I will have *you* brought up on charges."

Todd Hamilton snickered at the audacity of this hillbilly. "You have got to be kidding me! We're doing everything in our power to see that this conflict comes to a peaceful resolution, Governor, but you're making an absolute fool of yourself with your empty threats. With all due respect, I know that Barry Friar is an old friend of yours who worked for your election campaign, but you have to put emotional attachments on the backburner. Friar has changed. He's gone off the deep end and turned against his own country."

"Yeah, yeah, yeah," Boswell said, almost mocking. "Is there anything else?" He acted as if he was prepared to discontinue the conversation, much to Hamilton's dismay.

"Your Guard forces and highway patrol would be of service in apprehending this extremely dangerous criminal suspect." He appeared sincere and Governor Boswell realized that the feds really needed him for this manhunt. "I've e-mailed photographs and information on Fred 'Bull' Seibert to the Guard office, the PD's, and highway patrol offices. He escaped either on foot or on horseback and couldn't have gotten far."

"The only terrorist attack for which I have evidence is that which you and your camouflaged outfit have executed against a largely unarmed group of barbequing good-ole-boys. And speaking of the Montana State Guard, I'll be sending them up there to keep you and your boys from playing judge, jury, and executioner and murdering Barry Friar or his kids."

"Wha—" *Click*. He cut Hamilton off in mid-sentence.

Washington, D.C.

Todd Hamilton was still trying to process the conversation with the Montana governor when an aide knocked on his door. Hamilton called her in; she walked to his desk and handed him a faxed memo from the intelligence office in Helena. He snatched it out of her hand and read it quickly. It informed him of the telephone contact between Governor Boswell and Barry Friar before they could disconnect the line.

"Great! I must look like a freakin' idiot," he mumbled before dropping the memo into the paper shredder next to his desk.

*****

James Knight walked through the foyer on his way to the main assembly while reading the news alert on his cell phone. The assembly was buzzing with anxious conversations about the raid on the Militia of Montana compound.

"Hey, James," said someone who approached from the rear, "can we speak to you a minute?"

He turned and Bo Bennett, a congressman from Texas, extended his right hand toward him. Behind him were John Dobson and two other men he only vaguely recognized.

Knight shook his hand with vigor. "Good to see you again, Bo."

"Likewise."

Bo introduced him to the two other men. "This is Allen Chandler and Derek Williams from Montana."

He shook their hands solemnly. "I'm sorry about what's transpiring there in Garrison."

"That's what we'd like to talk to you about. Let's step into the back room."

Knight followed them into a meeting room adjacent to the foyer of the House of Representatives. When the door was shut, Bennett said, "This raid might help us win support for more aggressive measures to check Brighton's power grab."

"How do militia felons and child molesters shooting federal agents help anything except tyranny?"

The two Montana congressmen measured James Knight's skepticism for a moment. "I know Barry Friar," Chandler said, "as does Governor Ben Boswell. Those are lies, James. Lies! There's *no way* that this raid was justified!"

The others nodded as they sat down around a small round table. Knight released a faint smile, finally glad to have some of his allies against Brighton express a little ambition. "Can you prove it?"

"Barry Friar is a country pastor who loves his wife and kids," Williams informed him.

Knight held his cell phone up in the air for a moment. "They're saying he has sexually abused his children and is holding them hostage."

"They are lying through their teeth!" Williams stated emphatically.

Knight opened his cell phone and read part of his cyber-news alert out loud. "One of the militia members has confessed that the Friar children were being held against their will and that they were being ordered to fire on the federal agents."

"Tell me how a militia member, who was arrested outside of the house while trying to get inside, would know whether or not Barry Friar was holding his children against their will inside the house?" Bennett wondered out loud. "Tell me that. It doesn't make sense."

Knight looked at his watch. *Ten minutes till the next session.* "Let's get your governor on-line right now." Knight opened his briefcase and pulled out his webcam-equipped laptop computer.

James Knight and the Montana reps were enraged when they learned from Governor Boswell about the deaths and injuries to the Friar family. "You don't need to tell me that Barry's a good man," the Montana governor said to the Wyoming rep through their encrypted internet connection. "I don't believe any of this nonsense about him. I'm going public with my condemnation of the raid. I'll also speak to the state legislature this morning. I've already this day endured the lies and the spin of Todd Hamilton and Dena Halluci. I'm sick with it all."

"Have you spoken with the president?"

"She was unavailable. I'm sending the Montana Guard out to the Friar's farm right now to keep an eye on things." Governor Boswell could see that the conservative African-American representative was almost as livid as he and would probably be a helpful ally in Congress. "You guys need to get on the ball and get the impeachment process underway. For God's sake, Mr. Knight, you've got a Republican majority! You can't sit by and watch this unfold. Subpoena Todd Hamilton, Bill Erdman, whatever it takes. You've got to do something! Now!"

Chapter 12

Garrison, Montana

In the Rocky Mountain foothills of central Montana, a confrontation was brewing of immense proportions. Guard General Bob Bryan ordered the Montana State Guard to go up the hill to within clear view of the Friar's home, but the FBI refused to let them past their outer perimeter at the bottom of the hill.

"Tell *Mr.* Bryan that the FBI has jurisdiction over terrorist investigations," said Sergeant Roger Hammel. As the commander of the mission that had failed to meet any of its objectives in the raid the previous day, Mr. Hammel was rude, arrogant, and unbending. "Go home and watch it on the news."

"We obey orders from the governor of Montana," Captain Rod Sanders with the Montana Guard responded. "He has ordered us to—"

"We *all* take orders from the Commander-in-Chief, you little *peon*." Hammel interrupted with spite, leaning uncomfortably close to the guardsman and showing him his teeth. "We got militia terrorists up there who are shooting at us. You cow-milkers and potato-farmers can go home and leave this conflict to the professionals." His words dripped with sarcasm and mockery. He motioned to the 80 camouflaged guardsmen who carried automatic weapons and hand grenades as if they were prepared for war. The guardsmen stood around and within four armored personnel carriers and four Hummers equipped with .50 caliber machine guns down the driveway. "We don't need our nails done, so you can find something else to do."

"This is *our* state!" Captain Rod Sanders' knuckles were white around his rifle. He knew Barry Friar personally and so it took everything he had to keep from breaking Sergeant Hammel's nose for his insults of the Guard and of the Friar family. He'd never been so furious about the actions of the federal government. He was a firsthand witness to the federal government's horrifying, heavy-handed response to the peaceful protest at Bozeman and the images of suffering were etched deeply in his mind. "I have the order from General Bob Bryan of the Montana State Guard—"

"It's called the National Guard for a reason, ya moron!"

"...And Benjamin Boswell, governor of the state of Montana, to tell you to **stand down**!" He screamed those last two words at the FBI sergeant to be heard over his mockery. "We will take over negotiations with Barry Friar from here. Henceforth, you will be *assisting* us in *our* investigations in a manner that *Montana's* authorities will determine."

"Hey!" Sergeant Hammel snapped his fingers six inches from the face of the unintimidated Guard captain. "Wake up, fantasy boy!" He leaned into the face of the well tanned, graying weekend warrior of dense, muscular build and studied him for a moment.

Captain Rod Sanders kept his composure. "At the very least, then, until further negotiations between the governor and your supervisor can be concluded, we'll set up a watch within 50 yards of the Friar's home."

"What do hillbillies smoke in Montana? You aren't going anywhere near that hill!" Hammel was trying to get under the guardsman's skin and he was succeeding.

Captain Sanders turned, grinding his teeth together under a thick, graying goatee, and futilely trying to swallow the throbbing lump that burned in his throat. He appeared deep in thought as he made his way down the dirt drive to where his men were stationed about 30 yards from the federal perimeter. He stopped at the Humvee nearest the roadblock, and he rested his forearm on the open window.

"Are they gonna let us through?" the Humvee driver asked.

"Get General Bryan on the line," Sanders said quietly. He looked into the back seat, where a state investigator and a Guard physician were seated.

Captain Sanders glanced at them. "Hang tight. We're going to get you into that home."

Suddenly, they heard another gunshot on top of the hill, and their gaze darted to the home that they could barely see through the thick pine on the hill. Captain Sanders donned a headset and updated the drivers behind him of their present situation on a scrambled phone line. "Stay alert," he told them, "and follow my lead."

The driver of Sanders' Hummer informed him, "General's on line two."

Sanders put the phone to his cheek. "General Bryan?"

"Just tell me that you're in clear view of the house."

"They won't let us in anywhere near it, sir."

"Who?"

"The FBI. The ATF. A cocky FBI agent named Roger Hammel at the bottom of the Friar's hill. That's who."

"Listen, Captain," General Bryan pronounced each syllable slowly and purposefully so as not to be misunderstood. "Governor Benjamin Boswell and I have *ordered* you to get up that hill. I want the state investigator in there to interview the survivors and I want our doctor on the ground to try to patch them up as soon as possible. Neither the governor nor I will take 'I tried' as an answer."

"They're not budging, sir."

"Well, move around them! What are they going to do, shoot you?"

Sanders couldn't believe his ears. "You want me to go around them?"

"Do I need to repeat myself, Captain Sanders?"

"Forgive me for asking for clarification, but I want my driver to hear this order from your lips." Captain Sanders pulled the radio away from his ear so that the driver of the Hummer could also listen to the conversation. "You want us to go *around* their heavily guarded perimeter and get within view of the Friar's house?"

"Around 'em, under 'em, through 'em, I don't give a flip. I want you to set up a watch in close proximity of the house to keep an eye on those federal agents. They want vengeance, do you understand? They'll murder the survivors if you fail."

"And if they shoot at us?"

"Then defend yourself! Might doesn't make right, Captain! Just because the feds are guarding the property doesn't mean they own it. They are in the wrong and they have all the witnesses and all of the evidence in their control. The fox is guarding the hen house. We need to get a handle on the situation before any more blood is shed and any more evidence is destroyed."

Sanders was stunned at how far the superior general of the State Guard was willing to take this. He ran his fingers through his goatee. "And when federal charges are filed against us for killing federal agents, are you going to step up to the plate for us and take responsibility?"

"Proudly."

"You are prepared to go to prison for this?"

"I'm prepared to put a bullet through Todd Hamilton's brain if that's what it takes to stop the feds' murderous rampage in our state!"

Sanders cocked his head to the side and winked at the driver of his Humvee. "All right then."

"Don't call me again until you're within 50 yards of Barry Friar's home. Understand?"

"Uh huh." Sanders raised his eyebrows and scratched his head, finding himself in a precarious situation.

The general slammed the phone down on him.

Captain Sanders sighed as he handed the radio back to the driver and tapped a button on his headset. "Got the word from General Bryan. We're going with Plan A. Let's do it exactly as planned…"

"Plan A? You're serious?" a guardsman in an armored personnel carrier behind him responded.

"You heard me right, Plan A. Here we go, 60 seconds on my mark, three, two, one," he counted as everyone set watches simultaneously. "Get up that hill fast before they have time to adjust."

"What if they shoot?"

"They won't shoot…"

"What if they do?"

Sanders swallowed hard. "Then shoot back. They're the trespassers and murderers here. They murdered innocent people in search of a suspect they have no proof was even there. The lives of Barry Friar and his kids may very well depend on us."

Emotions in the Friar family wavered between great sorrow and hate – hate for the government, that anti-Christ Babylonian beast drunk with the blood of the saints prophesied about in the apocalyptic book of Revelation, hate for the wicked Jezebel of a president, and hate for the conscienceless beasts of the FBI and the ATF.

Barry sensed the malice rising in Theresa and Marion and decided to nip it in the bud. "God is our defender, do you hear me? 'Love them which hate you,' Jesus said. 'Vengeance is mine, I will repay,' saith the Lord. I don't want to hear any more bitter words." He was preaching to himself, too.

A loud megaphone stationed just outside the house interrupted Barry's counsel. The calm voice of the hostage negotiator thundered through the cracked and broken windows, **"Barry Friar, put down your weapons and come out with your hands up. You will not be harmed."**

Barry turned and studied his children. Their eyes were red with weeping and it was plain that Marion was in terrible pain. Nevertheless, they gripped their weapons tightly with a grim determination to defend their freedom to the end.

"Vicki!" the voice over the megaphone called out. Her name in their ears made them cringe with revived grief. **"Vicki, if you love your children, let them go and everything will go well with them. They will not be harmed and probably not even be charged with any crime..."**

"You killed Vicki!" Barry screamed at them. The negotiator paused when he thought he heard a voice coming from inside the building, that voice being amplified by microphones drilled into the walls of the house. Barry screamed it again, "You killed my wife, you animals!"

"Bet those weekend warriors are wetting their britches 'bout now," remarked an FBI agent at the bottom of the hill, his grin crooked thanks to a jaw full of chewing tobacco.

"The gall of those idiots!" Sergeant Roger Hammel leaned against the front of the Hummer closest to the barricade. He put the megaphone up to his mouth and walked in front of the barricade a few steps. "What ya waiting for?" he shouted to the guardsmen, the magnified sound of his mockery echoing through the foothills. "Stop sniffing your underarms and go home. What do you want, fireworks, want us to dance and sing for ya, entertain ya?" He did a fancy two-step on the road in front of the blockade as the armed agents behind him chuckled.

"Show those hicks how to line dance, Sarge!"

Sergeant Hammel made an obscene gesture with both hands at the Guard forces below the hill. Then he turned to walk back to his Hummer.

Without warning, several engines simultaneously thundered to life behind him down the hill.

"What the—!"

Sergeant Hammel turned to see several of the Guard's armored personnel carriers and Hummers blaze off the road to the left of the barricade and through a shallow ditch. Some of them drove up the grassy, woody hill toward a clearing that led up to the southern end of the open field in view of the Friar's home. With renewed vigor at the insults of the Bureau, the guardsmen accelerated aggressively over the rough terrain.

One Guard Hummer crossed the ditch and drove up the hill on the grassy shoulder of the ditch, parallel to the driveway. Once it passed the barricade and the FBI vehicles at the bottom of the drive, the driver tried to make another leap of the ditch back onto the driveway, sending clods of dirt and sod flying into the air. The Hummer almost flipped before the driver regained control and accelerated up the hill. A Guard personnel carrier continued up the hill parallel to the driveway on the far side of the ditch, driving over bushes and trying to evade stumps and trees.

The FBI agents at the blockade let out a collective gasp, stunned by the newfound audacity of the Montana guardsmen.

Sergeant Hammel spewed a string of vulgarities as he hopped back into the passenger seat of his Hummer. He tapped his earpiece. "Daren! Ray! Intercept them!" FBI vehicles spun wheels and spat dirt and gravel into the air as agents quickly gave heed to Hammel's urgent orders. An FBI personnel carrier followed on the heels of the guardsmen headed through the southern clearing in the woods up to the Friar's field. Once they caught up, they saw the machine-gun operator in the Guard's rear Hummer aim his .50 caliber machine gun at them, so they followed at a safe distance.

Hammel screamed into his radio to the FBI agents at the inner perimeter at the hilltop where the driveway spilled into the open field on the east side of the Friar's home. "They're coming up the hill! The Montana Guard is coming!"

Hammel prepared to turn the vehicle around and pursue up the driveway, but he changed his mind when he noticed a Guard Hummer and an armored personnel carrier idling below him on the driveway. If he abandoned the roadblock, they'd certainly pursue him up the hill, effectively collapsing the outer perimeter.

An ATF captain and an FBI agent in a van at the top of the driveway were discussing a bet they had on how long the siege would last when they heard Hammel's warning. They simultaneously grabbed their radios. "What? Say again?"

"The Guard's coming! Prepare for engagement! They're coming up both sides of the driveway and another force is driving west of you to try and exploit the clearing in the woods just south of the house."

The agents at the top of the driveway jumped out of their black van with white FBI letters on the side, just in time to hear the rumble of the roaring engines rapidly approaching. They both began to shout orders at their subordinates as they rushed behind the van, intending to use it for cover. They loaded and cocked their weapons as Hammel instructed them over their radio: "Use force if necessary! Keep them out of the field!"

"Lethal force?"

"Is there any other kind of force?"

One of the FBI agents in charge of maintaining the inner perimeter at the top of the gravel driveway began to shout into his megaphone toward the approaching camouflaged vehicles. "Stop! Stop immediately!"

At the bottom of the hill, FBI Sergeant Roger Hammel was stunned as the two Guard vehicles directly in front of him slowly pulled forward to within six feet of his barricade. Hammel shouted into the megaphone, "I order you to retreat from the site of this siege immediately by order of the United States government! Call your forces back behind the barricade or you risk an armed conflict and federal charges if you survive it!" He glanced to his right at the Guard vehicles that made their way up the hill toward the southern field, much to the dismay of the federal agents in the personnel carrier and the FBI Hummer following in their dusty wake over the steep, rocky terrain. He saw one of the FBI Hummers slide sideways off of a steep area of the terrain and flip onto its side, its roll halted by a pine tree.

Captain Sanders, who was in the Hummer below Hammel nearest the barricade, grinned to see a nervous look on the face of this cocky FBI sergeant.

The agent at the top of the driveway walked behind their wooden barricade, shouting into his megaphone at the Guard vehicles that were coming full-speed up the hill in a cloud of dust. "Stop!" He waved his arms over his head. "I order you to stop!" He felt a tug on his arm.

"Graham's got company!"

He turned to look at the field on the south side of the Friar's home. Agent Graham was disseminating snipers into positions around the home in the field and in the trees when the first Guard vehicle came out of the woods onto the field.

The driver of the Guard's armored personnel carrier pulled up through the southern clearing in the trees, over the rim of the hill, and entered the field in view of the Friar's home when ten camouflaged agents arose about 30 yards ahead of them. It appeared that they came right up out of the ground, their assault weapons hoisted to their shoulders and pointed toward their vehicle. The Guard Hummer was right on their tail.

"Captain Sanders," the guardsman in the passenger seat of the first vehicle shouted nervously into his radio, "we have a line of camouflaged snipers in front of us impeding progress to the house."

"And behind us," said the driver of the Hummer behind them into his radio. "We have snipers in the trees! Five o'clock and eight o'clock! We await instructions, Captain Sanders."

"Sergeant Hammel! What do we do?" the agent driving Hammel's Humvee asked. "The outer perimeter is collapsing. We need to reverse and offer support at the top of the hill."

"Ah!" Hammel exclaimed, frustrated. He looked back up the gravel drive and could see through the trees that the Guard vehicles had slowed to a stop in front of the barricade at the top of the hill at the FBI's inner perimeter. "Turn around! Get to the top!"

The driver did a quick three-point turn and sped to the top of the gravel driveway. Captain Sanders' men moved the barricade off the driveway and pursued Hammel up the hill.

At the top of the hill, Hammel came to a halt behind the Guard Hummer, and Guard Captain Sanders parked behind FBI Sergeant Hammel's Hummer, boxing him in. Sanders could see 20 federal agents lined up with fully automatic machine guns pointed and ready for action behind their vehicles and their barricade. He saw Hammel and his men step out of their Hummer, walk past the Guard vehicles in front of them, and join their men behind their orange barricade.

"Send Wilson to man the .50 cal on the feds' Hummer in front of us," Sanders ordered the senior officer in the Bradley behind him.

"Yes sir."

The urgency was even more extreme at the southern end of the field, thanks to a guardsman manning the .50 cal who continued to act like he would shoot at the federal agents nearest him. He shifted his aim from a nearby sniper, to the ATF vehicle behind him, to another sniper; he did so repeatedly, looking down his sights and tapping his finger against his trigger, daring the federal agents to do anything about it.

"Sergeant Hammel!" shouted the ATF agent who drove a personnel carrier behind the Guard vehicles through the southern clearing. They came to a halt when they came within 20 yards of the Guard vehicles. "Sergeant, we've reached an impasse!"

The agent driving the Hummer behind the Guard vehicles shouted to the soldier who stood behind their mounted machine gun, "Hold your fire!"

"They're aiming their .50 cal at us, sir!" the machine-gunner shouted back, his gaze darting back and forth between the senior agent and the guardsman manning the machine gun on top of the Guard Hummer.

"They're crazy!"

"Captain Sanders!" The guardsman in the passenger seat of one of the Guard's Bradley Fighting Vehicles on the southern edge of the Friar's property spoke into his mic, "Should we hold this position or retreat?"

The guardsman next to him had a look in his rearview mirrors, and corrected him. "We can't retreat!" The ATF vehicles behind them drew too close for them to reverse. They were hemmed in.

"We're surrounded, Captain Sanders, and outnumbered."

"Hold your position," Sanders informed them calmly by way of his headset mic as he stepped out of the Hummer and began to approach the federal blockade at the top of the gravel driveway.

Guardsmen exited the vehicles on each side of the gravel driveway, took cover behind their Hummers and Bradley Fighting Vehicles, and spread out to take cover behind several pine trees. The drivers of the Guard vehicles revved their engines as the machine-gunners kept their .50 caliber machine guns aimed at the agents squatting behind the roadblock.

"What do we do, Sergeant Hammel?" a nervous ATF agent beside him asked. "They're moving in the woods. They're flanking us."

Sergeant Hammel held a .44 caliber semi-automatic Desert Eagle handgun tightly in his right hand, contemplating the various contingencies before him. "Hold them where they are and await my signal," he barked angrily into his headset.

Hammel saw Captain Sanders walking up the driveway and Hammel, seeking to step up his aggressive tone with the feisty Montana Guard captain, rapidly stomped up to him. They met at the barricade, their fists clenched. "If you wanted a violent confrontation on my mountain, son," Hammel shouted at Sanders, "you're about to get your wish!"

"Your mountain?" Captain Rod Sanders was fed up with the infantile machismo of this arrogant Bureau agent. Captain Sanders put his pointed index finger within six inches of Hammel's determined grimace. "Is your cover-up really that important to you? Do you really want a war?" He stared deliberately into Hammel's squinty eyes.

"Only if you want to lose one!" Sergeant Hammel didn't miss a beat or flinch the slightest.

Rod Sanders huffed, turned, and marched back to his Hummer.

"Retreat back down this mountain," Hammel warned him, "or I'll arrest you!"

Sanders stopped ten steps away from the barricade and leaned against the Hummer that idled below the roadblock. "Whoever gets killed here today, I promise you that you will definitely be one of them." Sanders turned and shouted to his men as he made his way behind the Hummer, taking cover behind it, "Fire on my command!" The guardsmen behind him enthusiastically raised their weapons to their shoulders and clicked them off safety. The machine-gunner on the Hummer ducked behind his steel shields. Mortar rockets were loaded into the launchers of the Guard's Bradleys.

The federal agents behind Hammel began to shout nervously, "Sergeant Hammel?"

Hammel's countenance changed. "You have *got* to be kidding." He took a step forward, and shouted loudly, "You have got to be kidding me!"

Sanders stepped out from behind the cover of the Hummer, holding tightly to his handgun. "I've got orders to set up a watch within view of Barry Friar's house." Sanders pointed at the house in the center of the field 100 yards away. "If you don't accommodate me, then I'll take that position by force. I'm willing to die to fulfill my orders, how about you?" He paused for about ten slow seconds. "Make up your mind! Move or fight, ball's in your court. I'll give you a minute or two to decide if you want to fire the first shot. Because if you don't, I will." Captain Sanders ducked back behind the Hummer.

"Wait!" said Sergeant Hammel, placing his huge handgun back into his holster and putting both palms into the air. "Do you really want to fire on your government? Do you want another civil war?"

"This war won't be civil!" Sanders shouted from behind the Hummer.

"Wait!" shouted Hammel anxiously. "Um, wait! Let me make a phone call and see if we can accommodate —"

"I'll give you one minute," Sanders interrupted, "and if you're still on the phone with that *wench*, you'll have to move out of the way to finish your conversation because we're coming through, whether you like it or not."

"Hold on..."

"Fifty-nine."

Sergeant Hammel was shocked at the brazen fearlessness of these Montana guardsmen. He had witnessed such insubordination among hardened criminals, conspiracy theorists, tax protesters, and advocates of hate and armed revolt, but never among state employees. He jumped into the FBI van and slammed the door. "Get Todd Hamilton on the line!"

The numb agent to whom he directed the order just stared at him, stunned at the turn of events. He stammered, "This van isn't armored, Sergeant. We should abandon it for the cover of the —"

"I need Hamilton! Now!"

Sanders stepped back into his Hummer and donned his headset. The driver of the Hummer looked over at the confident Guard captain beside him. "Are you really gonna do this?"

Sanders, without glancing over at his driver, flicked a button on the dash to magnify his voice. "Forty-five seconds left!"

"What's takin' so long?" Hammel shouted at the agent that manned communications in the van. "Forget Hamilton, get the president on the line now! Get her on the phone now!"

"All right."

"Now!"

"I'm dialing, I'm dialing..."

"Come on!"

Barry heard the shouts through distant megaphones and engines roaring on his driveway and he grew curious.

"Wonder what that is?" Teresa asked.

"They're bringing in more troops to surround us and flush us out with tear gas," Marion predicted.

Barry held up a small mirror that he'd retrieved from one of the purses with a pair of tongs from the kitchen. He angled the mirror so he could see the commotion. "Well, I'll be!" Barry's optimistic tone surprised Marion and Teresa.

"Who is it?"

"It's the Guard."

Marion's bleeding had stopped but his arm was swelling terribly. His pain kept him conscious in spite of the blood loss that brought him to the edge of delirium.

"With the Guard in view of the home, they might not shoot us. We have to get you out of here."

"No way, Papa." Marion shook his head side to side. "I'm here for the duration."

"You're as white as a sheet. You're gonna bleed to death."

"And for a good cause!" he snapped.

Barry looked at his children and the sight of his infant son, Timmy, made his bottom lip tremble with a mixture of grief and fear.

Teresa must have read his thoughts. "The baby's fine. Mom knew she'd be busy with the barbeque, so she pumped some breast milk and stored it in the diaper bag." Teresa motioned to the blue diaper bag that lay on its side next to her behind the couch, contents partially spilling onto the floor.

"Teresa, I want you to hold a white blanket from that diaper bag up into the air with these tongs and walk out of this place with that baby in your arms."

"No, dad, please. They'll kill me."

"I am very, very proud of you. Both of you."

"I'm staying with you!" Teresa insisted, tears welling up in her eyes. "You're all I have. Please let me stay with you."

"Me too." Marion squinted in pain. "I can, I can shoot as straight with my left as I can with my right," he stuttered, holding his Glock .357 handgun in the air for a second with his good arm.

"**Vicki – how's little Timmy?**" came the amplified voice of the federal hostage negotiator. Knowing that with the approaching Guard forces his time to negotiate surrender may be drawing to a close, his voice was more hurried. "**You need to show that you aren't going to harm your children. Let them go!**"

The sound of the roaring engines and shouting from the direction of his driveway caused Barry to hoist the small mirror with his tongs again to try to discover what was happening. "The Guard's at the edge of the field," he said, angling the mirror to see. "They're arguing with the feds." Suddenly, a bullet shattered the mirror that Barry held in the tongs. Like the quick spark of a cheap, damp firecracker, his renewed optimism at the sight of the Montana Guard quickly faded in the face of the darkest of realities.

He winced and tried to pluck some shards of glass out of his hand. "They're not gonna let us leave alive."

The blast of the bullet near the house reminded Captain Sanders of the desperate situation the Friar family was facing. His adrenaline stirred anew.

The driver of the Hummer on the edge of the southern field exclaimed into his headset, "That was from a sniper in the tree line behind us, Captain Sanders!"

Sanders looked in his rearview mirror and saw that federal vehicles were speeding up the drive to support the federal perimeter. It was now or never. "Last chance!" he shouted through his headset. "Get out of the way or get ready to dance." By the looks on the faces of the federal agents who faced him, they believed an armed conflict was momentarily going to erupt and they didn't like it one bit. Shooting down teenagers with .22s is quite different from facing off against automatic weapons and mortars 20 yards away from a superior force with better position and cover. The Guard could completely annihilate them in 20 terrifying seconds.

"Wait! We're trying to get the president," Sergeant Hammel cried out through his hand-held megaphone as he sat in the passenger seat of his Hummer. "I'm willing to accommodate you, but you're going to have to be patient. The president doesn't carry a cell—"

"Sixty!" Sanders wasn't waiting around for the president to tell this FBI stooge that he wasn't allowed to give the Guard an inch, and they were going to lose their advantage if the FBI vehicles coming up the driveway reached their position. Rod Sanders gave the order and the two Guard Hummers and the two Bradleys lunged to the right and the left of the barricade, crossing over bushes, maneuvering around trees, and crashing through a waist-high wood fence.

"Fire only if fired upon!" Hammel shouted with his megaphone in one hand and a sat phone, which rang in the Oval Office, in the other. His men prepared to fire, but he prevented them. "Hold your fire!" The agents sighed with relief. Hammel hung up the phone before it was answered and turned to his driver. "Follow at a safe distance. Slowly!"

"Eat my dust!" Rod grinned as he looked into his rear-view mirror at the agents they were leaving behind. The guardsmen who took cover in the woods ran behind the Guard vehicles, intermittently aiming their weapons behind them at the federal forces.

The driver slowed as he approached the camouflaged FBI snipers who had set up a perimeter close to the house. These dozen agents had already tasted blood and had seen their comrades die the day before. They were battle tested and prepared to face off.

"Captain Sanders!" shouted the guardsman in the passenger seat of the Hummer at the edge of the southern field. When Sanders crossed the barricade, several more camouflaged snipers rose up from the thick grass all around the house. "Captain! Help me out a bit."

"Hold your position. We're coming."

When Hammel gave the order, the federal snipers retreated to the west and north sides of the house, causing the guardsmen to laugh, high-five each other, and pat each other's backs, elated. But their laughs came to a quick halt when they heard the roar of hovering Blackhawk helicopters. The Bradley Fighting Vehicles quickly took aim at the helicopters with their rockets in case missiles were about to be fired at them.

Sanders looked out of his window at the heavily armed birds circling overhead. "Follow my lead!" he shouted enthusiastically. He led the two fighting vehicles and two Hummers up the driveway to within 40 yards of the house, near the shot-up cars in front. One Blackhawk copter landed on the northeast side of the house and the other on the southeast side of the house, between the federal forces and the Guard forces. The third Blackhawk continued to circle the house.

Chapter 13

A stalemate ensued over the next 24 hours. The feds weren't budging another inch and the Guard wasn't prepared to kill federal agents in order to get into the house.

The walls seemed to be closing in on Barry Friar. His children kept him sane, but his fear and paranoia spewed the most terrifying images before his mind, testing the bounds of his faith. Flies were buzzing around his wife's carcass. He had stopped trying to swat them away. She was dead and those flies were just doing their job. He could see a cloud of flies orbiting the carcass on the stairs. The smell of death was everywhere. The bloodstains in the ceiling and at the top of the staircase had faded from bright red to a dull brown.

Barry found a black marker on the kitchen floor and was able to scribble on a white baby-blanket, "FEDS KILLED WIFE & SHOT KIDS! MEDIA?" He hung it out of a broken window, hoping to garner some more public sympathy.

Under the cover of the Blackhawk helicopters, the feds brought in tanks, which began to circle the house. The tanks crushed several cars that were in the way of the track they formed around the home. With the Guard present, the snipers stopped firing into the home. As the leaders of the Guard and the federal government traded insults and threats, despair was growing in the Friar's living room. The baby was drinking the last of his formula. Marion, who had been doing his part keeping watch during half the night, was now waning in and out of consciousness.

The electricity was disconnected, so their water pump was unable to pump water from their well; thus, Barry was forced to clean Marion's wound with water retrieved from the tank behind the toilet. With the spreading erythema, he feared that infection was setting in. On one occasion Barry turned and accidentally bumped into Marion's arm, and Marion screamed for about 20 seconds and then slipped into unconsciousness for about two minutes. When he awoke, he cried for his mother, and they all wept again. Their mourning echoed across the hillside, winning no sympathy from the soldiers who mocked their grief and waited patiently for revenge.

Teresa played with the baby as often as possible to keep him from crying. But the child longed for his mother and couldn't be consoled. Barry could hear Teresa's sobbing quietly during the night.

When the sun set at the end of the second day, the feds set up huge bright lights and large speakers all around the house. At midnight, they commenced the next stage in breaking down an enemy. The bright lights shone through the windows and the speakers blared extremely loud animal noises interspersed with heavy metal music. Sleep was impossible. The baby screamed himself hoarse, unable to rest because of the fearful noise and because of the cold that freely entered through the shattered windows.

In the morning, the children slept and Barry kept watch. He heard a new noise and crawled on his belly toward the window. He heard chanting.

"What is that?" Teresa roused from her slumber with the sleeping baby still in her arms.

"Sounds like protesters at the bottom of the hill."

A crowd of 150 gathered at the foot of the small mountain upon which the Friar's home was situated. It continued to swell with every minute as word of the siege spread. The FBI set up some barricades with orange barrels and yellow police tape to keep the protesters contained. Only the roof of the Friar's home was barely visible through the trees. The fog clung eerily to the mountain late into the morning. Having heard nothing about the Friar family's state of health since the siege began, they wondered and prayed for their safety.

Those who knew the Friars well took turns praising them for their faithfulness to God and each other. Some fellow hunters told of Barry and Marion Friar's hunting exploits. The soft-spoken wife of Sheriff Randy Woods was there to update them all on her husband. The crowd growled in disgust when she told them that he was being held without charge, without bail, without counsel, and without a trial. They gasped when she informed them of her son, Jeremiah's, disappearance.

An elderly pastor from a church down the road from Barry Friar's little country church rallied the crowd to a raging frenzy as he preached. "We have tolerated the immoral tax scheme which steals from the diligent to give to the lazy. We have tolerated the murder of innocent babies. We have tolerated the bloated, massive centralized government that intrudes into our lives in a thousand unconstitutional ways. We have tolerated the immoral sex ed programs in public schools that promote fornication and sodomy. We have tolerated the government's education system that pumps out incompetent, humanistic pagan youth fit for the New World Order. We have tolerated the perversion of justice in the government's cover-ups and unlawful sieges. We have tolerated the government's raid on churches that refused to act as government agents in collecting taxes from their employees. We have tolerated our government's unconstitutional empire building and, when we endured terrorist attacks as a result of our intrusive foreign policy, we tolerated our leaders' attempts to protect illegal aliens and rescind the God-given liberties of natural-born citizens. We stood still and did nothing as armed federal agents terrorized Montana patriots and gun-owners. Hundreds of good people have been arrested, many of them ripped from their homes in the middle of the night. Sheriffs, mayors, and governors have been kidnapped by FBI thugs for refusing to enforce the tyrannical and unreasonable dictates of this presidential administration."

As the crowd listened intently, he turned to face the federal agents who gathered behind their barricade at the gravel driveway's entrance that led up to the Friar's residence. "We have stood still and done nothing as year after year, election after election, and generation after generation, you" - he pointed at the stone-faced agents - "have trampled on the rights of good Americans, justified the wicked and condemned the just, did violence to the law of God and the Constitution of these United States. I am here today to draw a line in the sand!" The crowd began to applaud and shout affirmations of agreement as they turned with their cheerleader to face the agents at the edge of the driveway. "In the name of Jesus, we order you to release Barry Friar and those good men you have arrested! We order you to release Sheriff Randy Woods!" His index finger was pointing and the veins were bulging out of his tanned, wrinkled neck. "Fear the Lord God of Israel and repent! We say to you, no more tyranny!" He shouted "No more tyranny!" two more times, louder each time, then his congregation kept it going for another ten minutes.

When the chanting died down someone else started a new chant, providing good fodder for urgent news reports that broadcast the highlights around the globe. "Death to tyrants! Obedience to God! Death to tyrants! Obedience to God!" Fists were raised in symbolic defiance as the shouts echoed through the green Montana foot-hills and over the ragged, immovable Rocky Mountain ridges. The agents were attentive but didn't respond to the passionate rebukes and vague threats that were called out to them from a crowd of Montanans intoxicated with bitterness and rage.

A retired Marine who helped organize the protest walked to the podium with a cell phone in one hand and the other lifted heaven-ward. He'd been listening to the news through his Walkman and heard the Montana governor's comment on the siege. The Marine thought that this was the proper time to inform these people of just what lengths the federal government will go to destroy the people of Yahweh. "I have bad news!" he shouted. The crowd quieted. "I have bad news!" The crowd held its breath as he addressed them. "I want all of you to hold hands. That's an order. Hold the hand of the person to your left and right." After a pause, he said, "Barry, Marion, Teresa, and the baby are alive, but I have just heard Governor Boswell report at a press conference that Vicki Friar has been shot and killed."

A unified, bitter wail instantly erupted like lava from a trembling volcano. "Matt Friar has also been killed. Marion and Teresa Friar have been injured by gunshots."

There was much weeping as ladies and church members hugged and comforted each other. The young children present had looks of horror on their faces as they embraced their parents and each other. Though their love for America's heritage and people was steadfast, they were growing to hate their nation's government more and more every day.

The pastor went to his pickup truck and retrieved a fading yellow "Don't Tread On Me" flag. He stood on a lawn chair and began to wave it vigorously as tears of rage flowed down his face.

Some young people brought an American flag in front of the barricade on the driveway and burned it, much to the pleasure of the TV cameramen who zoomed in.

The Marine stepped forward and sternly rebuked the youth as he put out the fire. "They're the ones that destroy our flag and everything it stands for - not us!"

The guardsmen who set up in view of the Friar's house didn't expect to be left without food and water for an entire day, but the FBI had set up another perimeter below them and it was impossible for reinforcements to bring supplies without risking another showdown for which the FBI was much more prepared. The guardsmen were angry about the bright lights and the nightmarish music that blared into the Friar home all night long and were ready for action.

"Captain Sanders?" Governor Boswell spoke into his speakerphone from behind his desk.

Rod Sanders was getting stiff from so many hours inside his Hummer at the southeastern edge of the Friar's home, just outside the trek of the FBI tanks. He tapped his headset. "Yes sir?"

"The FBI is still refusing to cooperate with us," Governor Boswell informed him.

"We should have kept going when we got here yesterday. They've tripled their numbers, sir, and beefed up their perimeter above and below us. A tank and a Blackhawk haven't taken their guns off us for a second. All of our reinforcements are stuck at the bottom of the hill."

"I want those state investigators in that house. That's an order I have not retracted. They've cleaned up the carcasses, gathered up all the evidence, and have complete control over the witnesses by having them locked up somewhere. We can't trust their investigation. We *have* to get inside that home and speak to Friar. We have to send some medical care in there for the kids."

"Sergeant Hammel said that if they want medical care, they could come out with their hands up. They can't be reasoned with, sir."

Governor Boswell sighed. "I'm dealing with the same attitude with the FBI's head honcho in D.C."

"But they *can* be intimidated. We've proven that by getting up this mountain. They know they couldn't justify trampling on the Montana State Guard like they've done our citizens."

"Okay, Mr. Intimidator," said Governor Boswell, giving Captain Sanders a nick-name that would stick for the rest of his life, "you're the man for the job. Make Montana proud. You get those investigators and physicians into that house."

Sanders half smiled, half winced at the title that the governor had given him. He liked it. *Is it worth being brought up on federal charges?* he thought to himself. *Is it worth the deaths of some of your men?* "Can't think of a reason to die or get locked up in a federal pen," Sanders responded pessimistically.

"Excuse me? I don't want to hear that!" the governor rebuked his pessimism. "You *will* accomplish this mission, Captain Rod Sanders, and you will not be impeded by any miserable specks of humanity. No token defeats. You get into that house."

Ten minutes later, one of the two tanks parked on the north side of the house as the other tank continued to make laps around the home. Captain Sanders considered it divine intervention. If one of the tanks or Blackhawks intervened, his plan wouldn't work. Could they take on a tank and survive? *Maybe a grenade in the barrel would cripple it.* Sanders reached into a compartment in the dash and removed two grenades. He clipped them to his belt. Then he removed his cell phone and speed-dialed a number.

The guardsman behind the driver seat protested, "I don't know what you're thinking, Captain, but—"

"Here!" Sanders handed him his cell phone. "It's ringing my Pastor's office, Pastor Miller. You tell him that I'm gonna need some prayer coverage, now!"

"What?" The guardsman took the cell phone and Sanders stepped outside of the Hummer.

The FBI's barricades were set out in front of him in the shape of a "U." Sanders walked up to the blockade to the right of the Hummer, nearest to FBI Sergeant Hammel's vehicle.

Hammel was sitting on the footstep of the open door of his Hummer and didn't even look at Sanders when he motioned for him.

"Let's not be childish. You can't ignore me, Sergeant." Sanders tapped on the waist-high white and orange reflective barricade.

Hammel stood and faced the guardsman. "Those investigators aren't setting foot on this property!" he barked as he flicked a half-lit cigarette onto the ground. "No way!" Spit flew from his mouth in different directions as he hollered.

Sanders stayed calm. "Oh, we know you ain't gonna shoot us in the back, so stop actin' all macho."

"I'm in charge of this siege on these murderers and illegal arms dealers, Barry Friar and Fred Seibert," he barked, pointing at the house. "If you try anything like that suicidal stunt you tried before, I'll have you personally arrested and brought up on federal charges."

Sanders glanced at his watch and changed his tone. With the gravest frown he could muster he said, "There's something you just don't understand, Sergeant Hammel. Montana doesn't trust you. Now, if we discover that the men have committed legitimate crimes, then we'll have them prosecuted. But the sword has two-edges, Sergeant Hammel, because if we discover that you or your men have broken the law, then it will be *you* in the defendant's chair in front of a Montana jury."

Hammel's face reddened and he pointed his index finger at Sanders, and began to scold him like a drunk with a hangover would scold a boy who spilled his liquor.

The shouting had drawn the attention of several agents around the barricade and they walked up to listen to the argument.

"You're all a bunch of social mutants, you know that?" Hammel shouted at Sanders. "I've got a mind to shoot Barry Friar in the head just to watch you tinkle in your panties and cry your crocodile tears."

Those derogatory comments made Sanders grit his teeth, ready for a fight. He just stared into the eyes of Roger Hammel for a moment, studying him.

"What are you gonna do, weekend warrior?" Hammel said, mocking him, as the other agents laughed. "Huh?"

Six agents monitored the protesters at the bottom of the hill from behind some construction barricades. As if on cue, two of the protesters began to argue with one another. Shoving and pushing commenced and an argument soon broke out among several others.

"Uh oh," one agent mumbled to the other.

Soon, the fight progressed into a frenzied melee with dozens of locals punching, spitting, and tackling one another.

One of the federal agents contacted Hammel through his headset. "Sergeant Hammel, we're going to need more men at the bottom of the hill. The locals are getting into a big fight."

Suddenly two loud bangs rang out from the center of the crowd of fighting locals. The federal agents ducked and raised their weapons. The startled agent spoke into his headset, "Gunshots at the bottom of the hill. I repeat, we have shots fired at the bottom of the hill."

Hammel heard the gunshots and mumbled, "Please, no."

"The protesters are getting into a gunfight," the senior agent nearest the barricade at the bottom of the hill informed the FBI sergeant. "We're being threatened." The agent joined the others nearby who raised their M16s and began to search the crowd for someone with a gun.

"Good grief." Hammel sighed and backed away from Captain Sanders. "You six," - he pointed at six agents that stood to the right of him - "get in the Hummer and get down there. Call base to let them know what's happening."

"Yes sir."

Hammel turned away from Rod Sanders and spoke into his headset to the agents manning the inner perimeter at the top of the driveway to his east. "Weldon! Get some men down there and clean that up."

The FBI agents closed in on the protesters at the bottom of the hill to get the situation under control. "Who's got the gun?" the agents took turns shouting with their rifles at the ready. "Who's got the gun?"

None of the protesters responded. As they began to back up in response to the approaching armed federal agents, one of the agents noticed a large detonated firecracker on the ground.

"What's this?" He reached down and picked it up. It was warm.

Suddenly, the Guard Hummer beside Rod Sanders and Roger Hammel jolted forward with a roar and crashed through the wooden barricade the feds had set up directly in front of it.

Sergeant Hammel was aghast. He grabbed for his two-way radio, but stopped when he saw Rod Sanders pull a .45 caliber Colt handgun from a rear-seated holster and point it into the air.

"You see this little handgun?" Sanders asked calmly, stepping closer to Sergeant Hammel. Hammel froze in shock.

"What the... **Put that thing down!**" shouted Hammel, his face reddening. The four agents nearby raised their guns up to their shoulders, preparing to fire at Guard Captain Rod Sanders. They appeared confused, as if they didn't know if they should protect Hammel or pursue the Guard Hummer as it sped toward the front entrance of the Friar's home.

"Wait, just a minute," said Sanders calmly with his gun still aimed just above the head of Roger Hammel. "Watch this." Sanders switched it off safety and chambered a round. The four agents jolted with their fingers on their triggers, awaiting the order to fire from Sergeant Hammel.

"Hey! Hey!" several soldiers shouted. Even snipers at the perimeter of the property came out of concealment to aid Hammel, their weapons aimed at Captain Sanders' head.

"You're psychotic!" Hammel shouted. "Do you have a death wish?"

"These hollow points mushroom out when they strike your body," Rod said as he waved his hands outward, outlining the expanding mushroom-shape the bullet makes when it contacts its target. He spoke with a calmness that surprised even the agents who pointed their guns at his chest and head. Sergeant Hammel just stared at him with a look of shock on his face. "The question you have to ask yourself, Mr. Hammel, does one of these have your name on it? Will they bury you with one of these embedded in your brain?"

"Put that gun down or I'll have you shot!"

Sanders didn't flinch, but rather, spoke in a relaxed tone as he held his gun pointed into the air. "Right now, I see *your* attempts to block *our* investigation as an obstruction of justice." He glanced toward the home to see the state investigators and Dr. Lilly step out of his Hummer and make it to the foot of the stairs when four FBI agents intercepted them and physically prevented them from entering the home, their M16s aimed at their torsos. The driver of the Hummer stepped out and unholstered his handgun, and the second guardsman manned the .50 cal. Sanders turned back to the FBI sergeant. "We *will* investigate the crime scene and we *will* interview the suspects!"

He looked around at the four agents dressed in black who were equally spaced apart around him. "You boys can be brought up on state charges of obstructing justice if you interfere with Montana's attempt to look into these allegations. And if I see you shoot or try to shoot anybody else in our state, I'll shoot you myself. That'd be what you call, *justifiable* homicide. That may be all Barry Friar's guilty of, and that'll earn him the key to the city in Garrison. We still execute murderers in Montana and I can guarantee you that your employment in the FBI will win you no sympathy from our juries."

Hammel got a buzz on his two-way radio and Sanders took advantage of the distraction and tried to walk quickly past the agents who aimed their weapons at him, but Hammel stopped him. "Wait! I'll let you go, but you've got to take an FBI investigator with you. Wait a minute."

Captain Sanders took a deep breath. He fully expected his little drama to conclude with his arrest or his death, and was downright giddy that he was still in action. This was a small concession and he was willing to consent to it if it could get him into the house.

Hammel tapped on his two-way radio. "Weldon. You got Investigator Canton over there?"

Agent Weldon, who was in charge of monitoring the eastern perimeter at the top of the driveway, responded in the affirmative.

"Get him over here, now!" Sanders snapped. "Let him know that he's going to go in with the guardsmen posing as their physician's assistant."

Sanders glanced at the foot of the stairs in front of the Friar's home, where the white-haired Guard physician and the state investigator waited nervously, knowing that crosshairs were aimed at them from all over the field.

When Sanders saw the federal investigator in his white shirt and tie head out across the field, he walked briskly toward the front of the home and waited for him.

"How did you do that?" Montana state investigator Chavez asked, still trembling from the tense confrontation.

Captain Sanders didn't answer. He just smiled, finding it incredulous that they let him get away with what he just did. He mumbled, "Thank you, Jesus," as the tank turned the corner and aimed its rocket at them. The federal investigator slowly made his way toward them from across the field.

"What's wrong with you, Hammel?!" Hamilton was furious at the failure of the FBI to keep the Montana State Guard and the state investigator away from the Friars' property.

"When he pulled the gun, I just didn't know what else to do."

"So big and bad, weren't going to take anything from anybody, isn't that what you said? Now you're letting yourself get pushed around by a couple of weekend warriors from Outhouse County, Montana! Fine soldier you are. They're laughing at you, Sergeant, just laughin' their heads off at the whole Bureau right now!"

"Excuse me, sir," Hammel spoke as boldly as he dared, "but your temper tantrum's going to have to wait. I need an answer and I need it immediately." Hammel paced back and forth beside his Hummer while Todd Hamilton cursed behind his desk in D.C. "They're inside the tank perimeter and on the front porch, Mr. Hamilton, and they're preparing to enter."Who again?"

"A state investigator, a Guard field surgeon, and a crazy Guard captain named Rod Sanders. He has made it clear that he's not afraid to kill or be killed. I can't believe what he just did."

"This is a contest of wills, Sergeant Hammel, and we need to win it. It's poker with blank cards. They're all bluff."

"Our cards are blank too. That's the problem. They can't be intimidated. They know we aren't going to shoot them."

"Well, maybe we should! If they pull a gun on you again, I'd say the line's been—"

Hammel balked and interrupted. "Well, what do you want me to do? Shoot them right now where they stand? They're mannin' .50 cals, sir, and their Bradleys have mortar rockets. Now I'm content to let our federal investigator go in with them. He intends to pose as a physician's assistant. I need a decision now."

"Is your federal investigator armed?" Investigator Canton walked up to Hammel just as Hamilton asked the question.

"He's here, I'll ask him. Canton, are you armed?"

The investigator nodded as he straightened his tie, worn for the planned media interviews. "Always."

"If I know Canton," Hammel told Hamilton, "he'll be glad to take out Friar and company if the opportunity arises."

"You get your boys ready for a full-scale charge if gunshots are fired inside that house, understand? And tell Canton we don't want any eyewitnesses to contradict his recall of events. Our investigation will confirm his testimony."

"Yes sir."

Montana state investigator Chavez and the white-haired physician shook the federal investigator's hand when he reached them.

"I'll be going in as a physician's assistant," the federal investigator whispered, cautious about being overheard by the Friars inside.

"You're unarmed, right?" Sanders asked him.

"Of course."

Sanders raised an eyebrow and smirked, disbelieving him. "If you try anything, you'll be in a world of hurt. Do you understand?" The fed nodded more politely than Sanders expected. "All right then."

The federal agents that blocked their access to the front entrance backed away and Captain Sanders scaled the stairs. He shouted through a broken window beside the front door. "Barry Friar? I'm a captain in the Montana State Guard. I'm going to enter with a state investigator, a Montana Guard field surgeon, and a physician's assistant. Governor Boswell has ordered us to interview you and care for your medical needs."

From the shadows of the living room, Barry Friar aimed his AR15 at the four men who tarried on his front porch.

"Don't let them in, dad," Marion insisted with a whisper. "They're lying."

The door creaked open when Sanders attempted to knock. "We're coming in. Don't shoot."

Chapter 14

Deer Lodge, Montana

"And where are we going to get the explosives?" Lonny reclined comfortably on the narrow, sheetless mattress inside the small, dilapidated RV.

Bull was sitting backwards in a chair in the RV's kitchenette. They were just outside the border of the Deer Lodge National Forest at the foothills of a mountain among some untended pines. The RV was dusty and moldy, the carpet was stained and the sink dripped when the water was hooked up, but it was suitably stealthy for Bull and company. Bull laid his arms on the back of the chair and rested his chin on his forearm, deep in thought. Blowing up a federal building wasn't as easy as he had fantasized.

"You probably can't even get within 100 feet of federal buildings right now without some sort of a pass," Bull's pessimistic twin brother commented.

"That's right." Lonny nodded. "They're on high alert."

"Besides…" Stein paused to wiggle his black beret up and down on his head.

"Besides what?" Bull blurted out, irritated that his brother would start a sentence and then not finish.

"Besides, you don't want to kill innocent people to make a point. I mean, killing those who murdered our friends is one thing. Shooting Margaret Brighton in the face point-blank range with a double-barrel shotgun loaded with magnum, three-inch, double-ought buckshot - now that's an idea I could dig." Both Lonny and Bull chuckled and high-fived. "But I don't want innocent people to suffer."

"This is war, bro. You're going to have collateral damage."

"I want to shoot the tyrants," Stein responded, "the bureaucrats with the lists of patriots and gun-owners, the murderers – not secretaries and janitors."

"Well, what do you wanna do?" snapped Bull. "Want to go back up to Friar's place and take out a few more of those agents?"

Stein laughed and Lonny exclaimed, "You're insane."

"I'm serious! I can hit a couple of them from the top of that mountain with

my .450 magnum before they even know what hit 'em. If I can catch two of them standing next to each other, I can get a couple of them with one bullet! And there's no way they can catch me in those woods."

"They already have people on that mountain top, probably looking for you." Stein poked his brother in the chest. "Probably got satellites looking down on those mountains with infra-red imaging."

Bull swatted away the hand of his predictably cautious, smaller twin brother. "All three of us could probably take out ten of 'em without even thinking twice."

"You're thinkin' too small, Bull." Lonny leaned forward with his elbows on his knees. "We need to think through all of our options and come up with a bigger plan to maximize our influence."

"As well as our chances of escape," added Stein.

"I've got a lot of firepower right there in the trunk." Bull motioned to his camouflage-painted pick-up truck, wherein he kept a stash of gunpowder, bullets, and firearms. "We have to act quickly, move fast, and act again. We can't wait around while Brighton terrorizes our people."

Stein rolled his eyes at Bull's haste and impatience.

"Stein!" Bull barked, irritated. "Don't look at me like that! You know what? You're a follower. I'm a leader. Why don't you help instead of being so critical? Give me some ideas other than cowardly ones that send us retreating forever."

"Calm down, Bull. I'm just saying we don't need to do anything impulsive."

Bull whipped out his bronze butterfly knife and began to scrape its edge against the wooden back of the chair. "Why don't we order pizza, some cold beer, rent *Braveheart* for the umpteenth millionth time and then we can *grow old* in this RV talking about what we're going to do someday when we get that golden opportunity that'll *never* come!"

"Don't ruin the chair," Lonny told Bull, who didn't listen and continued chiseling crosshairs in the wood.

"I just want to make it count, Bull," Stein protested.

"Listen to me. I'm going to do something big and I'm going to do it now, like this week. If you're not with me, let me know. The amount of collateral damage I'm willing to consider acceptable is growing by the day."

"At least they got the Guard up there," remarked Stein.

"Big deal!" responded Bull, glancing up from his artistic vandalism. "What do you think they're gonna do against the feds? And how do you know that they aren't in on it?"

Lonny snapped his fingers and stood to his feet. "I got an idea. Why didn't I think of this before?"

Bull and Stein looked up at their lanky friend, who had a look of ecstasy on his face as if he had just won a bucketful of poker cash with a full house.

Bull stabbed his butterfly knife into the back of the chair, hopeful. "What?"

This is perfect! thought Lonny as he drove up beside the pay-phone at the nearest gas station. He punched in some numbers he'd memorized, as well as a code number that was assigned to him, which enabled him to call anywhere in the world without paying for it. *This will look good.*

The phone rang three times. The voice that answered was deep and masculine, "ID?"

"Four, three, one, apple. Two, one, five, charlie zebra."

After a pause, the person on the other end of the phone said, "Just a moment. I'll put you through as soon as I pull Mr. Conway out of a meeting."

There was another pause and the phone rang again. Mr. Conway picked up. "How are things, Baldwin?"

"Mind telling me why I wasn't notified about a Bureau raid on a group that I had infiltrated?"

Conway, the Director of the Northwestern Division of the FBI, sighed wearily and ran his thin fingers through the thin gray hairs of his balding scalp. "What do you want me to do, send you a telegram?" Conway was a short man with a stubby nose and red face. He had a meticulously manicured gray goatee. An explosive temper underscored his reputation, but his tone was unusually apologetic with one of his top undercover agents.

"I could've been killed! You could've blown my cover! It's taken me years."

"I know, I know. Sorry Joe. Spoke to Todd Hamilton about you and it was his decision to keep you in the dark rather than take a chance informing you. Do you have our boy?"

"Of course!" he said confidently. "I had him *before* the raid! You should have just asked for him. And call me Lonny as long as I'm undercover, will ya?"

"The president needed a show for ratings, Lonny. It wasn't up to me. But we can salvage the raid if you can bring him in."

"I can bring him in pink lingerie if you want. He's a chump, as malleable as play dough." The tension eased and Conway laughed. "But I don't think we want to make our move on him just yet."

"Why not?"

"He wants to bomb a federal site."

Conway gasped. "Well, it looks like you were in the right place at the right time, Joe."

"Lonny!"

"Lonny. Where and when?"

"Maybe your building in Billings. He's a blank slate right now. He doesn't have the means or detailed plans. He's only got a few guns and about 1,000 rounds of ammo. But I told him I could probably get the explosives for him from an uncle that works for the

237

railroad and he's buying it. I'm pretty sure I could convince him to do it wherever I want."

"You're good, Joe."

"Lonny!"

"Sorry, Lonny."

"I want you to get the explosives to me."

There was a pause on the other end. "We don't really need to do that, Lonny. We already got him on murder of at least one federal agent and—"

"He told me that he killed two while escaping from the Friar's property and he helped Jack Handel get away. Handel also killed several agents while escaping."

"Jack Handel? The militia leader?"

"Yep. Want his address? He's been shot in the leg."

"I still don't think we should risk giving this Seibert boy the ingredients for a bomb."

"But Mr. Conway, think about it. How much better would it be for our department if we could arrest him *in the act* of bombing a federal building?"

Hmmm. Conway mind was buzzing. He thought to himself, *I could get an audience with the president if we did that. Maybe get an appointment as the next national director.*

"And when you get to the top," said Lonny, sensing his predictable thoughts, "you'll have to take me with you."

"Are you sure you can stay on him? He's a paranoid, independent thinker and we wouldn't want him to run off with the explosives and do something without our knowledge."

"Hey, have I ever let the department down? He's a puppet in my hands."

"Okay, I'll try to get explosives approved. This request will have to go all the way to the White House."

"Old dynamite sticks'll do. Nothing too reactive."

Washington, D.C.

"Don't worry about our PR, Cameron!" President Brighton was fed up with her press secretary's obsession with outward appearances and media reports. Her cabinet was taking their cues that she would only be pleased with good news today.

"It's my job, Madam President," he responded. "The polls show that this siege—"

"It's going to turn around!" she interrupted. "You'll see that this will work in our favor. We need to just hold the siege until the ATF can confiscate the illegal firearms in the northwest. This is the perfect prescription for the problems we've had in the Rockies."

"Madam President, if I may," the Speaker of the House, Troy McAvery interjected in his commanding, bellowing voice. "It may help your agenda in Montana, but it may hurt your cause in the House and Senate. Now, your reputation could be salvaged if," he paused and glanced at Todd Hamilton, "if you would release the Bureau's results of the Columbus, Ohio, investigation."

Hamilton shook his head. "Not gonna happen."

"We can't do that," DOJ Director Vic Meyers affirmed Hamilton. "It's a matter of—"

"National security, I know," Congressman McAvery finished Meyers' statement. "I'm on your side, so you can save the spin for CNN. You should be aware, Madam President," – he glanced at Brighton – "that Congress' insistence that the investigation's details be released is growing. They find the stonewalling offensive and insulting. There have been serious proposals to hold you both" – he pointed to Hamilton, then Meyers – "in contempt of Congress until our subpoena is satisfied and—"

"The courts will uphold our right to stonewall!" Victor Meyers raised his voice, brazenly interrupting the House speaker. "The precedent's been settled for 20 years, Troy!"

The House speaker was offended at the DOJ director's interruption, but the president stepped up to the plate for Meyers. "Vic is right. Until those who have committed the act of terrorism that killed President Fitzgerald have been caught, we can't risk compromising the prosecution by releasing the evidence of their guilt."

Everyone just stared at the president. Since there were some congressmen in the room who didn't know that the explosion at the Columbus Civic Center was an accident, everyone else had to hold back the urge to remind her, *It was an accident, Madam President*. It was almost as if the president was beginning to believe her own lies.

"Congress isn't resting content with your distrust of our ability to hold state secrets," Troy McAvery coolly responded. "Need I remind you that you have a Republican majority in the House? The right-wing contingency is pushing hard for the details of the Columbus investigation, and we GOP moderates are looking every day more like Democrats in our defense of you. You should know that they're prepared to add teeth to their demands with a strong-armed, well-funded criminal investigation."

"*Criminal* investigation?" The president's chief of staff appeared stunned at Congress' partisan brutality.

"It's James Knight. His popularity is growing," McAvery said.

"His treason has been tolerated for far too long," snapped Brighton. "Maybe the DOJ can prosecute James Knight." Brighton's sneering proposal surprised everybody except the House Minority Leader, McGinnis, who grinned ear to ear. *There! I said it!* the president thought proudly. "Unless he's above the law that the rest of America's obligated to obey?" She cast a critical stare at Victor Meyers and his stout-faced assistant, Dunworth, who sat dutifully next to him.

"We'd have saved ourselves a lot of trouble if we'd done that a month ago when I first reported his violations," the minority leader commented.

Meyers responded by putting up his palms and shaking his head. "I, I, uh, I'm not arresting a Congressman for free speech unless—"

"Hate speech!" the president interjected, irritated.

"If you want the DOJ to penalize James Knight for hate speech, evict him from Congress first," Meyers proposed, his gaze darting back and forth between the House speaker and minority leader.

"It's more than hate speech," the president added, "it's treason!"

"A good reason to evict him from Congress then, or censure him, whatever." Meyers fixed his gaze on McAvery, as if he had just lobbed the ball into his court.

The Republican Speaker of the House protested, "Oh, no you don't. I'm not letting you lay that sack of bricks on my plate."

"If Congress doesn't have the courage to at least censure him," Meyers rebutted, "how can we trust that you'll stand by us when we've incarcerated your fellow congressman for hate speech and we've been subpoenaed by the Republican majority in the predictable investigation that's sure to follow? We're not exposing our backs to the American people for a flogging when you're afraid of getting a hangnail by helping us out."

NSA Director Warnell added through a wrinkled frown, "James Knight has done more to weaken our national security than all of our foreign enemies combined in the last ten years. I think the president's right."

In light of the recent terrorist attacks, half of the room would have chuckled at that overstatement if it weren't so politically incorrect to do so. Danny Connor couldn't withhold his snorting smirk, and the room bristled at the economic prodigy's disruption. He cleared his throat and mumbled, "Sorry."

McGinnis came to the defense of the House speaker. "The problem is that James Knight is saying what all the right-wingers want to say but don't have the courage to say. Letting him talk makes the conservatives appear more moderate and that helps them at the bargaining table. The progressives like Knight because he makes the right appear more radical, and that helps them at the bargaining table. Knight's a convenient mutant right in the middle of our debate. We just can't get the votes to censure him. He's too useful to both sides of the aisle."

The president unleashed a string of curse words aimed at James Knight. "I haven't figured out why you dopes at the DOJ are waiting for the dopes in Congress to do something," she mumbled without looking up. "The Josh Davis types wouldn't exist if it weren't for traitors like James Knight. You had better get your heads together and do something about him before I have my secret service do your dirty work."

McAvery grunted disapprovingly. "You do that, Madam President, and you'll bounce all your checks of political capital and the congressional subpoena for the Columbus investigation will be the least of your concerns. If you want a hysterical bipartisan attempt to impeach you, go ahead and bypass Congress to arrest Knight on your own."

The president ground her teeth at McAvery's bold rebuttal. "I'll take care of that subpoena for the results of the Bureau's investigation," she said, nodding at him and then Hamilton.

"How?" McAvery wondered.

"It's not a problem," she said, earning a cold stare from the director of the FBI. "What I mean is that the results of the investigation will be made public when we convict the ones responsible, and we're getting closer every day."

Danny Connor held his peace during the meeting, but the strange facial expressions exchanged between Todd Hamilton and President Brighton during that last comment troubled him. He made a mental note to inform Josh Davis as soon as the meeting concluded. There was more to this conversation than meets the eye.

Deer Lodge, Montana

"Jack! Hey, Jack!"

He rolled over and moaned. "Yeah?"

"How are ya this morning?" Bull stood in the doorway of the bedroom, his lanky arms crossed over his push-up-firmed chest.

Jack tried to sit up until the pain in his leg reminded him of his predicament. "Where am I?"

"You comin' down with 'old timer's' or something? It's been two days."

Jack looked around and his recall returned. "Oh yeah." He tried to sit up and pull his legs off to the side of the bed and a wave of hot pain flooded his body. He grabbed his right leg and groaned.

"It's not too bad," said Bull as he leaned against the open doorway in his hunting cams. "Went all the way through. Aunt Leanne said it probably nicked the sciatic nerve or something like that."

"Hurts bad."

"You lost a lot of blood. You're white as a ghost. I thought you might not make it. For a while there you fevered up, but you pulled through and it broke last night. You have hardly woken up since you got here. It'll take a while for Auntie's chlorophyll mix to build your blood supply back up. You owe me big time, Jack. I carried you through the woods all night and most of the next day. You gave me a crick in my back. Thank God you're so scrawny," he said with a grin.

"Thanks, I think." Jack winced in pain. "How many died?"

Bull frowned and glanced out the window. "Two dozen of ours and ten of theirs, last time I heard. Vicki Friar's dead. So is Matt Friar. It's Ruby Ridge all over again."

Jack shook his head side to side, appalled. "And Barry?"

"Holed up in his home, surrounded by snipers. The media's accusing Barry of molesting his kids and holding them inside against their will." Jack looked down and took a deep tremulous breath. "I think it's safe to say we're outnumbered, Jack." Jack looked up and their eyes met. Bull's eyes were firm, sharp, resolved. "But I saw you in action. You can take a few of 'em with ya."

After a meal and a 2-year-old oxycodone tablet from Aunt Leanne's medicine cabinet, Jack was feeling better. Bull's aunt brought him some old crutches she found in the garage, for which Jack was grateful. His thoughts went to his wife. He thought about calling her, but then realized that she only lived 20 minutes away from where he was. He contemplated buying some flowers, knocking on her door, and if *he* wasn't there, then maybe they could make amends. Probably not, but he had to try. His brush with death made him desperate for her forgiveness for the way he mistreated her for so many years. He couldn't sleep another night knowing that things weren't right between them.

"Aunt Leanne?" he hollered. "Come here for a sec." Momentarily a musty-smelling gray-haired lady in a dirty apron peeked into his room. "Can you help me up, ma'am?"

"What do ya mean, Jack?" she asked through floppy cheeks with a toothless slur. "Where are ya goin'?"

"I need to get up." His strained voiced relayed his pain as he tried to move his bad leg off the bed. It hurt, but not as bad as he thought it would. She came over and grabbed his elbow.

"You gotta bedpan on the other side of the bed, Jack."

"I need to leave. I have family business to tend to."

"You know you can stay here as long as you want?"

Jack sat on the side of the bed, his mind cringing at the thought of the pain he predictably would experience upon standing. He almost talked himself out of it, but the thought of seeing his wife again urged him on. He grabbed the crutches and pulled himself up onto them with a groan as Aunt Leanne held onto his right elbow.

"Okay," he groaned, holding his right leg out in front of him and putting all of his weight on his good left leg. He breathed deeply. *You can do this, Jack. See, it wasn't that bad.*

"Strong man, you are, Jack."

"Ma'am, do you have a vehicle I could use for a couple hours, one with an automatic transmission?"

"Do you really think you can drive in your condition?"

"I'll be all right," he mumbled through a painful wince as he tried to move his leg under the crutches. "I need to see the wife and…" He hesitated, recalling how his wife always despised being called "the wife." She thought the phrase made her sound like a possession rather than a person. "I need to see *my* wife."

Jack left just in time. The feds knocked on the door five minutes later.

"Where's Fred Seibert?" an agent shouted in Aunt Leanne's face as a younger agent held her at gunpoint. He stood over her as she sat trembling on the couch. Other agents gathered evidence in the bedrooms and guarded the front and back doors.

"I don't know."

"Where's Jack Handel?" he shouted a little louder.

"Who's he?"

The agent suddenly backhanded the elderly lady across the face. Her head jerked to the side. She faced him again, trembling more from anger than from pain as her lip begin to bleed.

"Now, I'm only going to ask you this one more time, ma'am…"

The slap was just the distraction Aunt Leanne needed. She dabbed her lip with a handkerchief, and then without warning, she reached back and pulled out a pistol she kept behind the middle cushion of the couch. She aimed it at the agent's chest. His eyes widened when he saw her pull the trigger.

Blam!

The agent that was guarding the elderly lady at gunpoint was distracted when his fellow agent slapping her. He never saw the gun until the senior agent fell to his back, breathless. The younger agent instinctively aimed his .45 Colt at her just as she recovered from the recoil of her weapon. He squeezed the trigger and killed her with one shot to the head.

Chapter 15

Garrison, Montana

Barry Friar's front door opened slowly and the four men walked gently into the shadowy room. Sheet rock and debris were strewn across the dusty floor. Bullet holes had carved erratic graffiti on the walls, wall hangings, and windows. Torn curtains waved eerily in the room from the cool Montana gusts that blew through the cracked and broken windows. Only the inharmonious creaking of the wooden floor beneath their feet broke the silence. Blood from the second floor had dried on the ceiling above them, casting an ominous gloom on their entrance.

Rod Sanders entered first with his hands raised. "I'm Captain Rod Sanders with the Montana Guard. We're unarmed."

"Get on the floor and shut the door behind you." The voice came from the direction of the kitchen.

Sanders looked back at Chavez and motioned for him to shut the door. "Okay, Barry. We're getting on the floor. Governor Boswell sent us. We have a video camera. We want your side of the story. We have a doctor."

"Get on the floor!" shouted Barry, upset at the their slowness to obey him the first time. "Now! All of you! Palms down in front of you!"

Rod Sanders did as Barry commanded and the others behind him followed suit. Sanders immediately noticed that the floor in the foyer was darker than the surrounding wood floor. It was sticky and damp like it had been soaked with syrup. Sanders looked up and saw Barry Friar's bearded face peek out from behind the couch, his eye peering at them down the sights on his .454 magnum pistol. "Don't move!"

Barry Friar crawled toward the window with his cocked pistol in his right hand. Barry's adopted son, Marion, poked his head slowly around the couch, aiming his handgun at the men. Barry held a shard of a broken mirror up with tongs so he could look around the front yard, paying close attention to the tank parked directly in front of his house about 20 yards away. He carefully studied the area around the vehicles that had been demolished by the tanks and scooted into a pile on one side of the house. He set his mirror down and crawled cautiously to Sanders.

"I'm Rod Sanders," he said as Barry Friar began to frisk him for weapons. "You know my father well, Doug Sanders."

"I know you." Barry frisked him carefully yet quickly, keeping an eye on the others who were lying down flat against the floor behind him. Barry put a hand on his shoulder and squeezed it gently. "I trust you, Rod."

Barry grabbed a leather bag that the state investigator Chavez was carrying. "That's a video camera, sir." Barry searched the pockets, took out the camera, ejected the video, and then placed all of it on the floor in front of the investigator. Chavez was clearly nervous and Barry took note.

He searched the physician next. "Are those black bags full of medical stuff?" The physician nodded. Barry set both bags upright and then shoved them across the wooden floor toward the couch. "Teresa, look through the doctor's bags." Barry's 12-year-old daughter leaned around the couch to grab the bags. When Sanders' eyes met hers, she stared at him momentarily. Her eyes were red and her face pale and thin. She pulled the bags behind the couch and began to hurriedly search each of them.

"Got breakable stuff in there," mumbled the doctor. "A little food, too. Formula for your infant."

"Nice of you to doctor us to health before they charge in here and kill us," Barry commented. "They're going to murder us just like they murdered my wife and son."

"Not if we have anything to say about it," Sanders assured him with confidence, still belly-down on the floor.

"We'll see."

Sanders studied Barry's facial features. He had dark circles under his eyes. His thin facial features were exaggerated with some mild dehydration. "Listen, Barry. You're *not* going to die. Governor Boswell sent the Guard up here to make sure of that."

"You think I'm foolish enough to believe that the Montana Guard is going to defy the feds?"

"I thought Ben Boswell was your friend," Sanders responded. "Don't you trust him?"

"Are you sure that you're not just a diversion, Captain Sanders? Are you sure that the feds won't charge this building any minute?" Barry moved to frisk the FBI investigator who posed as a medical assistant.

"They'll only charge this building if a gunshot goes off inside," Sanders replied.

"How will they know that it's my gun that goes off?"

Sanders looked back to make eye contact with Barry Friar. "We're unarmed, sir."

"What's this then?" Barry put a knee on Canton's lower back, grabbed his calf, and pulled Canton's laser equipped, compact .45 Glock out of his calf holster.

"It's just for self-defense, sir," Canton quipped nervously. "I wasn't going to use it or anything."

Barry slapped Canton across the back of the head, and Canton's chin thumped against the ground.

Sanders shook his head. "I didn't know, Barry. He said he was unarmed."

"Didn't I tell ya, Marion? Your dad knows what he's talking about. Keep your eyes on the doors, kids. If they know I've got this fellow's weapon they might just charge this place."

"Sir, I didn't know about that gun," Sanders reiterated.

"But you did know this guy was a fed, did you not?"

Sanders reluctantly nodded. "The only way the feds would let a state investigator in here is if a federal investigator came in here to assist Dr. Lilly. The governor said that if we didn't get in here quick then they'd kill you for sure."

As Captain Sanders spoke, Barry took a spool of thin twine and began to tie Canton's wrists together behind his back. Then he tied his feet together, and bound his wrists to his ankles so that there was an arch in his back. "Don't struggle against the twine," Barry told him, patting him on the back of the head, "or it'll cut into your skin."

"All right," said Barry, crawling away about ten feet. He sat on the ground next to the couch and set his .454 magnum revolver on the ground. He took the federal agent's handgun, ensured that there was a bullet in the chamber, and flicked it off safety. Then he grasped one gun in each hand. "Each of you can get up and sit down with your legs crossed Indian-style." Sanders, Chavez, and Dr. Lilly each sat up, brushing their hands against their clothes to remove the sticky residue that adhered to them from the floor.

"Nobody moves without my permission, got that?"

Sanders nodded.

Canton protested how tightly his wrists and ankles were bound. "My hands and going numb. You're cutting off my circulation."

"That reminds me." Barry pulled a half-used roll of duct tape out of one of his thigh pants pockets and crept back toward Canton on all fours. He put a long strip of duct tape over his mouth. "There. That's better."

Dr. Lilly pointed at Marion. "Can I take a look at that arm?"

"Teresa," Barry called out to her, "anything suspicious in the doctor's bags?"

"They're okay." She pushed them along the floor toward the white-haired physician.

"Teresa, keep an eye on the doctor while he examines Marion."

"I would like to film my interview with you," said Investigator Chavez as he prepared the video camera.

Rod tried to wipe this sticky film off his hands onto his camouflaged pants and was unable. It was a thin brownish substance that smelled musty. "What's on your floor?" asked Sanders, looking around him at the circular pattern of darker wood surrounded by wood of a lighter color.

"That's where my wife was killed. Shot through the head as she held the door open for my boy and me." Sanders wiped it again on his pants. "The flies were getting pretty thick, so we wrapped her as best as we could and put her in the closet behind you. I'd appreciate it if you'd take her body with you when you leave."

There was a moment of silence as each of the men turned to look at the closet door beside them.

"I'm sorry." Sanders turned back to face Barry Friar and was surprised to see his countenance void of emotion.

"From the beginning," said Chavez, turning the light on the camera in his right hand, "tell us what happened."

"Mr. Friar, you're not making sense," said Chavez, watching through the screen on his handheld camera. "They'll put your kids with one of your relatives."

Barry looked at the state investigator as if he just said he was from outer space. "You can't be that naïve. There's no way my kids will be placed with a relative."

"You don't know that."

"I know exactly what they're going to do." Barry raised his voice as he pointed toward the troops in his yard. "They're going to wind up in some locked house, some juvenile detention center. They'll have some court-appointed psychiatrist brainwash them and they'll end up hating God and their parents. They—"

"That's not true, dad!" Marion gritted his teeth as the physician placed the last few strips of tape on a fresh bandage on his wounded shoulder. "We'll keep the faith."

"That's right." Teresa nodded her head, politely protesting her father's doubt of their character.

"People have fought the federal government in court before and won," Rod Sanders reminded him. "You *can* get justice in the courts. Randy Weaver sued the federal government and actually won $3.1 million – $1 million for each of his surviving children and a $100,000 for him."

"And the sniper that murdered Mrs. Weaver was never prosecuted. You call that justice? They're going to try me for every single death on my land. That's the federal government's perversion of justice."

"The FBI's excessive force in this raid will put those deaths on their head, not yours," Chavez responded. "It's always been acceptable to repel excessive force, even when the force is legit."

"You don't have to convince a judge, Barry, just a jury."

"The government's probably labeled me an enemy combatant," Barry rebutted. "We are post-Patriot Acts One, Two, and Three. The right to a jury trial has been officially suspended for political enemies."

"But if you stay here, then you look just like the nut they're portraying you to be: paranoid, insane, and unwilling to do what's best for your kids." Sanders aimed his index finger at Barry Friar. "It's just a matter of time before they flush you out, Barry. If you want to waste your life, go ahead, but you need to let your kids leave with us."

"Promise me, kids, promise me that you'll read your Bible and pray every day." Barry Friar appeared unashamed of the tears that streamed down his cheek and onto his beard. "Promise me."

"Of course, Papa." Teresa gently rocked her little brother in her arms. Little Timmy cooed with a full stomach from the food that the physician brought. He playfully reached for his sister's necklace pendant that dangled just within his reach.

"Whatever happens to me," said Barry slowly, "know that I love you, and that I'm going to lift you up to God in prayer every single day."

"We love you too," said Marion as Teresa reached for and hugged her father's neck with one arm. Marion kept a close eye on their guests, gripping tightly to his gun.

Barry let go of Teresa and looked at Marion. "I'm proud of you, boy." Barry fought to maintain control of his speech as his emotions swelled deep within him.

Tears finally welled up in Marion's bloodshot eyes. "Though He slay me, yet will I praise Him."

"The Lord's your defender, not your slayer," responded his sister.

Marion's quote from the book of Job reminded his father of another. His eyes turned to the closet. He mumbled the words as a costly act of worship, a sacrifice of praise to God, "Yes, the Lord giveth and the Lord taketh away. Blessed be the name of the Lord."

Barry placed his palms on his children and began to pray for each of them in turn, blessing them, thanking God for them, and praying for their safety and that their spirits and souls would be preserved from the evil around them.

Rod Sanders and Carl Chavez listened intently as Barry prayed aloud for his children. The physician was so moved from the sincere passion of his prayer that he paused packing his supplies back into the satchels to bow his head until Barry was done.

When Barry Friar concluded, he turned to Captain Sanders. "Okay. We'll leave."

"You're doing the right thing, Barry."

Carl Chavez hit a button on his camera to transmit the encrypted video electronically to his department's vehicle at the bottom of the hill, just in case the feds tried to confiscate his camera when they left the home.

Sanders tapped a button on his two-way radio, stood to his feet, and spoke into it, "We're coming out, Sergeant Hammel. They're surrendering."

There was a long pause before Hammel responded. "We're waiting," he finally said.

Barry opened the coat closet door, which let out a long, mournful squeak, like the last exhale of a dying animal. There rested the carcass of Vicki Friar, covered with towels, leaning against the wall. Flies buzzed all around her. A large brown spot of dried blood marked the knit blanket that covered her head. Barry leaned down and lifted her cold, stiff corpse up in his arms. With Sanders' help, he stood and walked to the front door. Chavez held it open for him. The physician helped Teresa to her feet as she held her sleeping baby brother tightly against her chest. Chavez put his camera strap over his shoulder and helped Marion to his feet.

Thirty yards away from the front door, two dozen federal agents had their M16's aimed at the torso of Barry Friar as he stepped out of the house, carrying the blood-drenched body of his wife. A tank operator stuck his head out of the top door to get a better look at the domestic terrorist responsible for so many deaths. "There he is," one of them whispered. Their hateful eyes pierced Barry as he paused in the doorway.

Barry looked at them, staring down their barrels into their eyes. Though he felt no fear, he was hopelessly grief-stricken, daring to pray for death to ease his misery. He looked into their cold, blood-shot, merciless eyes, blazing through unshaven grimaces, and for a moment, he thought that they hated him more. Some of the agents were squatting, some standing, some pointing their guns, but everyone had a finger firm on the trigger. One agent who saw Barry's eyes fix upon him flicked up a middle finger in utter disrespect.

When Barry stepped off the last stair onto the blood-stained dirt, Sanders touched Friar's shoulder and whispered for him to put his wife down to allow the agents to handcuff him. Barry lowered his wife to the ground and kissed her gently on the forehead. He whispered his love to her one last time.

A federal agent raised his handgun at Barry Friar and his children, and pierced the tense moment with the shrillness of his order: "Get down on the ground, now! Face down! Hands on your head!" The agents made their way toward them, as wolves would prepare to pounce on an injured prey made weary by fleeing.

"Get down now!" Hammel shouted again, irritated at the hesitation of Marion and Teresa to get down on the ground. Rod Sanders walked up to Hammel to try to explain that Teresa was holding a baby and Marion had a severe shoulder injury when Hammel mumbled a foul curse at Sanders and backhanded him without warning. Sanders' head snapped back as the FBI agents nearby laughed. Sanders regained his composure and pinched his nose trying to stop the bleeding. He reckoned he deserved that for humiliating the sergeant in front of his men. If that were all the consequence he'd to face, he'd be more than happy.

The agents came to Barry Friar first, twisted his arms behind his back and frisked him roughly. They had no pity on Marion, who managed to slowly drop to his knees. They pushed him to the ground and twisted his arms behind his back, causing him to scream in pain and then pass out.

"He's got a bullet in his arm!" the physician warned them. "You'll make it start hemorrhaging again."

Roger Hammel stiff-armed the physician away and stepped forward to jerk Barry Friar up to his feet by the cuffs and lead him to the van. Barry heard his daughter, Teresa, scream behind him. He looked back and saw an agent pulling his crying infant son out of her arms. "It's all right, Teresa. Call upon Jesus' name! He will vindicate us!" Barry had one more glimpse of his weeping children and his dead wife's corpse before being shoved into a black windowless van.

Part IV

Judging the Law

Chapter 16

Southern Colorado Border

*T*he *ex-militia leader, Barry Friar, has been taken into custody and is facing charges from manufacturing illegal weapons to terrorism,* the newscaster announced on the radio. *Witnesses have confessed that he sexually abused his children and was holding them hostage against their will during the siege. Witnesses also stated that he knowingly harbored a suspect in the murder of at least two federal agents in Bozeman in the past month. The suspect, Fred "Bull" Seibert, escaped during the raid...*

"I'm tellin' you guys," Jared ranted as he pointed to the radio from the passenger seat, "that's the gunshot heard round the world. The resistance is growing stronger."

"I don't think we should get too excited about this fellow," Cal suggested from the passenger seat behind Jared. "He could be a counterfeit; they said he abused his children."

Elijah glanced at Cal in the rearview mirror. "They'll be saying that of you some day."

Cal winced, knowing that they already did.

"Shhh," said Sabina Manning from the rear of their mini-van with her youngest sleeping in her arms. "Keep it down."

Cal spoke in a quieter voice. "Maybe Montana's probably not the best state to head to right now."

Elijah shook his head. "Nah. The state that's sacrificing the most to resist the feds is the state that's going to be the most blessed by

God. As far as I can see, Montana's following the lead of Texas and South Carolina."

Jared shook his head. "Texas' leadership was too trusting of the feds, and South Carolina had too many dependent on government handouts. If the feds try to invade Montana, civilians need to be prepared to respond aggressively. We need to get us some more guns..."

David's cuffs were still tight around his wrists, but a pawnshop sledgehammer had broken the links. He ran his hands through his hair and tried to shake off Jared's hasty comment like a snake into the fire, but he couldn't get it off his mind. "Why is it, Jared, that your response to every trial is insubordination and violence?"

"Haven't you learned anything, Pastor?" Jared dared to reproach David in an impetuous tone, "If you haven't noticed, we're under a God-hating tyranny."

"The Bible says that the Lord *hates* the violent man—"

"Hey now," Elijah spoke up from the driver's seat. "I know everyone's on edge, but let's keep the fruits of the Spirit flourishing in our conversation, all right?"

Jared looked back at David with a hint of disappointment in his sarcastic grin. "Well, we know that there's at least one situation in which you would resort to violence to defend yourself," Jared said, recalling how David shot the soldier that held them at gunpoint on the side of the road.

"But I didn't enjoy it," David snapped. "It was a last resort to save lives."

"Is there any situation short of having your back to the coffin in which you would resort to violence to defend yourself?" Jared was stunned that David would oppose his comment after all that he and his family had been through.

"But violence is *always* your disposition, Jared. It's never love, joy, peace, patience, gentleness, kindness, and meekness; those are the fruits of the Spirit, even for warriors. Don't let sinners offend you so much that you try to be like Esau instead of Jacob. If I remember correctly, it was Esau the swindled who ended up bad and Jacob the swindler who turned out right. We should commit our way unto the Lord and trust Him to come to our defense, instead of always resorting to carnal remedies."

"Shhh!" Sabina repeated, gently patting the baby boy's back as he began to rouse at the sound of the invigorating discussion.

David's peaceful optimism in the midst of such tyranny irritated Jared. Jared bit his lip and gazed out at the sharp edges of the Rocky Mountains along the northwestern horizon.

"We're now entering a state officially recognized by President Margaret Brighton as the 'hub of treasonous resistance.'" Elijah thrust his fist out in front of him. "Here churches dare to preach against federal tyranny and everyone owns at least a half-dozen illegal guns!"

"Hallelujah!" said Jared as they passed the brown reflective sign that read "Welcome to Colorado."

David lifted his head from his hands and tapped Elijah, sitting in front of him, on the shoulder. "When we find a place and the dust settles, if it's okay with you, I'd like to borrow your van and go get my wife and kids."

Elijah's grimace informed David that he didn't like the idea. "I don't think it's wise to take a vehicle that fits this description back across the border into Texas."

"Not Texas. She's going to a safe house I've set up for her in Ohio. In my last conversation with Darlene, I gave her some code words that instructed her on where to go."

Elijah was surprised at David's foresight. "Didn't know that. Do you think she caught it?"

"I hope so."

Traffic thinned considerably when they crossed the border of the Coalition of Free Christian States. When they left Austin, they were forced to detour down back roads to avoid the federal roadblocks and auto accidents that clogged the roads and streets. Now they were relieved to have some breathing room on a wide highway. David and Jared were growing to appreciate Elijah's caution.

That evening, to David's horror, someone recognized him at a campground where they were setting up their garage-sale-purchased tents.

"Hey man! David's your name, right?" A hillbilly in well-worn, blue jeans and a red flannel shirt couldn't get over the fact that he was face to face with the same man who resolved the abortion clinic conflict that same fateful day that Governor Adams called the Guard out to shut down that clinic.

David acted as if he didn't hear his name called. He turned away when the man grabbed David's arm. "I was the Austin sheriff, Matt Wellington. How could you forget so quickly?"

David's eyes widened as the six-foot-four sheriff introduced himself. "What? I didn't even recognize you without your uniform on and with that fuzz on your face." He shook the burly hand of the unshaven sheriff.

"Yeah, that was me."

The handshake turned into a backslapping hug. "How's your shoulder?"

"Improving." They sat on a fallen log beside a campground campfire. "Gave up the sling just a few hours ago, but the pain med's startin' to wear off and it's beginnin' to throb so I might put it back on. Doc said it chipped the bone, but it's one of those fractures that do not require casts."

"Hey, Elijah!" David called out across the small campfire. "Come meet the sheriff of Austin."

Elijah came over from the other side of the fire and shook Wellington's hand. "It's an honor to finally meet you." Elijah smiled broadly. "You're the Hugh Thompson of our day and I want to thank you for standing up for righteousness at the abortion clinic."

"Hugh Thompson?"

"Yeah."

"Who's he?" Wellington asked.

"Ever heard of My Lai in Vietnam?" Elijah sat on the ground with his back to the fire.

Wellington nodded. "Isn't that the village in Vietnam where American soldiers killed unarmed locals?"

"When Thompson saw what was happening from his helicopter, he landed it between his fellow soldiers and some Vietnamese who were hiding in a shelter. He got out and tried to intervene to save the Vietnamese. He ordered the two soldiers in the chopper with him to fire on any Americans who tried to shoot the Vietnamese civilians."

David and Wellington were astonished.

"A government investigation would later tell of the rape and murder of 500 unarmed civilians at the hands of about 80 American soldiers. Those kinds of tragedies wouldn't happen if we have leaders like Hugh Thompson, and you, Sheriff."

Wellington grunted at the praise heaped on him. "Thank you kindly for the compliment, but it wasn't earned. I had never given a flip about abortion until the protesters forced me to take a side. I'm ashamed of my apathy, when I think about it."

Elijah motioned at a tent that was lit up across a grassy field. The lights inside caused the tent to glow like a light bulb in a field otherwise black with darkness. They could hear a guitar, a fiddle, and a harmonica playing and people were beginning to flock to the sound. "Guess what that is?"

David and Sheriff Wellington turned. David smiled when he saw it. "Looks like a Holy Ghost camp meeting."

David and Elijah slapped high-fives, and David said, "Ready for some church, Sheriff?"

"Someone told me that revival's breaking out all over the Coalition States," Wellington said. "God's doing something big here."

A stranger with a light brown beard and dark linen suspenders walked up to them and interrupted their conversation. "Pardon me for interrupting, but are y'all from Texas?" Beside the bearded man stood an identically dressed boy, who they presumed to be his son.

"Why?" Elijah asked.

"Is it as bad as they say?"

David nodded. "Worse."

"My name's Christopher." He reached down to shake David's, Elijah's, and then Wellington's hands. He seemed taken aback when he saw a handcuff on David's wrist.

"I was suffering for our faith," David informed, briefly raising his cuffs toward the man. "But God delivered me."

"I'm a pastor from Arizona. I've got half my church with me: 12 families, about 85 people. We want to live in the part of America that's outlawed abortion and euthanasia."

"Amen." David shook the man's hand a second time.

"If judgment's comin' to America, I'd rather be in the part of the country that's more likely to survive it."

"My name's David. That's Elijah and this," he placed his palm on the back of the burly sheriff, "this is the Sheriff of Austin, Matt Wellington, the first man to arrest an abortionist in America in almost half a century."

"It's an honor to meet you," he said, shaking Wellington's hand firmly. "Where are you all heading?"

"Montana," David replied. "Where are you headed?"

"Our destination is Billings, where we have a sister church." Christopher sat down next to Sheriff Wellington on the dirt.

"Is that your son?" David asked.

"This is my third son and seventh child, Henry."

"Hello," said Henry sheepishly as he sat on the ground next to his father in his matching homemade outfit.

Elijah reached over Christopher's lap to shake the young man's hand. "Good to meet you, little man." The boy smiled at the attention.

A 10-year-old girl ran up and plopped down in Christopher's lap. "Oooh, Daddy, look at that," she praised the campfire that lit up her eyes.

David's heart sank when he witnessed the affection between father and daughter. He so missed his girls. "How many kids do you have, Christopher?"

"Fourteen."

"Fourteen? Y'all sure got your hands full."

"Full of arrows," Christopher acknowledged. "Mind if we caravan north with you? Stayin' in groups is safer."

"Well, sure." Elijah gave David a thumbs-up. "If they're having a tent revival here for a few days, we may stay and worship with them for a bit."

David winced at the thought, and didn't return Elijah's thumbs-up. He certainly wanted to take part in revival meetings, but he missed his family and wanted to reunite with them as soon as possible. David forced a grin when he saw Christopher pat his little girl on the head.

Christopher discerned that something was troubling David, and he asked, "Anything bothering you, brother? Anything I can pray for you about?"

David took a deep breath. "My wife and my girls are behind enemy lines in Texas right now, hopefully heading to a safe haven I've set up for them. I hope to meet up with them soon." He bit his lip as fear of what may happen to them unexpectedly struck his mind and sped his heart rate. "It's a frightening time in America to have young children."

"It's a frightening time *not* to," Christopher replied instinctively.

David appeared surprised that someone would contradict his self-evident statement. "What do you mean by that?"

"Unless the Lord builds the house, they labor in vain that build it."

"Yes, Psalm 127."

"It's a dangerous time in America to build your own house, friend. If our heavenly Father wants to build us big families, but we build a small one instead, we labor in vain."

"But our children may wind up in prison, in the custody of Children's Services, or worse. We may be going to war."

"My children," he said, massaging his son's shoulder warmly, "are weapons for the kingdom. They're prayer warriors, statesmen, martyrs, and missionaries in training that will change the course of history. If my generation fails to win back our freedom, my children will charge the gates of hell and take back our Promised Land from our enemies."

David nodded, admiring the man's faith and passion. "I didn't feel like we could afford more than three."

"Consider the lilies of the field," Christopher quoted from Jesus' Sermon on the Mount. "Consider the sparrows. If our Father cares for these, are ye not of much more value than birds and flowers? O ye of little faith." Christopher noticed David's countenance become downcast, and he wondered if he'd said too much. "Forgive me if I sound curt, but professing Christians have birth-controlled away their posterity and their heritage, and it bothers me sometimes. Contraception, sterilization, abortion, and euthanasia are the four horsemen of America's culture of death, my friend. The pill and the prophylactic have been the hammer and sickle of the cultural revolution that has destroyed the country our great grandfathers grew up in."

"Can't argue with that." David felt a trembling in his bosom that reeked of conviction. Usually he was on the giving end of a good reproof, rarely on the receiving end, and he didn't like it at all. However, the Lord was speaking to his heart through this bearded farmer/pastor, so he paid close attention.

"The descent into tyrannical socialism is practically inevitable if the childbirth rate drops below 2.2 children per couple, America's been lower than that for 50 years."

"Is that so?"

"Thanks to Medicare and Social Security, children haven't been an insurance policy against want in old age. Now those government Ponzi schemes are going bankrupt and what are we doing? Americans would rather vote their kids and grandkids bankrupt and indulge in even more deficit spending than lose their old-age benefits."

David nodded. "I see where you're coming from."

"When our society purged Christian influences from the public square and began an age of self-imposed infertility in the sixties, the death warrant for our nation was signed. And how has the Christian family in America responded to our crisis? By turning to God's Word for the answer?" He shook his head. "No. We responded to the increased taxation by having fewer babies and encouraging our wives to enter the workforce. The devil's remedy for what ails us is more of the disease. Self-imposed infertility is the counterfeit cure for the crisis of self-imposed fertility. If Montana and the other states in the Coalition secede from the corrupt carcass of the United States but don't secede from the anti-child mentality that made tyranny inevitable, then our days are numbered, too." As he said this, several more of his children rushed over to sit beside their father and roast hot dogs on sticks over the fire. "Some places in Texas and Montana have had a major spiritual awakening," Christopher admitted, "but we're not out of the wilderness yet. Like Israel, the Coalition of Free Christian States may never make it to the Promised Land if the fathers don't turn their hearts to the children and the children to the fathers."

Christopher was the first of many godly leaders they met on the way to Montana. It seemed like God was pulling the Lots out of Sodom and taking the Elijahs out of Jezebel's strongholds, as if in preparation for a great judgment. The tens of thousands of families that packed up their goods and headed for Texas when Governor Adams outlawed abortion and euthanasia were now turning north toward the Coalition border. Thousands of Texas guardsmen and their families picked Montana as their new destination. Churches and whole neighborhoods daily joined together on the road, headed for some destination within the Coalition of Free Christian States.

The Lord, it appeared, was raising an army. It was an army of fathers turning their hearts to their children, and children turning their hearts to their fathers.

Colton, Texas

Darlene Jameson had zipped up the last suitcase when she heard the dreaded knock on the hotel room door.

Knock, knock, knock.

"It's Daddy!" 5-year-old Char exclaimed prematurely, jumping up and down in excitement.

"No, it's not your Daddy." Darlene had been so indecisive in the week since their conversation, but now her dwindling finances demanded action. The Greyhound bus was leaving in an hour. She'd made plans to take it to the home of the family David had prepared to care for her and her children in just such a scenario. There were so many unanswered questions about their last phone conversation, but she clung with hope to this one direction she received from David's code words. He had not abandoned them as it appeared, but why didn't he speak more frankly to her? Why did he use his secret code? Was she being watched? If so, how did he know? Was his confession of sin genuine? She knew it had to be.

As Darlene walked slowly to the door, she turned her mind from her unanswered questions to meditate upon the words of Proverbs

3, verses 5 and 6: *Trust in the Lord with all thine heart, and lean not unto thine own understanding. In all thy ways acknowledge Him, and He shall direct thy paths.*

She looked through the glass hole in the door and what she saw made her heart stop beating for a second. There were three men in suits with badges on their sports coats that read "FBI."

She placed both of her hands over her mouth and gasped in horror.

"Who is it, Mommy?"

Darlene regained her composure, turned, and knelt on the carpet in front of the door. "Girls, come here." She motioned for her daughters to draw close. "Remember what we talked about last night? Remember how I said that we have to trust God no matter what happens? Remember how I said that God's going to let us go through hard times to test our faith, but that He will always love us and care for us?"

The two oldest girls nodded soberly. The youngest was oblivious as she pulled on her mother's dress, whining to be held.

"Remember what I said about rejoicing in the bad times, too, not just the good times?"

Her daughters nodded.

"Don't be afraid and love God no matter what, okay?"

They nodded again.

Knock, knock, knock.

Those knocks on her door were like swings of a hammer against spikes in her hands and feet.

"Well, my precious daughters, we're about to have one of those hard times that will test our faith." She kissed them each on their foreheads and hugged them close, as the tears welled in her eyes. "Will you be strong for Jesus and make Him happy? Will you?"

They nodded confidently, trying to be strong and fight the fear that threatened to topple their little hopes and dreams. "Yes, Mommy."

Chapter 17

Washington, D.C.

"Our best interrogators know that she's withholding, Madam President." Todd Hamilton was enthusiastic in his report to the president through the encrypted laptop internet connection.

"How long until we know?" The president wasn't as pleased as Hamilton expected her to be. She was having PR problems and she needed David Jameson captured and convicted to save her agenda.

Hamilton shrugged. "It won't take long, Madam President. She's a fragile mother of three young children, not a Special Forces Green Beret. She'll break like a fresh cracker."

"She's an accomplice to one of the most devastating terrorist attacks ever on American soil, Todd." The president blinked hard.

Hamilton didn't know whether to remind the president that the explosion that killed President Fitzgerald was an accident or to play along in her alternate reality. "We actually don't know for sure whether she is an accomplice or—"

"We need her husband behind bars and we need it now! Do what you have to do to make her talk."

Todd Hamilton, Victor Meyers, Bill Erdman, and Dena Halluci, who were present via their laptops, jolted when the president raised her voice. It was as if the president had completely forgotten that the explosion was ruled accidental.

Halluci was discovering that the threat of Congress' investigations made the president very emotionally malleable. "Why don't we try and get Victor to expedite the prosecution of Barry Friar?" she proposed. "Publicizing all of the beliefs and crimes of this domestic terrorist will certainly help us a lot in the PR arena."

Victor nodded. "Certainly, James Knight is less likely to defend Barry Friar if his kids are justifying killing American soldiers from the witness stand."

Dena Halluci smiled when the president's face lit up with hope. "Knight will have to issue a public apology to salvage his career."

"You think so?"

"Absolutely," said Victor. "The timing is perfect. Friar's extremist views will win lots of sympathy for your hate speech EO's."

Erdman added, "The broadcast of his trial gives us the best opportunity to increase the popularity of your gun control EO in the northwest."

"Do you think that there's a clear conviction?"

Halluci snapped her fingers. "Of course."

Helena, Montana

Before Victor Meyers sat the four best attorneys in the Bureau. Surrounding them were a dozen of the most successful private attorneys in the nation, brought in as hired guns for the most publicized trial in years. They'd been working on this case ever since the pre-planning stages of the raid. Vic Meyers was the only one standing. "There will be no deals. We have to set a national precedent here. Anything less than a lethal injection or life without parole is a failure. Is that understood?" The lawyers reluctantly nodded. "So quit this talk about a possible compromise, exchanging information on other militia for a reduced sentence. We're not giving him any deals."

The lead prosecutor, Dan Porter, was the most experienced attorney in the group, as well as the wealthiest. Porter was a 40-year-old bachelor with more money than he could spend in five lifetimes. He was sure that this would be the most enjoyable case for which he had ever volunteered, but he thought the U.S. Attorney General was being naive.

"Listen, Vic." Dan Porter briefly raised his hand, but didn't wait for the AG to acknowledge him. "It's not too late for a military tribunal. If you want a guaranteed sentence of *life* at the least, then doing this without a jury trial is the only way to go. The government has lost similar cases in this state. What's a sure thing with a New York jury can fail miserably in Montana."

"I don't want to hear any of that nonsense, Dan!" Victor snapped, leaning forward with furrowed brow. "The president needs a jury conviction in Montana, not a jury conviction in New York, and we're gonna deliver. We'll pick our jury carefully. If you're not here for a kill, Dan, then you don't need to be here at all."

"The defense, sir," Dan Porter continued, undeterred by the uncharacteristic shrill tone of the DOJ director, "is going to argue that this raid was an unreasonable search and seizure and, therefore, a violation of his Fourth Amendment rights. Repelling excessive state force is justified in jurisprudence. The precedent has been set and we can't change it any more than we can change history. The defense is going to say that Barry Friar and company were just minding their own business, playing horseshoes and badminton, munching on potato salad and pork ribs when - *whamo!*" He slapped the wooden table, jolting his aids. "Out of the woods come 50 camouflaged soldiers firing automatic weapons at them. No warrant. No judicial oversight. They're going to say that as far as they knew, they were being attacked by armed robbers, illegal Cuban immigrants, a clan of Sasquatches in heat, aliens from outer—"

"All right! All right!" Victor interrupted his witty chief prosecutor and halted the chuckles that resounded from around the room. "Don't you think I know what the defense is going to say?" After a sigh, he spoke in an authoritative tone, "Barry Friar's radical beliefs are our best ally. We just get him to preach his bigotry and the jury will hate him for it."

"His counsel won't let him do that," a confident attorney spoke up. "Besides, Judge Waverly will dismiss the character evidence as inadmissible because, he'll claim, it unfairly prejudices the defendant."

"He's done that before," Dan Porter's chief assistant spoke up.

"Don't worry about Judge Waverly," Vic assured them. "He's our friend in this trial."

"Really?" Porter's assistant, who had spent many sleepless nights studying Judge Waverly in anticipation of this trial, wasn't convinced. "You're telling us that Judge Waverly is—"

"There are powerful forces at work here," Victor interjected with a wave of his hand, silencing his critic. "Judge Waverly will not dismiss the character evidence."

The attorney shifted uneasily and looked down at his legal pad as he thumped it with his pen. "That will work then," he said as he scribbled on his pad.

"If we want Barry Friar to lose a popularity contest," Porter interjected, "but not if we want him to lose his life."

"We quote the Militia of Montana that Friar directed justify defending themselves with violent force against the federal government. We let Barry Friar defend, on the stand in front of a disapproving jury, the very murders that Fred Seibert is accused of committing. We let him incriminate himself, which he'll be glad to do. He's a pastor. He likes to talk. We give him an audience and let him crucify himself like the Jesus he adores."

"*If* he talks."

"Friar's a preacher. He'll talk. Give him a podium and he'll preach his way straight to heaven. Moreover, we'll produce evidence that the murder suspect, Fred Seibert, was present at Barry Friar's target shootin' party that day. That evidence alone justifies the raid and strengthens the president's case for disarmament."

"It justifies an arrest warrant, but not an armed raid with automatic weapons, Mr. Meyers," said Porter. "That's what the defense is going to—"

"The warrant was too risky," Vic rebutted. "It was a gathering of skilled militia, not ordinary civilians. The warrant could have provoked violence and the accused would have fled."

Porter, unaccustomed to being interrupted, leaned forward, flailed his arms, and exclaimed, "It got violent anyway, and the accused fled anyway!"

Vic imitated Porter's aggressive demeanor. "It was the president's call, Dan!" Vic sat back in his seat and took a deep breath. "Terrorism is a federal jurisdiction. We couldn't trust local judges."

"Well, then why are we prosecuting with a local state judge?"

"I told you!" Victor shouted. "Waverly's with us!"

Porter leaned back in his chair and clasped his hands over firm abdomen. "It's coming down to a constitutional defense."

Vic Meyers grinned, as if he were unveiling a secret weapon to his subordinates. "We've got it worked out. In a pretrial motion, we're going to disallow the jury to consider constitutional matters."

"Vic, it's a state trial not a federal trial," Porter rebutted. "With the publicity of this trial, the judge would be crazy if he—"

"Dan! Come on! I'm the Attorney General of the United States of America! Don't you think I know what I'm doing? My letter of recommendation can get that judge out of the horse stalls in Outhouse, Montana, and into the District Court of Appeals or maybe even the Supreme Court. The defense won't be allowed to bring up constitutional arguments that fly in the face of well-settled constitutional precedence."

Porter raised his eyebrows at the DOJ director's perception of his own abilities. "I hope you're right."

"If Judge Waverly disallows the jury to consider constitutional controversies in the pretrial motions, then the defense has to give up its claim that the raid was an unreasonable search and seizure." The attorneys nodded. "That's our ticket to Barry Friar's jugular."

"You know that it's not just Barry Friar or the federal agents who charged Barry Friar's home that'll be put on trial," Porter said, "but also the executive orders of the president. If her agenda is more important than a conviction, then we need to face the potential for juror activism. There's a local juror activist group—"

"The Fully Informed Jurors Association," someone interjected.

"Yes." Porter nodded. "And they've done their job at making ours as difficult as possible."

"They've been a problem in IRS and drug conviction cases," Vic acknowledged, "but in a case of terrorism?" He shook his head side to side. "No way." Dan rolled his eyes to show his reluctance to embrace the U.S. Attorney's confidence.

"Come on, Dan," snapped Victor Meyers. "We have no reason to believe this jury will be any more enlightened or rebellious than any other jury we've ever manipulated" -the room full of attorneys smiled - "in the pursuit of justice. Most of the intelligent jury candidates get a doctor's excuse."

Victor Meyers' phone rang. He looked at the caller ID display and saw that it was the Department of Justice in Washington. He turned away from the room full of first class attorneys and tapped a button on his phone. "Meyers here."

"Ready for some wonderful news, Mr. Meyers?" This was Dunworth, the DOJ's second in command. "Just got a call from Barry Friar's defense team. He fired them."

"What?"

"Barry Friar is going *pro se*."

"Are you kidding me?"

"I'd never do that sir."

"What happened?"

"They insisted that he push for a deal, life in prison in exchange for information on the militia whereabouts. So he fired them."

"Just like that, one day before opening arguments?"

"Just like that."

"That is good news indeed."

Meyers turned to Porter, who was wide-eyed with anticipation to learn what had so excited the Attorney General. Meyers covered the receiver with his hand and announced, "Friar's going *pro se*."

The attorneys let out a unified gasp of disbelief. Porter sighed and turned to his chief assistant. "Well, our job just got a lot easier."

The pretrial motions did not go in Barry Friar's favor. The judge would allow the prosecution's character assassination strategy. Judge Waverly also uprooted Barry Friar's entire defensive strategy: the defense would not be allowed to present constitutional arguments that cast into question settled precedence in jurisprudence.

Moreover, Judge Waverly slated his trial to begin immediately. Opening arguments would begin on the morrow, July 2, the day before the president's disarmament EO would go into effect.

Barry Friar could sense that he was walking into a trap. His case was to be the national news story that would convince the public to turn in their weapons. He would be the poster boy for the president's gun control campaign.

The prosecution began the first day of the trial presenting a massive amount of evidence that Barry Friar had a deep-rooted hatred of the federal government. Dan Porter cast aspersions on Friar 's character in the most derogatory terms allowed. Some of the former members of Barry's congregation quoted his most radical sermons. Witnesses testified that he had insisted to them that *all* non-Christians were going to hell to burn forever. They quoted his teaching that the federal government was the anti-christ beast found in the book of Revelation. They cited many unpopular conspiracy theories that Friar had embraced: that the government murdered the Branch Davidians at Waco, that the government covered up the true perpetrators of the Oklahoma City bombing, that government leaders were complicit in the 9/11 terrorist attacks, and that they conspired to overthrow our constitutional rights and, ultimately, to merge us into a one-world government. They showed video footage of him discussing ways to flee from police forces, live off the land, hide weapons, pick locks, and practice guerilla warfare.

They also read parts of the notorious *Anarchist's Cookbook,* which they discovered in his library. It included recipes for homemade explosives derived from ordinary household chemicals. They quoted Barry Friar justifying violence against government agents in order to protect life, liberty, and property. They quoted his articles, his sermons, and even his private e-mails and letters to friends and foe alike.

As far as the attorneys and the reporters in the room were concerned, the judge could have shot Barry Friar dead on the spot and they would've cheered. Friar, acting as his own attorney, didn't object to any of the testimony and refused to cross-examine any of them, frustrating his sympathizers in the courtroom.

Dan Porter stood up to call his next witness to the stand. "Make him preach, Dan," one prosecutor whispered to him.

Porter whispered back, "He'll cite the Fifth, and I'll see you back in 15 seconds." He turned and announced, "The prosecution calls the defendant, Barry Friar, to the stand."

Barry Friar stood, nodded, and headed to the witness stand. The room full of attorneys and journalists was shocked that Barry Friar agreed to take the stand. In spite of a chorus of inharmonious whispers throughout the room, Barry Friar walked confidently to the stand, put his hand on the Bible, raised his right hand, but to everyone's surprise, he refused to repeat the oath.

The judge proved quite inflexible to Barry's first attempt to buck the legal system. "You *will* repeat this oath, Mr. Friar."

"I promise to tell the truth, Your Honor, but the very Bible I've got my hand on forbids me to swear an oath of any sort. Forcing me to take an oath to swear to tell the truth wouldn't justify a lie if I wasn't under oath, would it?"

Friar's question appeared to stump the austere judge. Friar wouldn't be the first to refuse to take an oath, but the judge didn't want to commence the trial with any loose leash on Barry Friar, knowing he'd probably try to buck the system with any slack allowed him.

"I will promise to tell the truth; that's all the law requires of me."

"All right, all right, Mr. Friar." The judge sighed heavily and nodded at the prosecutor.

"Mr. Friar," Dan Porter heaved the words with a contemptuous smirk, "you have heard the testimonies confirming your hatred of government authority. Have you changed your position in any way?"

"You've yet to present my position. You've mixed half-truths with innuendo. I love the federal government within its lawful jurisdiction."

That unexpected reply turned Porter chuckle. "Uh, excuse me?"

"The Bible says to honor the King. It says that civil authorities are God's ministers attending to justice."

Porter paced toward the jury with a mischievous grin on his well-manicured face. "Mr. Friar, how can you sit here and tell this jury," he said, motioning toward them, "that you love the federal government?"

Barry Friar laughed hard and Porter grew irritated. "Is something funny, Mr. Friar?"

"I just," he paused to compose himself, "I just find it amusing how you've tried to paint half a picture. You see, if I took all the yellow, red, and purple out of the Mona Lisa painting, you wouldn't

even recognize it. Try photocopying the Mona Lisa out of the ency-
clopedia some time. It's an inaccurate, hideous rendition of the—"

"Your Honor," Dan Porter bellowed, "please instruct the defendant to answer my questions directly, without all the rambling."

The judge grunted and looked down his nose condescendingly at
the defendant. "Answer the question, Mr. Friar."

"All right, I'm answering it. What you've done today, Mr. Porter,
is take bits and pieces of sermons and articles out of context. Your
strategy to this point is more indicative of your insincerity than it
is of my beliefs. Of course you can quote my saying that violence
against tyranny is justified. The United States of America wouldn't
exist as an independent nation if violence against tyranny weren't
justified; I'm assuming that even you justify our nation's existence.
You must consider the speaker's caveats when you quote him. I love
the government when the government is lawful, just as God wills
it to be, when its leaders abide by their constitutional limitations.
But when government becomes unjust and violates the God-given
rights of the people, the people may oppose the violence of their
leaders." Friar thoughtfully turned to the jury and said, "A jury trial
is a peaceful way that citizens may oppose the unlawful violence of
government leaders."

Judge Waverly and the chief investigator snorted their disapproval of Friar's implication. Porter pointed at Friar with both hands,
and then raised his eyebrows at the judge as if to say, *I told you so*.

The judge removed his spectacles and glared disapprovingly at
the defendant. "Mr. Friar, you'd better listen to me and listen to me
closely. Now, I'm going to give you some latitude since you are
providing your own defense, but you must avoid commentary on the
jury's rights and obligations."

Porter sighed and paced past the jury bench again. "Thank you,
Your Honor."

Barry Friar took a deep breath and leaned back in his seat.
Porter's gaze shifted from jury member to jury member. "Mr. Friar,
you urged young, impressionable men to shoot and kill federal
agents should they ever feel threatened by them. You repeatedly,
habitually, in tracts, in sermons, in articles and on internet blogs,
justified attacking the government with violence."

"If Judge Waverly were to pull a gun on you, Mr. Porter, wouldn't you defend yourself?" Friar turned and pointed to the judge with one hand while massaging his gray beard with the other. "Of course you would! Judge Waverly's position doesn't give him the power to do evil. The tracts and sermons you submitted are in evidence and can be read by the jury members in their entirety to examine the contexts of my quotes. If they do so they'll see that I do indeed love government when government is lawful. It is the tyrannical counterfeit of lawful government that symbolizes the Beast in the book of Revelation that's intoxicated with the blood of the martyrs. I'm no anarchist. I want justice, I plead for justice for me and my family," he said passionately, "justice that only the government can give me, justice that only this jury, operating as lawful agents of justice, can give me."

"Please don't insult us with your sermonizing, Mr. Friar," Dan Porter remarked critically. "This courtroom isn't your pulpit. Just answer my questions."

"Objection!" Friar blurted out, and then glanced at the judge. "I can still object as a witness, right?"

"Yes, you can object as a *pro se* defendant," the judge said with a curious grin. "Please approach the bench and quietly state your objection."

Friar and Porter approached the bench and Friar protested, "Mr. Porter is belittling the defendant in front of the jury. I didn't insult him at all. I answered his question precisely."

"The objection is sustained. Mr. Porter, spare us your derogatory commentary." Porter stared at the judge for a long moment, fearful of the impartiality he discerned behind the judge's eyes.

To Barry Friar's delight and to Dan Porter's disappointment, some in the jury, including a few who were most adamantly opposed to Barry Friar's far-right beliefs, nodded when they heard the judge sustain Friar's objection.

Dan Porter paced past the table of anxious prosecutors and whispered, "Plan B."

"The witness is not on trial here, you are!" The judge shouted at Barry Friar with a bang of his gavel as Friar attempted to cross-examine one of the prosecution's witnesses.

"With all due respect, Your Honor, that is an unreasonable—"

"Ah, ah, ah," the judge stopped him with a wag of his finger. "Not so fast. Approach the bench when you argue your objections."

Friar made his way to the bench with the enthusiastic prosecutor, Dan Porter, strutting in his wake. "Your Honor, that is begging the question," Friar said humbly. "My defense *must* address their offense. I *am* on trial, but I *must* be allowed to defend myself from the government in this courtroom. The Constitution and natural law are my allies. How can justice be secure if they're muzzled? If the government's case fails because the jury sees their force was excessive or unconstitutional—"

"I told you, Mr. Friar!" the judge angrily interrupted him, his voice straining with frustration. He paused and lowered his voice so as not to be heard by the restless jury. "Mr. Friar," the judge said quietly, yet sternly, "this jury will *not* be considering constitutional issues that higher courts have already decided.""Why do you presume that the decisions of other judges are set in stone, Judge Waverly? Reasonable judges have overruled the bad decisions of other judges on slavery in the colonies, on free speech, on—"

"You will keep your voice down when arguing your objections before my bench," Judge Waverly interrupted him, removing his spectacles. "Is that understood?" Friar nodded. "My reasons for not challenging the decisions of higher courts, Mr. Friar, are beyond the scope of your defense."

Friar put his hands on his hips and stuck out his chest, appalled at the injustice and wondering at the depth of Judge Waverly's corruption. "Oh, they are, huh?"

"Yes, so don't you even mention a constitutional amendment or duty again, or I'll hold you in contempt of court. Stick with the facts of your case. Is that understood?"

Friar reluctantly nodded, turned to glance at the jury and, as he walked back to his table, said, "My apologies to the jury for presuming to lecture them on their constitutional duties."

"Enough!" Judge Waverly slammed down his gavel. "I'm this far from sending you back to a concrete hole in the wall for a week and let you think about your disrespect of me and this court!"

Barry Friar turned on his heel, his countenance grim at the judge's reproof. "Your Honor, this jury is seated here *because* of their constitutional obligation," Barry said as firmly as he dared. "They have a right to know their constitutional duties! Shouldn't the justice system be objective and side with the law and the Constitution, and not take the side of the government? How can this jury defy the Constitution in their obedience to it?" Barry Friar knew he was walking a tightrope with this judge, but with his life on the line, what did he have to lose?

"The government is *not* on trial here! You are!" When Judge Waverly reproved the defendant, Dan Porter strutted back to his seat, grinning from ear to ear. He loved it when a plan came together. "Mr. Friar," Judge Waverly removed his bifocals and counseled him, "I've been very patient with you, fully aware of the gravity of the charges against you, the fact that you're not an attorney and that you've never done anything like this before. Nevertheless, if this continues, I *will* hold you in contempt of court and send you to jail and we'll have your case taken over by a public defender in your absence." As the judge scolded him, he pointed at him with his arthritic index finger as if he were a weary father correcting his incorrigible son.

Judge Waverly would have held Friar in contempt many objections ago if it hadn't been for Attorney General Victor Meyers, who pleaded with the judge to give Barry Friar some liberty. "Give him some loose rope," Victor reasoned, "and he'll hang himself."

A federal agent who looked more like a professional body-builder had the stand, responding confidently to the prosecutor's questions. "We approached the suspects who were shooting the semi-automatic weapons when one of the men fired at us with his illegal rifle. Three of my men took a bullet."

"So you returned fire," Porter clarified, "only *after* you were fired upon, is that right?"

"Yes sir. Terrence Van Winkle died instantly. He was a 14-year veteran who left behind a wife and two children, ten and eight years of age."

"You were friends with Mr. Van Winkle, weren't you?"

"Yes, I was."

"Do you miss him?"

"Yes, we all miss him."

"Objection!" Friar stood and blurted out. "Unfairly prejudicial to the defendant. I miss my wife and son."

"Sustained," the judge agreed with Friar.

Porter stiffened, took a deep breath, and stared at the judge for a moment, stunned that the judge would uphold this hillbilly's objection. He turned to the witness. "Thank you, Mr. Vaughn."

Barry Friar stood and prepared to cross-examine the witness. "You called our rifles illegal. Can you cite the law that made them illegal?"

"The President's Executive Order 22315."

"And when did that executive order go into effect?"

"Well, the guns were made illegal by the executive order."

"Your honor," Friar addressed the judge, "will you please remind the witness that he's under oath and that he should answer the question directly."

"The witness knows he's under oath, Mr. Friar."

"With that in mind, let me ask the question again. Mr. Vaughn, when did the executive order declare the guns unlawful?"

"The executive order was due to go into affect a few days after the raid," he reluctantly admitted.

"Oh, *after* the raid. So by what standard were they illegal on the day of the raid?"

The witness was speechless for a moment as Barry paced back and forth in front of the jury. "They weren't illegal when you raided my home, right? As a matter of fact, I think President Brighton postponed the date her gun control executive order was to go into effect in Montana, so they *still* aren't illegal here, are they?" Again, the witness was speechless.

"Judge Waverly, will you instruct the witness to answer the question?"

"No," the witness finally admitted.

Barry Friar smiled and winked at the jury. "Mr. Vaughn," Barry went on to his next question, "how do you know that Mr. Van Winkle didn't fire at the boys first?"

"The militia members were firing their guns before we charged."

"Were they firing *at you* before you charged?" Again, the witness was silent. "Your Honor, please instruct the witness to answer my quest—"

"No," the witness finally answered. "They were firing at tin cans."

"Was that legal at the time of your raid?"

The witness nodded. "Yes."

"Do you recall the testimony of Aaron Shotwell?"

After a pause, the witness responded, "I do not."

"Let me jar your memory. Aaron Shotwell is the 13-year-old boy who returned fire on you and your men only *after* his friend Ronny and Ronny's dad had been killed. He was one of the few eyewitnesses you missed as you shot people in the back while they fled toward the house."

"Objection!" Porter shouted.

"Sustained." The judge removed his bifocals and spoke to Friar with a critical glare. "Remember who's on trial, Mr. Friar." Friar never took his eyes off the witness.

"I am aware of Aaron Shotwell's deposition," the witness admitted, "but I don't consider that testimony credible. We certainly didn't intentionally shoot anybody in the back."

"Oh, have you not read the investigation?" Barry headed for the bench to look for the notes of the Bureau's investigation.

"We certainly didn't mean to shoot anyone in the back. Many of those killed shot at us as they ran toward the house."

"I see." Barry stopped and turned to face the witness. "Mr. Vaughn, what were the teenagers doing when you began to charge and shoot them?"

"They were firing illegal weapons." When Barry grunted in disapproval, the witness restated, "I mean, soon-to-be-illegal assault weapons."

Barry walked to the evidence table, picked up a Ruger 10-22 and an M16. "The boys were shootin' targets with these," he said, hoisting the .22 caliber gun into the air, "and you were shootin' us with these." He raised the M16 into the air. "Now, Mr. Vaughn, which one is the assault rifle?"

"Actually, both of them are."

"God, help us," Barry Friar mumbled as some of the jury laughed. "Where are you from, Washington, D.C.? That glorious crime-free, gun-free zone?"

"What? Why is that relevant?" The witness didn't get the joke, but the jury did. When they chuckled, the judge slammed down his gavel.

"Is it possible that they didn't hear you shout to put their guns down because they were *assaulting* R.C. Cola cans with their rifles?" Friar's comment drew more laughs from the jury before the critical eye of the judge silenced them. The witness grew uneasy and kept glancing to the rear of the room, so much so that Friar became suspicious. "Who do you keep looking at?" Friar turned his gaze to the back of the room. "Who is that back there? Oh, Mr. Conway. That's your superior, isn't it?" He pointed at Will Conway, one of Vaughn's superiors at the Bureau. "Have you been coaxed, Mr. Vaughn, into changing your statement by Mr. Conway or any of your other superiors?"

"Mr. Friar!" The judge slammed his gavel down as people turned to get a glimpse of the Director of the Northwest Division of the FBI. "Will you please approach the bench?" As the whisperings grew louder, the judge slammed his gavel again. "Order!" Then he turned his attention to the defendant. "Mr. Friar!"

"I know, question the witness, not others."

"Yes, please!"

"Can I place Mr. Conway under oath?" Upon hearing that question, Dan Porter laughed at the naiveté of this *pro se* defendant.

"No, you may not!"

"Why not?"

"This isn't a forum for you to flex your conspiracy theories, Mr. Friar. Now, question the witness."

Friar marched to the witness stand and stood nose to nose with the witness. "In your testimony, you said that I knowingly harbored a domestic terrorist, Fred Seibert, on my property. How did you come to believe this?"

"We learned about Mr. Seibert's presence at your farm before the raid."

"And is there evidence that he is a convicted terrorist? Is there any evidence that he is a convicted murderer? Has he been tried in a court of law and found guilty?"

"Not yet. We can't catch him."

"Well then, he is innocent until proven guilty, right?"

"Until proven guilty."

"Thank you. Now, where is this evidence that I *knowingly* harbored Fred Seibert while aware of the crime of which he is accused?" When the witness hesitated, Friar asked, "Is there any evidence at all that I *knowingly* harbored a terrorist?"

When the witness didn't answer the question forthrightly, Friar asked the judge, "Judge Waverly, please instruct the witness to answer the question."

"I, I don't know."

"Is there any evidence that anyone at my farm that day knew that there was a domestic terrorist suspect or a murder suspect in their midst?"

"The evidence, I think, is a matter of national security and hasn't been publicized. But we know that you were harboring a murderer and that he would be on your property that day."

"Oh please!" Friar exclaimed, thrusting his hands heavenward briefly. "Can you name one single person at my barbeque who had been convicted in a court of law for perpetrating any crime, much less murder?" When the witness didn't immediately respond, Friar shouted, "No! You can't! So stop pretending that you were justified in killing my wife, son, and friends because we were committing crimes or harboring a murderer!"

"Objection!" Porter jumped to his feet.

Barry asked another question before the judge could respond to Porter's objection. "Did you see me fire on federal agents, Mr. Vaughn, or is that testimony based upon hearsay as well?"

"Your fingerprints were on the guns, Mr. Friar," the witness testified.

"Hold up." Judge Waverly extended both of his hands. "When we have an objection on the floor, Mr. Friar—"

"My fingerprints were on many of the guns because they were my guns!" Friar raised his voice over Judge Waverly's. "Wouldn't you expect my fingerprints to be on them?"

"Mr. Friar!" Waverly bellowed.

Friar kept his gaze fixed on the witness. "You don't mean to imply that since my fingerprints were on those guns that I shot every one of those guns at federal agents, do you?"

"Objection!" Porter bellowed again as Judge Waverly's trembling right hand reached for his gavel.

"Well," the witness ignored the prosecutor, "I don't know."

"Wait!" Judge Waverly slammed his gavel three times. "The prosecutor's objection is sustained."

After a pause, Friar asked the judge, "What'd he object to?"

"Right now I'm objecting to, uh…" Porter had to think about it for a moment. "Judge Waverly, please instruct the defendant on whose on trial here."

"I'm on trial! All right?" Friar turned to face the jury. "But I have a right to defend myself to the witness who killed my wife, son, and friends!"

After another pause, the judge nodded at Barry Friar and Porter dropped noisily into his seat. Friar turned to the witness. "Isn't it true that you don't know if I fired guns at federal agents because you didn't see me? And no federal agent has testified that they saw me shoot a weapon at federal agents?"

"No, I didn't see it personally."

"Who saw me shoot at federal agents?"

"Um, I don't know. I was told by a superior."

"A superior?"

"Yes," said the witness. Barry cast a curious glance to the back of the room at Will Conway. "My superiors," the witness reiterated, "who are well informed of the investigation's details, told me that you fired at federal agents."

"Well," said Friar, "were they on the field that day?"

The witness shrugged. "I'm, uh…"

"Where's their sworn testimony? Where are their depositions under oath? When can I cross-examine them?"

"I don't know."

"Why are *you* telling us *their* testimony?"

Agent Vaughn's muscular jaw appeared to grind from side to side, as his eyes fixed on Barry's. Barry realized that the agent was trying to stare him down, so he stepped back for a moment to let him.

Agent Vaughn's adrenaline was surging in response to Barry Friar's aggressive questioning. He suddenly stood and pointed at Friar, "We did our job and did it the best we could! You're the killer, Mr. Friar!"

"Well, that just settles it then," Friar said, leaning back against his table and massaging his gray beard. "Let's just dismiss this jury and send the good judge home, and give you a sniper rifle to disseminate justice as you see fit."

"Fine by me," Agent Vaughn mumbled under his breath as he clenched his fists.

"What's that?" Friar stepped in closer. "Your Honor, please instruct the witness to speak up so that the court reporter can document his malicious comments."

Agent Vaughn crossed his arms over his chest and stood silent for a moment.

Barry wasn't intimidated by the outburst of emotion. "Your Honor, please instruct the witness to sit down." The judge didn't have to, because Vaughn complied with the request. "You might also want to let him know that I'm innocent until proven guilty."

"Which you will be!" Vaughn bellowed.

"We'll see." Barry stepped in closer, and asked, "Do you think it is justifiable to repel excessive government force in defense of life and property and in compliance with Montana law?"

Porter bellowed, "Objection!" just as the judge slammed his gavel.

"Mr. Friar!" Judge Waverly hollered. "I'm not going to tell you again. The government is not on trial here."

Barry didn't distract his gaze from the witness, who aimed a stiff index finger out of a clenched fist at Friar and raised his voice. "You and your friends refused to put down your weapons when we ordered you to do so and you began killing federal agents – good men! - with your *illegal* semi-automatic assault weapons! That's not repelling government force, that's murder!"

"Do we have to go through this again?" Friar rolled his eyes toward the jury with his hands raised in frustration. "None of our weapons were illegal, yet, sir. Do I need to tattoo it on your fore-head? The president's executive order, assuming that it's even legal," he said with a carefully calculated glance at the jury, "had not even gone into effect yet!"

"Well, semi-automatics had been outlawed, but you're right, those *assault* weapons were not yet illegal."

When Friar heard the witness referred to their .22s as "assault weapons" again, and he bowed his head and mumbled, "Oh brother."

"Excuse me?"

"How is this jury not to think you dishonest and disingenuous, Mr. Vaughn, when you keep misstating the facts?"

"Objection!" Porter interrupted.

"Oh," - Barry swiped a hand of frustration at the prosecutor - "cut it out!"

"Stop pontificating, Mr. Friar," snapped the judge. "Just ask your questions, then sit down."

Friar took a deep breath. "Mr. Vaughn, do you think that the president's executive order which made .22 caliber semi-automatics illegal is constitutional?"

"Objection! Irrelevant, lay opinion!" Porter hollered just as the judge slammed his gavel.

The judge pointed at Friar. "The constitutionality of federal law and presidential executive orders are not going to be debated in this courtroom and this jury will not consider such arguments, Mr. Friar. Do you understand?"

"Mr. Vaughn," Barry said, keeping his laser-like gaze on the witness, "what state were you in when you killed Ronny?"

"Montana, of course."

"Are you aware of the provision in the Montana Constitution that guarantees the right to keep and bear arms?"

"Objection! Irrelevant."

"Sustained."

"Are you aware of the provision in the Montana Constitution, the founding document of this state, that our land, our property, our goods were safe from illegal searches and seizures and from intrusive government raids?"

"Objection!" Porter raised his voice. "Absolutely irrelevant."

"Not to a Montana jury, it's not," Friar told Porter.

"That's for Judge Waverly to decide, not you."

"Objection sustained," the judge agreed with Porter.

Friar turned back to the witness, "Are you aware, Mr. Vaughn, of the Sovereignty Amendment in the Montana Constitution that restrains the federal government to specifically enumerated constitutional powers—"

"Objection!"

"...And that the Montana Firearms Act specifically forbids the federal government to intervene in Montana-made firearms?"

"Objection!"

"Sustained!" Judge Waverly sneered at Barry Friar.

The agent tried ineffectively to conceal a laugh and responded in spite of the prosecutor's stern objections. "I believe our Civil War answered this question, Mr. Friar. State law is subject to federal law just as federal law is subject to international law."

"Oh, really!" Friar turned to the jury and nodded. Whispers rose in the courtroom to a small roar until the judge thumped his gavel against his podium.

Barry knew that answer didn't set well with a jury full of Montana citizens. He let that answer hang out there for a moment before he slowly walked back to the jury. He rested his hands on the banister directly in front of them. "So, you think Montana law is subject to federal law just as federal law is subject to international law?"

"Absolutely."

Then, softly, as he searched the eyes of the jury, he said, "We'll see what this jury thinks about that."

"Tell me about the altered rules of engagement, Mr. Hammel."

"Objection!" Porter shouted. "Improper question to facts not in evidence."

"They are too in evidence."

"Hold up!" The judge silenced Friar and Porter with a wave of his hand. "Approach the bench."

"Your Honor," Friar said, "Mr. Hammel's sworn deposition cited in the FBI investigative report quoted an agent conversing with Mr. Hammel that mentioned the adjusted rules of engagement. Agents Locklear and Rawls confirmed this in their depositions. Hammel is their superior. This is an appropriate line of questioning."

The judge glanced down at his notes, winced, and then consented to Friar's point. "I suppose you are correct on that."

Porter grunted and made his way back to the prosecutor's table as Friar repeated the question to the witness. "Tell me about your altered rules of engagement."

"There was no altering of the rules of engagement. No, sir." Sergeant Hammel was adamant and animated in his response, shaking his head side to side and flailing his arms. "Not at all."

"Have you changed your mind since your deposition during the FBI's investigation?"

"No, I have not."

"Your Honor," said Barry Friar, "let me remind the witness of his previous testimony. On page 233 of the FBI investigative report, you were quoted as saying - Friar picked up the stack of papers on his table and read from Hammel's statement - "'We don't want to take *anybody* out if we can prevent it. No body bags!' you told Devon Rawls. And then Agent Rawls responded...?" Friar paused and looked at Hammel with raised eyebrows as if expecting him to finish the sentence.

After a sluggish moment, Hammel replied, "I don't remember what he said."

"Well, I can let you read your own statement if you like." Friar extended the stack of papers toward him with his finger on the paragraph.

Hammel didn't take him up on his offer, but simply said, "He offered a protest about the rules of engagement, didn't he?"

"Oh how quickly your memory returns," said Barry Friar with a carefully orchestrated smile at the jury. "This jury and I want to know about these altered rules of engagement."

"I'm not at liberty to say. According to my superiors, it's a matter of national security and irrelevant to the case."

"I do thank you for admitting to the jury that the rules of engagement were changed, but whether the change is relevant or not to this case is not for you to decide. That's something for this jury to decide," he said, pointing to the jury at his right.

"Objection!" Porter exclaimed. "It has already been decided in a pretrial motion that some details of the FBI investigation need to be concealed as a matter of national security."

"Your Honor, if they're accusing me and my friends of shooting at them first, we must discover what their rules of engagement were changed to ascertain the truth."

The judge sighed. "Very well."

Barry turned back to Agent Hammel. "To what were the rules of engagement changed?"

Hammel took a deep breath, his shifting eyes wandering around the room. "There are matters of national security which preclude the public from hearing many details of this investigation."

"This court has not granted you permission to withhold the answers to the question I'm asking you now, Mr. Hammel. It is quite pertinent to this case. How is it a matter of national security that you conceal from this jury the change of your rules of engagement that justified your firing on me, my family, and my friends?"

"Whether something is a matter of national security is an issue for people well above my pay grade. I was just following orders."

"Whose orders?"

Hammel smiled. "That's one of those details that must be concealed for the sake of national security. Suffice it to say that I was following orders."

"Of course. You're just following orders."

"Yes."

"Were you following orders when you ordered your men to shoot unarmed citizens like my wife?" He paused, expecting the prosecutor to object, but when he did not, he continued, "Can't you see that we are inclined to view the withholding of that critical information from this court as an act of self-protection? It looks more like job security than national security – can't you see that?" The witness glanced at the judge uneasily. Judge Waverly took a deep breath, tempted to reprove Friar for walking the line yet again. He decided to hold his peace.

Barry Friar picked up a two-inch stack of stapled papers and walked to the jury. "I have here some statements from federal agents who were involved in the raid and/or the investigation. I couldn't find hardly anything here on the rules of engagement," he said. He flipped through the pages with his thumb. "See all this black?" He pointed to the black ink that blocked out almost half of the statements. He turned to the witness, "Mr. Hammel, what happened here? This looks to the jury like some bureaucratic attorney is trying to cover the Bureau's flub-ups with a magic marker. It looks to us like they're trying to conceal evidence that would vindicate me."

"Objection! Speculation."

"Sustained. Mr. Friar, ask questions please."

Sergeant Hammel's body language appeared erratic and anxious as Friar interrogated him. So Friar thought he'd press harder to see if he could tease a confession out of him. "First you deny the rules of engagement were changed, and then you admit that they were. What other perjuries could we discover if only we could read under all this black marker?"

"Objection! This is improper impeachment of the witness, Your Honor."

"Sustained. Mr. Friar!" The judge leaned toward him and removed his bifocals in his condescending fashion. "Please refrain from making accusations. I'm going to ask that the jury," he said, glancing at the 12 of them, "put those unfounded accusations out of your mind and don't consider that derogatory comment in your decision."

"Speaking of the jury, help us get this straight, Mr. Hammel." Friar pointed to the jury and then at himself. "Help us make sense of this. So much has been blacked out, I need your help. Agent Rawls offered a protest about the rules of engagement. Something you said to him conflicted, at least in the mind of this 11-year FBI veteran, with the *adjusted* rules of engagement he had been given. What could it be? The traditional rules of engagement forbid you to fire upon someone unless you are being fired upon, right?"

"Yes."

"All you told him is that you don't want to kill anybody if you can prevent it. But he protested. Then you said to him, 'The rules of engagement do not preclude measures to minimize the casualties, Rawls! Take out the shooters as a last resort.' End quote. What in the world could the Bureau have changed the traditional rules of engagement to that would be in contradiction? What are we to think, Mr. Hammel?" Barry Friar's voice grew passionate, full of inflection. "If you won't fill in the blanks, then must we be forced to use our imaginations?"

"We did not break the law!" Hammel insisted.

"Well thank you for clarifying!" exclaimed Friar. "I suppose that the jury should just take your word for it, instead of judge the facts of the case for themselves."

"Objection!" Porter stood to his feet and inquired of the judge, "Must the defendant continue to berate this decorated public servant? Please, Your Honor! There's no evidence that the rules of engagement were adjusted to violate the law."

"Objection!" Friar shouted, his gaze darting toward the proud, starched attorneys behind the prosecutor's bench. "No evidence? Have you been listening to anything, Mr. Porter?"

The judge grinned. "Don't object to an objection, Mr. Friar. That's enough. Mr. Porter's objection is sustained."

"Tell me, Sergeant Hammel, what Agent Lex Morris said when he criticized your raid."

"I don't know what you're talking about."

"Right after you spoke with Rawls about those altered rules of engagement, Agent Lex Morris criticized the F.B.I.'s strategy."

Hammel broke out in a sweat, worried that the F.B.I. attorneys who scratched black marker over all the comments of the agents that implicated the Bureau, might have forgotten to scratch out the young Agent Lex's criticism. "I don't know."

Friar chuckled. "I wish I did, but all of this black marker..."

"Questions, Mr. Friar!" Judge Waverly bellowed.

Friar's body suddenly appeared to sag with fatigue. A long moment passed before he turned toward the jury. "I have no more questions for this witness, Your Honor." As he walked back to his table, he muttered softly, yet loud enough for the jury to hear, "This jury can see through this cover-up."

A loud smack of the judge's gavel startled everybody. "That's it!" Judge Waverly shouted. "You're spending the night in jail, Mr. Friar, for contempt of this court!"

"Well, surprise, surprise," he mumbled in his best Gomer Pyle accent, prompting many chuckles throughout the room. "I was planning on spendin' the night there anyway."

"You are that close," the judge said as he held up his index finger and his thumb just a few inches apart, "to a mistrial, Mr. Friar. Then a public defender will take your case without your presence. Do you want that?"

"Oh, that'll get me justice," he mumbled, offering his wrists to the police officer. "No thank you," he said, glancing at the jury. "You can't trust a corrupt system to punish itself, but maybe this jury of my peers will give me justice."

"Silence! Get him out of here!"

"We're idiots," Victor Meyers whispered to an aide beside him in the rear of the courtroom. "We should have never consented to a trial before a Montana jury."

"Was he a lawyer in a previous life?" the aid whispered back.

"He participated in some jurisdiction meetings at his community library where people are taught how to defend themselves in court and win," Meyers whispered. "But the government's inside man in those meetings never thought he was much of a threat."

"Well, it's not like he's doing a good job," he said as Barry Friar was led out of the courtroom in cuffs.

The DOJ director clicked his tongue in his cheek. "On the contrary, this is just what Barry Friar wants. He wanted us to drag him from the courtroom in cuffs. It's the perfect backdrop to his charge that the justice system's on the side of the government. The jury pities him. Just look at him smile. This is all part of his plan."

Chapter 18

Deer Lodge, Montana

❝ According to the fellow in charge of the city park, she'll be speaking here." Bull pointed to an area on a map of downtown Portland, which was spread out on the kitchenette table in their camper. "It's exactly where Fitzgerald spoke three years ago and other politicians speak there annually. We have three weeks before her speech." He highlighted the area on the map with a yellow highlighter. "We can plant the explosives just under the ground right here late one night. Maybe we can try to get temp jobs working with the company in charge of stage setup, or in charge of cleaning the city's parks. Something that'll get us close.'

"It's a suicide mission," said Lonny, popping Bull's balloon with a shake of his head. "You don't know how those Secret Service fellows operate. They switch things around. They look everywhere for anything suspicious and they have a short fuse for calling the whole event off. The dogs'll smell our TNT from a half-a-mile away."

"We'll bury them deep."

"And how are you going to detonate it if it's deep? I don't feel right about it."

"That's all you've said with every plan I've come up with so far!" Bull's face reddened as he placed the cap back on the highlighter and set it on the table. "How about some constructive criticism for a change? I think that every third president has at least been shot at—"

"And there are more people in prison for trying it than there are shots fired," Lonny rebutted. "It's crazy, Bull."

"At this point, I don't really care if I get caught. I want to blast that witch before she destroys our country. She gave the order to murder a bunch of our friends, she's incarcerated hundreds of good people, and she wants to euthanize our grandparents in nursing homes."

"Yeah, but—"

Bull raised his voice over Lonny's. "On top of that, on top of that, she's trying to disarm Montana citizens right now! Come on, Lonny! If we take her out, we'll teach generations of would-be tyrants a *huge* lesson."

"Just forget about the president, bro." Stein placed his right hand on Bull's shoulder for a second. "It's not going to happen."

Bull cursed and with an open palm he angrily smacked the map of Portland. Then he crumpled it up and threw it on the bed against the wall. "Well, what do you want to do?" he shouted, irritated at Lonny and Stein's skepticism.

"We've got the explosives. Let's use them wisely a little closer to home." Lonny opened up the city map of Billings, Montana. "Let's take out the FBI building in Billings." He spread his map out on the table. "The Tenet Federal Building. It's an easier target and we'll be free to strike again. It's right here." He uncapped the yellow highlighter and highlighted the city block where the building was located.

"Fine. Anything's better than sitting here talking and dreaming. But when we're done with this job, we go for the 'wicked witch of the west' wing of the White House, all right?"

"Maybe, when we're done with this," responded Lonny, nodding. "Even King David had to kill the lion and the bear before moving on to Goliath."

"Okay."

Lonny pointed at the intersection on the map where the federal building was located. "The Tenet Federal Building in Billings; it's your key to fame, Bull."

Bull grinned at the flattery and Lonny thought to himself, *This is too easy.*

Billings, Montana

Todd Hamilton's smile was broad as he puffed a cigar behind his desk on the top floor of the Tenet Federal Building. The proposed headline of tomorrow morning's newspaper was sprawled out in front of him. It read, *Operation Offense Begins*. He winked at Will Conway, the red-faced, stub-nosed regional Bureau director, who sat at the head of a large table with dozens of FBI bureaucrats. They all had their eyes fixed on the projected image of the newspaper headline on the wall. Hamilton nodded at the newspaper editor. "If the public's tipped off, there will be federal charges."

"I know, I know," said the editor. "My own staff won't see this until 3 a.m. at least. You have my word."

"Very well then. Good luck."

The editor left and the room full of Bureau administrators shook hands and congratulated each other on their breakthroughs in local media outlets. Hamilton tried to settle them down so they could bring the meeting to a satisfactory conclusion.

With the shooting death of Ernie Harris, the manhunt for Fred "Bull" Seibert, and the well-publicized trial of accused child molester and murderer Barry Friar, public opinion was beginning to turn in their favor. Hamilton had personally taken over much of the Bureau's responsibilities in Montana. The FBI would no longer remain on the defensive in the Rockies. They had the manpower in place and now it was time to aggressively disarm suspected militia and popular hate-mongers.

He commissioned a 300-pound mount of African-American muscle, Butch Nichols, to take over the reins of the FBI's role in Operation Offense in Bozeman and a half-dozen surrounding towns. Agent Nichols began to brief the room full of administrators on the plan to search for guns in the homes of known or suspected militia. The ATF would cooperate in the raids. It was the evening before the deadline of the president's executive order, but the agencies were stepping up the process for militia members and their family contacts for fear that those weapons would go underground.

Agent Nichols leaned forward with his elbows on the large mahogany table. "First pass is already in action. Twelve magnometer-mounted vans and squads will start scanning any minute."

Hamilton grinned and leaned back in his swivel chair. "Boeing has just completed an order for 1,000 of these babies, so let's get it right. This is a test run for what we're going to be doing soon on a scale a thousand-fold greater. Are there any other comments or questions?" After a pause, he stood to his feet and said, "You're dismissed then. We'll review our successes at 7 a.m."

As ATF and FBI administrators gathered their briefcases and headed out of the office, Hamilton approached Will Conway and put his hand on his shoulder. He leaned close and, careful that no one nearby could overhear, he whispered into his ear, "How are you handling the plan?"

"Which plan?"

"You know, the president's plan. The plan for Tenet."

Conway's face turned redder than his usual sunburned complexion, and beads of sweat broke out on his balding head. "I don't know what you're talking about."

"The president let me in on it," Hamilton told him matter-of-factly. Conway appeared angry as he stomped to the room's corner and motioned for Hamilton to follow.

"How do you know about this?" Conway exclaimed in a harsh whisper, his back to the others in the crowded room. "The president told me that this was a secret mission between her and me."

"And me."

Conway swallowed hard. "And who else?" His blood pressure rose with the thought that the list of people aware of his secret mission was longer than he could've imagined.

"Oh, don't worry," said Hamilton, swatting at his fear as if he were swatting at a pesky gnat. "Just do what you need to do and move on, Will. If things go south it'll be because *you* became untrustworthy. Just follow the plan."

Lolo, Montana

"Robert Kemp - this guy's been active in the militia for four years. Pretty serious wacko." The FBI agent perused the abbreviated rap sheet inside the windowless black van. "It's his parents' house, but he lives with them. Scan it carefully."

The colorful magnometer screen set off an eerie glow inside the windowless van. The ATF technician identified various metallic parts of the house: "Fridge, washer drier, pipes... Ah ha!" He pointed at the screen and tapped it to magnify the image. "Second floor, probably bedroom closet. It's a gun safe. It looks like there are some guns outside of the safe in the bedroom as well. See that?" He pointed to an erect white object on the screen. "That's probably a gun sitting up against the wall. By the look of that," - he tapped the screen to magnify the image again - "it's got a high capacity magazine on it. Large caliber."

"What's the heat sensor tell you?"

"Two bodies." The technician pointed at the glowing red images on another screen. "Downstairs. Sitting in the living room. No guns as far as I can see in that area of the house. No, make it three bodies. Probably a kid in a second upstairs room."

"We're a go," the agent with the rap sheet on Robert Kemp whispered into the microphone impaled in his Kevlar helmet. "Second floor, northeast bedroom. Unsecured contraband." He set his notebook down and reached for his M16. "Two bodies downstairs, one upstairs near the contraband. Prepare to move. Be careful."

The black van 20 yards behind the magnometer-equipped van carried five ATF agents and seven FBI agents, wearing matte black outfits, carrying automatic weapons.

A plain-clothed senior agent patted a technician on the shoulder, and said, "All right, jam 'em." The technician tapped a button that released a powerful signal that jammed all telephone communications. "They're jammed."

The plain-clothed agent turned to senior squad leader, a six and a half feet tall and 50-pound overweight ATF agent named Rock Bradley. "We want in and out in three minutes."

"Affirmative," came the gruff reply. "Jim, back door. Dan, east side. Trey, west side. Mark, on my tail. Miller, let's get it on. Everybody on safety." Bradley barked out orders as his SWAT team rushed to their positions.

When Agent Bradley arrived at the front door, the ATF veteran reached with the butt of his rifle and smashed the bulb in the light fixture next to the door.

Knock, knock, knock. "Bureau of Firearms!" shouted Bradley.

"What in the world!" the gray-haired gentleman in his early fifties spilled his Good Earth tea on his boxers. He jumped off the couch, brushed the hot liquid off his shorts and turned toward the front door. "Uh, just a minute!" He glanced at his equally frantic wife, unsure of what to do.

Knock, knock. "Open up now!"

"Josephine's upstairs," she whispered to her husband as the loud knocks continued to echo through the home's wooden floors and walls.

"Go get her." The owner of the house moved to the door and peeked through the eyehole. "Do you have a search warrant?"

Bradley's face was one inch away from the hole, so all the homeowner could see was the agent's cheek. "Don't need one. Patriot Act. You've got illegal guns and multiple phone calls have been made from this location to the sheriff's office in a conspiracy to interfere with federal communications. An active member of the Militia of Montana is also known to reside here."

"We don't have any illegal weapons. What are you talking about?" The old man reached for his cell phone on the corner table by the door.

Agent Bradley appeared to read his mind. "Your phone communication has been temporarily disconnected, so don't bother trying to call."

"Kick it down!" came the order through Bradley's earpiece. "Second body going upstairs toward gun."

Bradley took one step back and thrust his right foot as hard as he could just under the doorknob.

Smash!

Wood shattered and splinters careened in different directions as Bradley's well-trained kick destroyed the bolt-locked wooden door. A piece of the door hit Mr. Kemp in the forehead, lacerating his brow. He was knocked onto his back, only to look up and see a federal agent pointing an automatic M16 rifle in his face. Other agents raced up the stairwell shouting orders to freeze.

"Leave 'em alone!" Mr. Kemp shouted at the agents that were chasing his wife up the stairs.

"Shut up!" Agent Bradley ordered with the gun barrel in Kemp's face.

The two agents jumped four stairs at a time on their way up the stairwell and turned in time to see one of the bedroom doors slam shut. Behind the door, they heard a crying child. They flung the door open to see Mrs. Kemp holding their 3-year-old granddaughter, who screamed when she saw the agents pointing their guns at her. It was a child's room; the guns were in the adjacent room.

"What do you want?" screamed Mrs. Kemp. "Leave us alone!" she squealed as she backed up against the wall, hugging the terrified girl.

"Where are the guns?"

"What are you talking about?" she said, trying to calm down her terrified granddaughter.

"The guns! Where are they?"

"They're in the next room."

One of the agents kept Mrs. Kemp and her hysterical granddaughter at bay with his weapon while the other went into the adjacent room.

The agent entered to find an unloaded semi-automatic AR15 leaning against the wall behind the bed and a locked gun safe in the closet. A full clip for the AR15 was on top of the safe.

"Bradley, everything's under control upstairs," the agent said through his helmet mic as he fondled the lock on the gun safe. "Get Alan up here to unlock the safe."

Bradley shook his M16 in the face of the elderly Mr. Kemp, who was tending to a splinter that stuck deep in his forehead beside his bleeding abrasions. "Get up!" shouted Bradley.

The homeowner struggled to his feet, nursing his bloody forehead with his white sleeve.

"Go open your son's gun safe."

"For what?"

"You've got illegal assault weapons in your home."

"They're not illeg—"

"If you don't want to go to jail, you'll open it up for us and surrender your arms to the government."

Mr. Kemp made his way up the stairs with Agent Bradley right behind him, intermittingly poking his gun barrel into his back. "You are under no obligation, sir, to obey an unconstitutional order."

"Shut up!" Bradley ordered, following it up with an angry curse.

Mr. Kemp turned the corner at the top of the stairs and saw his terrified wife and granddaughter. He tried to comfort her. "It's all right, dear. They're taking Robby's guns."

"Where *is* your son, Mr. Kemp?" asked Bradley.

"He's in custody from the raid on Barry Friar's home. Are you telling me that you didn't know that?"

Bradley notified the lead agent in the magnometer-equipped van of the new intelligence data through his helmet mic as he pushed Mr. Kemp into his son's bedroom. He pointed to the gun safe as the other agent stood in the corner of the room with Robby's AR15 in his hands.

"Aren't we supposed to get some compensation for turning these in?"

"Not today. Open the safe."

"What's that? Did you hear that, dad?"

"I don't know." The Hispanic father of four stopped swinging on the front-porch swing so he could listen more closely. "It sounded like a crash."

"What's going on at the Kemp house?" The 14-year-old boy stood to get a better look over the bushes adjacent to the front porch.

His father set his rocky road ice cream down on a small wicker table next to the swing and stood up on his toes to see over the azalea bushes. *Two black vans. Front door of the house is open. Front porch light is off, but it, it looks like the door has been kicked in!*

He squinted to see that the upper half of the front door was hanging from its hinges at an erratic angle.

The father darted inside his house, pulled his .45 semi-automatic handgun off the top shelf of his closet, and ran toward the Kemp's house to investigate. As he crossed the street, he looked through the front living room window and saw a silhouette of what appeared to be a rifle casting its shadow on the beige curtain. He stopped in his tracks and suddenly realized that the Kemps were being burglarized.

When two mysterious characters in black rushed out the broken front door into a dimly lit sky, causing the upper half of the door to swing noisily on its deformed hinges, the Hispanic man saw that their arms were full of firearms. The curious neighbor chambered a round in his handgun and yelled, "Freeze! Those aren't yours! Put them down and get out of here before the cops arrive!"

He reached for the cell phone clipped to his hip. He pushed and held the button "9" which should have speed-dialed 911. Instead, there was a buzz on the phone that informed him that his phone was out of commission.

When the 14-year-old on the front porch heard his father's yell, he ran inside to retrieve his .22 caliber rifle from the gun safe to get a piece of the action. His mother was in the basement with his siblings. She heard his running upstairs and yelled, "What's going on?"

"Someone's stealing the Kemps' guns." The boy hurriedly turned the dial to open the combination lock.

"What? Where's your father?"

The boy rushed from the house and slammed the door behind him without answering his mother's question.

The woman reached for a wireless phone on the wall, but heard only static.

Agent Bradley was on his way down the stairs with the last of the guns when he heard a loud crash of metal. He darted out the front door to see the two agents who were carrying the Kemps' weapons standing with their hands in the air and the guns lying at their feet. One of the agents was trying to reason with the neighbor. "We're with the Bureau of Firearms. We searched the house and found—"

"Shut up!" shouted Agent Bradley to his comrade. Bradley walked confidently down the stairs, set the weapons he carried down on the stairs, and then marched confidently to within ten feet of the neighbor.

"That's close enough," the neighbor shouted with more authority than Bradley expected. "Who are you and where are the Kemps?"

"Put the gun down," Bradley said calmly.

The neighbor winced and grew angry. "What did you do to the Kemps?"

"We're fine!" Mr. Kemp shouted through the broken front door. "We're okay. They're taking Robby's guns."

"Who's 'they'?"

Bradley tapped the white ATF acronym on his sleeve. "Guess."

"Are you sure you're okay, Mr. Kemp?" The neighbor saw Mr. Kemp's bleeding forehead and was concerned that he was being forced to say those things against his will.

"Yeah." Mr. Kemp walked out onto his front porch to try to calm his neighbor. "Don't get yourself into any trouble. Go home." Suddenly, a nervous FBI agent put his rifle barrel into Mr. Kemp's belly, stopping him in his tracks and causing him to gasp.

"Back in the house!" he ordered the elderly man.

The neighbor wasn't eased with Mr. Kemp's solacing words. He knew what was happening. The government had begun its disarmament campaign. The Kemps were indeed being burglarized - by professionals!

Bradley could see the worrisome grimace on the Hispanic neighbor's face in the light of a nearby street lamp. "Go inside your house and pretend this never happened," Bradley tried to reason with him. "If you keep pointing that gun at us, you'll be charged with a federal offense."

"You guys can get in those vans and leave and I'll pretend this never happened," he shouted, tensing his grip on his handgun. That comment stirred the ire of Agent Bradley, who was growing angrier with every moment this meddling neighbor's refused to lower his weapon. They had a busy schedule and this punk was slowing them down.

"We're not going to your house, just the households of militia and other suspects."

"The Kemps are good folk," the man said, pointing his gun at Bradley's chest. "Thou shalt not steal."

"We're not stealing. They'll be returned once their son is released from incarceration."

"Dad! I'm coming!" The 14-year-old boy rushed through the yard with his rifle.

His mother stepped out onto the front porch to fetch her son, protesting his involvement. "Get back here, William!"

The father turned to his son and ordered him, "Go back inside the—"

In the middle of his sentence he felt and heard an excruciating crack behind his left elbow. Before he could turn around to face his foe, a heel kick to the ribs knocked the breath out of him. He fell flat on his back. His head was dizzy from its smack against the cement, his elbow was dislocated in a contorted position, and his lungs burned as he strained for a gasp of air. Bradley had taken his handgun away in a split second and tucked it under his own belt.

"Leave my dad alone!" yelled the boy as he raised his squirrel-hunting rifle to his cheek.

The father's lips screamed, "No!" but no sound came out. He heard the rattle of silenced M16's and then the thump of his son's lifeless carcass against the sidewalk.

"No!" the father moaned, coughing.

"Get out of there!" a senior agent ordered Bradley through his headset as the agents on the front porch carried the guns to the van. "You're going to wake up the whole neighborhood."

The boy's mother came running to the side of her dead child, weeping with unfathomable grief.

"Let's pull out." Agent Bradley motioned to the vans. "Someone call 911."

Hamilton, Montana

The black magnometer-equipped vans began to yield disappointing results. It seemed like everybody was forewarned about the raids. Homes were empty. Gun safes were open and vacant of the coveted arms.

"Anything? Anything at all?" the senior FBI agent inquired of the magnometer technician. The farm residence they were now searching was the home of a known conspiracy theorist and retired arms dealer, a suspected militia sympathizer.

The ATF agent pointed at the colorful monitor in the darkened van. "That's a gun safe, all right, but look." He moved the mouse and brought the pointer to the area in front of the white rectangle on the screen. "The safe's door is open. I'm telling you, they've been tipped off. They're gone and so are the weapons." The ATF agent looked up at the FBI agent who stood next to him, actually expecting him to call off the raids. "We're wasting our time."

"Shut up!" he snapped. "These guys are taking their guns some-where. Now where?"

"They probably left with their guns in their cars or they stored them in underground bunkers on the property."

"And you can't see those?"

"Not with the magnometer."

The FBI agent cursed and kicked the wall.

The technician glanced at the heat sensor image on a second screen. "Hold on, I've got bodies moving behind the house."

"Where?" The agent looked down at his laptop to study the schematic of the property.

"Back porch. It's a weak signal because of the distance, but it's human-sized, for sure. I see two now. They're moving away from the house towards the barn."

"They might know we're here. We have to move quickly. Agent Bradley?"

"Yes sir," Agent Bradley responded from his van 20 yards behind the magnometer-equipped van.

"Two suspects behind the house are heading for a barn. They could be aware of our presence, so move swiftly."

"Yes sir." He began to bark out orders to his crew.

In less than five seconds, the back door to the van flew open and ten agents, gripping automatic weapons, moved quickly toward the house.

"Here you go, Doug," said the father to his 18-year-old son as he handed him the last of their rifles and a heavy briefcase full of ammo.

"What exactly did they say?" Doug asked his father as he set the firearms down into a hole that he had dug in the floor of their barn.

"They said that the feds are raidin' militia to confiscate their firearms a day early."

"How'd they know?"

"I told you: they're friends of a neighbor who was killed by the feds during one of their raids tonight."

When he received the tip, Doug's father sent his wife and daughters to a neighbor's house as the men began to hide their arms in a secret location in the barn.

The young man repositioned the weapons in the three-foot-deep rectangular-shaped hole while his father rushed to the back porch for the handguns. He had planned to make it bigger and insulate it, but they ran out of time.

His father ran back into the barn a few seconds later, carrying three handgun cases in one hand and another heavy wooden box of ammo in the other.

"Why would they come to our house anyway?" Doug asked. "You're not militia."

"I've organized TEA parties. I'm a gun owner who stockpiles. And I don't buy used guns, so the feds know I've got a lot of 'em. I've got too many unreliable guns from gun shows to trust a used gun."

Doug took the last gun case out of his father's hand and set it gently into the hole. His father handed him a loaded nine-millimeter handgun and Doug put it under his belt.

"Come on, Doug, hurry! Let's close it and shovel this manure on top. Then we have to take the shovels out of the barn to the woodpile so it won't be easy for them to dig under the manure."

"Dad, I'm sorry, but I didn't have time to make it as deep as you wanted, so I need to reposition some or the door won't shut." The boy dropped back down into the hole and moved the guns around.

"Hurry."

"I've got a question for you, dad."

"What?"

"If we're going to hide our guns when we need 'em most, why are we taking the risk of keeping them at all? I mean, what good are these guns going to do buried under manure in our barn?" As he spoke, he removed the weapons and began to re-stack them more tightly in the hole.

"You mean, as opposed to letting the government steal them?"

"These guns could still get us into a lot of trouble?"

"Well, sure," he grinned, "if we get caught."

"Why are we taking the chance?" Doug asked forthrightly.

"Son, my father told me if America ever takes away your guns, then she ain't worth living in anymore."

"But whether they're confiscated or they're buried and can't be dug up without the risk of being arrested, the feds succeeded. For all practical purposes, we're disarmed. So why are we taking the chance in keeping them?"

The father sighed deeply and sat down on a bale of hay. "I suppose if we ever have the opportunity to fight for our freedoms again, then we'll have the means to."

"If we ever have the opportunity? When will that be? When everybody else is disarmed? What good are these 25 guns going to do us if they're all that exist in the whole city?"

"Son, other people are hiding their guns, too."

"But there are more guns in town today than there will be tomorrow. If you're taking the risk of hiding the guns from the feds in hopes that one day we'll have the opportunity to fight for the right to keep 'em, then for the same reason, wouldn't we be more effective at fighting for that right now, when the chances of success are the greatest because the people haven't been disarmed yet?"

Good question, Doug's father thought.

"If a disarmed America is not worth living in," Doug said, "then maybe an armed America is worth dying for. And can you think of a better time to do it than now, when more people are armed and we actually stand a chance of victory?"

The cutting words pained the elder's mind. Doug's dad felt like a coward right at that moment. His son's gem of wisdom had cast a yellow glow onto his soul. He regrettably admitted, "Truth is, guess

I'm willing to risk my freedom to hide my guns, but not quite willing to risk my life in fighting those trying to steal them."

"If we aren't willing to risk our lives," Doug said as cautiously as he dared lest he be counted disrespectful, "then it seems to me that they've already won." He shoved the last gun into the hole. "It's just a matter of time and then—"

"Freeze!" the agent appeared in the barn's doorway behind Doug's father, causing them both to chill with fear. "Hands up! Let me see them!" With his weapon shouldered, Bradley carefully approached through the open barn door as a horse neighed in its stall.

Doug and his father put their hands up.

The agent informed his comrades through his helmet mic, "Got 'em in the barn, armed to the teeth."

The next five seconds lasted what seemed to be an eternity to Doug and his father. Here was probably their last chance to defend themselves against disarmament, against what they admittedly considered to be the apex of American tyranny. With a nine-millimeter handgun at Doug's waist, and an AR15 with thousands of rounds of ammo at their feet, they stood a chance, a very slim chance. They could shoot and retreat out the back door of the barn into the woods. Would they survive a shootout? Probably not. Surely more agents outside of the barn greatly outnumbered them. Would their neighbors come to their defense?

Doug's father could hear approaching footsteps outside. Even if he and his son could only shoot a couple of the troopers before being killed themselves, maybe that's all it would take for the feds to call off their raid on the families that were next on the list. Maybe their deaths would motivate Americans to rise up. Their freedoms *were* worth dying for. *Everybody dies*. The question is, do they want to die under the boot of a tyrant, or fighting against that tyrant with a fully loaded AR15?

Ten seconds later, those courageous imaginations became moot points as father and son became surrounded with black-clothed FBI and ATF agents pointing their full-auto machine guns at their chests. Their brave thoughts stalled and their cautious minds tossed them into the trash heap of all of the brave thoughts of an innumerable host of cowards and slaves throughout history. One of the agents reached forward and pulled the nine-millimeter Taurus out from under the young man's belt.

"You made the hole too small," the agent commented.

"Yep," said Doug. "A little."

"What were you planning on doing with these?" Bradley asked as he kicked the gun case that protruded from the hole in the barn floor.

"Putting them in a safe place for you," said Doug's father with a sarcastic tone.

Agent Bradley found that humorous. The six and a half foot frame of Rock Bradley heaved an intentionally obnoxious hackle. "That's what I figured."

Two agents frisked Doug and his father for weapons as Bradley questioned them. "Any more guns anywhere else?"

"No," he responded instinctively, hoping they wouldn't find the remnant of their handguns on the back porch.

"We've got handguns on the back porch," an agent informed Bradley through his ear mic.

Bradley grinned. "Then you won't mind if we take the ones someone left on your back porch."

The father sighed and looked at his son, who dropped his head.

"Do you know where all of your militia buddies are keeping their guns?"

When the man did not quickly respond, Bradley raised a rifle and aimed it at his face. "Where's everybody stocking their guns?"

The man refused to answer, matching Bradley's cold, careless stare with one of his own. Bradley aimed the gun at the face of the young man instead, who appeared equally unmoved. The boy's father didn't flinch or show any emotion.

"We can take you to jail or you can leave a free man – you'll have an empty gun case, but at least you'll be free." A couple of the agents chuckled and received a bitter grimace from Doug's father as a result. Bradley motioned for other agents to start taking the weapons. "The choice is yours. Where's everybody taking their guns?"

"I'm not a part of the militia," he said as he slowly lowered his hands. "Almost all of the friends I had in the militia are dead or in jail from your raid."

"Do you know where Fred Seibert is?"

"Don't know him."

Bradley grinned mischievously as he paced a circle around Doug and his father. "I can personally see to it that you stay out of jail if you can give us some information that can help us seize the illegal weapons that your friends are hiding."

"Maybe you should check in the barns behind their homes," proposed the gray-haired man as he pointed at the hole his son had dug.

"Yeah," said Doug with a snicker, "under the manure. It's a special type of manure that you have to shovel by hand. Shovels don't—"

"Shut up!" Bradley yelled.

"When am I going to get reimbursed for these guns? You're supposed to give me 25 % of the fair market value."

"Not today," said Bradley as he motioned to a nearby agent and then pointed at Doug. The agent unlatched some plastic cuffs off of his belt and began to handcuff the young man.

"What are you doing?"

"I'm arresting your son."

"For what?"

"Didn't tell ya,' did I?" Bradley quipped, leveling his rifle at the gray-haired man's blushing forehead.

"Dad? Can you bail me out?"

The agents laughed heartily at hearing the son's request.

One of the agents said mockingly in a high-pitched voice, "Dad, bail me out."

"If you want your son to be free," Bradley said as he retreated out the barn door, "give me some answers that can help us disarm your buddies in accordance with the law."

"Law? Hah!" The old man gasped at the agent's audacity to presume that he was following law.

"Fight 'em, dad."

Those were the last words the father heard his son say as the young man was led out of the barn and into the darkness.

The man slumped down on a bale of hay in front of the empty storage area in the barn floor. He felt like his body had aged a decade in five minutes. His whole body grew numb and began to ache. It was fear of losing his boy that kept him from fighting. His boy would face prison and maybe even torture and he'd have no way of fighting back. A Scripture came to his mind: *The fear of man is a snare.* The old man shook his head in shock. It was when he tried to think of how he would inform the boy's mother of what happened that he began to sob.

Washington, D.C.

"A 14-year-old boy. The boy's father thought that the agents were thieves stealing his neighbor's guns. One of our agents disarmed his father and the boy shot at us. An agent fired back and the boy's dead." Bill Erdman spoke to the president through their encrypted laptop connection.

President Brighton's heart sank. She frowned into the camera on top of her monitor where she also saw the faces of FBI Director Todd Hamilton, AG Vic Meyers, ATF Director Bill Erdman, and her Chief of Staff Dena Halluci. It was 6 a.m. and the president was being driven to a cabinet meeting in a limousine. She desperately wanted to hear some good news from her most trusted staff members, but all she heard since she lifted her head off of her pillow were extremely disappointing results from the first hellish night of Operation Offense.

The president wrung her hands, already imagining the panicky editorials in the morning news. "Oh, we'll have to change that story." She leaned into the camera. "You know the problems I'm having in Congress right now."

"Will Conway has a press conference scheduled soon," Hamilton said, referring to the director of the Midwest Division of the FBI. "He's optimistic that he can exploit the boy's death to harness the public rage and convince people to turn in their neighbors who are hiding arms."

"Madam President," Victor Meyers interjected, "you'll be equally displeased with the progress in Alabama and the Carolinas."

She sighed and braced herself for the worst. "Tell me."

"We've got a dozen sheriffs and mayors vowing publicly to keep their own illegal firearms today. A few in Mississippi and Georgia, too. The Georgia governor's loyal and he's trying to keep the outlaws in line but having problems with enforcement due to insubordination in his Guard and highway patrol. They're publicly daring us to prosecute them. It's having the predicted ripple effect throughout their precincts with as many as 49 percent of semi-automatic gunowners surveyed anonymously admitting that they won't turn in their illegal firearms by today's deadline."

"All right, let's pull a 'Randy Woods' on 'em." The president's coined phrase evoked a confident nod from Vic Meyers and Bill Erdman. They knew what that meant. They were to prosecute the most popular in the most humiliating manner feasible.

"I have bad news about Woods," Vic Meyers informed her. "It looks like the Bozeman Sheriff Randall Woods'll be out by the weekend."

"What?"

"A federal judge ruled his incarceration unconstitutional."

"Who?"

"Judge Kanka."

"She can't do that!" The president clenched her fists. "Who does she think she is?"

"She mentioned your EO that suspended *habeas corpus* in her ruling and said that it was unconstitutional."

"What? That's classic Patriot Act fodder. That's been upheld over and over."

"I know."

"If you want to keep Woods under the anti-terrorism statutes," Hamilton recommended, "you've got to declare him an enemy combatant and lock him up in a drawer. Hate-speech crimes and obstruction of justice charges are insufficient."

"All right," the president responded with a sigh, "let's do that."

Vic shook his head side to side and took a deep breath. "If you do that, Madam President, it will be costly politically. Up to this point, you've never accused him of terrorist activities, but only of

310

not enforcing your EO. A change in your game plan after Kanka's ruling could devastate your agenda."

"Okay, let's not take that route yet. I'll personally send some marshals to pick him up and move him. The judge's decision is unenforceable as long as they don't know where he is."

Hamilton stuttered. "Uh, um, Madam President. Do you really want to face off with the judiciary? If it goes all the way to the Supreme Court and they rule in Judge Kanka's favor, then—"

"The president is co-equal with the Supreme Court. I'm over-riding Mrs. Carol Kanka and I'll do the same to the Supreme Court if I must. We're not letting Randy Woods go. I've looked into this Sheriff Woods," she spoke with open contempt. "He could make the volatile situation in Montana much worse very quickly. He *hates* the federal government, and his constituents love him for it. Hamilton, I want you to put some people on Judge Kanka. Interview her staff and check out her recent cases. I want to know where she gets entertained, what her husband does, who she's on the phone with, where she goes to church, the websites her kids visit, and any religious or political affiliations. Look for something, anything, that'll help us cast aspersions upon her and this decision."

"I can do that," said Hamilton with a weary sigh as he jotted down some notes.

"Dena? How's the public responding so far?"

The chief of staff patted a stack of papers on her desk that summarized various public opinion polls that had been taken recently. "The terrorist attacks have turned public opinion slightly in your favor with regard to your anti-terrorist statutes and your disarmament EO in most states. The official story we've put out on South Carolina has helped us everywhere except in South Carolina, just as the official story we distributed on the Bozeman riot deaths helped us everywhere except in Montana."

The president was optimistic. "As we would expect."

"Of course."

"I have a meeting with Cameron Weaver this afternoon and we intend to discuss ways to combat the negative press. Vic? How's the case against Barry Friar?"

Vic widened his eyelids, opened his mouth, took a deep breath, and exhaled it noisily. That was a question he preferred not to answer honestly. "The guilty verdict's a done deal."

"Good."

Then softly, he added, "Probably."

Chapter 19

Helena, Montana

Barry Friar was at the end of a long chain of questions to a federal agent who was a witness in the case. "Can't you understand that as far as we could see, Mr. Quentin, you were trespassing?" The judge's eyes squinted and he gripped tighter to his gavel as Friar neared forbidden territory, but Porter beat him to the punch.

"Objection! Question elicits a legal conclusion."

"Sustained."

Friar reworded the question: "What did you expect us to do when you shot our dog and charged the field shooting at us?"

"We can't question orders on the field. Our superiors have all the information, and we have to trust their decisions."

"Did you know that we would have helped you apprehend the suspect if you'd have just asked? If you would have shown up with a warrant and arrested him, then you'd have had him in custody and—"

"Objection! Speculation and lay opinion. Your Honor, please remind the defendant who's on trial here."

"I apologize, Judge Waverly," Barry said humbly. Then he turned back to the witness. "You've got to help this jury out, Mr. Quentin. Let me get this right. You suspected I was going to commit a felony and that I was harboring an unconvicted murderer?"

"That's correct."

"So you barge onto my land with machine guns a-blazing, shooting, dismembering, and disemboweling dozens of men and boys because you suspect that we *might* one day commit a felony, and you suspect that we *may* have been harboring a terrorist?"

The witness reluctantly nodded. "We raided your property because of our suspicions and we fired in self-defense."

"My son was unarmed when you shot him! How can you say that you did it in self-defense?"

"He shot at us a moment before. How was I supposed to know he had dropped his gun? I never would have knowingly shot at an unarmed civilian." Barry could see that the agent was somewhat disappointed at himself for shooting an unarmed civilian, so Barry let a pregnant pause drag on in hopes that the witness would say something else. The witness swallowed hard. "I'm sorry about the death of your son, Mr. Friar, but I have to follow orders."

"There's that ubiquitous answer from the federal agents again." Friar turned back to the jury. "He was just following orders." He glanced at the witness. "You justify the raid on specious grounds and when your reasons are refuted, you revert back to the FBI agents' default excuse that you were just following orders."

"Question, Mr. Friar, question," the judge reminded him.

"Do you, Mr. Quentin, think you have an obligation to obey unconstitutional and immoral orders?"

"Objection!" Porter stood up from his seat. "How is this relevant to the defendant's guilt? Moreover, this trespasses upon the pretrial agreement that inquiries into afore established constitutional precedent would not be undertaken!"

"Withdrawn," Friar responded without turning away from the witness. "Did the adjusted rules of engagement allow you to shoot and kill teenage boys as they ran injured and unarmed away from you, fleeing for their lives?"

Porter prepared to object but the witness answered Friar's pointed question before he could. "I am not at liberty to—"

"That's right," Barry interrupted with another snap of his fingers and a wave of disrespect. "You're not at liberty to inform this jury of the truth, the whole truth, and nothing but the truth. You're not at liberty to tell this jury about those adjusted rules of engagement that allowed you to shoot my unarmed boy in the back."

"Objection, Your Honor!" Dan Porter stood to his feet with manufactured rage.

"I'm done with him," Friar mumbled as he returned to his seat. "Get this murderer to a city of refuge before someone who loves my boy does something sensible and—"

"Mr. Friar!" Judge Waverly slammed his gavel. "Control your emotional outbursts! This is a court of law!"

"This man put a hole the size of a softball through my unarmed son's spine! I think I'm controlling myself quite well."

"Mr. Friar! That's enough!"

The next day in court, Barry Friar tried to be more subdued, but when one of the FBI snipers was called to the stand, Porter was back to his enthusiastic objections and Judge Waverly was banging his gavel again.

"So, you're the man that shot my unarmed wife in the face?"

"Yes," he answered just as the prosecution sternly objected.

"Objection!" Porter bellowed. "Don't answer that!"

"He just did," Friar rebutted.

The judge slammed his gavel. "Mr. Porter! That is not a proper objection and the witness already answered the question. Please coach your witnesses *before* they're on the stand."

"May I approach the bench, Your Honor?" Porter asked.

When he and Barry arrived at the judge's bench, Porter asked, "May I have the defendant's comment struck from the record?"

"It's a statement of fact," Barry protested.

"It was stated in a derogatory manner," Porter argued.

"It was a statement of fact, Mr. Porter," Judge Waverly agreed with Barry Friar. "Stating facts in a derogatory fashion does not merit an objection."

"Even when it is a federal agent being spoken of in a derogatory fashion?"

Judge Waverly took a deep breath and sunk down in his chair. "Let's just get this over with, Dan. Spare us the excessive objections."

"May I have his objection struck from the record?" Barry asked. The judge grinned at that question.

"No," he said, "you may not."

"He objects every chance he gets, just to try and throw me off. He's objecting to a question that the witness already answered. Can't I get some kind of ruling that limits his objections to, maybe, less than one a minute, kind of like a golf-handicap for an inexperienced player?"

Waverly was showing his pearly whites now with an ear-to-ear grin. Porter shook his head and rolled his eyes at the defendant's stupidity. "Oh, Mr. Friar," the judge responded, "prosecutors have a way of doing that to *pro se* defendants. You'll have to adapt. Return to your witness."

Barry sighed and turned to face the witness. He rubbed his graying beard and asked, "So, you're the man that shot my unarmed wife in the face while she was breastfeeding her—"

"**Objection!**" Porter stood and shouted, causing the courtroom to erupt into laughter.

"Objection!" Friar whined in a high-pitched voice, turning toward the prosecution's bench to mock Porter.

The judge slammed his gavel and laughed out the words, "I object to both of you. Mr. Friar, finish your question. Mr. Porter, no more objections for an entire minute. Got that?" Porter turned to his table and shrugged, evoking smiles from his fellow prosecutors.

The agent in the witness stand was the only one who didn't find the humor in this exchange. Stone-faced, he responded to Barry's question, "I did not intend to shoot her. I returned fire."

"Are you seriously claiming that you did not intend to shoot her? You were a hundred yards away. Please don't embarrass your fellow snipers with that story."

The dark-skinned sniper cleared his throat and held his peace.

"I thought you were a crack-shot with the Bureau, Quentin?"

"I intended to shoot *you*, Mr. Friar."

"Well, I'm sorry you missed," Friar replied as he walked toward the jury. "Weren't you aware that my wife, kids, and other women were in the house, you know, cooking, cleaning, breastfeeding their

316

babies like good mothers do? Why did you shoot through an open door like you did?"

"I couldn't see anybody in the line of fire except you. My cross-hairs were on you. It was an unfortunate miss, but an appropriate shot."

"Was I shooting at you?"

"No, but you were running for cover," the agent stated calmly. "Men in your direction were shooting at us. If you shot at us from the cover of the house, we would've suffered more casualties."

"Did you know that you blew off my wife's jaw and half of her face?" He reached over and, without looking at it, held up a poster of an autopsy photograph of his wife toward the witness, then the jury, and then the courtroom audience. "I wiped up the blood and wrapped her body with a blanket and put it in the closet when she started attracting flies." His voice cracked and a painful moment of silence passed as the on-lookers studied the gruesome photograph of Vicki Friar.

"Objection! Why is this relevant to the defendant's guilt?"

The judge sighed. "I'm going to sustain this objection. You need to ask questions, Mr. Friar, not make statements."

"Yes sir." Barry turned back to the sniper. "Is the jury supposed to forgive this act of violence against my unarmed wife based upon your confession that you were trying to shoot a different unarmed person?"

"Objection! There's nothing to forgive because the witness is not on trial!"

"Sustained. Would you like a recess, Mr. Friar?" Judge Waverly's sympathetic tone caused Dan Porter to shift uncomfortably in his seat. This show of emotion only hurt his case against Barry Friar. He couldn't afford anyone on that jury to feel pity for this domestic terrorist.

"What in the world are you trying to do to us?" Judge Waverly shouted to Todd Hamilton through videophone in his office.

"Calm down."

"These notes from the FBI sniper that shot Vicki Friar," Judge Waverly said, waving a manila envelope in front of the web camera, "were sent fourth-class mail – **fourth-class!** In the middle of the trial! This evidence appears to contradict his testimony of this morning!"

"It was an oversight. It's not a problem."

"Oh yes it is! I'm going to have to fine the FBI for this. This makes the Bureau look *real bad*. How could you send such critical evidence in the middle of a trial of this magnitude via *fourth class mail?*"

According to the sniper's drawing of the front door through which he shot Vicki Friar, he was able to see her. On his drawing, the sniper outlined the top of her head seen through the cracked door. The newly discovered hand-written note became a thorn in the side of the FBI and the prosecution. Judge Waverly fined the FBI $1,400.

"Dan Porter!" Victor entered Porter's office without knocking, marched up to the desk, poked an index finger out of a clenched fist and leveled it 12 inches from Porter's nose. "You're screwing up this case!" Spit flew out of the corners of his mouth like shrapnel, causing Porter to blink and the attorney next to Porter to wipe his pant's leg.

The four prosecuting attorneys expected to get scolded, but they didn't expect such an emotional outburst from a man of such stoic demeanor as Victor Meyers.

"The bailiff told me that Barry Friar has that jury in the palm of his hand, thanks to you!" the DOJ director rebuked them. "You have not exposed his extremist views adequately." He hammered off a list of the prosecution's misfortunes one by one, tapping one finger at a time. "You've let him tease the jury with this jury nullification nonsense. You've let him wade into constitutional waters. You've let our witnesses waffle on their stories. You've let him caress the jury with irrelevant sentiment without objecting."

"I've objected more in this case than I have in the previous ten cases put together!" Porter shouted back. "You were supposed to have the judge on our side. What happened?"

Victor began to pace the room, visibly upset. "You were supposed to challenge him, get under his skin, and make him preach his conspiracies."

"If you think he's gained the sympathy of the jury now," Porter said as he leaned forward on his elbows, "can you imagine how they'd sympathize with him if I'd badgered him about his beliefs while he, the *pro se* underdog in a tussle with the mighty U.S. government, continued to appeal to the First Amendment prejudices of the jury? This whole trial is like a caricatured illustration of Barry Friar's whole point."

"What point?"

"You know, that the government's too big, too powerful, that you trample the little guy for a self-serving agenda."

"Oh man," Victor complained under his breath as he pressed his palms against a wall. "If we're not careful, we're going to blow this case."

"It's the FBI that's blowing the case! Judge Waverly has held the Bureau in contempt."

"I know, I know."

"What am I supposed to do when my witnesses conflict?"

"You're supposed to coach them, Porter!"

"The FBI has its own witness coaches, Vic. And Barry Friar is doing a knock-down great job of planting questions in the jury's mind that the Bureau's telling half-truths in order to conceal evidence that could acquit him."

"And why in the world are you letting Barry Friar delve into constitutional issues?"

"Me? I'm not letting him do it, Judge Waverly is! Maybe you need to get in there and put some pressure on him." Porter pointed toward the judge's chambers one floor up.

"I already have." Victor moaned as he took a seat. He raised his eyes toward the ceiling and took a deep breath. "Maybe it's time we talk about a plea bargain," he fretted. "Or else just give up hope in this state trial and put all our chips on the federal trial."

"Barry Friar wouldn't take a plea bargain," Porter predicted. "This man thinks that this trial is his life's purpose and he'll die for his principles. If you think it's going bad now, Vic, wait until you see who they're calling as a witness in the morning."

"Who?"

All observers were stunned when Barry Friar called his first witness. He stood up, smiled, and projected his voice throughout the courtroom. "The defense calls the governor of Montana, Benjamin Boswell."

The back door opened up and, instinctively, most of the room stood to their feet to see Benjamin Boswell walk down the center aisle.

He entered with a politician's smile, high-fiving the hands of those near the center aisle who put their palms out to him. Dan Porter trembled when he saw the members of the jury smile, applaud, and nod admiringly at the popular Montana governor.

At the sound of the applause, the judge slammed his gavel. "This is a courtroom, not a county fair," he snarled. "Hold your peaGovernor Boswell took his oath on the Bible and sat down comfortably behind the witness stand. The whispers in the room prompted the judge to thump his podium with his gavel. Barry Friar walked toward the governor with a warm smile.

Friar extended his hand and Governor Boswell took it in his own, calloused, muscular hand.

"It's good to see you, Governor."

"You too, Barry."

Barry backed away to his bench and leaned against it. "Governor Boswell, please inform the jury how you're involved in this case."

Boswell took his seat and turned his gaze to the jury. "Barry Friar and I have been friends for 21 years. He was of great assistance to me in my political campaigns over the years, and I was the best man at his wedding to his wife, Vicki..."

Washington, D.C.

"This is not good." Dena Halluci sat beside Margaret Brighton in the Oval Office as they watched the courtroom proceedings together, but the chief of staff appeared to be the only one worried. A federal agent sat among the courtroom observers with a secret camera that broadcast the video directly to the president's desktop computer.

"There're two ways to look at it, Dena," the president replied lightheartedly. "It's good for Friar or" - she looked at her and smiled -

"it's bad for Boswell." Halluci grunted as she ran her fingers through her hairspray-stiffened shoulder length hair. She was impressed with the president's insightful ability to find the good in any situation. "By the end of this day," the president added, "it'll be *real* bad for both of them."

Helena, Montana

"I was on the phone," Governor Boswell testified, "with Todd Hamilton. Mr. Hamilton informed me that the man wanted for the murder of two federal agents in Bozeman was being sheltered at Barry Friar's *compound*. That's what Mr. Hamilton called Barry's humble, hand-made hilltop home," he said with a snicker. "I'd be just as likely to call his bathroom a temple." Those words sparked laughs throughout the courtroom.

"Order!" Judge Waverly shouted with more volume than most in the room thought necessary.

"Mr. Hamilton told me that they had evidence of a conspiracy to commit acts of terrorism on government buildings. He also informed me that Barry Friar had sexually abused his children. I told Mr. Hamilton that I doubted that when my secretary interrupted me and told me that I had Barry Friar on the other line. I then put Mr. Hamilton on hold and spoke with Barry, who straightened out the story. He told me that camouflaged soldiers came out of the woods shooting automatic weapons at them. He told me that—"

"Objection. This is hearsay."

"Overruled," the judge quickly replied. "It confirms previous testimony given by the defendant and others. Continue, Governor."

The governor nodded courteously. "I told them to throw down their guns and surrender, but he was fearful that they would simply be killed. He told me that federal agents were shooting at him even though he was disarmed. They had already killed his son and wife though they were unarmed. He told me that Teresa and Marion had been injured. He asked for my help in calling off the troops and then we were cut off."

Barry let a long still moment pass as he leaned against the table behind him. "When you spoke to Todd Hamilton after we got disconnected," he finally asked Governor Boswell, "what did he say?"

"He told me that you were inside holding your children against their will."

"Against their will? Did he offer any evidence of this derogatory claim?"

"No. I recognized that he was lying, but he's the director of the FBI, so I was naturally on my guard." *Oohs,* and *Ahhs* echoed through the building, causing the judge to snarl at the governor in disapproval.

"Ob – jec – tion!" Dan Porter slurred in disgust as he slapped the table with his palm on each syllable. "Does the witness have to slander United States investigative agencies in his answers? This is preposterous!" he wailed with both hands raised in frustration.

"Calm down," the judge urged the prosecutor. "Governor Boswell, please spare us the political humor."

"Yes, Your Honor. Mr. Hamilton also told me" – Governor Boswell turned his gaze to the jury - "that Marion and Theresa Friar were in danger of being killed by their father. That's when I called him a liar."

"And why do you think he was lying?" Barry asked.

"Because I've known you for more than two decades! You would never do that. I've never known a better father or husband, nor children better raised. Then I told Mr. Hamilton that I knew about the deaths of Matt and Vicki, and the injuries to Teresa and Marion. I told him that I knew that FBI agents were attacking and shooting civilians without just cause."

"Tell the jury how you saved my life."

"I called out the Guard. At risk of being fired upon by foul-mouthed federal agents, Captain Rod Sanders, who gave his testimony here yesterday, maneuvered his way into your home and brought you out safely. No thanks to the president's unconstitutional executive orders or the obstruction by the FB—"

"Objection!" Dan Porter blurted out, standing to his feet.

"That kind of talk can get you placed in contempt of court, Governor," the judge retorted with a furrowed brow. Judge Waverly solemnly removed his spectacles and turned to the jury. "I'm going to ask you to disregard the comments of Ben Boswell, please. The governor's opinion and even your opinion of the president's policies have no bearing on this case." He donned his bifocals and turned back to Governor Boswell. "This is not the place to air your political grievances, Governor. It just muddies the waters of justice. Is that understood?"

"How can the jury justly weigh this case independent of the facts surrounding it?" the governor respectfully asked.

"Some facts are not relevant, such as your opinion about the president's policies."

"I'm a strong proponent of an independent jury, Judge Waverly."

Barry Friar smiled as the governor followed the script he laid out for him.

"Independent of coercion, yes. But not independent of law, of which I am the judge." Judge Waverly then turned to Friar. "Inform your witness of our agreement, Mr. Friar. If he speaks another word of this nonsense, we'll get rid of this jury and start the trial over with a new one, and with the counsel of my choosing. Is that understood?"

"Yes sir, Judge Waverly." Friar nodded at the judge's exhortation, but added, "But it was not 'our agreement,' sir, it was unilateral."

"Enough!" Judge Waverly slammed his gavel again. "Inform him of my decision then. And in the future you will approach the bench with those kinds of comments. Is that understood?"

Barry Friar nodded as the judge slammed his gavel again and ordered a ten-minute recess.

Billings, Montana

Bull's heart pounded with anticipation as he waved casually to a security guard in the parking lot. The guard, whose shift just ended, waved back without a second glance. Bull drove his rusting, camouflage-painted pickup truck toward the front entrance of the Tenet Federal Building.

The dynamite sticks obtained from Lonny were stacked in the back of his pickup in a manner that allowed one to see clearly all the way through the cab's windows. The simple radio-operated deto-nator had a wire connected to one stick in each box.

Stein parked the get-away car in a lot across from the building, where he patiently sipped his fourth fast-food coffee in two hours. They had done their homework. They carefully planned Bull's entrance to coincide with the shift change of the security guards. They speculated that the security cameras would be temporarily unmanned at that time.

The problem would be getting close to the building. The force of an explosion diminishes exponentially as the distance away from the blast increases. The truck had to be close to an internal column in order to destroy it and maximize the damage to the building and the loss of life. The federal government was careful to keep parking lots a safe distance from the buildings.

Bull did not want this to be a suicide mission. He wanted to sur-vive to strike again. He didn't fancy himself a martyr for the militia, but rather, a living warrior-icon. His brother planned to pick him up in his old Chevy Impala just before detonation. They meticulously studied the roads in downtown Billings, and had a plan for any type of sustained chase the enemy could possibly attempt.

"Wait here," Will Conway ordered the subordinate in an authori-tative tone. Conway set down his briefcase and opened the door to another room. He unfolded his cell phone as if to make a call.

"Yes sir," responded the senior agent assigned to the mission. This agent was one of a dozen fully armed agents who were plan-ning to rush the get-away car as it approached. Six others in a nearby room were to apprehend Fred "Bull" Seibert with sudden, over-whelming force from the side of the building and prevent him from detonating the bomb. Technicians manned state-of-the-art jamming equipment in order to be a safeguard against the wireless detonation that Bull was planning. Other armed agents were instructed to set up a perimeter. They were told to take Bull and his brother dead or alive, preferably alive, but under no circumstances should they delay in taking that detonation device away from the terrorist driving the pickup truck packed with explosives. Any shots at Fred Seibert must be instantly lethal and under no circumstances should the course of the bullet strike the vehicle or anything within it.

Conway picked up his briefcase and walked through the door. Before shutting it, he added, "Don't leave this position until I personally order you to do so. And don't interrupt me. Got that?"

"Yes sir." The senior agent, dressed in full swat gear, glanced at the 11 agents beside him as they held their weapons aloft, mentally preparing for their mission.

"This is a critical phone call, Agent Leahy. I need to confirm some things." Conway raised his cell phone briefly as he shut the door. Once it was shut, he quietly locked it and put his cell phone back onto its belt clip. He quickly walked to the other end of the room and opened another door that led into a hallway. He walked into the hallway and twisted the bolt lock on the door. He began to walk rapidly down the hallway into a stairwell and down the stairs. He exited the building and closed the door gently behind him. He glanced at his watch. Time was running out.

"He's not answering his cell!" Lonny shouted at the Tenet Building phone operator through the radio communications device that was inserted into his right ear. He told the Seibert boys that he was going to video the explosion from a nearby building, but he watched from his parked car closer to the Tenet building in case something went wrong. "I need for you to find him for me!"

"I tried calling his cell and he's not answering for me either."

"Put me back through to the room he was using as his office."

Lonny tapped the steering wheel anxiously when no one answered the phone. He let the phone in Conway's office continue to ring.

The armed agents in the office anxiously glanced at the phone as it rang on the desk over and over for several minutes.

"I think we should get that. Maybe it's important."

The agent in charge stomped over to the phone and picked it up. "May I help you?"

"Who's this? Where is Will Conway?!"

"Mr. Conway stepped out."

"I need to speak with him now!" His hurried tone worried the agent. "I'm your undercover man outside. Is this one of the agents responsible for apprehending the terrorist suspect in front of your building?"

The agent's mouth went dry. Something was wrong. "Yes. This is Agent Leahy, senior commander of the operation."

"I need you to find Conway immediately!"

"Conway stepped out to make an urgent call. He'll be back momentarily."

"Get him now!" Lonny shouted.

Lonny's urgency made the agent's heart skip a beat. "We have explicit orders from Conway to wait for his instructions."

"That building's going to have a huge hunk taken out of it in about two minutes if you don't move."

"He was clear with his instructions, sir."

"Where is he?" Lonny asked in a coarse, raised voice. He glanced around briefly to make sure his rage wasn't noticed by any passers-by. "I need to speak to him *now*, Agent Leahy!" The shrillness of Lonny's tone increased as he watched Bull pull his truck to the far end of the employee parking lot unnoticed. "Now!"

"He said he doesn't want to be interrupted under *any* circumstances. He's probably on the phone with the president."

Lonny's respiratory rate increased as he watched the befriended militia fanatic walk toward the waist-high chain that prevented his truck from getting closer to the building.

"Was Mr. Conway sick? Could he have passed out or something?"

"He was fine, sir. I think you need to just calm down. Trust him. He's never let us down."

"Where are you located?" Lonny snapped.

"Third floor, northwest corner of the building."

"Third floor of the…? What? You're not even in position! The terrorist is on the southeast part of the building!"

"We are exactly where we are **supposed** to be, sir," the agent responded, irritated at the undercover agent's lack of faith in their regional director's supervision.

"You might not even get there in time even if you left now!" Lonny hollered. **"Where's Conway?!"**

The agent blew out an irritated sigh and rapped his knuckles on the door. "Sir, sorry to interrupt, but your inside man needs to speak with you. Says it's urgent."

There was no answer.

"He said that he must speak to you now, Mr. Conway. It's urgent!" The agent banged on the door again. "Mr. Conway?"

"This is too easy. I can't believe we're pullin' this off," Bull mumbled to himself. Giddy with self-adulation, he grabbed the chain held aloft by two waist-high poles 15 feet apart. He noticed a young woman in her twenties smoking a cigarette near the front entrance. She was looking the opposite way. Bull pulled on one of the poles. To his fortune, it easily pulled out of the ground. He wouldn't need his four-foot bolt cutter after all. Bull laid the pole and chain down, walked to the other side and did the same with the adjacent pole, effectively eliminating the barrier.

He walked back to his still idling truck. "Come on, Stein, be there, be there." He took one last sip of his Rockstar energy drink and set it in the cup holder on the floor. He looked through the rear-view mirror for the familiar Impala.

In the parking lot on the way to his car, Conway waved to four employees who returned with their fountain drinks after a short Subway Sandwich lunch break.

"Good afternoon, Mr. Conway," one of them said respectfully. He smiled and nodded.

He started his car and quickly pulled out of the parking lot into the back street. He glanced at his watch again. It was 12:21. *At 12:30,* he reminded himself, *I'll call a press conference for 3:30.* He was on his way to Bob Evans, hoping that'd he'd get to eat some of his turkey club before the blast. It would be a long day. He picked up the phone and speed-dialed the number of the restaurant to put in his order.

Bull pulled over the curb carefully, over the chain that he had laid on the ground, and onto the freshly cut green lawn toward the building.

"Now! Now! He's driving toward the building! **Now!**" shouted Lonny.

"Mr. Conway!" Lonny overheard the senior agent shout as he banged on the door. The agent twisted the doorknob. "It's locked!"

Lonny shouted, "Apprehend the terrorist now!"

"Conway said to—"

"I don't care what Conway said! You're going to be dead in 30 seconds if you don't move now! In self-defense, for God's sake, stop him!"

"Conway!" The agent twisted the doorknob in vain. He stepped back and kicked the door in with one great thrust. He was shocked to find the room vacant.

The senior agent pulled the gun out of his holster and gave the order to his subordinates. "Mulestop! Execute Mulestop!" That was the code name for their operation. "Step it up. We're late." He led his men down the hallway and into a stairwell in a full sprint, their rifles at the ready.

Bull backed the truck to within two inches of one of the main concrete beams in the building construct.

"Perfect!" He removed the keys, opened the door, and bolted full speed across the lawn and into the employee parking lot. He was keenly aware of the .45 caliber handgun that was in an inside-the-pants concealed holster. He was relieved when he saw Stein's Impala finally turn into the lot.

The security guard in the building's foyer was sipping his diet Pepsi and munching on Fritos as he chatted with another employee about the upcoming NFL football season.

"Operation Mulestop underway!" came the urgent message on the security guard's radio.

The security guard's smile faded to a confused grimace. He tapped his radio. "Identify yourself!"

"Agent Leahy – execute Operation Mulestop!" came the hurried, panting voice. "Mulestop!"

"Say again?"

"Conway said he briefed you. Execute Operation Mulestop!"

"I don't know what in the world you're talking about, Agent Leahy! What is Operation Mulestop?"

There was no response from Leahy, who had just turned the corner of the building with his men. He caught sight of the suspect sprinting across the parking lot. Leahy ran toward the vehicle parked next to the building and ordered his men to apprehend the subject.

The security guard stood up, puzzled, and glanced at his security cameras for the first time in two minutes. He saw the truck, the driver sprinting away from it, and the armed agents giving chase. His eyes widened and breathing quickened.

"We've got a terrorist attack on the building!" the security guard shouted. He picked up the desk phone, tapped in four numbers, and spoke into it, "Code Red! Code Red! This is not a drill! Evacuate through northwestern exits immediately!"

Mr. Conway had disconnected the amplification system and no one heard the order. The security guard did set off the alarm and workers slowly got up to exit the building in response to what they thought was another drill.

Bull heard an alarm siren behind him and turned his head to see several black-clothed agents charging him, aiming their weapons as they ran. He breathed a curse as he sprinted. Bullets sprayed dirt onto him as they struck the ground, shot low intentionally to avoid the cars that drove the road beyond him. Bull reached the Impala and was about to jump into the seat when he saw Lonny's pickup truck skid into the driveway entrance. Lonny was shouting with his head out of the window, "Stop! Don't detonate it! Abort, Bull! Abort!"

"What!" He looked carefully and noticed that Lonny had his own gun drawn. *Lonny*, thought Bull, *what are you doing?* He jumped into the car and Stein did a 180-degree turn to face Lonny, who was coming right at them.

"Detonate it!" Stein shouted as he accelerated toward the exit. A bullet struck the side of the car and another pierced the windshield. "Quick!" Stein caught sight of Lonny's pickup charging toward them on the opposite lane. "What's Lonny doing? He's going to get himself killed!"

"He's telling us to abort the mission."

"Why?"

Bull stuck his torso through the open window as Stein sped toward the exit. Bull aimed his semi-automatic handgun and rapidly unloaded six bullets into Lonny's upper chest and face. Lonny's car careened off the road and smashed into a telephone pole, which teetered and collapsed, sending electric sparks zapping into the air.

"What are you doing?" griped Stein, exasperated. The agents behind them lay on the ground to take better aim. Several more bullets struck the car, sending shards of glass all over the vehicle. Stein ducked, swerved the Impala, and scraped against a stop sign. Bull ducked quickly back into the car window just in time to miss being behind by the stop sign.

"Where'd you learn to drive," he said mockingly.

"Why'd you kill Lonny?"

"He betrayed us." Bull pulled the detonator out of his pocket, flipped open the clear plastic cover, and prepared to set off the bomb.

"How can he be a traitor when *he* got the explosives for us?" Stein's eyes were on the road as he sped up to merge into the four-lane road that ran in front of the Tenet Federal Building.

A terrifying thought gripped Bull Seibert's mind as he flipped the switch. *Oh no! Lonny gave us bad explosives...*

The Impala's tires squealed as Stein turned into the main road in front of a honking pickup truck, his black beret falling off onto his lap. Bull pressed the button and the bomb exploded with magnificent power. It was massive, deafening, and mind numbing, surpassing all of Bull's expectations. The force of the blast thrust the get-away car sideways, slinging it six feet into the road, fortunately not into oncoming traffic. The tremendous force – like a fist of hot air through the open windows – caused Stein to hit his head on the steering wheel, leaving a blanched, then momentarily, bleeding gash on his forehead.

Bull gasped at the force of the explosion. He looked back to witness the entire four floors in the front of the building come crashing to the ground in a torrent of smoke and debris.

"No way!" Bull exclaimed as goose bumps went up and down his body in a wave. He thought he had enough explosives to take out one column, maybe. But the whole front of the building was coming down!

"Go! Go! Go!" Bull was dissatisfied with his twin brother's mellow driving, so he put his foot over onto the gas pedal and grabbed the wheel. "Come on!"

"I got it!" Stein dabbed his bleeding forehead with his palm. He put his black beret back on and winced as the beret scraped against his head laceration.

"Oh man!" squealed Bull, laughing as he turned to watch the clouds of dust and debris rise in great expanding billows high into the Montana sky. "Man! I never!" He stuck his head out of the broken window and shouted a quote from Thomas Jefferson into the direction of the blast: "The tree of liberty must be refreshed from time to time with the blood of patriots and tyrants."

He laughed sadistically as he turned back toward Stein. "Yes!" Bull raised a high-five at his brother, but Stein was too busy weaving in and out of slowing traffic to celebrate.

They pulled left onto a secondary road, following the escape route that had been mapped out, carefully slowing down to follow the speed limit. "Something's not right, bro," Stein remarked. "We're not looking at all the cards on the table. You just shot the fellow that got us the explosives. It doesn't make sense."

"I know, I know." Bull turned on the radio to listen for news stories of the explosion. "Lonny must have been turned somehow."

"Hello, Mr. Conway." The waitress lowered the piping hot turkey club down in front of him.

"Thanks Jan." He hastily reached down to pick up his sandwich.

Five bites later, the Montana sky groaned and the ground shook, causing the drinks on the table to tremble. One waitress dropped the platter of food she was holding over her head and it crashed to the ground.

"What in the world was that?" someone cried out worriedly.

Conway took another bite and sipped his coffee as customers headed to the windows to see what had caused the earth-shaking roar. He looked down with hungry eyes at his half-eaten sandwich and tried to console himself. At least he wouldn't have to pay for it.

"Was it an explosion?" someone asked.

Conway stood to his feet, walked to the window, and changed his countenance when he saw the smoke rising above the storefront across the road. "Oh no, please no. It's the Tenet. It's my office!" He picked up his suit coat and rushed for the front door. Once he pulled out of the Bob Evans parking lot, he opened his cell phone, tapped 11 numbers and coolly spoke two words. "Wrong number."

Helena, Montana

During the ten-minute recess, Judge Waverly verbally blistered Barry Friar for publicly questioning his authority and disrespecting his rules. When the court resumed, Friar was more cautious as he questioned Governor Boswell. The Montana governor spoke at length about the Guard's adventure in trying to get state investigators into the Friar home during the siege. The jury was on the edge of their seats as the leader they so admired unfolded the drama before them like a master storyteller.

In the final moments of the governor's testimony, an athletic gentleman wearing a three-piece suit and a military buzz cut walked through the back door in a hurry. He rushed up to the prosecutor's table and handed Dan Porter a typed white sheet of paper. Dan Porter read the paper, dropped it, and let it float to the table. He dropped his head into his hands and appeared stunned with what he read. He whispered something into the ear of the prosecuting attorney next to him, and then he picked the paper up and they read it again together. A moment later, the same athletic gentleman stepped back into the room with a legal-sized manila envelope with the red words "TOP SECRET" stamped on it. Porter opened it, peeked inside, and then set it back down.

"Hearing your testimony," Barry Friar said to Governor Boswell, "the jury must conclude that either you or the FBI is lying."

"Well, it's not me," the governor said matter-of-factly, shifting forward to the edge of his seat with his elbows on the table in front of him. "I've told the whole truth without any black-marker exclusions."

Barry glanced at Porter and smiled. "Your witness."

Dan Porter stood slowly and picked up the manila envelope. He walked toward the governor, opened his mouth as if to speak, but paused. He looked at Barry Friar and then the jury. "Approximately five minutes ago, the Tenet Federal Building in Billings was destroyed by a terrorist's bomb." The room erupted in gasps of unbelief. Two persons in the room immediately stood up, took out their cell phones, and began to dial phone numbers as they rushed from the room.

Judge Waverly appeared stunned by the announcement, yet disappointed that the prosecutor would make such an irrelevant announcement in the middle of the governor's testimony. "Approach the bench!" Judge Waverly ordered in a bellowing voice.

A pale Dan Porter, followed by a confused Barry Friar, gathered in front of the bench. "What in the blazes are you talking about?" the judge barked.

"This!" Porter extended the manila envelope toward the judge. The judge opened it and perused it anxiously. "May I submit it into evidence, Judge Waverly?"

"Submit what into evidence?" Barry Friar wondered out loud, his eyes wide with trepidation. "The defense must be made aware of it first, right?"

"What is this?" Judge Waverly asked, removing several large photographs from the envelope. The whispers rose in the room, prompting the judge to slam his gavel hard three times. "Order! This is still a court of law!"

Porter glanced at Friar with a disapproving snarl. "There has been a terrorist attack in Billings. And *you know* who did it! Hundreds have been killed and many more injured."

"What? I have no idea what you're talking about!"

"The explosion," Porter said, turning to the judge, "the explosion was the work of a domestic terrorist."

"Even if it was, why is this relevant?" Friar's suspicions of what the answer to that question might be haunted him, making his head spin with suspense.

The judge's eyes slowly rose from the piece of paper in his hands until his eyes met Barry Friar's. Friar didn't like what he saw in those eyes at all. There was a fresh malice and a renewed animosity behind those eyes, that terse jaw, and those grinding teeth that made his heart speed up. The judge dropped the paper to his desk and broke out in a sweat.

"It was Fred 'Bull' Seibert," Porter announced to Friar as he took several large photographs from the stack of papers in front of the judge. The prosecutor raised an eight-by-ten-inch glossy photograph for Barry to see, careful to let the jury behind Friar catch a glimpse of it. It showed Bull stepping out of a pickup truck in front of the Tenet Federal Building in Billings with a black MOM hat on his head.

"What?"

Porter began to show him the other photos as well, of the car fleeing and of the building collapsing.

The room full of journalists, jurors, and attorneys gasped and whispered frantically as their internet-accessible cell phones and laptops began to tell the story. Judge Waverly appeared confused and didn't intervene as the whispers rose to a level that he ordinarily wouldn't tolerate.

One of the elderly female members, whose son worked at the Tenet in Billings, began to have a panic attack. She began to hyperventilate and the woman next to her tried futilely to comfort her.

"What's going on?" Governor Boswell asked, unable to make sense of the conversation before the bench.

"You're still on the witness stand," Porter shouted at the governor in a disrespectful tone, "so you may speak only if spoken to."

One of the governor's bodyguards approached rapidly from the rear of the room and whispered something into the governor's ear. Governor Boswell jumped to his feet. "Judge Waverly, I request your permission to leave due to an urgent state matter."

The judge had his eyes fixed on an eight-by-ten photograph he held in his grasp, and remained speechless. Porter inquired of Governor Boswell, "Do you recognize this man who is responsible for bombing the Tenet Federal Building just a few minutes ago?" Porter extended the photograph to him.

"Objection!" Barry Friar blurted out as loudly as he dared. "That's, this is unfairly prejudicial to the defendant and completely irrelevant!"

"I do not!" Governor Boswell responded to the prosecutor's question. He stood and turned to Judge Waverly. "I will return for the cross-examination, but I need to leave!"

The judge simply sat there with a blank look on his face, studying the photograph of the ruins of the Tenet Federal Building.

"Judge Waverly!" Barry Friar shouted.

Porter stood erect and aimed a critical index finger at the governor, and in a tone more appropriate for a Pentecostal preacher than a prosecutor, began to reprove Boswell in the harshest tone. "The man you are defending knows him well, Governor Boswell! He trained him! He taught him everything he knows - about guns, about warfare, about government conspiracies, about fighting the feds and putting a halt to the anti-christ, one-world-government!"

The governor's beeper went off and he headed for the side door without even looking at the number. The judge picked up his gavel to stop the governor from leaving, but his trembling hand dropped it, and he reached down to pick it up again.

"It's Fred Seibert, Governor Boswell!" Porter announced. Ben Boswell stopped dead in his tracts as his bodyguard held the side door open for him. "Fred 'Bull' Seibert," Porter repeated, "the same man whom Todd Hamilton asked you to help find. Remember? You refused to call the State Guard to help the FBI with the manhunt of the terrorist suspect who fled from Barry Friar's home on the day of the siege. Now look what Fred Seibert has done!"

"Governor Boswell!" The clearly shaken Judge Waverly stammered out the words and tapped his gavel lightly three times against the table. "I, I did not give you permission to leave."

"Objection, Your Honor!" Friar exclaimed, standing on his tiptoes and raising his voice. "Am I not supposed to be pre-notified of all evidence to be displayed before this jury so that I can formulate a defense and prepare for cross-examination?" The judge wasn't listening; he was too busy telling Governor Boswell that he couldn't leave. The judge's speech was slurred and it appeared as if he was having a stroke.

"I must leave now!" said Boswell, rejecting the judge's order to stay. "There's a terrorist attack on Montana soil and my people need me." The governor disappeared out the side door and his bodyguard shut it behind him.

The rustling and whispering of the audience grew into a roar. The initial shock turned to grief and fear. Many tried to make calls on their cell phones but the lines were jammed.

With a loud whack of his wooden gavel, the judge called for a recess. "We'll resume, we'll resume in the morning." He then called for an aide to help him from the room.

"Are you all right, Judge?" Friar asked.

"I'll see, I'll see you in the, in the morning." Judge Waverly placed his arm around the legal aid's shoulder and was led slowly from the room.

Barry Friar shook his head and tried to absorb the gravity of what just happened. He turned to watch the famed prosecutor, Dan Porter, pack his photographs into his briefcase at the prosecutor's table, where six stunned attorneys whispered frantic questions to him that he did not dare answer.

I'd like to know, Barry wondered, *how Dan Porter got those photographs even before the governor knew about the crime*. During this whole trial, it was the prosecution and the judge who threatened to pronounce a mistrial to try to keep him in line, but now it was he who was considering it.

The prosecution team seemed comfortably confused about the day's conclusion, but Porter remained very quiet and sober as he walked out the rear of the room, past a cloud of anxious reporters shouting out unanswered questions. Porter's case against Barry Friar had improved considerably, but Americans were dying and he couldn't be happy about their crisis. In Dan Porter's mind, a mistrial was a possible response to his announcement during the trial, but that was a worst-case scenario. In light of how the jury appeared to be sympathetic with Barry Friar and Governor Boswell, a mistrial may be their best option. Furthermore, Porter knew that news of Friar's intimate connections with this terrorist, Bull Seibert, would soon become common knowledge and would stain any jury he could get in this state. Moreover, Boswell's refusal to help with the state-wide manhunt for Bull Seibert would mitigate his influence on the jury.

"I'm not taking any questions," Porter announced as he followed his attorneys from the courtroom.

Barry Friar lent his wrists to the two guards who would take him back to his cell.

Billings, Montana

As Will Conway sped to the FBI office building, he speed-dialed a press agent and scheduled a press conference for 15:30 hours. He arrived to witness the carnage just as the first emergency response vehicles arrived on the scene.

The front half of the building had crashed to the ground in a chaotic mass of crumbled cement, smoking boards, and twisted metal. Much of what remained standing was in flames. Ruins, interspersed with lifeless carcasses, were strewn across the lawn as chaotically as the emotions of the on-lookers. Rage, sadness, tears, and despair filled the eyes of the Americans who stood behind barricades of rapidly erected police tape, watching in horror.

The ambulances parked in the streets and the police shut off the main road directly in front of the building. Most of the paramedics found their skills useless as they stood in shock at the wreckage that was spread out in front of them. Some of them tended to minor wounds that were inflicted upon the passers-by. Some of the injured reclined on the debris-cluttered lawn. The bravest rushed headlong into the building to scour for survivors. The gentle breeze blew papers haphazardly across the streets, parking lots, and lawns adjacent to the building.

Other FBI employees fortunate enough to be tardy returning from their lunch break arrived just in time to receive orders directly from Mr. Conway. "Get those paramedics and firemen away from the building!" Conway pointed at some emergency workers heading inside the half-standing building. "We could have other bombs in there! Get them out of there and get the bomb squad out here right away!"

A few firemen had already made their way inside the rear part of the building to help survivors out of the maze of debris to safety. They carried out four unconscious victims and led out six wounded persons who could walk. Then their superiors told them to stay out-side the perimeter that the FBI was setting up around the building, for fear of undetonated bombs inside.

"Mr. Conway!" a female subordinate rushed to his side and got his attention. "Mr. Conway!"

"What?"

"Do you know what was in that building?"

Conway feigned a puzzled look on his face, and then his brow relaxed as he pretended to suddenly realize the implications of this event. "Where were they stored?"

"On the east end of the building, second floor." She pointed to the missing edge of the building. "That room is gone, sir. What do you want me to do?"

One survivor was climbing down into a ravine of pancaked con-crete slabs in the direction of a crying voice below when his name was shouted through a megaphone above. "Is that you Loudenslager? Get outta' there! Loudenslager! There are other bombs in there!"

The employee reluctantly obeyed his superior's orders and reversed his course. The crying voice of the wounded day-care worker in the basement, who held the fractured body of somebody's 2-year-old daughter in her arms, went unheeded.

Loudenslager stomped right up to the superior who managed the megaphone. "I told them about this!"

The superior lowered his megaphone, his bewildered gaze fixed on the trembling countenance of the enraged subordinate. "What?"

"I complained to administration about all the ordnance the ATF was storing there!" he pointed at the top of the building on the far side of the ruins.

"What? Where?"

"On the eastern side of the building. It was after hours. They wouldn't do anything about it! I told them that it was unnecessary and dangerous!"

The superior leaned forward and whispered harshly into Loudenslager's ear, "I don't know anything about that. Who'd you tell?"

"Administration."

"Exactly who?"

"I told Will Conway face-to-face."

The superior winced and looked over his shoulder to make sure that no one overheard Loudenslager's complaint. "You go complaining to anyone else, you just might wind up as one of the casualties. Now get out of here and keep your mouth shut."

"Everybody back!" The firemen busied themselves pushing back the crowd that had gathered to help find survivors. "There could be other bombs. Get back!"

The fire trucks slowly inched their way nearer to the building to try to put out the fires with their powerful water hoses, but firemen were disallowed from entering the building until it could be cleared. Many observed in rage, craving vengeance. Others simply mourned, and many with missing family members wept bitterly. In vain did observers implore the authorities to begin to rescue survivors.

Conway was immovable. "No! We're going to hold off the rescue attempt until the bomb squad arrives. I want that first floor scoured for any more bombs before we go in. You got that? Keep everybody back!"

"The bomb squad was in *that* building, sir!" protested one of Conway's employees.

"We have a squad on their way by helicopter," Conway responded. "Just keep the peace. We'll get everybody out when it's safe."

That was one order that the 17-year-old son of a secretary who worked on the second floor couldn't obey. His mother could be in there pinned by a column, bleeding, suffocating - he had to try to help her. Ten minutes passed and everybody was just standing around, waiting and watching, everybody except a few firemen who were engulfing a part of the building with huge jet streams of water. The young man wiped his tears, snuck up behind a fire truck, and darted toward the building.

"Stop that man!" shouted a federal agent into a megaphone. Two policemen gave chase, but turned around when the boy jumped through a waist-high broken window into a smoky room.

"Let him go. Let him go." The FBI superior waved the policemen back to the perimeter and out of the danger zone. "Just secure that section! The bomb squad will be here in a minute."

As the helicopter landed on the lawn about ten minutes later, the 17-year-old young man carried a half-conscious woman with a crushed hand and a hemorrhaging spleen through a crack in the wall in the part of the building that was still standing.

"He's got someone!" one of the pedestrians shouted as the news cameras zoomed in. "He's bringing someone out."

The young man carried the woman away from the building, tears filling his eyes, bloodshot and stinging from the dust and smoke. His body was soaked from the stream of water that the fire trucks sprayed on the ruins. "They're not all dead," he murmured to the first FBI agent who reached him. The FBI agent nodded and wrapped a fist around the young man's soot-covered wrist. A fireman took the woman from him and led her toward the nearest ambulance. The young man pointed to the building. "We gotta go get 'em."

"I'm sorry son. It's too dangerous."

"I'm going back!"

The agent tightened his grasp around the boy's wrist and reproved him before he could make another break for the building. "No more stunts like that, little hero, or you'll wind up dead! They're bombs on that first floor that need to be disarmed. That whole building could collapse on you and bury you alive."

"You don't know that," the young man replied, jerking his sweaty arm out of the grasp of the plain-clothed federal agent. "I know we can save somebody else, but I don't know that I'm going to die trying. Come on, man, people are bleeding to death in there!"

The agent grabbed the boy's wrist tighter this time, and pulled him away from the building. "See, look." The agent pointed at the bomb squad that was just getting off the helicopter. "The bomb squad's already heading inside."

The bomb squad went in with the dogs, searching the first floor, room by room in the uncollapsed part of the building, scouring for bombs or suspicious packages. Local news stations reported that they were taking so long because they were dismantling undetonated explosives in the building. The ATF would later deny that charge, in keeping with the official story that a single bomb in a truck outside the building was solely to blame. The national media outlets dismissed all testimony that contradicted the final approved story.

Twenty long minutes later, the pronouncement went out, "All clear!"

Then the search and rescue began. For many trapped and bleeding in the debris, it would be too late. Many in the basement drowned from the waterline rupture and the water spray from the fire trucks. Many of the injured bled to death or died of smoke inhalation.

Chapter 20

New York City, NY

"May I speak to Mr. Trump?" The dark-skinned Arab with a heavy accent looked quite out of place in the waiting room full of young and beautiful aspiring Trump sycophants.

The plastic-surgeon-sculpted secretary appeared taken aback with his attire. Although usual for a NY City subway, his all white cotton outfit, long black beard, and white skullcap didn't fit the profile for Trump, Inc., job applicants. Applicants sat around the large comfortable waiting room in leather chairs, reading fashion magazines and chatting with each other inconspicuously. They all turned their attention to the guest with the white Muslim garb.

"Do you have an appointment?"

He shook his head. "No."

The secretary tried hard not to laugh at the man's ridiculous request to see Mr. Trump face-to-face without an appointment. "May I ask your name?"

The Arab stuttered his response. "My name is, my name is, just tell him, just tell him that I must speak to him immediately."

"I'm sorry, Mr. Trump doesn't make appointments through me. Hold on, I'll get one of his assistants to help you." She picked up the phone and tapped a number.

In a few minutes, a thin assistant in a mini-skirt came into the waiting room and extended a hand toward the staunch guest who stood upright in the middle of the room with his hands clasped behind his back.

"Hello, Mr.?" She paused with her hand out-stretched, expecting the strange guest to give his name and shake her hand. He did neither.

"I need to speak to Donald Trump immediately."

She pulled her hand back to her side. "Mr. Trump sent me to assist you. What can I do for you?"

The Arab man looked around the room, walked away from the aid and back to the secretary. "Ma'am, can you please get Donald Trump on the phone and tell him that I need to speak to him? Tell him it's a matter of life and death."

The urgency in the man's voice disturbed both the secretary and the assistant. The Arab man saw the fear in their faces as the secretary picked up the phone and dialed three numbers. He knew that his time was short. Beads of sweat broke out on his brow as he backed up and unexpectedly stood up on a chair beside the door. He opened his white gown to display a bomb strapped around his chest, connected by duct tape and wires.

"Allah Akbar!" he shouted before pushing a button on a device in his hand.

A hundred square feet of the first and second floors was instantly obliterated, sending glass, sheet rock, and scalded body parts flying into the street.

Corporations with branches in Muslim lands were the next targets of the Islamic fascists. Contracted security guards of leaders of corporations operating businesses in the Middle East were implicated in atrocities against civilians, public intoxication, and blasphemy against the Muslim faith. These orchestrated attacks were in response to those charges. Twelve large corporations were targeted with suitcase bombs or suicide bombers, resulting in the deaths of 88 Americans. None of the targeted CEOs were injured in the attacks.

Washington, D.C.

Todd Hamilton typed on his computer in his office in the Hoover Building, preparing a detailed report for the president. He paused

343

his typing to watch a video on his computer, which reviewed the damage to the third floor of the Empire State Building. He breathed a sigh of relief that the building didn't crumble as a result of the explosion. To him, the multiple terrorist attacks in the waiting rooms and offices of private corporations were just a blip on the screen compared to the Tenet Building attack, but to the public, the attack upon civilians was devastating.

The phone rang and his gaze darted at the Bluetooth that rested on his desk. He snarled at the unwelcomed interruption. By the sound of the ring, he knew that this was Hamilton's secure line. It was a day of endless bad news, so he took a deep breath and prepared for the worst. He glanced at the caller I.D. on the lower right hand corner of his computer screen. It was the director of the FBI's northwest division. He hurriedly picked up his Bluetooth, tapped a button on its side, and placed the device over his right ear.

"Hello, Conway." The face of the highest-ranking Bureau administrator west of the Mississippi shined up on his monitor. Hamilton faked a smile at the clearly perturbed FBI administrator.

"Please tell me what is going on!? Are these bombings—?"

"This isn't our doing, Conway." Hamilton interrupted him. "This comes as a complete surprise to us as well."

"You expect me to believe that this is completely coincidental?"

Hamilton nodded confidently.

"Are you sure our Seibert suspect wasn't working with the Islamists? What are the chances that these attacks would take place one day apart from each other?"

Hamilton was growing troubled with Conway's angry tone. Hamilton leaned into the camera on top of his monitor. "You said yourself that your man on the inside knew the Seibert boys better than their mother. If Fred Seibert were cooperating with the Islamists, you would know it. Believe me, Conway, these terrorist attacks are a complete surprise to us and to the CIA, with whom we have been in close communication throughout the day."

"Are you absolutely sure that no one in the Bureau had any foreknowledge of these attacks?"

Hamilton shook his head back and forth. "I told you already. We didn't know about this."

"Who did it?"

"*Jihad* rag-heads again, operating independently."

"Of course," he responded with a hint of sarcasm, disbelieving the official story already.

"The important thing is that it's probably over and it'll assist us in our implementation tremendously."

"So our whole plan for my building was unnecessary? Today's terrorist attacks would have been sufficient to—"

"Not true, Conway!" Hamilton tried to console him. "The Tenet operation was *absolutely* essential. We *had* to take out all of the material pertaining to our investigations of the Columbus, Ohio, bombing that was being stored in Tenet. That was *critical* to our agenda. The calls in Congress to produce those findings will come to a screeching halt as a result of the data destruction. Furthermore, our main problem with disarmament is in the Rockies, as you know. The Islamist attacks nearest to the Rockies were northern California and Chicago, and they wouldn't have had a great affect on the folks in Montana, Idaho, Utah, Wyoming and the Dakotas. The plan for Tenet was absolutely necessary in order to implement our strategy in the most troubled parts of your territory."

Conway cursed the timing. "If we'd have waited until well after the president's deadline for disarmament in the Rocky Mountain states, like I initially requested, none of this would be necessary!"

That comment made Hamilton's brow wrinkle and he leaned even closer toward the monitor. "I don't want to hear anything like that again. You hear me? It's done. It was for the good of the country. The president's pleased."

"It was unnecessary, Hamilton!" Conway was emphatic. "We should have waited." His voice cracked as he spoke and his face reddened. The display of emotion broke Todd Hamilton out in a sweat of worry.

"Calm down, Conway."

"I've got 168 employees dead for 'the good of the country,'" he snapped sarcastically while pointing at the monitor, "and *not one* of them had to die."

"There's no way we could have predicted these terrorist attacks, Conway. Get a hold of yourself. We did the best we could with what information we had. Don't fritz out on me and become a liability. You've been CFR for what, 35 years? You know how hard we've worked to get to this point. Hold your mud."

Conway sighed deeply and looked at his hands while he twiddled the thumbs. Hamilton frowned and changed the subject. "How's the rescue?"

Conway took a deep breath, but kept his gaze fixed on his clasped hands. "We held off the rescue for two hours and got a good body count. No one even suspects internal munitions except some wacko conspiracy theorists and suspicious observers, the most influential of which have already been silenced. We've had to take out a few noteworthy private detectives who were getting too close."

"You did what you had to do."

"Some state reps are suspicious, but our hands are clean. It's pinned on Seibert's car bomb pretty firmly and his militia by default. Media's helping. Tide of public opinion out here is already turning."

"Great." Hamilton smiled at the good news but was disappointed that Conway's countenance didn't reflect it. "Hang in there, Will. You're doing a good job. I'll be meeting with the president in half-an-hour and we'll discuss your promotion. Who knows, she's been so displeased with my performance that you just might take my job!" Hamilton laughed, trying to lighten the mood, but there was no smile or eye contact from Conway.

Conway ran his stubby fingers through his gray hair. "I need that crime scene destroyed as soon as possible. There's already been talk on the floor of the Montana state legislature to have an independent investigation and Governor Boswell has endorsed it."

"Of course he has." Hamilton leaned back in his chair, undisturbed by the announcement.

"I have encouraged the independent investigation publicly in order to neutralize any suspicion of me, but we can't have anybody discovering the evidence of the internal bombs."

"We'll take care of that just like we did in Oklahoma City," Hamilton assured him with a smile. "Don't worry. I'll just need a statement from you and some state reps on how the healing would be expedited if you could speedily clean up that wound in the heart of Billings."

"I'll fax it to you in a few minutes," Conway said before flipping off the monitor.

Hamilton slapped the button on his speakerphone, disappointed with the conversation. He unlocked his briefcase, removed a sat phone, and prepared to make a phone call.

Billings, Montana

"Thank you, thank you." Conway tried to wave quiet the crowd of hundreds who stood on the lawn in front of the Tenet Federal Building wreckage. His thin, gray hair had been hair-sprayed firmly to one side, and his red complexion had been pampered with make-up, thanks to a friendly CNN make-up artist. The crowd of onlookers applauded his leadership in the rescue efforts that saved hundreds of people from the building in the past 16 hours.

"Thank you. But it is *I* who should join *you* in applauding the true heroes of Montana: the local policemen, emergency medical personnel, firemen and women, and Federal Bureau agents who saved many Americans here today. If you were involved in the rescue efforts, please, stand to your feet." Rescue personnel stood proudly all over the lawn. Conway began to clap and the crowd followed his lead, clapping and shaking the hand or patting the shoulder of the hero who stood nearest.

"We appreciate you more than you know. You're the glory of America."

When the applause subsided, he looked into the camera and spoke in a grave tone. "It is a day of grief and tragedy for Montana and for the United States of America. The bomb of a domestic terrorist has struck at the very heart of our democracy. It is with much sadness that I inform you of the deaths of 168 Americans from every state in the Union, and the injury of 680. Many of the injured remain in critical condition."

Conway took a deep, cleansing breath. "It's time to make some changes, America." As he admonished his listeners, his voice was confident and strong, like a dependable tower rising from the midst of an ocean of shifting waves. "There is an evil in our midst, a domestic threat that seeks to destroy our way of life and drive fear into our hearts to manipulate us to conform to *their* extremist agenda. This small minority of fanatics has declared war on America." Many of the civilians held their breath, bracing for what was sure to be the introduction of even more intrusive federal regulations and security measures. At the foot of such carnage, how could they refute the heroic FBI administrator?

"It is for the sake of those heroes who rescued your friends and family from this wreckage," he said, pointing to the half-destroyed building that lay in ruins behind him, "for the sake of the dead, for the dying and the injured, that I ask for your help. Though many of us might disagree with some of the actions of our president's administration, please, let us not resort to hate speech or the violence that resulted in, in *this*" - he pointed to the wreckage again - "this evil!" He fought off a sob in his throat and a tear fell down his cheek, and a journalist snapped TIME magazine's photograph of the year. Conway didn't even wipe the tear, but mustered the strength to raise his voice to an uncomfortable level: "My country, good or bad! Right?" Several applauded at this statement and the tension in the crowd eased.

"We *must* pull together, for the sake of the heroes, for the sake of the victims, we *must* obey the law of the land! I ask for the citizens of Montana to place their trust in our time-honored process of justice, which, for all its faults, is still the best system in the world. Trust in our government of the people, by the people, and for the people. We will tolerate nothing less than full compliance with all of the laws that your elected representatives and leaders have passed – all of them!" The crowd stilled and he could sense resistance building. "If you don't like it, join me in working for change at the ballot box. God knows I'm votin' to change it." The audience sensed that Conway was shooting from the hip and probably taking quite a risk in saying such a thing publicly. A flurry of reluctant applause rippled through the otherwise still crowd. "I'll probably get in trouble for saying it, but it's true. Trust the American people to make the changes that need to be made through the democratic process. Work within the system of law. Lawlessness and anarchy will only bring suffering. Our disunity will destroy us from the inside out, like a malignant cancer. We can't stop this" - he again pointed over his shoulder at the ruins - "unless we are unified. Our nation *will* conquer fear, we *will* conquer our terrorist enemies, we *will* conquer the hate, but we must do it together or *we* will be the ones conquered."

Conway swallowed hard as the applause was not forthcoming as he expected. The federal agents on guard at the perimeter shifted uneasily. "I ask now for a moment of silence out of respect for the men and women who died and for their families. No." He paused and shook his head. "Forget that moment of silence, let's make it a moment of prayer."

A long moment of quiet stillness followed his conclusion, as Conway bowed his head reverently, his hands clasped piously in front of him. It was a strange sight: an FBI administrator bowing his head to pray as the nation watched in awe. Momentarily, Conway turned to shake the hands of some colleagues and heroes that stood on the elevated platform next to him. The applause was soon forthcoming. How could you argue against that patriotic call for unity and prayer in light of the terrifying backdrop of crooked cement slabs, haphazardly thrown chairs, blood-stained furniture, shattered sheet rock, twisted steel beams, and death?

"You did well, sir." The local chief of police shook Conway's hand and followed him from the platform. Conway shook a few more hands and offered his condolences, relishing the praise that his subordinates heaped upon him. He kissed the cheek of a senior agent's widow and patted the soft, blond hair of the 5-year-old son, who wiped the tears out of his red eyes and tried to appear brave. Conway was led to a silver-gray Crown Victoria, where his bodyguard was waiting to drive him to his next destination. Conway turned to wave at the few who had gathered around to say goodbye.

"Mr. Conway! Mr. Conway!" A reporter managed to slither past the barricades and get her microphone within two feet of the regional FBI director. "Where are you going now?"

Conway's voice trembled with restrained grief. "Home." He ducked into the car and waved through the window.

Halfway down his quarter-mile driveway just north of Billings, the chauffeur slowed to a stop in his gravel driveway.

"Aww. Don't slow down," the retired FBI sniper Lon Horiuchi complained from 200 yards away. His crosshairs were on Conway's second button from the top. He raised his crosshairs over Conway's temple. "You don't have to make it that easy."

"Is everything all right?" Conway uttered to the driver, who was as motionless as a statue. Conway looked behind him and to each side to try and figure out why the car slowed to a stop.

The driver muttered without looking back, "Just a minute, sir."

Conway glanced uneasily at the nearest door, noticing it locked.

The marksman in the woods put a bullet through the vehicle's side window, instantly killing Conway with a shot to the cranium. The chauffeur then made a frantic phone call.

The official investigative report of Conway's untimely death would break a Bureau record in its findings and conclusions. An AR15 semi-automatic rifle with the serial number scraped off would be found in a creek near the scene with the fingerprints of Jack Handel on it, the notorious leader of the homegrown terrorists in the Militia of Montana who had escaped the raid on the Friar's farm. The gun had an internal serial number on the trigger mechanism that linked the gun to Barry Friar.

Brighton's crime control statutes would see a boost in popularity in the Rocky Mountain States as the common people grew more fearful and suspicious of assault weapons in the hands of right-wing extremists like Jack Handel, Barry Friar, and Fred "Bull" Seibert. And now Barry Friar's case had one more huge obstacle to overcome in his pursuit of the jury's sympathy.

Chapter 21

Helena, Montana

In the prosecution's closing arguments, Dan Porter showed why he was the most sought-after attorney in the world. He vividly contrasted the loving families and children of the slain agents with the government-hating, homophobic, anti-choice, religious extremism of Barry Friar. That was the red carpet for his *coup d' grace*.

"Intelligence had linked the wanted domestic terrorist, Fred "Bull" Seibert, to Barry Friar," Porter bellowed as he marched back and forth in front of the jury. "He had been recruited into the militia by Barry Friar, trained by Barry Friar, and he was on the field with Barry Friar the day of the raid, armed with Barry Friar's semi-automatic weapons banned by the United States government." He halted in front of the jury and aimed a critical finger at Friar. "Those were the very same weapons *his* militia used to shoot down men and women who had served their country honorably. It was Barry Friar's weapons in the hands of trained killers like Fred Seibert and Jack Handel that cut down so many men on the outskirts of his property. Character witnesses quoted Barry Friar admitting that he would not turn his guns in if they were ever banned and he urged others not to turn in their guns either. Moreover, it has been proven that Barry Friar manufactured a shotgun that was shorter than federal regulations allowed. Barry had violated federal gun laws and was conspiring to continue to do it againDan Porter began to pace again as he ran through the list of the dead and maimed federal agents.

"Somebody is responsible for the needless deaths of those American soldiers. They perished in the line of duty, upholding the law and defending their nation from ruthless criminals and violent fanatics like Barry Friar and his friends Jack Handel and Fred Seibert. Don't dishonor the memory of these American heroes by giving Barry Friar anything less than he deserves. Don't let the pathetic veneer of a self-proclaimed patriot and family man obscure the time-honored tradition of American law and justice." He aimed his index finger at the defendant with a stern grimace on his well-tanned face. "Don't spit on the coffins of those who died in the line of duty by giving anything less than a guilty charge to the man *most responsible* for their deaths. Don't join with the terrorists who hate our country and defy our laws. Give Barry Friar justice!"

When Porter sat down, all eyes turned to Barry Friar. For a moment, he just sat there and did nothing. His mind was on his friend Jack Handel. He had heard in the morning news reports that Handel was accused of shooting an FBI administrator, and although he knew that to be a lie, it encouraged him to discover that at least Jack Handel had survived and escaped. His thoughts went to his three surviving children, Teresa, Timmy, and Marion. He prayed that they were keeping their faith in God. He wondered what lies they had been told and what they thought about him. His thoughts wandered to his dead son and wife. Had they even been buried? Or did they lie dissected on a cold, stainless steel medical table in some FBI crime lab, or naked in a bathtub of formaldehyde?

Judge Waverly cleared his throat. "Mr. Friar?"

Barry stood to his feet and steadied himself with his palms on the table. He could sense that spirits were heavy after the wave of terrorism that swept such fear and grief across the nation. First it was the destruction of the Tenet Federal Building, which was pinned on a Montana militiaman, and then it was the Muslim bombings of American businesses. Then it was the assassination of the FBI administrator whose leadership had been credited for saving so many lives in the aftermath of the Tenet's destruction. The sympathetic countenances that the jury had been showing him during the final days of the trial were now suspicious and cold. They hated terrorism, and Barry Friar had been painted as the poster boy of everything anti-American. He took a deep breath and walked toward them.

"Innocent until proven guilty. It's been a hallmark of justice ever since the giving of the law at Mt. Sinai. You don't execute people until they've been convicted. The Bible says that God hates the hands that shed innocent blood. So do I. I'd love to be on Jack Handel or Fred Seibert's jury if they did that for which they are accused. But accusation does not equal guilt, as we all know too well from the arrests and detentions of our friends and neighbors as a result of the president's executive orders of late." Some among the jury nodded, causing the prosecutors to begin to whisper to one another.

"My unarmed son, Matt, was shot in the back as he fled camou-flaged attackers shooting at him from the woods. Of what was he found guilty? What crime did he commit? Resisting excessive government force? Is that a crime? If so, what jury heard his case before he was executed? My dear lovely wife was shot in the face by an FBI sniper." He paused and took a deep breath, trying to prevent the burst of grief in his bosom from rising to a sob. His emotion caused Porter to roll his eyes and the jury to shift uncomfortably in their seats. "My son, Marion, was severely injured by the gunshot that killed his mother. He clenched his teeth and wept for days, suffering indescribable pain, in and out of consciousness, unable to hold food down. What was their crime? Where was his jury trial?"

He turned and walked in front of the prosecutor's bench, standing directly in front of them. He searched their eyes. "Half of the time all the prosecutors have done is attack *our* faith. But the Constitution protects the free exercise of my religious beliefs even if your government and these prosecutors here spit on the Bible and believe that my faith in every word of that good book is nothing but religious fanaticism. Their primary virtue is tolerance and non-judgmentalism but they" - he pointed at Dan Porter - "are the chief violators of their own moral standard. They are intolerant of Bible-believing Christianity, the faith of our American forefathers."

He turned back to face the jury. "I'm thankful that God has granted me a jury trial. Many men better than me were denied one: Sheriff Randy Woods, local pastors, local statesmen, fathers, mothers, many of my friends and your friends who had the nerve to criticize

Margaret Brighton and her dream of a socialist country where babies are killed at taxpayer expense, where Alzheimer patients are murdered in order to cut Medicare expenses, where churches are forced to marry sodomites or lose their tax-subsidized status, and where all political dissidents have been disarmed. Hundreds of Americans have simply disappeared since the president's suspension of a right to a jury trial recently ruled unconstitutional by Judge Carol Kanka and predictably disregarded by President Brighton.

"Not only is your government responsible for the death of my wife, the death of my son, and all of the others who died on my property. But they're responsible for the deaths of the American soldiers who, as you have heard time and time again, were just following orders. Who gave those orders? Who changed those rules of engagement and to what were they changed? Those answers, we were told, were concealed from you for what they called 'national security.'" Barry shook his head as if in disbelief, and then said sarcastically, "National security – yeah right. Did all that black marker across the FBI's report make you feel safer?

"I think the only reason they let me have a jury trial is because they thought they could beat me and set an example that would discourage other patriots from resisting. If the state trial fails to convict, they'll still keep me locked up for the federal trial, which they can suspend indefinitely under Margaret Brighton's executive orders. So what do the feds have to lose? The one thing they didn't count on is a righteous, independent Montana jury that will pull the mask off of their subterfuge." The judge took a deep, audible breath at hearing those words, but didn't interrupt. "Montanans understand the abuses of the federal government better than anybody. Homes have been raided, privacy rights violated, and property confiscated. A 14-year-old boy was killed in the city of Lolo, Montana, a boy who tried to defend his father from FBI and ATF thugs who were confiscating firearms even before the President's executive order went into affect. Today, you have the opportunity to do justice in one such case. This jury trial is the mercy of God poured out on our nation for this one, brief span of time, when the people are given a fleeting opportunity to right the government's wrong and acquit the innocent. God has given you, the jury, that power and I pray you are a good steward of it.

"Our forefathers designed this federal government to be restrained by the Constitution. They designed a system of checks and balances to keep this government from getting out of control. One of those checks and balances is the jury system. Our government cannot persecute innocent civilians with perverse, man-made laws without the help of the jury. You are the teeth of the government's legislation and President's executive orders. Our government can't give me a lethal injection or torture me in solitary confinement for the rest of my life without *your* help. You are representative of the people of Montana. They," he said, pointing at Porter and some of the Bureau's agents sitting behind the prosecutor's table, "can't continue to persecute us without *your* help. Don't help them abuse the people. Don't deliver yet another wound upon my wounds." The prosecutors grew uneasy and whispered anxiously to one another.

"Uh, Mr. Friar?" Judge Waverly spoke up and motioned for Barry Friar to stop talking. "Hold up." The judge glanced at the jury. "Let me clarify for you so that there is no confusion," he explained calmly and methodically. "You jurors are to decide innocence or guilt based upon the law as *I* explain it to you." He tapped his chest with his thumb. "You are *not* to decide the law for yourselves. Do you understand me?" The members of the jury and the prosecution nodded, and the judge turned back to Friar. "Please, Mr. Friar, don't contradict my instructions to the jury in your closing comments. It doesn't help your case."

Barry Friar nodded and bit his lip as he turned back to the jury. "'The right of the people to keep and bear arms shall not be infringed' the Second Amendment plainly says. The Fourth Amendment of the Bill of Rights forbids unreasonable searches and seizures. Jury, it's your choice whether you want to do justice or injustice today. I beg of you not to disregard the Constitution and the Bible for the opinions of lawless bureaucrats and tyrants."

Judge Waverly grunted uncomfortably, taking the sting of Barry's reproof personally. Barry Friar was walking the line and the judge's blood pressure was rising. He recalled the mini-stroke on the day of the Tenet bombing and thought it best for his own health to keep quiet and let Barry Friar ramble to a close.

"The government did more to discredit their own agencies than they did to convict me of anything criminal. All the prosecution did was cast aspersions upon the motives of those they're defending with their thick, black markers. I have broken no law, except a federal gun law, and in that case, I was following the orders of an undercover federal agent who intentionally misstated the law to me when I did some work on a shotgun of his. Why wasn't he charged as an accomplice? Why wasn't I allowed to see my accuser face-to-face and cross-examine him? The government has not convicted me of anything criminal." Friar took a deep breath. "The guns on my property that day were all legal. They can't even prove that I fired a single shot at a federal agent." He turned to face the horde of formally dressed FBI agents who sat behind the prosecutor's table. "And I certainly would've been justified in doing so, given that they shot my son in the back and my wife in the face, probably following those adjusted rules of engagement in their unprovoked attack on my home. This injustice needs to stop, and it starts with you, dear jury. It starts with you, today."

Just as the judge prepared to interrupt again, Barry Friar turned and addressed him, "Judge Waverly has been very patient with me and for that I thank him. However, he has told you that he doesn't want you to consider constitutional issues. He wants you not to consider the strongest evidence for my defense – the law of the land."

Judge Waverly shook his head at that comment and glanced at the prosecution.

"Did the government deprive me of my God-given right to life, liberty, and property that day? Was their force excessive? Was their seizure of my property and siege on my home reasonable? Were the deaths of my family and my friends justified? Was their cover-up of evidence critical to my defense truly necessary for national security?" He paused and his eyes welled up with tears. "You decide, jury." He concluded with a cracking voice, full of emotion: "God help you to do the right thing. He's watching and He will hold you accountable on the final Day of Judgment." Friar nodded at the jury, and some nodded back, much to Dan Porter's dismay. Friar turned and walked slowly back to his chair, the stillness of the moment punctuated by the slam of Judge Waverly's unforgiving gavel.

Dan Porter walked hastily up to the bailiff, who had his ear pressed up against the crack between the door and doorframe. "Hear anything?" The jury was taking longer to deliberate this case than he expected, and that was a bad sign.

"That foreman has turned up the volume on his CD player," he whispered. "He set the CD player facing the door, to be sure that we couldn't hear them. Can't make out a single word over the Bach they're blaring."

Dan Porter shook his head and walked away. The foreman was not showing encouraging signs.

Three long days of debating had worn out everybody except the tall, gray-headed foreman of the jury, an elder in a Pentecostal church who managed to get on the jury only because he was a retired public school teacher. Each of the charges against Barry Friar was considered, the evidence for his guilt, and the defense's rebuttals. Arguments were heated. Predictably, the veracity of Barry Friar's defense depended upon the jury's willingness to consider constitutional issues.

"But we are more than the judge's voice," the aged foreman said confidently at the end of the long rectangular table in the middle of the room. "Otherwise, what's the point of being judged by a jury of your peers, instead of just letting the judge decide? How can we ignore Barry Friar's rights? We all have a constitutional right to resist excessive government force."

"The judge won't let us consider constitutional matters," a thick-skinned construction worker reminded them.

"Federal judges don't grant our constitutional rights and so they can't take them away. According to the Constitution, our rights come from God, Judge Waverly's protest notwithstanding."

"You're joshing' me," a disabled African-American female juror said critically. "You want to reject what the judge says, just like that?"

"Of course not." The foreman shook his head side to side. "He's welcome to his opinion and we need to take what he says very seriously. But I wouldn't murder someone if the judge told me to, would you?"

The woman shook her head. "No."

"Well, neither will I be an accomplice to injustice because the judge tells me to." The foreman slapped the long wooden table in front of him, and thundered, "My conscience isn't for sale! I'd be a fool to trade God's law for man's. How can I ignore the Constitution that grants us the right to a jury trial in the first place? How can *we* ignore our moral obligation to do justice and love our neighbors as ourselves? There are a lot of forces at work here pushing for their own agendas. Our agenda is justice and the Constitution is our friend in this endeavor."

"You must have the nads of a gorilla to take on Judge Waverly like that," the construction worker told the foreman. "If we honor the judge's instructions, then he's guilty. Hands down guilty." The other jurors nodded.

"Y'all just don't know your rights as a juror," the foreman told the reluctant jury. "Juries are the people's last safeguard against government abuses, the last check in our government's system of checks and balances." The blank stares the elderly foreman received revealed to him that his lofty confidence was not moving them.

"It sure looks like they're trying to hide something," a pre-law student sympathetic with the foreman's points said. "They wouldn't even let us see half the evidence from the FBI investigation."

"We're *not* lawyers," protested the elderly lady in a high-pitched voice as she fondled the sleeves of her green sweater that she obviously had knitted herself. "We're just common folk. How can you say that you know more than Judge Waverly and the other attorneys?"

"We're not saying that, Mrs. Annabella," said the foreman in a gentle, yet forceful tone so as to be heard in spite of her faltering hearing aid. "There's this principle in American law called 'jury nullification' or the jury veto power. Juries have the authority to decide guilt or innocence regardless of the instructions of the judge or the law. Even the Supreme Court of the United States has consistently endorsed the traditional power of the jury to nullify a law or a specific conviction. You know what Thomas Jefferson said about jurors, Mrs. Annabella?"

She didn't look up.

"I was a history major and I teach history part-time at Knowland Heights High School…"

The elderly lady perked up. "I have a grandson at Knowland."

"You do? What's his name?"

"Tony Price."

The foreman smiled. "I had Tony last year. Intelligent lad."

"Thank you. Anyway, I'll never forget Jefferson's quote about jurors. He said, '[As] jurors, the people exercise the greatest proportion of judiciary powers.' Thomas Jefferson said that you, Mrs. Annabella," - her eyes now met his - "have more power than Judge Waverly. As a member of the jury, you are *more important* in providing justice than he is or Congress or the president or even the Supreme Court. You know why? Because you, Mrs. Annabella, all of us jurors," he said as he looked around the room, "have the final veto power over all of our laws." Mrs. Annabella didn't respond. She shrugged and looked down at her sleeve as she twiddled with a loose bit of green yarn.

"Jefferson also said, 'I consider trial by jury as the only anchor yet devised by man, by which a government can be held to the principles of the Constitution.'"

"Wow. He said that?" The pre-law student was amazed.

The foreman nodded. "If a politician abuses his position of authority and tries to take away our rights, it is the right and obligation of the jury to tie down the government with the chains of the Constitution. One of my favorite founding fathers, John Adams, said, 'It is not only the juror's right, but his duty to find the verdict according to his own best understanding, judgment, and conscience, though in direct opposition to the direction of the court.' You see, if our leaders persecute Christian folk who have done nothing wrong, we have the right and obligation to spurn their malice and *not* to convict. I *refuse* to be an accessory to the government's abuse of Barry Friar. We represent the people of the United States, not the government."

"I've sat on a jury two times in my life and I've never heard this before," said Mrs. Annabella with a tremor in her voice.

"Me either." A young businessman loosened his silk yellow tie.

"You know why? Because the courts stopped informing jurors of their rights in the 1890s. It is up to us to do our own homework now. But jury nullification of bad law gave our country the freedom of the press. It was through jury nullification that slavery was overturned in state after state even before the Civil War, the Salem Witch Trials were stopped, and anti-strike laws were overturned. The government cannot use bad law to deprive anyone of life or liberty without the consent of the jury."

"This is true," the pre-law student added. "It's not popular today in the courts, but this is fact, not fiction."

Mrs. Annabella mumbled incoherently as she pulled her lipstick out of her cracked, fake-leather purse. The foreman saw that clearly she was not convinced.

"Mrs. Annabella, may I ask you a question?"

She looked him in the eye. "Yes."

"Do you agree with the laws outlawing guns or the taxes that Brighton passed without the consent of Congress?"

After a pause, with trembling voice, she said, "No, I do not."

"Do you agree with the FBI arresting pastors during church services because they preach against the sins condemned in the Bible? Do you agree with abortion-on-demand and gay marriage?"

"No, but it's not my place to disagree with Judge Waverly," she screeched.

"Do you think the government has a right to shoot unarmed folks like Matt Friar in the back as he runs away from armed trespassers? Do you think that the government has the right to shoot Mrs. Vicki Friar in the face as she's unarmed, holding her baby?"

"Of course not!" she squealed as she crossed her arms over her purse in her lap.

"Well, then don't enforce those bad laws, Mrs. Annabella. It's that simple. The buck stops here, with you, with us, the jury. If we think the president's executive orders are unconstitutional and unjust, then don't condemn innocent people with them. With a 'Not Guilty' verdict, we can put a halt to these abusive unconstitutional raids that have been taking place all across America. That's our right. That's our duty."

The door opened without a knock and in stepped the bailiff followed by one of the prosecuting attorneys. "How's it coming?" the bailiff asked in a cordial tone. "Y'all need any—"Uh, hold it." The foreman raised an index finger and interrupted. "Please step out of the room if you will. You're not allowed to be here."

"What's going on?" inquired the prosecutor.

"What do you think is going on? Leave."

The prosecutor looked confused.

"Just give us five minutes and then we'll take a break. You don't want to be charged with jury tampering, do you?"

"Okay." The prosecutor backpedaled out of the room with the flabbergasted bailiff in his wake. "Five minutes." The other jurors were stunned at the authority that their foreman demonstrated.

"I don't know if you all realize this," the foreman continued once the door was shut, "but this jury decides not only the fate of Barry Friar, but may also decide the fate of Margaret Brighton's political agenda as well. They know that," he said, pointing at the door, "but they don't want you to know it. We need to prayerfully pass down a 'Not Guilty' verdict and let the world know that the people of Montana will not be accessories to the unconstitutional and tyrannical abuses of its citizens."

He looked at the gentleman closest to the door and winked at him. "Let's take a break now. What do you say? Go ahead and let them know they can enter."

"Yes sir." The man nodded and jumped to his feet as if grateful for the request. He marched proudly toward the door, as if he had just been ordered to do so by the man who held the keys to American liberty in the palm of his hand.

The courtroom was packed and tensions were high. Barry Friar had his eyes closed, praying silently. Tall, muscular bodyguards surrounded Governor Ben Boswell in the row behind Barry Friar. The jury foreman handed the decision to the officer without emotion, who handed it to the judge.

The judge took one look at it, glanced at someone in the back of the room, and ruffled his baggy cheeks. Barry Friar's hopes rose. With a grunt, Judge Waverly handed it back to the officer, who handed it to the foreman.

"For the charge of first degree murder, we find the defendant, *Not* Guilty," the foreman read, which unleashed a wave of sighs and smiles on one side of the room and gasps of disbelief on the other. He read each charge: conspiracy to commit terrorist acts, hate speech, gun law violations, kidnapping, murder, followed with the jury's judgment.

"Not guilty."

"Not guilty."

"Not guilty."

"Not guilty."

"Not guilty." By the time that the last charge and verdict were read, Barry Friar was grinning ear to ear and the courtroom erupted in chaos.

The judge slammed the gavel once and then rushed from the room without another word.

As Barry turned and hugged Ben Boswell, four men in black suits and ties approached from the rear of the courtroom.

"Barry Friar. We have a warrant to take you into federal custody."

"Now just a minute!" the governor intervened. "He's been declared 'Not Guilty.'"

"By the state of Montana," the elder agent responded without hesitation as the other three agents placed their hands on their concealed weapons under their jackets. Boswell's bodyguards also placed their hands on their holsters.

The agent raised his voice and stepped back a step. "This man has been charged under federal law and he's going to receive a federal trial. We have 50 armed agents in the adjacent courtroom who are watching us through surveillance cameras. Don't do anything stupid. We *will* take him into custody, Governor Boswell."

Barry glanced over at the governor and winked as he offered his wrists to the federal agents. "I was prepared for this, brother. I was planning a prayer and fasting vigil for you anyway, so the solitary confinement will suit me just right. Keep your faith in God and keep fighting for righteousness and justice. Keep an eye on my kids for me, if you can find them."

"Will do. We're praying for you!"

"Governor Boswell! Governor Boswell!" A reporter thrust a microphone into his face in the courtroom foyer. "What do you have to say about the 'Not Guilty' verdict?"

Flanked by his bodyguards, Boswell said, "These are the first raindrops of a hurricane of revolutionary thought that's sweeping across this land. There is a law higher than the laws of human government to which the people of Montana will give priority. The jury rendered a decision that was right and just in the eyes of God, and that is compatible with the Constitution." The governor winced, and said, "I am extremely disappointed that Mr. Friar has been taken into federal custody."

Another reporter angled a microphone toward him as the camera behind her zoomed in. "After the manner in which the federal government has treated the leadership of Texas and South Carolina, don't you worry that the government will step in and remove you from power, citing national security interests?"

The crowd of reporters and journalists pressed in tight around him and Boswell smiled unexpectedly. "The sacrifices of Texas, South Carolina, and all Christians and patriots who have suffered under federal tyranny will be the tithe for the harvest of righteousness and justice that God will send His people. If I must also pay into that tithe to keep Montana free, then I am willing to do so." He looked into the camera. "But I want to forewarn President Brighton, Todd Hamilton, Victor Meyers - listen to me!" He aimed his finger at the camera. "If you bullies come and pick a fight with us, we'll make you pay dearly. Montana will go down fighting."

"But Governor Boswell!" The reporter pressed in closer as the governor's bodyguards tried to make a path for him to the front door. "What do you have to say to the terrorist suspect in the Tenet Federal Building explosion, Fred Seibert, who's still at large? Or Jack Handel, the suspect charged with murdering FBI administrator Will Conway? What do you have to say in response to Todd

Hamilton, who said that your incompetence was partly to blame for the escape of these suspects?"

"To Fred Seibert and Jack Handel, I say, Montana's coming after you, turn yourselves in. To Todd Hamilton, I say..." He paused as he moved between his bodyguards toward the foyer.

"What? Governor Boswell?" The reporter frantically changed her position so that her cameraman could get a good face shot.

"To Todd Hamilton, I say, Montana's coming after you. Turn yourself in."

Baltimore, Maryland

With the help of his friend in the president's cabinet, world-renown underground journalist Josh Davis was writing another article that would turn out to be the most read piece of journalism in American history, even though the federal government would criminalize its publication. Davis' army of fans and volunteers would distribute it by hand and over the internet all over the world. For him, this wasn't for fame or money anymore. Since he was hunted by the feds, there was no way to collect income from his articles. He didn't make a dime. No, Josh Davis was a-changing. He knew that his articles were fuel for the next American Revolution. He knew that his pen might cost him his freedom, maybe even his life. But he was willing to pay that price.

Danny Connor was rubbing off on him.

Washington, D.C.

"You need to hear this, Madam President." Dena Halluci read a highlighted portion of the Davis article to the president as they drove in a limousine together on the way to the National Press Conference. "'I fear that the patriots and heroes of our generation may very well be those who defy the federal government. The Barry Friars, the Pastor Anthony Hendersons, the Henry Adams, the Ben Boswells, and the Sam Kepplers...'"

"Sam Keppler?"

Halluci nodded. "He was the 17-year-old boy who disobeyed the direct orders from the FBI administration after the Tenet Federal Building explosion. He snuck past the barricade and rescued an injured woman. Josh Davis praises him for it."

The president sighed and fixed her gaze on a cloud formation that peaked at her through a layer of morning fog. "Who benefited the most from the destruction of the Tenet Federal Building?" Halluci continued to read, "The president's agenda. All the records from the Reproductive Rights Convention explosion in Columbus, Ohio - the very same records that Congress has repeatedly subpoenaed and which the president has refused to provide - were destroyed when the Tenet Federal Building tumbled to the ground in a heap of smoking ash. Why weren't these records converted to electronic format and stored at more than one facility, as is government policy? What a convenient oversight! Furthermore, how could a pickup truck barely packed with enough explosives to destroy one of the cement beams destroy 11? When 13-year FBI veteran Mike Loudenslager complained to regional FBI director Will Conway about the large amount of ordinance that the ATF was storing in the part of the Tenet Building that was destroyed, why was his complaint, lodged two days before the explosion, was ignored? Why was the ATF storing ordinance in the Tenet Federal Building, which did not meet the federal criteria as a safe storage place for explosive ordinance? Why did all of the ATF employees that had offices at the Tenet Federal Building call in sick on the day of the explosion? What a convenient illness! And why was Mike Loudenslager found dead on a gravel road outside of Billings' city limits with a bullet in the back of his brain and cash still in his wallet soon after giving this interview? What a convenient random execution!"

Halluci paused and looked at the president, as if she expected her to either deny these facts or add some missing information that could resolve the apparent mysteries. Instead, the president cursed Josh Davis with her lip trembling in anger. Halluci gave her a moment to regain her composure.

"Continue," the president mumbled without looking at her.

"Here's his conclusion. 'Sam Keppler lost his mother that day, but he saved a woman's life and earned America's respect. Sam Keppler is an American hero. Governors Gary Cropp and Henry Adams are American heroes the likes of Samuel Adams and Thomas Jefferson, who also were avid advocates of resistance to and independence from a similar tyrant in a different age. Give me 1,000 more like them who will courageously defy federal law to obey God's and I'll put tombstones on top of the graves of America's tyrants.'"

"Treason," the president exhaled through gritted teeth. She glanced at Halluci with a fiery ambition in her eyes. "That's treason."

Given the president's accusation, Halluci thought it best to omit the last sentence, which read, "The hope of America are those godly patriots accused of treason by America's tyrants."

Part V

A Rose in the Desert

Chapter 22

Missoula, Montana

Kneeling in a dark room teeming with pastors and church leaders at the largest church in Missoula, surrounded by men weeping for revival, praying for the lost, and interceding for the Coalition of Free Christian States, David Jameson felt like he was on the verge of despair.

With borrowed cell phones, he had done everything he could to discover the location of his wife and daughters. The hotel where she was staying had no knowledge of her whereabouts, as she never checked out. She just disappeared. The hotel manager was more interested in collecting unpaid debt than in finding Darlene and his daughters. Those who lived at the home in Ohio where he had planned for her to stay hadn't heard from her. The bus stations and train stations in Austin had no record of ticket purchases for his wife or three daughters. Each of the airlines that flew out of Austin's airport denied selling her tickets. The campgrounds near the hotel informed him that she had not leased a campsite. Every car rental agency within 50 miles denied renting her a car. The hospitals and police departments had no record of her being admitted. Children's Services denied that they had taken custody of his daughters. He even called local banks to see if she'd taken out a loan, and local used auto dealerships to discover if she'd purchased a car. Every investigation was a dead end.

He feared the worst: Darlene had been taken into custody. He pressed his head against the cheap maroon carpet in the darkened prayer room of the little church that had called a citywide 24-hour fast. He had no more words to pray. All he could do was groan and cry out to God. God had never used him more in ministry, but the cost was his brokenness and his frequent fastings, birthed out of his extreme grief and concern over his family. Like a single rose rising out of the dearth of a vast expanse of a dry desert, David's passion for revival and his mountain-moving prayers were birthed out of the most excruciating circumstances of his life.

David, Elijah, Jared, and the Manning family found Montana in the throes of a spiritual awakening. Almost every church was over-flowing with passionate worshipers and repentant sinners at almost nightly meetings. Elijah, Jared, and Cal were meeting regularly with groups of new converts at the campground where they were staying. They baptized sinners in a creek near their tent. The Spirit of God came upon hundreds in just a few weeks.

Since David was a wanted man, he limited his personal contact to pastors and church leaders, who held a deep respect for him because of his obvious wisdom and anointing. When David laid his hands on someone and prayed the prayer of faith, heaven seemed to move on his behalf. Pastors regularly invited David to preach from their pulpits, but he refused and deferred to Elijah instead. If someone were to recognize him, his ministry and his freedom would be put in jeopardy. When he was invited to preach, he would offer to intercede for the pastor during his sermon instead. And then he would lay his hands on that pastor and pray for the power of God to flow through him as he preached. Many preachers confessed that they had never felt anything near the 'cloven tongues of fire' mentioned in Acts, chapter, 1 as when David laid his hands on their head and prayed for them.

There was joy in knowing that God was using him, in spite of his struggles with doubt and worry. There was joy in knowing that revival had come to Montana. There was joy in knowing that he was living in a state that had banned abortion and was trying to honor the Lord. But when his thoughts drifted to his wife and daughters, he imagined how much they could be suffering right at that moment and he found it extremely difficult to be joyful. He found it very difficult to put his faith in God and lay his wife and daughters into Jesus' hands, to put aside his doubt and lift a voice of thanksgiving and praise to his loving heavenly Father.

He thought about how Abraham must have felt when God called him to sacrifice his son, Isaac, the promised seed given to him in his old age. How hard it must have been! He thought about Jesus in the Garden of Gethsemane, wrestling with whether to submit to the Father's will and endure the scourging and crucifixion. As David Jameson moaned and wept there on the carpet in that dark room of that little church, he could now understand how Jesus must have felt when He sweat drops of blood and asked His Father if the cross could be avoided.

The words of Jesus in Gethsemane rang in his mind. He could see in his mind's eye his dear Savior, with His eyes heavenward, cry out the words to His heavenly Father. David's lips moved to speak those words, but no sound came out. A dark cloud seemed to hover over him, snatching his breath away and terrifying him with nightmarish thoughts. He whispered a request to the Lord for strength, and then opened his mouth to speak the Lord's words: "Not my will, but Thine be done."

As has happened hundreds of times since their flight from Texas three weeks ago, his fear, doubt, and despair took wings and flew away, leaving him with an ocean of peace in his heart and rivers of living water flowing from his spirit. He raised his head, looked heavenward, and said those words again, "Not my will, but Thine be done." He smiled. God was such a good God, so trustworthy. David basked in God's love, confident that God was taking care of them.

Questa, New Mexico

"So what'dya think, Stein?" asked Bull.

Stein wiped the butter from his mouth with the back of his hand and smiled. "You're good, bro, you're good."

Bull laughed as Stein took another bite of his pan-fried squirrel, a staple for the Seibert brothers since their flight to New Mexico after the Billings bombing. The sun was setting at their campsite and the low cloud cover reflected an eerie orange-yellow glow onto everything.

"Without the pellets," said Stein with a grin.

"Yeah," responded Bull. Eating wild game speckled with shotgun pellets was routine for the Seibert brothers, but Bull was careful not to use any of his guns unnecessarily. He caught this squirrel in a snare trap erected on a branch propped up against an oak tree laden with acorns.

"You know, poaching's illegal also."

"What isn't?" snarled Bull. "I'd like to poach Brighton and every slug in that Congress, if I could, and roast them on a pointed stick."

"Yeah." Stein nodded as he sucked on a squirrel's hind leg. "So what's next?"

"With all of the terrorists' bombings the day after ours, I feel like fate has blessed us. Barry Friar was acquitted. Freedom's invincible." Bull grabbed the tongs and selected another squirrel thigh from the hot pan propped up on bricks over the embers. He placed it on the plate and blew on it to cool it off.

"Uh oh," said Stein, looking down the lane. He saw four shiny black SUVs coming down the dirt trail and his eyes went wide. Bull turned slowly and caught a glimpse of the SUVs and his heart began to pound. He cursed under his breath, and looked around to try to formulate a quick plan of escape.

"Don't move a muscle, boys." The calm voice that came from behind them was calculated to keep Bull and Stein from getting startled, but Bull quickly stood up anyway to face the tattooed fellow-camper who approached them from behind their tent with a cocked handgun pointed toward Bull's chest.

"Jeff!" Bull faced his foe, disgusted with himself for trusting their friendly, redneck fishing neighbor with whom they drank a couple beers and traded hunting stories the previous night.

"Sit down, buddy or I'll kill ya. Don't care if you're dead or alive, but you're going with us."

"Us?" Stein wondered.

Bull glanced down at Stein, whose back was to the undercover FBI agent. Stein was still watching the SUVs that picked up speed as they made their way toward them down the gravel drive, kicking up clouds of dust in their wake. They were about 90 yards away when Stein looked up at Bull. "It's over, bro. It's over."

Bull looked and saw Stein glance over at the hot pan resting on the bricks in the campfire between them.

Bull put up his hands and turned sideways so as to make himself a smaller target. Stein raised one hand into the air, but with the other he reached for the iron handle of the hot pan full of steaming butter and squirrel quarters. He winced in pain as his hand singed against the pan, then he let out a blood-curdling yelp as he lifted the pan and flung it at the undercover agent's face about five feet away.

The agent ducked the hot pan, but hot butter splattered onto his face, neck and into his right eye. He screamed in pain as he aimed the weapon toward the brothers.

Blam! Blam! Blam!

A moment later, the agent had regained his composure and was able to open his left eye. The taller of the two suspects, Fred "Bull" Seibert, was lying on his back, unconscious on the ground with a gun-shot wound to his abdomen. It looked like he wasn't breathing. The other Seibert brother had disappeared. The black SUVs screeched to a halt and their doors flung open. The agents jumped out and rushed onto the open, unmowed grassy field, pausing occasionally to shoot their handguns at Ed Seibert, who sprinted into the woods.

The undercover agent cursed loudly and pulled a cell phone out of his pocket with one hand as he held his other over his blistered eyeball. He pushed a button. "One suspect down, the other is fleeing east toward the forest. Agents giving chase. Get the dogs and the copters out here! And I need a Med-evac!"

Winston, Montana

Jack Handel stared at the CNN station from his bed in his studio room at Motel 8, the only hotel in town that took cash. The breaking stories came every hour now. Congress issued subpoenas to every member of the president's cabinet for the congressional investigation into the thoroughly documented allegations in Josh Davis' article. Fred "Bull" Seibert, the militia trainee that was accused of blowing up the Tenet Federal Building, was severely wounded in a shoot-out at a New Mexico campground, and a manhunt was underway for his brother. Anti-abortion terrorists targeted abortionists and clinic workers with violence and vandalism. Gun battles erupted all over Texas as the feds tried to enforce disarmament and martial law in the rural communities. Barry Friar was acquitted in state court and then immediately taken into custody for a federal trial that, as predicted, would never happen as long as the president's suspension of *habeas corpus* remained in effect. In spite of the president's threats to the Coalition's leaders, thousands of Americans all over the country were packing up their guns and flooding into the Coalition States. And just when Jack thought it couldn't get any messier, he was accused of murdering FBI administrator Will Conway.

What could Jack Handel do about any of it? He was a discouraged outlaw with a bullet wound in his thigh, a pitiful man whose wife and children hated him, a lousy hillbilly too impoverished to buy some fishing hooks and too honest to steal them. As far as he was concerned, he was on the lowest rung of the ladder of life. He had killed at least three federal agents in the raid on Barry's farm. The Militia of Montana was all but gone; the boys were either jailed without bail or in hiding. Because of the interrogation that he knew fellow militia members were undergoing, he felt it wasn't safe to contact any of his old friends. Jack was a hunted man.

If there was ever a time that his nation needed his skills and military experience, now was that time. He was an expert in guerilla warfare. He knew how to live off the land. He knew how to build a bomb out of ordinary household chemicals. He was an experienced leader of a civilian militia with the respect of tens of thousands of Montana patriots. If the feds tried in Montana what they did in South Carolina and Texas, he knew he could make the federal occupation a tour of misery.

As he watched Governor Boswell's press secretary hold a press conference to defend the mission of the Coalition of Free Christian States, he realized that his dream was coming true: civil magistrates were beginning to defy the federal government and re-establish the kind of government our forefathers envisioned, where freedom could flourish. The revolution of liberty for which he had been praying was happening right before his eyes.

Yet, as he lay there in that cheap hotel room nursing a bullet wound, all Jack Handel could think about was his wife. He could still feel her hair in between his fingers. His hands tingled at the thought of caressing the small of her back. He could still see her eyes, those beautiful, crystal clear, light green eyes.

Did she really love her new man? Jack knew that he didn't deserve Dixie anymore. A dozen times he dialed her number, but he always hung up before it rang. Jack knew that he was reaping what he sowed. His failures were her occasions for adultery. Jack withheld the kindness and intimacy that Dixie desperately needed and the forbidden fruit was more attractive as a result. She was responsible for her own sinful choices, but he rolled out the red carpet for her boyfriend's seductive whispers. It was as Barry said: the buck stopped with Jack Handel. The faults of his wife and children were of his making. He was a spineless coward, who couldn't fix his own wounds, much less his nation. For years he talked big, but that was all it was – talk. Jack Handel was a loud-talking bucket of misery, an absolute failure. Truly, a man is no stronger than his weakest link, and for Jack, this was his trampled marriage vow.

But God was a God of mercy and grace, undeserved favor, wasn't He? When God forgave a man, He not only washed his sins away, but sometimes He restored that which was lost through sin. Sometimes. Sometimes, the scars of a sinful life remained, even after the wounds were healed. But "He that spared not His Son upon the tree, how shall He not freely give us all things?" The Bible verse offered him hope for a miracle. He clenched his hands and whispered, "Oh God, is it possible?"

Would Jack's repentance to his estranged wife even make a difference? For him, the fruit of repentance was to take his vow "Till death do us part" seriously, regardless of the consequences. At the end of the fractured bridge of his marriage and his life, he finally decided that he must keep his promise. He was going to pray for her to come back and wasn't going to give up until she did. If not this week, if not this year or the next, then maybe when they were old. He wasn't going to *ever* give up. His heart ached worse than his wounded leg at the thought of living life without her.

Oh God! Please help her. Help her to forgive me.

The saltiest tears began to flow down the face of this hard, calloused man. He flicked off the television with the remote control and clasped his hands in a tearful plea. The room was dark and quiet now. Jack was alone with his God and his throbbing heart.

He began to meditate upon a Bible passage he read earlier in the day: Psalm 51, which was King David's prayer of repentance after he committed adultery with Bathsheba and ordered her husband murdered. After David sinned, he prayed, "Against thee and thee only have I sinned." Jack was beginning to realize that he sinned not only against his wife and kids, but he sinned against his God.

With his eyes heavenward, he opened his mouth and spoke the words, "Against thee and thee only have I sinned." He knew that God was merciful. That was Jack's only hope. God gave His Son to die on the cross, so that whoever trusts in Him should have everlasting life. Jesus healed the sick, picked up the fallen, forgave the sinner, and exalted the humble. He looks to dwell in those who have a poor and contrite heart. The deeper the pit, the greater the grace.

"God, forgive me for what I have done," he prayed from the bottom of his heart, his tears graduating to a deep sob. "Help me, Jesus, help me."

That was all that his Father wanted to hear.

A newfound confidence filled Jack's heart in the morning. He tried to walk on his bad leg and found the pain more manageable. He knew that Dixie didn't watch the news, but word of mouth would certainly reach her ears of the government's accusations against him, so he only had a short window of opportunity to speak to her and convince her of his change of heart. He decided that the time had come for him to take a little drive and knock on a door. He could wait no longer.

Knock, knock, knock.

What an inconvenient time to have to take a leak, thought Jack, shaking his good leg to hold off the urge as he stood on his crutches at his wife's front door. His mouth went dry, his palms broke out into a sweat, and at that moment Jack wished that he had put on more deodorant. His breakfast churned uneasily in his stomach, tempting him to leave quickly before someone answered the door. He focused his thoughts on the speech that he'd rehearsed. He had to prove to her that he was a changed man and that he loved her. He swatted a fly with a trembling hand at he stood at the front door of the double-wide trailer. He closed his eyes and tried to remember their wedding day, trying to fight off the temptation to get back into his car and drive away. *Till death do us part...*

The door opened and a dark skinned, muscular man with damp, shoulder-length brown hair and a five o'clock shadow stood before him. He wore a tattered tank top and was as hairy as a shag carpet. His face was covered with acne scars. "Hello?" The man's voice was deep and scratchy, injured from a lifetime of tobacco smoke.

Jack stuttered an uncomfortable response. "Uh, hi, uh, how are you?" This was the first time he had seen his wife's lumberjack boyfriend, who was several inches taller and 80 pounds of muscle heavier. Buddy was first-string varsity, whereas by comparison Jack was second string J.V. Jack hoped that the Marine Corp tattoo on his right forearm made up for his lack of size in the sight of this testosterone-saturated monster of muscle.

"Fine. What can I do for you?" The man had a blank look on his face, like he was thinking more about the conclusion of the Sylvester Stallone flick that he was watching on TV than he was about the mission of the thin fellow at his front door.

"Well, uh." Jack suddenly forgot the eloquent speech he had carefully planned. He looked away and wiggled his nose at the strong odors of whisky and cigarette smoke that emanated from the man. "Um, I..." Jack paused and looked down.

The beefy fellow took a step back into the trailer and prepared to shut the door. "When you remember what it is that you wanted, come back." He swung the door shut and Jack stuck the tip of a crutch into the door to keep it from shutting.

"I'm Jack Handel." He inhaled deeply and concentrated on stilling his quivering hands.

The man swung the door back open and it smacked the inside of the wall. His eyes were wide and deep as caves. Jack cleared his throat. "I'm Dixie's wife, I mean, husband. Dixie's my wife."

The man took a step toward Jack and mumbled, "So, you're the ex-husband she's told me about?"

"No, I'm not her ex-husband," he calmly stated, shaking his head, "I'm her husband." He tried to look past the intimidating physique into the house for Dixie's familiar face, but the lights were off and the window shades were drawn, so he couldn't see anything.

"Well, she told me that you were her *ex*-husband. If I remember correctly, the fault for the separation was yours and the divorce is as good as done."

"Yes sir, you are correct on that first point," Jack admitted, faking a smile and gripping his crutches tightly. He was, after all, relieved that this fellow hadn't recognized him as the man wanted on the news for shooting the FBI administrator. He didn't look like the kind of fellow that would watch the news, maybe the NFL, Nascar, and MMA re-runs, but not the news. If he'd known that there was a reward out for Jack's capture, he'd probably have tackled him to the ground by now. "The fault was my own and the divorce has appeared inevitable. May I speak to Dixie?"

"You mean you gonna' try to get Dixie to kick me out?"

This wasn't going as Jack planned. He grinned sheepishly, and then tried to display a more sober countenance, fearful of provoking this scar-faced, bar-room brawler to violence. "Uh, I just want to talk to—"

"You're trying to steal *my woman!?*" The lumberjack raised his voice, flexed his pecks and crossed his hairy arms over his chest.

Jack winced and felt his face flush. "She's still my wife, sir. I just want to talk to her."

The man cursed, pointed his finger into Jack's face, and yelled, "She's been with me for the past six months! I ain't going anywhere, pal."

Jack's pulse throbbed in his head with the rising adrenaline and escalating tension. "You know, let's talk about it some time, but not now. Right now I'm here to see Dixie."

"You just can't take a hint, can ya?" The man took one step toward Jack.

Jack yelled past him into the house, "Dixie! It's Jack! Can I speak to you for a sec?"

"Why don't you get outta' here!" The huge man took another step through the doorway till his nose was inches from Jack's forehead. Jack was careful not to flinch, since he knew that the scent of fear emboldens such men. The man's breath was a mixture of whiskey and mint, and Jack contemplated what type of mouthwash he used to cover up his liquor odor from Dixie. She hated liquor breath.

"Go back to your target shootin', you paranoid freak!" Jack was on crutches and handicapped but scenarios of punches and counter punches whizzed through his mind anyway. He would have to connect the first punch in order to stand a chance. He flexed his bad leg to see how it would handle a rumble, but the leg throbbed with the movement. He calculated that the man was too close for him to swing a crutch effectively.

Jack leaned to the left a bit to try to see past the man into the house. "Dixie!"

The man raised his right hand as if he was going to slap Jack. Jack took as big of a step back as he dared with his injured leg. Thankfully, a small hand reached through the doorway and grabbed the man by the shoulder.

"Bud, it's okay. Go back inside," came the familiar voice from inside the trailer. She'd been waiting just inside the door, trying to measure Jack's sincerity. "If he just wants to talk, that's okay." Jack's wife stepped through the door next to her boyfriend. She put her hands on her hips and stared Jack up and down as she bit her bottom lip.

Jack immediately noticed that she had lost some weight in the past year. Her skin was more tanned, her freckles more pronounced, her auburn hair appeared lighter, and her jeans and her "Harley's Bar" T-shirt were tighter than he was accustomed to see her wearing.

"Bud," she said as she glanced at her boyfriend over her shoulder, "let us alone so we can talk for a minute."

Bud turned and walked back inside the house with a disapproving grunt. She shut the door behind him. There she stood before him now, leaning against the door. It had been a long year since their separation and his heart raced like a schoolboy's on a first date.

She cracked a familiar grin. "Jack, it's good to see you."

"Hello, babe." Jack spoke softly to avoid upsetting the linebacker who was sure to have his ear on the other side of the door.

"Still can't make up your mind, huh?" She tapped her own chin and then motioned to his. Jack looked down and massaged the stubble on his chin. Dixie always preferred him unshaven or bearded, but disliked the untended look that characterized him whenever he forgot to shave for a week or two.

Dixie glanced at his crutches. "What happened to you?"

"Injured a leg out on the field with the boys," he responded with his pre-planned understatement.

"Oh, yes," she nodded, "out on the field, out with the boys as you would say, preparing for the government take-over. Did you shoot that FBI fat cat they accused you of killin'? Not that he probably didn't deserve it."

His face blushed. She knew that he was accused of shooting the FBI administrator. "No way." He shook his head. "Probably someone who escaped from the raid on Barry Friar's farm with a gun that I had handled some time in the past, so it must have had my fingerprints on it. But I didn't and wouldn't do that. They'll catch the guy that did soon and I'll be cleared, I'm sure."

Dixie half-grinned at him and his heart warmed as his hands chilled. "With tanks killing people in Montana's streets, maybe you deserve more credit than I've given you."

"No, no, Dixie, I was all wrong." He took a deep breath and took one step closer to her as he stared into her eyes. "Dixie, that's one of the main reasons I'm here today. I owe you an apology." Jack could feel a hot bubble rise up in his throat as he said those words. Humility was as foreign to his constitution as romance. He had never apologized to anyone since his dad made him confess to a Wal-Mart cashier that he had stolen a pack of gum when he was 12.

Dixie just looked on with her hands in her pockets, finding Jack's apology to be as strange and unbelievable as a two-headed horse.

"Dixie, I 've been doing some thinking, and I, I did you wrong, you and the kids." His voice trailed off to a whisper and he looked down briefly to keep his composure. "I didn't love you like I should have. Dixie, I am so, so sorry, and I want you to forgive me and...." He hesitated and tried to calm the anxiety that made him swoon. He bit his lip and looked away from her. "Dixie, I know it took many years for me to betray your trust as your husband, and it might take awhile for it to be restored, but I vowed to love you and to care for you till death do us part, and I want to try and keep that promise."

Dixie's eyebrows were now raised in disbelief. She took her hands out of her pockets and stood erect.

"I want to give it another shot, Dixie. Give me a chance to love you right." Jack removed his right hand from his crutch handle and reached for her hand, but she pulled away.

"Uh, Jack? Um, I can't believe this." Her voice was curt and insensitive. She furrowed her brow and licked her lips. "Why now?"

"Well, I wanna make it right. I owe it to you and I owe it to God, who I believe has forgiven me for being such a jerk. I hope you'll forgive me, too."

"Jack, I..." Dixie swallowed hard. "Are you for real? Do you realize I'm in another relationship?"

"That was made pretty obvious to me just a few seconds ago."

"I just can't up and tell Buddy to leave. I buried you, Jack."

Jack nodded. "I know, Dixie, but with God's help, we can resurrect our marriage." He reached for her hand again and this time she didn't pull away. Hope rose in his heart. "Please, Dixie, please forgive me." His lip trembled as he held her hand. He looked down and a hot tear dribbled down his nose.

She stood there in utter disbelief, shaking her head. Jack Handel, hard-nosed, stubborn, overly critical, hard to please, impetuous, always too busy for dinner, too calloused for romance, too busy to wrestle with the kids, too pessimistic to watch the news without railing against tyranny, too paranoid to take a walk in the park or drive to the city without a loaded pistol in his concealed holster and a knife in his pocket. Now here he stood, crying like a baby, caressing her hand, begging for her to take him back.

"I can't believe this," she mumbled, shaking her head. "I'm sorry but I don't think I love you anymore."

"I don't deserve your love. I know that it'll take time, but give me a chance. Remember our marriage vows?" He paused and measured her reception to that comment. She looked as if she doubted his sincerity. "I want to stand before God knowing I did everything in my power to keep my vow to you."

She shrugged, looked down, and pulled her hand out of his. He reached for it again, but she reached for the doorknob instead.

"I'm sorry, Jack. If you'd have done this a year ago, I could stomach it, but not now. It's been too long." She opened the door and stepped through it into the dark unlit living room.

Jack held the door open and said, "Dixie, all I ask for is your forgiveness. Please."

"No, Jack."

"I'm at the Motel 8 if you change your—"

Buddy stomped to the door and got between Jack and Dixie. "Why don't you get your fingers out of my door before I smash 'em!"

Jack's emotions went from gentle to angry in a split second. He stared into Buddy's eyes and ground his teeth together; the bar-bouncer took that as a challenge. "Want to try something, crip?" He stepped through the door and inched closer to Jack.

Jack looked away and stepped back. "Maybe when my leg's healed, but not today. I'm leaving."

"You better!"

"But I'll be back." He looked up and caught sight of Dixie's eyes over Buddy's shoulder. "I'll be back for Dixie, if she'll have me."

"You got nerve!" Buddy started to stomp out the door toward Jack until Dixie grabbed his arm from behind.

"Leave him alone, Buddy. He just wanted to apologize. Let him go."

Jack was hobbling toward his car with his crutches, but when he heard Dixie's gentle voice, he stopped and turned to her. "Dixie, I'll always love you."

Those words ignited dynamite in Buddy's inflated ego. He was livid. He followed Jack down the driveway, cursing and daring him to say another word. Jack feared getting struck from behind, so he stopped and turned, and was nose to nose with Buddy as Dixie walked out of the door toward them.

"You had your chance, Jack! But you picked your gun-slingin', John-Birchin' paranoids over your wife and left her to raise the kids on her own for a decade. And now you have the gall to come back here and torment her with your apologies?" The furious lumberjack slouched to bring himself eye-level to Jack's calm face. "I got a mind to kick your tail for even daring to come and take *my* woman!Jack smiled and tried some humor to calm Buddy's temper. "For $35 a year, you can join the John Birchers and get yourself a hat, a coffee mug, and a ten percent discount at Western Outdoors."

"Buddy!" Dixie trotted up to Buddy, put one hand on his shoulder and another on his chest. "Back off. Just go back inside. Leave this to me."

"Buddy, I empathize with you," said Jack after Buddy took a few steps away. "Dixie is a lovely woman and I wouldn't want to lose her either if I was you. I squandered the years I had with her. But we're still married. Separated, but married. She's my w—"

Without warning, Buddy lunged toward Jack and swung an open palm at Jack's face.

Smack!

Jack was knocked off balance; his body thumped against the car and he cringed, preparing for a second strike. He dropped one of his crutches and placed his weight on his bad leg, which punished him with searing pain that shot up his hip into his back. He leaned against the car, dizzy, unable to see straight for a few seconds. He grabbed his stinging face to check for blood. There was none, just a red imprint of Buddy's huge, calloused hand. Jack tried to gain his balance and his composure. Buddy would have struck again if Dixie hadn't stepped between them.

"Bud! That's enough!" she screamed. "You've proven your point. Enough! Let's go back to the house!" She grabbed Buddy's arm and urged him toward the house. He reluctantly went with her, cursing Jack out loud.

Jack came to his senses and opened the car door. He turned to see Dixie as she was stepping into his house. "Good to see you again, Dixie." She closed the door without looking back.

Jack got into the car, peeked at his beet-red cheek and his bruised eye in the mirror. He smiled and whispered hopefully, "I think she still likes me." He started the car and mumbled, "Ah, Jesus, You can still turn this around."

Dixie, still floating from her second cappuccino on an empty stomach, snapped the scissors enthusiastically at the erratic strands of her customer's pepper-black hair. "I was flattered, Steph, really I was, but the guy's time is up."

"But that was so romantic." Her customer, face heavy with make-up, thought Dixie should forgive her husband after his display of humility and affection. "Asking you back like that with crutches and taking a slap from your boyfriend. Makes my heart melt, you know. He must *really* love you."

"Or else he's on a head trip." Dixie paused cutting to study her work.

"I love it when my Johnny gets on a head trip like that, which he does, once in a while," she said, referring to her husband.

Dixie turned on the hairdryer and whisked it back and forth over the puffy hairdo. "He kept referring to God and all. With all this religious fanaticism in the churches, you'd expect it to hit home some day. He's probably just in a mid-life crisis and feeling lonely." She paused and looked at her customer in the mirror. "No. I'm not going to let him hurt me again."

"I know what you mean," Stephanie sympathized.

"Can you blame me?"

She shook her head back and forth. "Of course not."

"For 15 years, he wasted my life. He was a stranger to the kids. They're all out of the house and all hate him now. I stayed with him because I really loved him, but even true love has its limits. He about drove me crazy," she said with an exaggerated roll of her eyes like all women do when men act like idiots. "He was all salt and no sugar. That can wear down a woman after a while."

"That's a shame."

Dixie put her hairdryer down and turned the chair around so that her customer could see herself in the mirror. "What do you think?'

The young woman tweaked her bangs and gazed at her hair in the mirror from various angles. "I like what you did with it, Dixie."

"Good." Dixie faked a smile. "Anything else?"

The woman stood and reached for her purse, "Yeah. Answer a question for me. If you could be absolutely certain that Jack was sincere in his apology and wanted to love you right, would you give him a chance? I mean, you *are* still married. Maybe he's learned his lesson."

Dixie took the cash her customer handed her and shook her head. "I don't know."

"You've got a lot to think about." The girl looked over and saw a dark, handsome gentleman enter the store pushing a stroller with a chubby toddler in it. "Hey Johnny!" She walked over and gave him a kiss on the lips. Dixie looked away. The customer spoke to Dixie over her shoulder as she pranced out of the shop, "Give him a chance, Dixie. We've been there and God's made second chances golden for us. I'm prayin' for you." Those unwelcomed words pained Dixie's heart.

Stephanie was her last customer after a long day of cutting, brushing, curling, and coloring hair. Her back and arms ached and the cut hair penetrated her clothes and made her scratch, but it paid the bills. All Dixie could think about all day was Jack. All she talked about all day to every customer was her husband. She almost couldn't believe that he asked her back. It seemed like a strange dream. She despised how the whole event had obsessed her mind. Her heart's wires must be crossed or something. Jack certainly did act like a new man. The more she thought about him and the way he humbled himself before her, the way he told Buddy off like that and got smacked in the face for it, the more her heart warmed to him. She couldn't believe it, but she actually began to ponder the fact that she liked the new Jack a lot better than the old one.

She counted the money in the cash register, put it in the safe, and exited, locking the door behind her. It was 6:05 p.m. She almost didn't look forward to going home. Buddy's drinking problem was starting to affect their relationship. *I reckon that's what I get for shopping for guys in a biker bar.*

She walked down the sidewalk on the windless evening toward the parking lot. She turned the corner and stopped dead in her tracks when she saw it. She dropped her purse, stunned. She wiped her eyes with her hands. *No way!* Her car was decorated and covered with rose petals! A poster, held in place under her windshield wipers, read, "To the love of my life. Give me a second chance." Dixie looked around. Only two empty cars remained in the lot. There was a diner next door, but Jack was not in sight. She walked up to the car, and was startled when a man stood up behind the vehicle.

"Jack!" she half screamed.

Jack was also startled. "Dixie? Uh, hi!" he said with an embarrassed smile as he scratched one of his ears. "What'd ya think?" He brought his crutches under his arms and stood without making eye contact.

She walked to the back of the car, careful to stay an arm's length away from him, and gazed in disbelief at what Jack did to her bumper. A string held a row of empty Sunkist cans to it. *Just like on our honeymoon.*

"Those Sunkist cans are not as easy to come by as they used to be," he commented.

On the back of the windshield, the words, "My husband loves me!" were sloppily written in shaving cream.

"I was worried you'd be upset if I used shoe polish like we did on our wedding day, because you'd have to wash it off. Shaving cream falls off on its own."

She tugged at one of the rose petals and saw that a dab of shaving cream held the petal to the car. "It still leaves a film," Dixie complained.

"I can wash it for you later if—"

"Jack!" she blurted out. "What are you doing?" She was glad that the dim light of the parking lot was unable to reveal her blushing cheeks.

Jack searched for the right words as he reached for the spool of fishing line and the small travel-size can of shaving cream sitting on the car bumper. He shoved them into his front pockets as he fumbled for the words. "Dixie, I'm trying to say…" He paused and took an awkward step closer to her with his crutches. "I'm trying to say, I love you."

Dixie's heart jumped. Her body tingled from head to toe. Goosebumps rose up on her skin in waves. *What's happening to me?* she thought to herself. *Why am I falling for this idiot again? He wasn't this good in high school.*

"My Dixie." He set his crutches against her car, slowly knelt down on one knee, wincing from the pain in his thigh. He reached for her hand.

Jack, on his knees in front of me! I can't believe this! "No, Jack." She quickly jerked her hand away.

Jack's heart dropped and his emotions sagged. He fought off self-pity and tried hard not to be offended. Risking further rejection, he forced a smile at her and slowly grabbed her hand again. She let him hold it this time. He took a deep breath and gently squeezed her hand. He looked up at her face and thought he saw a tear in her eye.

"Dixie? Please forgive me. Please." He paused to swallow the emotion that stuck painfully in his throat like a cold, hard-boiled egg. "I have been a terrible husband and father. Please give me a chance to make it right."

He kissed her hand and his heart skipped a beat when she let him. He closed his eyes and kissed it again gently. She felt her body lean towards his. He reached for her and pulled her close. She let him and he found himself hugging her torso. She was so warm to him. *Oh God! Let it work out.*

He felt her touch his hair, and try to wave his cowlicks flat like she used to do. He could sense her heart soften toward him. He asked again with a soft whisper, "Please forgive me, Dixie."

"Oh, Jack." Her words were gentle and easy as she slowly knelt down in front of him beside her decorated car. He supported her weight as she knelt. It felt so good to touch her. He put his hands in the small of her back and looked into those eyes. Oh! How he had sorely missed those eyes! *It's going to work!* His body went numb as he studied the contour of a single tear drip down her cheek, taking the pink powder with it like a plow lifts the hard soil off the farmland, revealing the tender, moist soil beneath. The shallow river of wetness in a landscape of freckles dimly reflected the street lamps overhead.

He looked at her lips and she swallowed hard. He began to move his own lips toward hers when she stopped him. "Jack." The voice wasn't as gentle this time. "Jack, I'm sorry. I'm flattered, but I'm sorry. I'm in a serious relationship. You've been very kind and I appreciate all of this." She glanced at the car and smiled broadly. "But I'm in a relationship."

"Dixie, please." His voice was urgent as he put a finger over her lips to silence her protest. "I'm your husband, and I forgive you for that."

"Forgive *me*?" Dixie winced, as if Jack just poked her in the eye for no reason at all. "Forgive *me!?*" She stood to her feet, irritated, wiping her eyes, ashamed of her tears. "I don't need any forgiveness from you, Jack," she exclaimed coldly.

"Dixie, I didn't mean it like... well, yes, to be honest with you, love, you do need forgiveness." He was still on his knees, practically begging her now. "You need God's forgiveness just like I do. You're my wife."

"Jack!" she snapped, turning her gaze to the street lamp overhead. "You have no right to tell me what *I* need." She placed her hands on her hips and rolled her eyes as she always did when he disappointed her.

The familiar tone of voice and posture reminded Jack of the brick wall that remained between them for so many years and he grew nauseous. Hope began to slip between his fingers. He grasped once more for his fading dream and tried to turn the attention toward his own guilt. "God's forgiven me, Dixie. God's forgiven me."

"Well, I'm afraid that's all the forgiveness you're going to get right now."

Jack was confused at the sudden change in her demeanor. "Dixie? Wait!" She opened her car door and began to step inside when Jack grabbed her forearm. She shrugged him away and stepped into the car. He held the door open. "Dixie, please. Can't we talk for just one more moment?"

She started the car, revved it once, and without looking at him, said, "If *I* want *your* forgiveness, I'll ask for it!" She slammed the door shut, shoved the transmission into drive, and skidded the car out of the parking lot and onto the road, almost colliding with another vehicle as she did.

Jack just stood there for a moment, trying to take it all in. *So close!* He should have known that it wasn't going to be easy. Barry Friar's words echoed in his mind, "Don't take 'No' for an answer, Jack. She'll come around. God didn't give up on you, don't you give up on her. Have faith."

As if trying to shelter her tender heart from the rain of arrows and unwanted emotions that were now swarming upon her, Dixie held up an umbrella of hate and bitterness. She cursed and tried futilely to hold back the tears.

"Sorry to be the bearer of bad news, Dixie." Dolly's tone was melancholy as she sat at a booth across from her friend in the coffee shop.

"Are you sure it was him?" Dixie's eyes welled with tears as she spoke with trembling lips, her cheek pressed against one of her palms as her elbow rested on the table.

Dolly, her co-worker at the beauty salon was confident. "When he recognized me, you could tell he was embarrassed to be seen with her."

"Did you know her?"

"Yeah. I think she frequents Harley's," she said, referring to the biker bar where Dixie and Buddy met.

"Are you sure you saw them kiss?"

"They did more than kiss, Dixie. She was all over him and his hands were all over her, and I mean," she repeated with wide eyes, "*all* over."

Dixie squinted away her emotion and turned her attention to a couple in the parking lot getting out of their car together.

"Hey, you." Dolly snapped her fingers. "You okay?"

"I can't believe it."

"He was drunk, Dixie. A dozen beers will turn a prince into a frog."

Dixie sighed and rolled her eyes at Dolly's implication that Buddy's drunkenness somehow lessened the severity of the infraction. She leaned back in the booth with her shoulders slumped forward and her fingers typing on her kneecaps.

"Why don't you take a sick day, Dix?"

"What am I going to do, Dolly? If I kick him out when he's drunk, he'll beat me up again. If I kick him out when he's sober, he'll kill me. Staying with him appears to be my only option. But that's no way to live my life, in fear of a dozen cans of Miller 'low-life' and Bud's backhand. The tender moments I live for are getting less and less frequent. I don't want to look back in ten years and regret the choice I make today."

"Why don't you stay with me? Don won't mind," she said, referring to her husband.

"You've got two teens in a two-bedroom single-wide. You're crazy."

"Well, what are you going to do?"

Dixie wiped her damp eyes, exercising caution not to smear her mascara. "What I have to do is confront him. If it's true, then—"

"It's true, Dixie."

"And if it is, he's got to go." She began to cry freely. "Oh, God."

"I'm so sorry, Dixie."

Buddy wasn't drunk as usual, but he was getting there. His shirt was off and his leather Lazyboy comfortably reclined. He took another swig of his Miller. "Who told you that?" he snapped.

"Does it matter?" Dixie's cheeks cluttered with the tears that vainly invited his pity. She stood with her hands behind her back, out of the way of the television that he pretended to watch during their arguments. "Is it true?"

Buddy cursed. "Why don't you trust me?"

"Should I? Why won't you tell me the truth?"

"It wasn't the way it looked, Dixie." He shook his head, careful not to make eye contact as Dixie's tears began to flow freely again. "I'd had a few beers and she had—"

"You were all over her, Buddy!"

He looked away from the TV and gazed at her angrily. "I want to know who lied to you about me. I want to know who's trying to break us up!"

"You already admitted that you were drunk and it wasn't the way it looked, which means to me that it looked pretty bad."

"All right! So what!" Realizing that he wasn't going to get away from the facts of the case, he thought it appropriate to make light of them. "So I kissed an old girlfriend after having a few beers. There's nothing serious between me and Vivian."

Dixie tried hard to control her emotions, especially when she realized her weeping wasn't softening Buddy's heart in the slightest.

He wasn't even apologetic. He was mad at getting caught. "How long?" Buddy didn't answer. "How long have you been kissing her, Buddy?"

Buddy repeated her question as he pretended to watch TV, "How long?" Then he coldly said, "Since high school, baby. Even more recently since you took less of an interest in me."

At this point, Dixie broke down. "Oh, Buddy!" She leaned against the paneled wall of her trailer and began to cry bitterly. This irritated him. He finished the last few ounces of his beer and tossed the empty can over the kitchen counter onto the kitchen floor, missing the trashcan by two feet. He raised his voice at her. "What are you complaining about, Dixie? Are we married? Have we said any vows to each other? No!" This made Dixie weep all the harder, her face now buried deep in her hands as if she could hide there from the pain of the betrayal.

"Stop ruining my sit-com with your tears." He grabbed the remote and turned the volume up on the television to an uncharacteristically loud level. "You're cheating on your husband with me, so who are you to judge?"

"Buddy!" Dixie clenched her fists and stomped her feet. "You said you loved me!"

"Did I ever say I stopped? Huh, Dixie?" Their eyes met and Buddy looked away.

"So you're just going to sleep with me when you're here and sleep with her whenever you want?"

"We ain't..." he paused, his guilt showing in his grimace. "I suppose you could do better with your gun-toting, mud-crawler of a husband."

"Don't lie to me Buddy!" she screamed back through grinding teeth, stepping closer to him and pointing at him now with a critical finger. "You're not making things better with your half truths! Are you sleeping with her?"

He cursed the moment and clenched his fists. He stood at the intersection of two paths and was left with a choice: humility or pride, stubbornness or confession, rise up in anger or break down and mourn over his sin. He knew that he was his own worst enemy with all of his bad habits. But momentum was carrying him in a predictable direction; he spurned the prick of his conscience and heeded the beckon of his pride and anger. "You'd better count your blessings, woman! I'm the best thing that ever happened to you."

"You're a lousy cheat, Buddy!" Dixie plopped down on a chair near his, grabbed the couch pillow on the floor beside her and buried her head in it. When her grief didn't provoke any sorrow in him, she raised her head and looked at him again. "Do you think I'm some kind of whore? Do you think my love is some kind of commodity that you can treat like an old shoe and throw it in the corner when a new one comes along that better suits your fancy? You're pathetic!"

Without warning, he leaned forward in his chair, swung the back of his right hand and smacked her jaw. It sent her head flinging back against the chair. She screamed at the top of her voice from the stinging pain, and then screamed again out of anger.

He aimed an index finger at her, poking out of a white-knuckled fist. "You better speak to me with some respect, woman! I'm not your husband. So stop expecting me to act like one."

"You're never going to be either!" She rose to her feet, risking more of Buddy's fury.

"What?" he barked, leaning toward her.

She cradled her bruised jaw with her hand. "Get out, Buddy. You can't hit me."

He didn't budge, but turned up the TV even louder.

"Get out!" she said, raising her voice over the TV. She turned her gaze to the door, hoping beyond hope that her husband would knock again right at that moment.

"You get out," he mumbled, his eyes fastened on the television screen.

"It's my house!"

Buddy stood up to her, until his chin was one inch from her forehead. "Don't bust an attitude with me, little girl."

She took a deep breath and turned her eyes away from his. "Just get your stuff and—"

Whack!

Another right hand under her left eye sent her reeling against the paneled wall, writhing in pain as she hugged its dust.

He cursed her and would have hit her again, but Dixie put up a halting hand and threatened him in a high-pitched squeal: "I'll call the police, Buddy!" He held his backhand aloft, pondering various contingencies and considering the unthinkable. "You know, Buddy, that if I call the police again, you're going to jail for a long time this time."

He held his backhand in position, gritting his teeth. "I will launch you into a world of pain, you little—"You'd better kill me then, because I'm not going to let you get away with it!" she screeched. "The neighbors have probably already called the police, Buddy, so get!" She pointed vigorously at the door.

He cursed her under his breath, lowered his right hand, and stomped into the bedroom. She was normally easier to intimidate than this, and he was disappointed in the outcome. He slammed the door behind him with all his might, shaking the trailer.

Why did you ever go back to him, Dixie? she reproved herself. *You fool! You knew it was going to come to this. You knew he was a drunk who only wanted a sexual fling. What were you thinking? He doesn't love you.*

As Buddy packed his things in the bedroom, she walked over to the mirror on the wall and studied her wounds. There was no bleeding this time, but the eye was already starting to blacken in the typical fashion. She had seen it before; it was usually her right eye with Buddy. He was right-handed and preferred the backhand to lessen the likelihood of knocking her out or giving her a laceration that required an ER visit.

The cycle had repeated itself about three times over the past year. He'd hit her when he was drunk and angry, and then she'd threaten him or call the police. But he'd be at her door by the end of the week, flattering her with heartfelt apologies with big tears in his eyes, and his right fist clenched around a dozen red sweet-smelling pink roses. How could she refuse him like that? She was so predictable. He was strong and charming when he was sober and entertaining when he was jolly drunk on booze and lust. After 15 years with Jack, it felt good to be wanted. She'd forgive Buddy for his outbursts of rage and accept him back, and he'd be romantic and as sweet as a bucket of honey for a while. Then he would get drunk again, they'd argue over something, and he'd transform back into a cursin,' right-fist swingin' monster.

Buddy slammed every drawer in the bedroom as loud as he could while he packed. Then he burst into the living room with as much ruckus as he could muster, banging into anything and everything on the way down the hallway. His stomp came to a halt in the middle of the living room. Dixie had feigned that she was wiping the dining table with a wet rag, which was in the corner of the living room, but all she was really trying to do was get the table between her and her abuser. Buddy carried a small suitcase in each hand. They were her suitcases, but she held her peace.

"That's it, Dixie. Last chance." She looked up at him with trembling lips. "This is the last straw, I'm not coming back."

She walked into the kitchen, grabbed the largest kitchen knife she owned, and stomped to the front door. "Good riddance," she mumbled as she opened the door for him. He stared at the black-handled knife that she held in her hand and was stunned by her confident demeanor. This was unlike her. She stared into his eyes. "You will *never*," she screamed that word, "hit me again!"

"Or what? You gonna stab me?"

"I'm just leveling the playing field." She stiffened her neck, gripped her knife tightly, and braced her back stiff against the wall as his heavy footsteps approached. The breeze of Buddy passing her through the door out of the house was refreshing. She took a deep breath.

"Vivian's better in the sack anyway," he mumbled without looking back, one last stab into her heart before he slammed the door on her for the last time.

Dixie stood there alone, staring at Buddy's Lazyboy through stormy eyes for what seemed like hours, sensing only the wrenching of her heart and the bounding of her pulse in her temples. Then, in a fit of desperation, she raised her kitchen knife, and prepared to quickly sweep the blade across her wrist. She would have made the cut, but a feeling roared into her heart that stopped her cold. She'd been fighting this feeling for several days, ever since Jack came back into her life. Now, she welcomed it. It was a feeling of regret for leaving her husband. It was a sense of dishonor for cheating on him and leaving a bad example for her children. It was a feeling of shame for hooking up with a bar-brawling bozo like Bud, and for tolerating his unstable mood swings and his cruelty for so long. But these weren't feelings of despair, because now she knew that her husband still wanted her. Jack's knock on her door had given her hope. The thought of Jack was keeping her alive.

She opened her eyes and suddenly realized how close she had come to spilling her life's blood onto the floor of her living room. It drove fear into her heart, fear of dying, fear of judgment, the fear of God. She thrust the knife out in front of her as if fighting an invisible demon and she screamed from deep down, a long, shrill scream. Then she tossed the knife over the counter into the kitchen, leaned against the wall, slumped to the floor, and wept over the mess she had made of her life.

Jack was hobbling to the waiting room to fetch his pizza when he saw her across the foyer of Motel 8. He stopped dead in his tracks and his heart dropped into his stomach. His eyes must be tricking him. "It can't be," he mumbled. *That can't be Dixie. My Dixie?*

There she stood wearing the white lacy dress that she wore on their wedding day. She looked as beautiful as he could ever remember. She was a red rose on the banks of an oasis in the middle of a dry desert void of color. His heart throbbed when he saw her smile at him.

"Dixie?" He spoke her name so softly as to not be heard, not believing his eyes. Then he said it louder, "Dixie?"

She began to walk to him from across the Motel 8 foyer. "Oh, Jack!" she said as her walk progressed to a run.

She reached him with a full embrace and a kiss on the lips. Jack dropped his crutches and held her. On-lookers smiled and pointed as they kissed long and passionately. Even the pizza delivery boy stood and watched.

"Oh, Jack," Dixie breathed in a mournful tone. "I'm so sorry." She looked deep into his moist eyes and he smiled and wiped the tears off of her rosy cheeks with his thumbs. "Can you ever forgive me?"

"I already have, Dixie." He embraced her again, his breath taken away by the passion of the moment. Just one hour ago, on his knees in prayer by his hotel bed, his dream of being reunited with his wife seemed so far away. Now, here she was in his full embrace in her musty wedding dress, her body pressed firmly against his and her arms clasped tightly around his neck. Truly, the greatest test of faith is at the foot of the Jordan River on the very edge of the Promised Land. It really is darkest right before the dawn. He was so glad he held on through the night. He couldn't believe that it was happening. "I do forgive you, Dixie. With all my heart, I do." When he said that, the memories stirred and they looked into each other's eyes again.

She cradled his face in her hands. "You are so, so different. I don't ever remember you being so gentle and thoughtful." She swallowed hard and moistened her lips. "I'm here to stay, Jack."

"What happened to your eye?" Jack furrowed his brow as he examined the bruise under the make-up that her tears washed away.

"God knocked some sense into me." She smiled widely, causing the skin over the bridge of her nose to wrinkle.

The sight prompted a flood of long forgotten emotions to pour over him like waves, melting his heart. In the last decade of their marriage, intimacy had been so rare. He savored that warm smile as a starving man before a steak dinner would savor the smell before saying grace. Jack embraced her tightly again. "Thank God." He nestled his nose under her chin and kissed her neck.

"Do you really love me?" she whispered the question in his ear.

He pulled away from her and gazed into her eyes. "With all my heart. And I always will."

"I can't believe you love me like that, Jack. Even when I was sleazing around with someone else. You still loved me?"

"Yes."

She kissed him so tenderly that he began to weep.

Jack heard the creak of the metal door in the hotel foyer, and he saw out of the corner of his eye the forms of two police officers walking into the motel. He quickly backed away from his wife, grabbed her by the hand, and pulled her into the hallway.

"What's the matter?" She grew worried as he led her quickly down the hall, hobbling from his bad leg.

Jack and Dixie's embrace and kiss had caught the attention of the first police officer that entered. When they rushed off after seeing the officers, he became suspicious. He walked to the hallway and turned the corner. He eyed the pair of crutches lying on the ground. With concern on his facial features, he walked back to the counter where the younger officer was speaking to the clerk.

"I need your roster," the younger officer said. "We need to—"

The senior officer interrupted. He put his elbows on the counter and leaned into the employee. "Any cash paying customers?"

"Cash paying? Do you have a court order?"

"Show us the names and room numbers of your cash payers," the elder officer said as he handed her the court order. She began to read the long court order and he jerked it out of her hands. "You can read it later. Tell me the names of your cash payers now or I'm arresting you."

"Um." She chewed on her lip as she nervously reached for the phone. "I should probably call my manager."

"You'll be calling her from jail if you don't answer my question now!"

"Okay." She typed into the computer for a moment. "We only have one."

"Don't print it off, ma'am," the elder officer said to the hotel clerk. "Just tell me the name and the room number."

"Jack, where are we going?" Dixie said as they held hands on the way to Jack's pickup truck in the parking lot.

"I blew it. We shouldn't have drawn attention to ourselves."

"What?"

"The officers. They saw us kissing and then run off. Did you tell Buddy where I was staying?"

"No. Well, I don't think so. He may have overheard you tell me when you first visited." Jack opened the passenger door of the truck for his wife. "Don't you want to get your stuff out of your room?"

"I've got my cash and don't have much else to go back for that's worth the risk." Jack started the truck and pulled out of the parking lot onto the road. He kept glancing into his rear view mirror to assure himself that they weren't being followed. "Dixie, I love you more than anything and I'll not let anything come between us, but you have to trust me. We have to live on the run for a while."

Dixie smiled. "I understand. I'm with you for good."

He reached over and squeezed her hand. "Till death do us part, babe."

She echoed his sentiment as she straightened the wrinkles in the skirt of her lacy white dress. "Till death do us part, Jack."

Chapter 23

Albuquerque, New Mexico

"How're you doing today, sir?" Stein smiled warmly at the Greyhound bus driver as he stepped up on the bus and handed him his ticket. His black beret with the Confederate flag ironed on it was stuck under his belt, and he gripped a black duffel bag. He wore stolen Ray Ban sunglasses to help conceal his facial features.

"Fair to midland." The bus driver took his ticket and shifted in his well-worn black vinyl seat.

Stein slowly walked the aisle toward his seat in the fifteenth row. He searched each passenger's eyes carefully, yet inconspicuously as possible. He was a wanted man and the last thing on earth he'd want to do is get on a bus with someone who would recognize him and turn him in for the hefty reward being offered for information that would lead to his arrest.

He was relieved to discover that he was the only passenger in the fifteenth row. He set his duffle bag in the seat next to the aisle, donned his black beret, and sat next to the window. He took the newspaper out from underneath his right arm and plopped into his seat with a sigh. *I made it!* he congratulated himself.

His three-day flight from the authorities had led him through a desert, a mile long sewage canal, and into the home of an elderly couple where he stole some clothes and a car. Then he drove to a Bank First branch in Gallup, New Mexico, where an easy robbery with a plastic pistol raked in $25,000. His hand rested on the duffle bag that sat on the seat beside him. He took comfort in the fact that the bank was insured so he didn't really steal money from the customers, but rather, the dough would come from the insurance company's coffers. His conscience was only mildly disturbed at his theft; in war, he reasoned, extraordinary circumstances demanded extraordinary measures. As he settled down into his seat, his thoughts went to his brother. He had learned from a radio news report that Bull survived. He grieved for him, for he knew that they would torture the sanity out of him. The thought of Bull suffering energized him.

As the bus pulled out of the parking lot, Stein held a magazine and a newspaper in his hands. "Touring Washington, D.C." the caption of the pamphlet read. He tucked it inside the newspaper and opened the gray *Human Events* newspaper to the article he'd been reading on the Middle East conflict. A boxed quotation caught his eye, "Suicide attacks have an 85 percent success rate." One of his favorite Bible characters ended his life in a suicide attack: Sampson pushed down the pillars in the Philistine temple, killing himself and all within the building.

Hmm. Eighty-five percent.

Deer Lodge, Montana

"What a wonderful breakfast, my love." Jack Handel dabbed his thickening goatee with a napkin.

"No more 'greasy spoons' for my favorite felon," Dixie responded with a smile.

Jack was taken aback by her comment. She didn't know that he was at Barry Friar's farm during the raid and had killed federal agents to escape. "What do you mean?"

"You've been falsely accused of killing that FBI administrator from Billings, haven't you? Plus, you're a Bible-believing Christian and a militia leader. That practically makes you an enemy combatant all by itself now-a-days."

He grinned sheepishly as his wife boasted in him. "Oh, yeah." They bowed their heads together as Jack said grace. "Amen."

Dixie was in the mood to chat, but Jack was already into his buttermilk pancakes. "Honey, what's our plans?"

Jack swallowed and looked up at her. "I think we have a nice set-up here. This little log cabin get-away belongs to one of your friend's parents. No connection to me. They're not right-wingers. I can hunt and fish more out here as my leg heals. There's lots of untouched forest 'round these parts." He wagged the sausage at the end of his fork. "Plenty more where this came from." He pointed his sausage at his wife. "You can still work, right? No one knows about us. That's good. We should keep it that way. If we keep our distance from forest rangers and cops, all's well. At least, we're together. God'll take care of us."

"As you've been teaching me about God and I've been praying more about us and our country, I feel like," she searched for the words, "I feel like..."

He bit into his sausage. "Like our country is without hope? Like we can't stop the tyranny?"

She nodded. "I feel like I'm swimming upstream, but the current's so strong in the opposite direction that instead of making progress, I'm being pushed downstream anyway."

"Me too, Dixie." He set down his fork and reached for her hand. He squeezed her fingers gently in his palm. They felt cold.

Her countenance suddenly winced and for a moment Jack thought she was going to cry. "I feel that if we just stay here and do nothing but try to live out our lives, then we're being selfish and we become part of the problem with the country." Her tears began to flow freely. "We're not doing anything or even planning anything to try to help others or fix our nation."

He squeezed her hand in both of his. "I'm just so glad to have you back, Dixie."

"I know. But what about everybody else? People are losing their freedoms, Jack. Things are getting worse."

He let go of her hand and his smile faded to a stressful grimace. "Well, what can we do?"

"If there's anything we can do to help keep our country be free and help others through their trials, then that's what I want to do."

"I've been praying about the same thing, Dixie, for a long time. And I think I've got the answer."

"What's that?"

"Wait. The Bible says to wait on the Lord. The problems will come to us. We don't need to go looking for them. I'm confident that we'll be in the right place at the right time. Right now, we need to heal our marriage and fortify our faith for the tough times that are coming. Darker clouds are on the horizon, Dixie, and they're rushing this way. Be patient, my love. It won't be long and you'll miss this string of lazy sabbaths."

Dixie always thought that Jack had squandered his family in pursuit of his conspiracy theories, gun hobbies, and militia activities, trying to turn the country around the best way he knew how. Now, for the first time ever, Dixie thought that he needed to put his training to use, get out there and make a difference teaching people how to defend their freedoms. Instead he was sitting back, waiting, and savoring his time with his wife. Yep, his priorities were straight all right.

Dixie didn't know it, but the storm clouds were closer than they had supposed.

When they were cleaning the kitchen after breakfast, Jack called out to Dixie, "Hey hon, turn that up." He motioned to the radio beside the phone. She turned up the volume. A moment later he exclaimed, "Lord, have mercy!"

"What?"

Jack stopped wiping the table with the wet rag and moved closer to the radio. "They're talking about Bull." He set his elbows on the counter to get closer to the speaker.

"The media's always talking *bull*." She grinned, impressed with her wit.

"No, Bull Seibert." Jack turned up the volume. "He's alive after all."

She cocked her head sideways trying to recall the face that matched the name. "You mean the taller Seibert twin? Ain't he accused of killin' somebody?"

"He shot two federal agents at the Bozeman riot and was the fellow accused of blowing up the FBI building in Billings."

"Really?" She raised her eyebrows in disbelief. "That was him? Did he really do it, or are they just trying to pin that on the militia?"

Jack plunged his hands into the sink and started doing the dishes while his wife rinsed and dried. "They caught up to him in New Mexico a few weeks ago and shot him. I guess he's gonna make it."

The radio announcer proclaimed, *The twin brother, Ed "Stein" Seibert, is thought to be the mastermind of the bombing of the Tenet Federal Building in Billings. He continues to evade authorities in New Mexico and the manhunt is being extended to nearby states.*

"Bull was always a radical." Jack wiped his forehead with the back of his suds-covered hand. "Stein had his head screwed on right. His only fault was his admiration for his crazy brother."

"You and Bull were close?"

Jack sighed. "Bull was the bad apple of our last training group. He had a chip on his shoulder regarding *all* authority, not just the federal government. He was unteachable and disrespectful." Jack dried his hands with a towel and sat down on a chair at the dining room table. "He did save my life though. Can't take that away from him."

"Really? How?" She sat beside him at the table.

Jack could have kicked himself for saying that.

Jack appeared deep in thought and so Dixie asked again, "How did he save your life, honey?"

"Huh? Oh, sorry. Um." He paused and scratched his head. "I don't even know whether to believe those allegations against Bull anyway. I don't believe the liberal news media any more than I believe the press releases of Margaret Brighton."

"How did he save your life?" His reluctance to forthrightly answer her question added suspense to the moment.

Jack was hesitant to worry his wife with things she didn't need to know. Finally, he threw up his hands and slapped his thighs. Then he glanced adoringly at his wife and smiled.

"What?" she said, grinning back.

"Remember the federal raid on Barry Friar's farm against the militia?"

"Yeah."

"I was there." He looked into her wide-eyed gaze and knew that she wouldn't be content with anything less than the whole story. Like the typical woman, she'd demand all the details: what he did, saw, heard, prayed, and, of course, what he *felt*. That would be the hardest question to answer.

One flesh, he reminded himself. *No secrets.*

"*You* were there?"

He nodded. "I was there. My leg wound was caused by a bullet."

"But you said you got it out with the boys."

"Yeah, out on Barry's farm with the boys."

Here came the first of a hundred questions.

Two hours later, his wife was pacing the room as Jack sat on the couch. "I can't believe it, Jack. You killed those men!"

"It was self-defense, hon." He waved his arms emphatically as he spoke. "They were shooting us down like dogs. I have a right to defend myself." He pointed out the window as if there were a dozen soldiers waiting for him outside. "Just be thankful I was able to get out of there alive, dear. The only other alternative was prison. They're throwing the book at everybody that got caught or surrendered. Barry Friar's an anomaly in that a state jury acquitted him, but with the suspension of the right to a jury trial, he'll probably never get his federal trial; he will never see the light of day. Everybody else that survived that raid is being labeled an enemy combatant and being locked away for life. If that ain't the color of tyranny, what would it look like? If resistance wasn't justified then, when in God's name would it ever be justified?"

She stopped pacing and stood in front of him, her hands on her hips. "So the charge against you for shooting the FBI administrator, is that true?"

"No, of course not."

Dixie plopped down in the loveseat across from her husband, leaned back and looked at the ceiling with worried eyes.

Jack felt sorry for raising his voice. He sighed, went over and sat down next to her, and placed his hand gently on her shoulder. "I'm sorry for yelling."

"It's okay," she responded softly. "It was a lose-lose situation for you, huh?"

Jack sighed. "As far as I know, only Bull, Stein, and I made it out alive. Man!" He slumped his shoulders and wagged his head in disbelief, "It's so surreal. It's so hard to believe that I'm a wanted man."

"Why didn't you tell me you were shot in the leg from that raid?"

"If the FBI questioned you and didn't believe your story, it could be you rotting in solitary confinement or being water-boarded in a soundproof room."

Dixie's face had the look of fear on it for a moment, and then she dropped her forehead into her hands. She appeared to be studying the stains on the beige carpet until Jack looked beneath her hands and saw a tear drop hanging from the tip of her freckled nose.

He patted her on the shoulder. "It'll be all right."

She sniffed and looked up at him. "I pray so."

"Tell me, Dixie," Jack said soberly. "If you had known all of this, would you still have gotten back together with me?"

It took Dixie only a few seconds of reflection. "Of course I would have." She leaned toward her husband, grabbed both of his hands, and turned to kneel down in front of him. "I love you, Jack. We'll get through this together, you, me, and God."

They stared into each other's damp eyes a moment, and then Jack squinted away his tears. "That's good to hear."

The phone rang, startling Jack. "Did you give this number to anybody?"

"Uh, just one friend, Dolly. She works with me. We're close."

"I thought you weren't going to tell anybody."

"I trust her, Jack."

They let the answering machine pick it up. "Hey," the voice came over the answering machine, "I'm looking for Dixie. If you know where..."

Dixie recognized the voice. "It's Dolly." She walked over and quickly picked up the phone. "Hey Dolly."

"Oh. Hi, Dixie! Where've you been?"

"Jack and I are having a second honeymoon. We're back together."

Dolly didn't sound excited at her friend's renewed feelings for her husband. "Oh, really?"

"Yeah. I've had some vacation time and so we're spending it together. How are things for you?"

"Um. There were some FBI agents snooping around, looking for you at work today."

"Looking for me?" Her troubled gaze darted to her husband.

"What?" Jack sensed Dixie's unease.

"They said you could be in danger because of Jack," Dolly continued. "They said Jack was wanted for shooting some senior FBI director in Billings."

"He didn't do it, Dolly."

"They said they've got his fingerprints on the gun and that they have two witnesses who put Jack near the crime. I've got the guy's business card right here."

"I know about the accusation, but it's not true, Dolly."

"How do you know for sure?"

Jack tapped her on the arm. "What's not true, Dixie?" Dixie waved him off and cupped her hand over her other ear so as not to be distracted from her conversation with Dolly.

"I couldn't believe my ears, Dixie. From what you've told me of Jack, I just can't believe he'd do something like that. I mean, you said he was a bad husband, but a murderer? I didn't believe a word they told me, Dixie."

"What did you tell them?"

"I told them that I'd let them know if I saw you or Jack. Of course, I wouldn't do that. I tried to find you because I wanted to let you know not to come around."

"Okay, Dolly. Thanks."

"I'll let you know if anything else is up. Please stay there, Dixie. Don't venture back here if you can help it. Not if you want to stay with Jack."

"Thanks Dolly. I'll talk to you later."

She hung up the phone and turned her attention to her husband. She walked over and stood in front of him. He rose to his feet and placed his hands on her elbows. "What happened?"

"FBI agents were at my workplace looking for me, asking about you. They told Dolly that they had eyewitnesses that placed you near the crime."

"Those liars!" growled Jack.

"What are we going to do, Jack?"

"Well, they have certainly bugged your office phone. They might know where we are now. We need to get away, babe. Maybe I need to leave for a couple days."

"Don't even say such a thing, Jack." She pulled his body tight against hers. "I'm not saying goodbye to you in a time like this."

"I don't want to get you into trouble."

"I'm not in trouble. Dolly said that they just wanted to question me."

"But if I got caught, they'd try you for aiding and abetting a felon."

"You're not getting caught, Jack. Hey." She put her palms on Jack's cheeks. "I'm not going to let you go."

Jack inhaled deeply and breathed out slowly. "Dixie?"

"What?"

"Do you trust Dolly to keep your secret?"

Dixie breathed deeply, looked down at her hands, thinking. Dolly was known to gossip and speak ill of others behind their back, yet be outwardly sweet and kind to their faces. She always wondered what cruel things Dolly must say about her to others when she wasn't around. "I don't know, Jack. First things first. Let's put our trust in God." Jack embraced his wife as they prayed together.

"Yes, Mr. Whittenberg, please."

"Just a moment. May I ask who's calling?"

"Dolly Dresden."

After a brief moment, the FBI agent answered the phone. "Hello?"

"I'm the blond woman you spoke to at the Hair Shop this morning."

"How could I forget you Mrs. Dresden?" He flattered her with a flirtatious sway in his deep masculine voice. "What can I do for you?"

Dolly giggled childishly. "First tell me about this cash reward I could get for helping you catch him."

"The $10,000 would be in your bank account by the time the handcuffs were on his wrists, Mrs. Dresden."

"You're sure Jack Handel did this thing?"

"It's the most cut and dry case I've ever seen in my 15 years in the crime-fighting business, Mrs. Dresden. No doubt about it."

"Well, I know where he is. But I want the money first."

"Uh." The agent paused and laughed. "Mrs. Dresden, you'll get the money once we've arrested him."

She laughed back. "I promise I'll give it back if you can't catch him. Do you think I'm going to steal it from you?"

"I don't make the rules, Mrs. Dresden, but like you, I have to follow them."

"Then you must have another way of catching him, because I'm not telling you a thing until the check clears my bank."

"Excuse me?"

"Better yet, bring cash." Dolly sensed the rising temper on the other end of the line and tried to play the victim to gain sympathy. "I'm sorry, Mr. Whittenberg, but I've been regulated out of business once, audited twice, and had my lion's share of experiences with federal agents. Ninety-nine percent of 'em give the rest of 'em a bad name."

"You know, Mrs. Dresden, we could indict you for *not* turning in his location. In effect, you're harboring a—"

"Well, if you're going to threaten me like that, we'll just make it $20,000," she retorted before slamming down the phone.

The agent pulled the phone away from his ear and glanced at it awkwardly for a moment as if it were a pet that unsuspectingly bit him. A moment later, he called her back. She picked up the phone with a grin as she scraped her bright red fingernail against her tooth. "Wanna be friends again?" she said in a bashful tone.

"$10,000 cash?"

She smiled. "I'm a patriot. $10,000 cash."

"I won't be able to get it to you till the morning," he said in a less friendly tone. "We'll re-acquire the cash if for any reason at all we are unable to catch him."

Dolly rolled her eyes. "Duh."

Jack and Dixie awoke at first light and began to pack, preparing for their departure. Jack planned to convert all of the meat in his freezer into jerky so it wouldn't go bad on the road. But his meat hadn't all thawed yet. So he headed for his deer stand with a crossbow at 5 a.m., just a quarter-of-a-mile away from the hillside log cabin get-away. Dixie finished packing and headed into town to work out at the gym.

Jack spied a whitetail doe through some brush and raised his crossbow, waiting for his shot. He squeezed the trigger and sent an arrow whizzing through the air. *Heart shot!*

After he tracked, cleaned, and quartered the doe, he set it up on his wheeled carrier and headed back home at the crack of dawn. He walked across a two-acre field toward the log cabin, which was barely discernible due to a dense fog that was just now beginning to lift.

When he was within 50 yards of the cabin, he heard a car pull up into the driveway. But the engine was quieter than Dolly's little Honda with its tremulous muffler. He was immediately suspicious and froze. The fog was stubbornly licking the ground longer into the day than normal, so he couldn't see the end of the gravel driveway. In a moment, he heard a second set of tires. That's when he dropped to the dew covered ground and hugged the grass. He could now hear several cars pulling into the driveway, and then several sets of footsteps. He thought he heard a handgun chamber a round.

His worst fears were realized. They'd been discovered!

The fog was lifting quickly and if anyone gave a cursory glance into the backyard, they might see him. Yet he couldn't stand up and run because they would certainly see him from the full-length dining room windows with its full view of the backyard.

He had to think fast. He crawled on his belly as quickly as he could to his right, aiming for the concealment of four cypress pine trees with branches all the way to the ground. The federal agents inside scurried about, searching for evidence and placing listening devices inside the home, and Jack wanted to avoid their shifting glances through the windows.

When he reached the cover of the cypress trees, he stood up and ran as fast as his wounded leg would let him toward the woods at an angle that would prevent him from being seen through the dining room windows. Only one thought filled his mind, *I've got to get to Dixie!*

As the agents prepared their hasty exit, one senior agent glanced into the backyard. "What's that?" He pointed at a game-hauling device with two, six-inch wheels 30 yards away.

He rushed over and discovered that a freshly quartered deer was tied to it. He knelt down and brushed his hand along the brown fur. It was still warm.

"He was here." The senior agent stood to his feet and began to study the perimeter. He pulled his gun from its holster and the eight agents quickly began to scour the edge of the property for signs of the suspect.

After a few minutes of futile searching, the senior agent's disappointment was evident in his voice. "We spooked him." He cursed his luck and flipped the game-hauling device onto its side. "Let's go. We've got to find his wife before he does."

Jack knew that the feds would scour the town for all the usual places Dixie frequented, but they may not know about her gym membership, which was only a couple of weeks old. The gym was ten miles away on the outskirts of town. He prayed to intercept her between the gym and home, but his leg was paining him pretty badly. When his wound began to swell and bleed again, he had to rip his shirt and apply a pressure bandage to it. He glanced at his watch as he hobbled. He prayed that she wouldn't cross paths with the agents as they fluttered about searching the small outlying communities for her.

"God help us." Jack tarried in the woods 20 yards away from the intersection he hoped that she would pass. He was panting heavily from his painful jog up and down the deer trails. He had cuts on his face from sprinting past thorns and bushes. "Please let her come this way. Don't let her get captured…"

He was there only two minutes when he saw her yellow Honda pull up at the stop sign. He limped as quickly as he could up to her car and banged on the passenger-side window just as she turned the corner.

"Dixie!"

"Ah!" she screamed. "Jack!" She slammed on her breaks and unlocked the door. "What in blazes are you doing?"

He got into the car breathing heavily, soaked with sweat. "Thank God. Turn right at the intersection."

"What?"

"Just do it!" He pointed at a street sign 50 yards ahead. "Turn right. Quick!"

Part VI

The Downside of a Tyrant's Remedy

Chapter 24

Washington, D.C.

"That won't work, I'm telling you." Danny Connor dared to raise his voice during the president's cabinet meeting. He turned to the Secretary of the Treasury. "You're telling us that our nation's heading over a cliff of economic disaster, Mr. Hammond. We're keeping it just out of reach through borrowing and the Federal Reserve's inflating of the money supply has investors more reluctant to invest in us. You're telling us the dollar's collapsing and bankruptcy appears inevitable if we continue business as usual. Yet your prescription is more of the stuff that got us into this mess! There must be a plan to avert economic calamity *without* causing one at least as bad as that which you're trying to prevent."

Most of them just stared at Danny with blank faces. Politicians specialized in producing short-term political gains without consideration of long-term consequences, so they weren't accustomed to thinking in terms of the honest answers the question demanded. Their remedies were only to increase their chances of re-election or re-appointment, never to actually avert the impending national disaster. Now, prescribing the hard medicine was the only way to get re-elected or re-appointed. Time had run out. The finish line was close and they didn't have the time to catch up.

Danny studied the bland, emotionless countenance of the Secretary of the Treasury, and began to worry that his fiscally conservative rhetoric was distancing himself from them. To secure his cover, he asked, "Give us a plan for getting us out of these problems without abandoning the president's agenda. How can we afford our gun control measures?" He glanced at Bill Erdman, the ATF director. "How can we afford to imprison all those we're planning on prosecuting?" His gaze shifted from Vic Meyers to the Public Education Czar and the NEA president. "How can we afford our education campaign for hate criminals?"

"We'll find a way to pay for it, Mr. Connor," the president responded dryly without looking up from her laptop. "Do you have any productive contribution to make besides sharp criticisms?"

"'Hey! Look! Don't go over that cliff!' is an important contribution when we're headed for one," Danny responded humorously.

The Treasury Secretary smiled at the economic prodigy's wit. "I believe we can get more loans for now, the Federal Reserve can monetize the debt and—"

Danny puffed his cheeks out and scoffed, "Please, Mr. Hammond! If you want to strengthen the hand of those trying to impeach the president, go ahead. Getting another credit card so you can afford the minimum payments on all your other maxed cards just deepens the inflationary pit into which we're sinking."

Mr. Hammond laughed. "A good physician learns the disease well before he ventures a remedy," he said. "We can fix this."

"Your remedy is more of the disease!" Danny snapped. "Raising taxes any more will cut productivity. Raising welfare risks a Republican takeover. We have tens of trillions of dollars of unfunded liabilities, Mr. Hammond, because of so much borrowing, and you can't borrow your way out of—"

"We were about to answer those questions, Mr. Connor," the president interrupted Danny. She looked away from her notes and into his eyes. "If you will please be patient."

Danny Connor sat back in his chair. "You asked for my opinion, Madam President. In order to afford our agenda without sacrificing an election, we've got to be economically realistic."

"Mr. Hammond was just setting up his plan. Now hear him out."

Danny folded his hands across his pink silk tie and his buttoned blue blazer. "I'm all ears."

"There is another fiscal factor we must consider here," said the Treasury Secretary. "Medicare pays out billions of dollars annually for the elderly and disabled. About half of the entire Medicare budget goes to pay for the end-of-life care of about ten percent of the Medicare recipients. *Half*," he raised his voice for emphasis, "is spent on the patients with the poorest quality of life. Why are we breaking our economy's back to pay for health care for terminally ill elderly patients in their final months? Many suffer terribly during that time."

Where is he going with this? thought Danny with a furrowed brow.

"Medicare and the Social Security trust funds are dry, bone dry. We're spending more than we're taking in and the negative balance is increasing exponentially. Next year about 90% of our budget will go to pay these unfunded liabilities and the interest on the debt. It's unmanageable as is—"

"I thought we had a few more years before Social Security caught up with us." Congressman McGinnis looked worried. This was a bomb to his ambitions. He always believed that he would be out of office by the time the safety nets went bankrupt.

"What planet have you been campaigning on? That *was* true a dozen years ago, but not anymore." Hammond looked at McGinnis with spite in his eyes. "The data you're thinking of was based on figures that assumed Congress put the money back that they took out of the Trust Fund. And it didn't take into account increased liabilities for Medicare, socialized healthcare, nor drug entitlement legislation."

Danny Connor was getting irritated at the minority whip's reluctance to admit the obvious. *Was he really that oblivious to the fiscal facts?* "You all know that there has never been a trust fund ever since F.D.R. dreamed up the Social Security plan," Connor stated. "We spent the surplus every year. The trust fund is a vault of IOU's from Congress."

"Congress' Ponzi scheme is coming to an end," Hammond added with a nod.

McGinnis began to angrily protest the Treasurer's hypocritical audacity to criticize Congress' fiscal responsibility when the president interrupted: "We don't have time for this! Those are the facts, gentlemen. Deal with it. We need to be fully aware of the critical predicament we are in for a reason. In the past several months, I have proposed some novel, revolutionary changes in government for the good of our nation, but those changes cost money that we just don't have."

"*Lots* of money!" the Treasurer agreed.

"Peace and prosperity is costly," Brighton said. "We *have* to enforce these statutes. We have to investigate, prosecute, and see these measures through to their completion. We're raising taxes, of course, but as Danny said, raising taxes has fiscal consequences and negatively affects our re-election efforts. So there is another avenue of cost-saving I'm going to pursue with more vigor." She took a deep breath, and everyone could see that she was finally coming to her point. "We are going to take advantage of the Supreme Court's ruling on physician-assisted suicide to revive the safety net of Medicare and Social Security and save hundreds of billions if not trillions of dollars. I'm directing Hammond to work with IRS and HHS administrators to make euthanasia more profitable and practical for Americans. We're in a financial crisis that popular euthanasia will help us remedy. Not to mention the benefit to our overpopulation and ecosystem crisis. It's the remedy that we need and we need it now.

That pill was hard enough to swallow, but the president's face flushed as she ventured into a more emotionally charged proposal with more significant personal consequences.

"My husband, many of you know him," she strained to say, nodding at a few of those around the room who considered him an acquaintance, "has been suffering terribly from metastatic bone cancer for the past eight years. The cancer is in his lower spine and hip bones. He's partially paralyzed below the waist. He's had four surgeries and dozens of rounds of chemotherapy and radiation, which has only prolonged his misery. He has severe allergies to the best medicines for this condition. His pain is unbearable at times. Excruciating electrical pains," she pointed at her leg and grimaced, "shoot down his legs with any movement whatsoever. He is on large doses of narcotic pain medications, which toss him back and forth between fits of delirium when the medication peaks and times when the pain is so unbearable, he actually cries for death. I would never wish this nightmare upon anybody. Jerry and I have discussed this in detail, and he agrees to a dignified death under the care of his physician in our home."

Press Secretary, Cameron Weaver, almost fell out of his chair. "No, no, no, no..."

Dena jerked in her chair, her body stiff and eyes glazed over as if she had just seen a ghost. "That would be disastrous, Madam President. You can't mean it."

The president raised her voice to plead her case. "We want to avert financial disaster in our country, don't we? And my husband and I want to avert the disaster of a painful prolonged death."

"You can't do this!" Weaver objected, shaking his head firmly side to side. "The press will have you for lunch. This is too, too volatile."

The president closed her eyes as if withholding some wave of emotion, and looked down. Her cabinet members knew that this must be painful for her, but it was difficult for them to conceal their disdain.

Weaver leaned toward the president with his elbows on the table. "We're sorry about your husband, Madam President, but you've got to do what's best for your administration."

"We can't let you do it," Dena Halluci insisted. But when Dena caught the president's glare, she knew the president would not change her mind.

"We've been considering this long before the case even appeared before the Supreme Court, and long before our federal budget needed the financial relief that it would receive from the promotion of euthanasia in our culture. We're overpopulated as it is, and this will help us." The president paused to search for the right words, and with a tear in her eye, she said, "This will help us to heal the earth."

Danny took a deep breath and put his palms down flat on the table, trying his best to keep his moral objections under the radar.

"You just don't know how terribly we have suffered! Jerry knows that this is not only best for his health, but he believes it's his patriotic duty. He wants to go out a hero. A dignified death under a physician's care is not something to be feared. We'll show the nation compassionate care. We'll lead the way."

"But Madam President..."

"You are over-reacting!" the president blurted out, visibly upset by the scornful glances of her cabinet members, czars, and Democratic congressional leaders. "This hysterical over-reaction is the very thing we're trying to overcome in the American psyche!"

"And someone *should* try to overcome it, Madam President," said Dena, "but *not you*." She spoke as softly as she could so she wouldn't stir up the president's volatile emotions. "The public's reaction will be ten-fold more hysterical than what you are witnessing in us. It's going to hurt your image and negatively affect your agenda."

"Madam President, if I may?" The Secretary of Health and Human Services and former oncology professor at the George Washington Medical School raised a finger and the president nodded at him.

"The medical community has been lobbying for legalized euthanasia for decades. You've never seen the suffering that I have, the kind of suffering that the president has witnessed in her husband." The president wiped her nose with a tissue and nodded as he spoke. "We know what compassionate care entails for the moaning patient wracked with pain in a hospital bed. The law's prevented us from being compassionate, but that has been remedied. Now, the primary obstacles to appropriate end-of-life care are the unreasonable taboos of our culture. I think the only thing that could be more influential in the arena of compassionate, dignified dying than the Supreme Court Case that legalized it in all 50 states, is the president and her husband's bold, public exercise of their right to die." He glanced adoringly at President Margaret Brighton. "Their courage could crack the dam of unreasonable taboos that stand in opposition to the sanctity of the physician-patient relationship in the process of passing into the next world. We need to encourage the president, right now. This is very difficult for her."

"You all just don't realize how much we've suffered," the president whispered, summoning pity. "We're going to do it. We realize that if we do it in a corner, away from the eyes of the public, the radical right will still harshly criticize us; plus, we'll lose an opportunity to influence the culture. Why should we be ashamed? Why not do it publicly and make converts? We'll move the discussion to the dinner table and make compassionate end-of-life care more acceptable to the American public. Rather than always following the consensus, why not make a new one?"

"This is where the bankruptcy of the Medicare system becomes an important consideration, gentlemen," said Mr. Hammond, tying it all together. "This could *save* Medicare and prolong Social Security. If Americans will become more comfortable with euthanizing their elderly parents and grandparents, as well as their incompetent, handicapped family members, we could save *trillions* of dollars. We can prolong these safety nets for another decade or so."

"We won't be unloading this on the public all at once," the president assured them. "During my announcement tonight on our new euthanasia initiatives that we're incorporating into the tax code, I'll be introducing my wheelchair-bound husband. That'll soften the blow of my tax proposals and win sympathy for our 'Death With Dignity' campaign. When they see how terribly he suffers and how emaciated he is, they'll understand. The media will help us."

"You're amazing, Margaret Brighton, just amazing." The progressive icon, Senator Tom Tindale crossed his arms over his chest, proud of their leader and wishing he had her courage.

"*Jerry* is the amazing one. This was all his idea. I'm just a heartbroken wife who's going to miss her husband terribly." Her bottom lip began to tremble and she reached down to get a tissue out of her purse.

"You're in our prayers, Madam President." Congressman McGinnis reached across the table and gently squeezed her hand.

"Thank you, Jim."

McGinnis let go of the president's hand and glanced at Danny Connor, who feigned a sympathetic nod to prevent arousing suspicion. Danny's thoughts were on the glee with which his friend Josh Davis and his mighty pen would tackle this issue in his next article.

"When?" Halluci asked.

The president swallowed hard. "We want the pain to end as soon as possible."

Cameron shook his head and glanced at Dena, who rolled her eyes and shrugged her slim shoulders slightly. From this vantage point, their job was damage control.

Margaret Brighton put her make-up on extra-thin today. She donned a special type of waterproof mascara. When the tears flowed, she wanted to avoid the black streaks on her face. It was a big day. The whole world was watching. What Abraham Lincoln was to the American slaves, she would be to the handicapped and terminally ill. Today, the religious dogmas that impede America's progress were coming down like a sandcastle in a hurricane. Her husband's euthanasia would have the impact of the novel *Uncle Tom's Cabin* before the Civil War; it would turn the tide of public opinion and set a new cultural standard. Popular euthanasia was critical to her financial plan for her gun control and hate-speech executive orders, which were vital to America's peace and security. Therefore, her husband's death was best for America – it was that simple.

To the president, this was not just political. It was also deeply personal. When her husband suffered, she suffered, and his comfortable death would end her suffering. She loved him, but enough is enough. He'd lost control of his bowels and had to wear a diaper now. Oh, the humility for a grown man to endure diaper changes three to four times a day. He had open sores on his buttocks. The pain of any leg movement was beyond excruciating. Why should the law let us love our pets more than our parents? We'd put a beloved dog out of its misery at the vet's office if it had to endure what we let our loved ones endure. It was time to die with dignity.

Jerry Brighton had begun having second thoughts the past couple days, and they had more than one argument about it. He claimed that his main concern was that he would miss his wife of 30 years – he admired Margaret dearly. He made the comments expected of a man staring death in the eye: *I want to see my wife grow old... I want to see the grandkids graduate from high school... I can tolerate the pain... Maybe they'll have a medical breakthrough that will cure cancer... What will happen to me after death?*

"I'll see you again in the afterlife," Margaret tried to encourage him.

"What afterlife? You always said that heaven and hell are on earth."

"Well, who knows?" She shrugged. "Maybe we'll be incarnated."

"Then how do I know I'll see you again?"

"Maybe there is an afterlife."

"Maybe?! I've got one life, and I'm not going to gamble it all on a maybe! What if there is a heaven and a hell in your afterlife?"

Those conversations did not end well. Margaret was upset that he was changing his mind after being so confident about doing it earlier. They had made all the plans. It had been advertised on nationwide television. Oprah had come out of retirement to interview them before and after the procedure. But his second thoughts were ruining everything. What an embarrassment this would be!

After a brainstorming session with her most trusted advisors, they developed a remedy. They would stop his anti-depressant medications. Those medicines were only covering his symptoms, not curing him anyway. Let him feel the full weight of his misery and death will appear more welcoming.

It worked like a charm. The morning of the scheduled euthanasia procedure, he was as depressed as he was in pain. He claimed that he would kill himself if a physician didn't do it. Margaret Brighton would not have her plan spoiled by her fatally ill husband. Pragmatism reigned. He was going to die and the country would love her for it.

It would be picturesque. The grown children and one grandchild would surround the bed. They'd sing one of his favorite songs. He would smile, shed a tear with his wife, they'd kiss one more time and then say goodbye. The injection would be given and he'd fall asleep and feel no more pain. Then he'd drift to whatever ecstasy his next life held for him.

To give the most comfortable setting, they decided to have the procedure done at home. The dimly lamp-lit bedroom with family pictures on the wall and a window overlooking the White House lawn would be more conducive to a comfortable euthanasia.

60 Minutes, who purchased the video rights to the event, had two video cameras in the room, one in each corner. They were aiming for breaking the world record for the number of viewers at one time, which it was predicted they could only do if they broadcast the event live. Margaret Brighton, always hungry to pioneer new paths to fame, consented. Weaver and Halluci begged the Brightons to pre-record, but the president insisted that the euthanasia and its accompanying emotions be authentic.

The *60 Minutes* director decided to have Margaret stand on Jerry's left side, holding and caressing his hand. The mildly autistic grandson would sit at the foot of the bed. His inability to comprehend what was happening would make childish outbursts of grief less likely with him than with the other grandchildren. The two grown Brighton sons and their wives would be seated on stools on each side of the bed. The physician would wear his white lab coat to create the presence of competent medical supervision and to take advantage of the public's trust of physicians. He would sit at the head of the bed on the other side of the president.

A *60 Minutes* make-up artist met President Brighton in the hallway to make the finishing touches on her face.

"Margaret?" Jerry smiled faintly when he saw her in the hallway.

"Hello dear." She walked to his side and grabbed his hand. "You're my hero." She kissed him on the forehead.

"I'm going to miss you so much," he whispered.

"Me too." She looked up at a videographer, who stood behind one of the cameras. "Are we ready?"

"We're live in one minute and 22 seconds. I'll give you a ten second countdown."

The autistic grandchild sat on the edge of the bed staring at his fingers. His mother kissed his cheek and whispered something into his ear. The boy turned to look at his grandfather. "Grandpa?" the 8-year-old boy spoke, as he rarely does. He looked confused by the lights, cameras, and the sad countenances on everybody's face.

"The doctor's going to take care of him," his mother said as she straightened the little boy's clip-on bow tie.

The *60 Minutes* film director nodded at the president. "Ten seconds! Don't you worry, Madam President. We're live in seven, six, five, four, three, two, and..."

Brighton began with friendly introductions of her family and a brief, melodramatic oratory about how she would miss her husband terribly. She cried briefly, yet regained her composure appropriately. Her eldest daughter stood up and gave her a warm hug, and Jerry patted her hand and told her it was okay. Jerry comforted Margaret –it was perfect!

Margaret explained how she was glad that he was finally going to be out of the horrible misery that this terminal cancer was causing him. She bent down, kissed him on the forehead, and told him that she loved him. He reciprocated. Every eye was full of tears, except the child's.

"Is Grandpa okay?" the 8-year-old boy slurred in a loud voice. "Who cry, Mommy? Who cry?" The autistic child was showing a rare emotion. The mother discerned that the *60 Minutes* director disapproved because of the intense frown he had behind the camera.

"It's okay," his mother whispered. "Grandpa's sick. See that man over there? That's the doctor. He's going to help him."

"Okay, Grandpa?" The child tried to move away from his mother toward his grandfather. His mother shushed him to try to quiet him down.

Margaret turned and spoke to him in a stern voice. "Grandpa's going to be okay. Be quiet now." She nodded at the physician, which was his cue to begin the lethal injection of a barbiturate into his I.V. line.

Margaret looked down at her husband as she caressed his hand, and when she saw his eyes, she panicked for a brief moment. *Oh no!* she thought. *Be quiet. Don't say anything.* "It's okay, dear. Your pain will be gone in a few seconds." She nodded at the physician again, as if to inform him to increase the rate of infusion.

"Who cry, Mommy?" the autistic grandson whined. "Grandpa?" His mother picked him up from the bed and tried to comfort him, but he wanted to go to his grandpa's side, and her restraint prompted a screaming fit. His arms flailed and his voice was shrill.

The president motioned for the child to be removed when her husband got her attention. "Honey," Jerry said, looking up at his wife, "I don't want to die."

No! Margaret thought in her mind, trying not to look angry. *Keep your mouth shut. Don't say anything!* Outwardly, she held her peace.

The doctor glanced at the president, unsure if she wished him to continue. She winked at him to encourage him. "It'll be all right."

The president glanced at her daughter, who had begun to remove the 8-year-old boy from the room. Unwilling to leave his grandpa, the child fell onto the floor and began to throw a temper tantrum. "I be with Grandpa!" he squealed as he clenched his fists around the edge of the white blanket that draped off the bed. She began to drag him out of the room, taking the blanket with him. The president grabbed the blanket to keep it from being taken off the bed and there was a brief tug of war.

"I don't want to leave you." Jerry grabbed his wife's right hand with both of his. She let go of the blanket and he pulled her hand to his cheek.

He began to sob as the president whispered harshly into his ear. "You're ruining this for me. Be quiet." The president's cheeks flushed. She glanced worriedly at the anxious *60 Minutes* director, and then she gave him the sign of the thumb across the throat, letting him know that she wanted to cut the video.

The director rolled his eyes, stopped recording, and then loudly exclaimed several foul words. He glanced at a frustrated-looking elderly gentleman in a three-piece suit at the door of the room. "I told you we should have pre-recorded."

Helena, Montana

Governor Ben Boswell was on his knees praying in his home-office. The lights were off and the room was dark as he poured his heart out to the Lord.

His wife lightly knocked on his door. "Dear," she said softly, "there's something that you should see."

He sighed deeply, his heart heavy with many burdens. "Can it wait?"

"The president's killing her husband."

His head turned to the sliver of horizontal light that escaped into his office under the door. "Now?"

"You haven't heard?" He stood and exited the room, squinting from the bright light. "They've been advertising this all day."

Ben Boswell plopped down in his seat in front of the television, shocked at what he was witnessing. He couldn't believe his eyes.

His wife rested her hand on his shoulder and spoke with a faint voice. "We've been letting the government get away with murder for a long time."

He shook his head and clenched his fists over the corners of the armrests. "Well, we're not going to let them get away with it in Montana."

Arlington, Virginia

"Unbelievable!" Congressman James Knight watched the small television from his living room. When Jerry Brighton shut his eyes for the last time, his grimace of horror fading to a sedated calmness, Knight uttered, "God have mercy on that man." When he saw the president swipe her thumb across her throat to end the recording, he mumbled, "God have mercy on that woman."

The troubling thought came to him, *If she murders her husband, whom she claims to love, what do you think she's going to do to you, whom she claims to hate?*

The brave and bold James Knight suddenly became just a little frightened. He rubbed his clammy hands against his pants as the future suddenly grew more ominous and foreboding in his imagination.

Little Rock, Arkansas

Stein stood in front of a wall-mounted television at the Greyhound bus stop. Without warning, he clenched his fists and lifted up his voice, "Stinkin' witch!" He glanced over at those around him, who were startled by his shouting at the screen.

"The man's been suffering a lot. Have pity." A young, frail woman with short hair wearing several bead bracelets and neck-laces looked with disdain upon the unkempt, black-clad character beside her. She uncrossed and crossed her legs repeatedly, unable to adequately verbalize her disgust with her loud-mouthed neighbor.

Stein turned back to the television, stunned that he appeared to be the only one upset at the sight of the president murdering her husband on television. Under his breath, he mumbled, "All right." He sighed deeply and turned his mind to thoughts of vengeance. "All right, Margaret Brighton, all right."

Southern Montana

Elijah bit his tongue as he listened to the radio report of Jerry Brighton's final moments. Jared sat beside him in the front seat and David behind him, while most of the Mannings napped in the backseats and on the floor. Their trek north was slowed considerably by their attendance at several revival meetings inside the Coalition's borders. Many meetings had to be held outdoors because of the size of the crowds, and the influx of Christians into the Coalition made the atmosphere just heavenly.

"I can't believe this!" Jared called out to Cal in the rear of the minivan. "Cal! Wake up! You won't believe it"

"What? What happened?" Cal sat up, startling the child who was snoozing in his lap.

"The president euthanized her husband." Jared glanced at David in the seat behind him, surprised that David wasn't more interested in what was happening in the White House. "Whatcha' doing, David?"

David ignored the question as he quietly studied map of the United States spread across his lap. He was trying to calculate how long it would take his wife and family to reach her destination in Ohio. Maybe she found someone to give her a ride.

"How ironic," Elijah mumbled. "Now the generation that aborted their children is going to be aborted."

"The president's a sick freak!" Jared blurted out, unable to articulate his emotions into any language that wasn't derogatory. "Our country's so far gone. I can't believe this?"

"Shhh," Cal urged Jared, leaning forward to check on his wife who was still sleeping in the middle seat in front of him. "She was awake most of the night. Let her sleep."

"Sorry."

"This can't be good for her agenda," Elijah opined. "Maybe now James Knight will rally enough support in Congress to get impeachment back on its feet."

"At least now we have hope in the American jury," Cal commented softly. "The Barry Friar 'Not Guilty' verdict changed everything. Jury nullification is making a comeback."

"Are you kidding?" Jared shook his head, amazed at Cal's naiveté. "Juries won't be hearing any more cases whose outcome could have an impact on the president's agenda."

Jared glanced back at David, whose head was bowed low over his map. "You all right, David?"

Unbeknownst to everyone in the van, David Jameson was in tears. He clasped his hands together and blinked rivers of tears down his cheeks and onto the map before him. He was halfway through day three of a three-day fast, during which he barely spoke. He spent the entire day praying for his family, his country, and reading his Bible. Now, as he listened to the report of the president euthanizing her husband before the entire country, his heart was breaking. The English language lacked words strong enough to express his grief and heartache. All he could do was groan in prayer with as much fervency as his cramped conditions would let him. He knew that God's longsuffering was being tested, and that the nation was in danger of utter annihilation under God's gavel of judgment. He prayed for the men and women he knew who stood between where the nation was now and its final calamity, men and women with the incense of praise in their hands who stood between the plague and the healing: James Knight, Josh Davis, the pastors and prophets behind bars, the leaders of South Carolina and Texas, Montana Governor Ben Boswell, and his missing wife.

Washington, D.C.

The *60 Minutes* director was irate, but the other cameraman in the hospital room tried to ease the tension. "Okay, we're at a break. Everybody take a deep breath. It's not the end of the world."

The autistic child's tantrum grew more pronounced as the mother tried to usher him from the room. She managed to pry his fingers off of the blanket, but he grabbed onto a decorative curtain with one fist, then two, and wouldn't let it go when his mother ordered him to. His screams were full of rage and fear. "Grandpa! Okay, Grandpa? Grandpa!"

President Brighton's hand was still in her departing husband's tight grip. She looked at him with spite. As she tried to pry his clammy fingers off her hand, he shocked her by suddenly opening his eyes wide and gazing into hers. He gripped her hand with both of his and his grimace appeared ghostly.

"Please, Margaret." His words were slurred and raspy. "I don't want to die. Make him stop." He let out another strong sob as he pulled her against his chest and hugged her tightly, almost pulling her into bed with him. "I'm sorry," he mumbled. His eyes closed and he blew out his last breath in a snoring grunt. His arms went limp and Margaret pulled away.

The mother who embraced her angry 8-year-old son in the doorway wept bitterly as she watched her father's life fade away before her eyes. This show of grief only frightened her son all the more. His shrill screams caused the nearest cameraman to put his hands over his ears. The mother pulled her child away from the curtain. It came off of its rings and followed them both out of the room. "Okay, Grandpa? Grandpa!" The child was dragged away kicking, crying, and lurching his body back and forth in violent protest.

After an uneasy moment, the physician put his stethoscope on the patient's chest and pronounced, "He's comfortable now, Madam President."

"Good for him!" she blurted out, disgusted with how the event had transpired. "Is that how it's supposed to happen?"

A sweat broke out on the physician's face. "No, Madam President. The medicine must have reacted with his chemotherapy or his narcotic combination, or something."

The *60 Minutes* director quietly breathed another foul word. He walked to the foot of the bed, unsure of what to say to comfort the president. Attempting to assuage her predictable criticism, he said, "I told you that we shouldn't have had the kid in it."

The president just stared at him coldly as she brushed away a lone tear.

"We went to a commercial when things got out of control, but you shouldn't have motioned for us to stop the cameras with your thumb across the throat. That probably wasn't appropriate, Madam President."

She reached down and closed her husband's partially opened eyes. His facial features were contorted, his lips frozen in an unspoken word begging for mercy from his killers. Margaret wheezed an incoherent curse, followed with "Moron." Words could not express her abhorrence of her pathetic, weak husband's double-mindedness. He was always such a push-over. Worshiping his wife never made up for his lack of backbone. She jerked her husband's blanket up over his face.

"Now what?" she blurted out angrily.

"Now we have the interview," the director said calmly. "Let's do it just like we planned. We'll need tears and we'll need you to focus on how much he suffered." He glanced at his watch. "Oprah will be here any minute. If anyone can redeem this, she can."

Chapter 25

New York City, New York

"It's murder!"

"Come on, Mr. Knight, don't you think you've been over-using that word a bit recently?" O.J. Simpsonite, the ex-con, NFL bad-boy became America's most popular radio talk show host when Rush Limball lost half his brain after a stroke during his second gastric bypass surgery, Sean Hammity was imprisoned for the attempted murder of the ageless Congressman Ron Paul, and Gwyn Beck was admitted to a psych ward with an eating disorder after Fitzgerald was elected by a landslide.

"Of course, it's murder." Knight leaned into his microphone and pressed his earphones tighter over his ears while sitting in the studio of New York City's largest FM radio station. "The elderly and handicapped are next on the list of those to be killed in the American Holocaust."

"Just ten minutes ago - you heard her! - she made it clear that only those willing to die in such a painless and dignified manner would be euthanized," O.J. rebutted, massaging his graying mustache.

"Oh, but you've got to read the fine print of the Supreme Court ruling. If grandma is determined to be mentally incompetent, then her family can overdose her, collect on her insurance policy early, *and* get a tax break."

Mitch Paine, the University of Texas professor in charge of the Congressional Subcommittee on Dying with Dignity, was the euthanasia proponent on the show sitting on the other side of Knight. He wore his flowery hippy shirt and had his hair pulled back into a pony tail. He leaned toward the congressman from Wyoming. "What do you think about the poll this morning which shows that most Americans and most physicians want legal euthanasia? If you'd rather die a slow, painful death from cancer rather than with your wits and your loved ones gathered round, that's your prerogative. If you don't want euthanasia—"

"Don't have one," Knight finished his sentence. "I'm well familiar with that slogan from the pro-abortion campaign. It's an appropriate comparison."

"It's similar in that the proponents of legal euthanasia and legal abortion don't want people to get euthanized or get aborted," Paine argued, "they just want people to have the choice."

"It's also similar in that a murder takes place in both cases," Knight rebutted.

That comment stoked Paine's ire. "Murder defined by whom? You? Your priest or holy book? Tell me why the state should respect your religious dogma at the expense of all others?"

O.J. agreed with Paine. "We live in a democracy, Mr. Knight. If most Americans want it, why shouldn't they get it?"

"There are limits to a democracy, O.J. If most Americans want to enslave blacks again, we wouldn't let them. Why? Because we should be ruled by good law. We're not to be ruled by the majority, or else when the majority wants racism and slavery, we'd have no basis to condemn it, would we? The founding documents of America make it plain that the right to life comes from God and is inalienable."

"You mean 'unalienable,' O.J. suggested.

"That's the old English term in the Declaration of Independence, but the contemporary word for it is 'inalienable', which is something that cannot be taken away, or cannot be revoked."

"Except for women – right, Congressman?" Paine interjected. "They don't have the inalienable right to do what they want with their body according to you..."

Knight grinned. "Sure they do. As long as it's *their* body..."

"Except for gays - right, Congressman?" Mitch Paine began to mock him. "They don't have the inalienable right to marry according to you."

Knight grinned even wider. "Oh, they can marry just like heterosexuals, they just can't marry someone of the same sex. Gays and heterosexuals are equally forbidden the opportunity to redefine marriage."

Paine took a deep breath and brought their conversation back to the subject matter. "The American Medical Association, who brought the suit that resulted in the Court's decision on euthanasia," Mitch Paine interjected, "has said that the primary intention of the physician is not to kill patients, but to alleviate suffering. The death of the patient was not an end, but a means to an end. We should have a right to death with dignity, instead of perpetual surgery and futile medicine to extend life unnaturally."

"You're confusing two different issues," Knight responded. "First of all, we have always had the right to reject medicine and surgery. That's not suicide. If we're incompetent, our loved ones have the right to make decisions on our behalf. What the AMA endorses is not simply discontinuing medicine and withholding futile surgery. They want to intentionally over-dose patients."

"It's about choice!" Paine insisted. "A free people should have the free choice to do what they want with their own body."

"A choice to cause," Knight tapped his index finger against the table, "another's death is murder, Mr. Paine, not medicine! Barbiturates in high doses are not FDA-approved to treat cancer or depression except for barbarians and butchers."

"That's absurd!" Paine shook his head in frustration.

"Is this just one more reason to impeach President Margaret Brighton?" asked O.J. with a sarcastic grin.

"She's encouraging and paying for the slaughter of the elderly and handicapped. I think that she deserves life in prison or the electric chair. I suppose we could do that without impeaching her."

"Oh, please!" Paine exclaimed. "Your default position is always hate speech and violence! How do you stay out of jail?"

"We hung Nazi war criminals by the neck till dead, even though what they did was legal where and when they did it. There's a law that is higher than human government – it's the law of God. Our mass-murder-in-chief wants to hire assassins to kill tens of thousands of elderly and handicapped people to save Medicare money. If that's not a capital crime, there's no such—"

"She's a Christian who goes to a church, Mr. Knight!" Paine adamantly insisted. "She loves God just as much as you claim to!"

Knight laughed embarrassingly loud, and then proclaimed, "Yeah, a church that marries gays and has late-term abortionists teaching Sunday School. Some church!"

"It's a Christian church."

"It's a social club of pagans and sodomites."

That comment made Paine fighting mad. Even the usually subdued O.J. Simpsonite grew tempted to turn off the congressman's microphone. "You're violating the nation's hate speech laws and should be locked away, congressman!" Paine practically screamed into the microphone, his ponytail bobbing with his head wagging. "You're a pathetic bigot!"

James Knight tried to make eye contact with his apoplectic opponent in debate. "First, you tell me that it's a free country and then you say you want to lock me away in prison for exercising my free speech rights? Which is it? Is it free only for anti-Christians like you?"

"O.J., you've heard how he has actually encouraged rebellion," Paine said, glancing at O.J. and angrily pointing at Knight. "He wants states to criminalize euthanasia in defiance of federal law."

"That's right," Knight admitted.

"James Knight wants Americans to break the law!"

"No. Break the lawlessness and keep the law. Murder is unlawful. The government's policies are contrary to the law of God and unlawful."

O.J. appeared perplexed as Knight's rhetoric appeared to cross the line. "You are actually encouraging states to criminalize euthanasia in defiance of federal law."

Paine added, "He also publicly encourages citizens to keep their firearms in defiance of federal law."

Knight grinned. "States have no obligation to respect unlawful Supreme Court decisions and executive orders."

"Unlawful according to who? You?"

"Unlawful according to the laws of nature and nature's God."

"Ah!" Paine smiled, wide-eyed. "O.J., this is what it comes down to. James Knight wants a Christian country that embraces his particular interpretation of his particular holy book. Since he can't get it through the democratic process, he wants to do it through instigating open rebellion in the states with an utter disregard for our constitutional separation of powers."

"Oh, stop pretending you care about democracy. When the democratic consensus wanted prayer in school or Ten Commandments plaques in our courtrooms, you opposed it. You only wave the flag of democracy when people want communism or when they want to slaughter their preborn babies or their handicapped family members for a tax break. And don't pretend like you care about the Constitution either! Your president has suspended the right to a jury trial for thousands of Americans who were exercising their free speech rights in a manner that she despises."

"Your party's most famous president, Abraham Lincoln, suspended *habeas corpus* in the Civil War," Paine said spitefully. "You political conservatives have harped on President Brighton for suspending the right to a jury trial in a time of national crisis, but Abe Lincoln, the Great Emancipator himself, did that exact same thing. He imprisoned thousands of critics without a trial or legal representation. Lincoln feared that several of Maryland's legislators might join the South's call for independence, and so he locked them up in Ft. McHenry without legal representation or a trial. How's that for the birth of the Republican Party?"

Knight didn't defend Lincoln as the professor expected, but instead said, "Not only that, but Lincoln even approved an arrest warrant for the Chief Justice of the Supreme Court who wrote an opinion condemning Lincoln's suspension of trial by jury. Lincoln also shut down over 300 newspapers and magazines that were critical of his invasion into the southern states. All this was not only unconstitutional, it was immoral, just like President Margaret Brighton's persecution of political opponents."

O.J. seemed surprised with Knight's criticism of Lincoln. "You seem very critical of a president who emancipated your forefathers from the chains of slavery."

"The Emancipation Proclamation didn't protect slaves in the North, and it let the South keep their slaves if they'd return to the Union. Did you know that three slave states stayed in the Union? Lincoln enforced the Supreme Court's infamous 1857 Dred Scott Decision in which they said that slaves were the property of their masters and runaway slaves should be returned to their masters. That's why the Underground Railroad had to go all the way to Canada. In 1861, Lincoln supported a constitutional amendment that expressly made slavery irrevocable."

Mitch Paine intended to embarrass his Republican opponent by bringing up Lincoln's suspension of *habeas corpus* during the Civil War. He didn't expect this to be turned against him. "The point is that during times of national crisis," Paine said, "government must, for the greater good, be able to silence traitors who stir up rebellion among the people."

"And our government *has* that right, Professor, but our Constitution grants that right to Congress, *not* the president. And it limits that right to be exercised temporarily under extreme circumstances, not to silence unpopular religious speech."

"Unpopular religious speech? That's what you call it? You want to criminalize 'Death With Dignity' and encourage anti-abortion vandals and snipers to be armed to the teeth and you call it 'unpopular religious speech'?"

"That's not true."

"You're problem, Mr. Knight, is that you have no respect for the separation of church and state. No wonder you can't get a democratic consensus to uphold your sadist Deity's rules in society: no gays, no women's rights, no reproductive choice, no government welfare—"

"I do *not* respect the separation of *God* and state that you propose, Mr. Paine, and neither did our American forefathers. You want a godless nation, but I long for our country to be one nation under the God of our forefathers once again – the one *true* God!"

"Mr. Knight," O.J. interrupted, leaning forward with an authoritative wave of his hand, "we have 15 seconds until commercial break. Tell us, are you God's holy warrior sent to defeat the president?"

"It's not just 'my God' she's fighting against, as if there are others. There is only one God, the God of the Bible. If a remnant of the country repents, God may bless some states with victory over tyranny."

"Like the Coalition of Free Christian States?" O.J. asked. Knight nodded confidently.

"So now you're urging secession?" Paine couldn't believe his ears. "Is that what you want? Would you sacrifice the lives of tens of thousands of Americans in a Revolutionary War to liberate *fetuses* and hatemongers from the federal government? All in the name of your genocidal Deity! Preposterous!"

Knowing that last impressions are lasting impressions, Knight kept his cool and looked straight into the camera. "The states should ban abortion and physician-assisted suicide as God commands, and if they must secede in order to do so, so be it. Until we do justice for the slaughtered innocent, President Brighton and the armed forces of the United States will be the least of the states' concerns, because the gavel of God Almighty's Judgment will fall against us."

Washington, D.C.

"I've heard that James Knight is blitzing the talk shows and lecture circuit again," Brighton ranted, her gazed fixed on Todd Hamilton, who sat across from her desk at the Oval Office. "He's praising the Coalition, encouraging them and other states to secede, and continuing his venomous, traitorous diatribe against me."

Hamilton sighed, foreseeing another one of the president's infamous emotional outbursts. "Yes, I've heard him.""Are you going to do something about it?" She straightened her back and glared at him critically with her mouth slightly agape. "Or are you just going to let him stir up rebellion?"

Hamilton extended both of his palms toward the president. "He's a congressman, Madame President. When Congress censures him, we'll arrest him."

"I don't understand." She tilted her head to the side. "Why do you need to wait for them to do their duty before you'll do yours?"

"May I make a recommendation first?"

She looked down at her laptop and typed something. "What kind of recommendation?" she asked without looking.

"Dena and I think it's best for your reputation and your agenda to at least meet privately with Knight and see if he can be tempered. That way, if and when we do arrest him, we'll have proof that we exhausted lesser means first."

"Dena agreed to this?"

"Yes. Meet with James Knight first, Madam President, and see if he'll quiet down for the good of the country. Let's see if your charm does its magic as it did at the last Conservative American Conference, where you turned a lot of your enemies into friends and your bitterest enemies into friendly foes. Some tender-hearted diplomacy across the aisle can save us a lot of heartache in the long run."

James Knight sat in the aisle reading his notes before the commencement of the House session. He glanced over at a 21-year-old female Republican aid in a crisp navy blue suit-dress who sat two seats over. "Good morning, Mrs. Willis."

"Good morning, sir," she said respectfully. She briefly turned her eyes away from her laptop to nod at the congressman.

He looked back to carefully peruse his notes. "God give me strength," he whispered. Being the oracle of righteousness in Congress was lonely business. Many of the conservatives who praised him in private loathed him in public. They loved him when they were appealing to the grassroots to get elected in the primaries, but despised him when they were appealing to the moderates in the general election. The conservatives on the right appealed to Knight's distasteful, strict idealism to make themselves appear more mainstream. The liberals on the left pointed at Knight to make the mainstream Republicans appear more extreme.

Moderate Republican Speaker of the House, Troy McAvery, informed Knight that he had an opportunity to speak this morning about some of his lesser proposals to limit the executive office's power. Knight was enthusiastic about the opportunity to make his case. All of his attempts at impeachment failed since it was discovered that the records of the investigation of the Reproductive Rights Convention explosion were destroyed in the Billings bombing. But he hoped that there were still steps that could be taken to restrain the executive's over-reaching. Thanks to Josh Davis' articles, the internet videos of the tragedies in South Carolina and Texas that the media refused to show, and the general disapproval of the president euthanizing her husband on television, religious conservatives were rallying to a tipping point.

Just do the right thing. Don't worry about the political consequences. Don't worry about who you offend. Just don't offend God. Knight pursed his lips and nodded as he basked in the hope of heaven. *Make God happy – that's all that matters.*

He felt a brush on his shoulder and looked up to see the chaplain's disapproving scowl as he walked past him to the platform. The chaplain prayed his typical generic prayer in his usual dry fashion while the congressmen and women in the House generally ignored him, walking about and conversing with each other.

As the House speaker stepped up from his lavish leather chair to the podium, whispers started to crescendo throughout the building.

That's unusual, thought Knight.

He glanced over to the congressional aid beside him, and then leaned over and whispered to her: "What's going on?"

"You haven't heard?"

Knight looked around him in wonder, curious as to what caused the whispers to increase in intensity and some to hastily exit the chamber. "Heard of what?"

"The explosion at the Columbus Civic Center was an accident."

"An accident? You mean the explosion at the National Reproductive Rights Convention? Josh Davis' article claimed that it was an accident, but that's based upon anonymous insiders and not confirmed by any hard facts."

"There was a leak from a Bureau agent involved in the investigation. Josh Davis recorded and posted the interview online."

Knight sat back in his chair, stunned. He watched the Speaker of the House delay introductions in order to read an e-mail message on his hand-held. Knight unclipped his cell phone and made a phone call to his office to confirm the rumor.

President Brighton was digging deep into the well of her colorful vocabulary to spew forth her most derogatory of insults for the betrayal in the Bureau. "Who is this son of a gun, this right-wing, hatemongering son of a gun?"

"Calm down, Madam President."

"Calm down?" She shouted at Todd Hamilton through her laptop connection, absolutely apoplectic at this betrayal. "Your subordinates are destroying my administration on nationwide television and you want me to calm down?!"

"No one's destroying anything, Madam President." Hamilton's secretary notified him over his desk intercom that his next appointment was in the lobby. Hamilton waited until the president was done with breathing hysterical curses at him and the Bureau with her tobacco-masculinized raspy voice.

"I'm preparing to meet with him right now. We'll get to the bottom of it and do what we have to do to shut him up."

"What do you have on him?"

"He's a 14-year veteran of the Bureau, former New York City P.D., a Republican, and a professing Christian." The president cursed the Christian faith as Hamilton continued, "He's the number three man in the convention explosion investigation and that traitor Josh Davis got into his head somehow and convinced him to talk. But don't worry, we'll shut him up."

Knight closed his cell phone after confirming the rumor through a reputable source. He planned to convince this Congress to take small steps in limiting the powers of the executive branch and the judiciary, but this turn of events, along with the recent televised killing of the president's husband, might just give him the edge in a renewed impeachment effort. The news quickly spread throughout Congress and the whispers and mumblings were peaking just as the House Speaker began the introductions.

Knight looked around and bemoaned the poor attendance. He recalled how Congress was such a grave disappointment to him during his first few weeks of service in the House. He found it incredulous that hardly anyone even showed up for the meetings. The absentees were out golfing, enjoying fine dining, attending parties and concerts, sleeping late, traveling overseas for tropical vacations, feasting on the gifts from lobbyists' and special interest groups - everything except the faithful performance of constitutional duty. Of course, thanks to C-Span, the congressmen were always present to make their speeches and to cast their vote on issues crucial to their constituencies, but they were rarely present to hear the speeches and debates of their fellow congressman.

James Knight received a gentle nudge on the shoulder and turned to face a fellow conservative congressman. "Bo Bennett, how are you?"

"Fine," responded the Montana rep.

"I presume you heard," said Dobson, the other Montana rep that stood beside Bennett.

"About the interview? Yes."

Dobson leaned forward and placed his palm on Knight's shoulder. "I just want to let you know that the Montana contingent is behind you if you want to renew impeachment efforts."

"So's a senior Democrat." The voice behind Knight was familiar, but those words didn't fit the reputation of the person who spoke them. Confused, Knight turned to see the white-haired chairman of the Ethics Committee, a Democrat from Arkansas in his sixth term.

"Theo Jefferson?" Knight exclaimed, distrusting the senior Democrat's sincerity. "Since when have you had sympathy with anything I've proposed?"

After an uncomfortable pause, tears welled up in the elderly man's eyes that made Knight and the Montana reps uncomfortable. "Since about a week ago." He squinted away his emotions and tried to maintain his stately composure. "My son's been arrested."

"What?" exclaimed Dobson. "For what?"

"He's a pastor back in Fayetteville. I haven't walked with the Lord for years but he has. He's been arrested for preaching against..." The elderly man began to cry and Knight grew embarrassed for him as those nearby began to pay attention.

"Are you going to be all right?" Dobson stood and patted the senior Democrat's shoulder.

The elderly rep pulled his right hand out of his pocket and unfolded a hand-written letter that his son had written him from jail. "Oh, my son. Y'all please pray for him."

"We will."

"He's so much more of a man than I am."

"You can be that man again," Knight told him. "Do you see your need for God's forgiveness?"

Jefferson wiped his tears and swallowed hard. "Oh yes. I'm a long-gone prodigal son, but I'm coming home. If the Father will have me."

Knight smiled and looked into the aging congressman's tired eyes. "He's not *the* Father, He's *your* Father, if you trust in Jesus. Of course, He'll have you back."

Jefferson carefully folded the note and put it back into his pocket. "But now God wants me to tear down the idols I've built for the last 25 years. I'm terrified and excited all at the same time." He turned his gaze heavenward, breathed deeply, and blew it out noisily. "I'd change parties if I thought the Republican Party wasn't equally corrupt." He turned his gaze upon James Knight. "I don't mean to offend you, James."

Knight smiled. "No offense taken."

"James, I want you to know that I am behind you in what you want to do here. I know standing with you will probably cost me my re-election, but that's a small price to pay."

"Well, praise God." Knight extended his hand and clasped Jefferson's. "Will you help me get this impeachment vote on the floor? This FBI leak might give us the edge."

"Even the Democrats are chattering at how Brighton has insulted Congress with her bottomless EOs and her stonewalling of our sub-poenas," Jefferson commented. "Some from fiscally conservative districts may lose their re-election because of her, but they're too scared of her attack dogs to break ranks."

"I put forth a formal request with Vic Meyers yesterday to have an independent investigator look into the raid and arrest of the Texas and South Carolina governors and their cabinets. They also arrested several reps, judges, and police officers."

Dobson and Bennett raised their eyebrows curiously. "Any headway?" Dobson asked.

Knight shook his head. "The DOJ is as silent as death. But now with this leak from the Bureau, who knows? McAvery did agree to recognize me as the first speaker this morning on the condition that I limit discussion to the topics to which he agreed. If I change the subject, he may try to cut me off." Knight glanced at the House Speaker in the distance. "I might need your help if I'm cut off."

"We're behind you, James and we're praying for you." Jefferson whispered to him.

Troy McAvery was pushing for unity in his morning introductions. McAvery voted with the liberals on every issue except tax cuts. He was more effective at increasing the size of government than the Democrats, because of the conservatives' willingness to capitulate to him in order to win his support on their bills.

McAvery concluded his introductions, "...And so in the light of the present contention, I think it in the best interests of the American people to try to preserve the social peace, rather than promote political division, which I am sure is very tempting at this moment. We need to cooperate. Today we'll begin with opening remarks from the gentleman William Watson from California."

Mr. Knight's eyebrows rose as the House speaker called another representative to speak. *I was supposed to be first this morning.* He held his peace as Congressman Watson discussed the failure of federal mandated price-controls for California power companies. He introduced his bill to federalize the power companies, as Mr. Knight patiently waited for the next opportunity to speak. *Maybe he's going to call me next.*

"Thank you, Mr. Watson. Next, we proceed to the gentle lady Angela Ferris from California."

What happened? Why won't he let me speak?

Knight rushed to McAvery's office after the assembly concluded, hoping to catch him before he left. He knocked on the locked office door, but there was no answer.

He let out a long sigh of frustrated tension. He turned and walked slowly down the hall when the House speaker stepped out of another office and almost ran headlong into Knight.

"Troy! Just the man I have been looking for."

"Oh, James," he mumbled as he quickly looked down and straightened his tie.

Mr. Knight followed him toward the elevators. "What's with the cold shoulder today? You agreed to let me speak this morning."

"I'm sorry, James. Plans change."

"May I have dibs tomorrow morning?"

"I thought my introductory comments would have given you a hint. I don't think it is wise to indulge in topics of such a divisive and hyper-partisan nature."

"But this is a *bipartisan* attempt to limit the executive."

"Not now." McAvery pushed the elevator's button and waited anxiously for the doors to open.

"Do you think I want to bring division, Troy? It's President Brighton and Todd Hamilton who've brought division through establishing military dictatorships in Texas and South Carolina. You've heard about the FBI leak."

The House speaker raised an index finger and rebutted, "I think he's back-tracked on that story."

"Yeah, I heard, in response to a job offer at the FBI that tripled his salary."

"I haven't heard that."

"I have a few friends in the Bureau. It's true. This campaign to persecute religious dissidents has been built on lies from day one."

"Don't you even try to make a case on the conspiracy theories of that traitor Josh Davis." An aid walked up and stood next to the House speaker, also waiting for the elevator. He held his peace and looked away from Knight, hoping that if he ignored the right-wing congressman he'd slink away.

Knight moved closer to him. "I have 78 supporters in the House." The House speaker's eyebrows rose a bit. "We got almost ten just today, including Democratic Ethics Chairman Jefferson from Arkansas."

"Theo Jefferson?"

Knight nodded. "And Brendan from South Carolina, Severyn from Colorado, and Rollins from Nebraska," he said, referring to several influential Democrats.

"South Carolina and Texas reps don't count, James. The case could be made that the reps from the ten Coalition states are too severely compromised in their commitment to the government to be trusted."

"Oh, come on!" Knight raised his voice and spread out his hands, frustrated at the House speaker's reluctance to be reasonable. "Why are you doing this to me? History won't judge success based upon the amount of boats you don't rock."

"I'll take the stairs." McAvery darted across the hall into a door with a glowing exit sign above it. James Knight was growing suspicious. He was right on McAvery's heels.

"Why have you done a one-eighty on me? We have always disagreed on things, even strongly, but you've never treated me with such contempt."

McAvery walked down the stairs, out the door, and into the parking lot. Knight held the door open for a moment as McAvery rushed toward his car. "Troy!" The House speaker didn't so much as turn around to look at him.

Knight went back into the stairwell and saw a small manila envelope on the ground. He picked up the envelope and grew curious when he saw the words, "FOR MCAVERY'S EYES ONLY" printed in caps in black ink on the front. On the rear was written, "Will exchange originals for no waves."

He opened the envelope and stared in disbelief at the first of several lurid photographs just as the metal door began to bang and rustle. McAvery was trying to get the right key into the keyhole. Knight knew that McAvery was returning to pick up his dropped photographs. He opened the door and McAvery stepped hurriedly inside the hall.

"Who's the adulteress, Troy?" Knight extended the envelope toward McAvery.

McAvery snatched the photographs from Knight and hung his head in shame. He reached to open the door but Knight held it shut. "The administration is blackmailing you to protect them, aren't they?"

"Open the door."

"I can't let your desire to preserve your reputation impede your obligation to our country."

"I had an affair," McAvery confessed with his eyes fixed on the doorknob. "It's, it's not presently active."

"'A fair' is a place where I take my kids for cotton candy and rides. You committed adultery," scowled James Knight.

"It was brief and it's over."

"Is the brevity of your infidelity supposed to lessen its gravity?" He motioned to the manila envelope in McAvery's clutches. "She's got to be half your age, Troy. You think betraying your country is going to cleanse your guilty conscience?"

"I want to protect my wife, not myself."

"No, no, no," said Knight, shaking his head and poking his index finger into McAvery's chest. "Don't kid yourself. You don't protect your wife through lying. That only postpones and magnifies the distrust and pain. How can God forgive you if you continue to live a lie?"

"No." He turned briskly away from Knight and glared at the doorknob, hoping Knight would take his hand off it. Instead, Knight got in between McAvery and the door.

"She could never forgive me. Please, James!" His eyes began to moisten. "This could tear my family apart and I could lose my position in the House."

"Your family's already torn apart and the quickest way to heal the wound is to repent and confess. Lies don't heal."

"They're going to give me the originals if I don't make waves. I have no choice."

"No choice? That lousy excuse for sin is the worst of all excuses. You *can* do right and you *will!*"

"I can't. I can't."

"You will!" Knight raised his voice as he pointed his finger into McAvery's chest again. "You'll confess to your wife and not let yourself be blackmailed. I'll not let the nation suffer because of your sin. Congress must confront Margaret Brighton's tyranny!" McAvery pushed Knight out of the way and reached for the door-knob, but Knight grabbed his forearm. "Whoever is blackmailing you is going to continue to do it to get whatever they want out of you. Accept the guilt and make amends while you can. The cover-up is worse than the crime."

"Get out of my way!" McAvery jerked his arm out of Knight's grasp and walked through the door to the parking lot. Knight followed, exasperated.

"I won't let you do this!"

The House speaker stopped dead in his tracks in mid-stride, turned around, and shouted, "You had *better* keep your *trap shut*, if you know what's good for you!"

"I'm more concerned about the fate of this nation than I am about what's good for me or your so-called reputation, that pathetic veneer on your career that's more like a painted-on clown's face than anything genuine. As your friend, I'm more concerned about what God thinks about you than even what your wife thinks about you. Marital unfaithfulness is one thing, but letting this blackmailer impede Congress' obligation to protect this country is just a step below treason."

McAvery winced and turned to continue toward his Lexus. "Say a word and it will be your word versus mine, and you'll have to prove it. There are powerful forces at work here, James. That manila envelope came in a package with a White House insignia on it."

At hearing those words, a chilling numbness crept up Knight's back into his neck and down his arms. James Knight stood in the middle of the parking lot with his jaw agape. A gnaw of hopelessness crept into his chest that even the most fervent of prayers was slow to halt.

"I know, sir," Knight pleaded in his 23rd phone call of the morning, "but we have to try."

"Why can't you just be content to cooperate with the Republican Party?" The South Carolina Republican representative was urging Knight to back off his political aggression and let the non-binding partisan resolutions against the president do the talking. "We've made our views known, now let it lie."

Knight shook his head and hoarsely declared, "The GOP resolutions are powerless to stop the president. Your own state leaders risked so much to be on the right side."

"Some of them, yes, but—"

"How can we betray their cause? Join me in the call for impeachment."

Click!

Knight gasped, raised the cordless phone into the air as if he were going to throw it against the wall, when suddenly there was a knock on the door. "Lord, help me," he exhaled as he placed the phone back onto the receiver. "Come in."

"Daddy? Are you okay?" His 3-year-old daughter peeked in to see what was wrong with her father. She'd hardly ever heard him raise his voice as he'd done on the phone several times in the past few hours.

"It's okay, honey." He forced a smile at her. "Daddy was talking to a bad man and he got a little upset. It's okay."

"Was it a *paw-wi-ti-shun*?" she said, grinning, expecting her father to be proud of her brand-new, albeit awkwardly pronounced vocabulary word.

"Yes, it was a politician, honey."

"Oh." She furrowed her brow. "Was it a *we-pub, we-pub, uh, wepub-wickan*?" she forced out, glancing up at her daddy. James Knight just laughed and patted her tenderly on the head. "Want some of my juice?" She raised a sippy-cup up toward him.

"No thank you."

James' wife stuck her head in the door. "Any success, my love?"

"No." He sighed heavily. "They're all so full of fear."

She walked over to him as he sat in his chair behind his desk. "Your duty is to obey God," she encouraged him, wrapping her arms around him from behind, "and leave the results to God."

He looked down with disappointment at the list of conservative reps in his notebook. His phone suddenly rang and he answered before the second ring. "James Knight here."

"This is Dena Halluci, the president's chief of staff."

James Knight felt like he was punched in the chest. He cupped his hand over the microphone and said to his wife, "I'll be out in a minute." His wife and daughter exited and he said, "What can I do for you, Ms. Halluci?"

"Much. President Brighton would like to have a personal meeting with you?"

"With me?" He was startled at the request. "Just me?"

"Yes."

"Well, sure." He swallowed his trepidation as he reached for a pen and a pad to write on.

"Can you meet with her in the Oval Office tonight?"

"Tonight? I suppose I can do that." Knight found it difficult to measure the president's sincerity through the emotionless voice of her chief of staff.

"Very well. I will notify the president that you'll meet with her alone in the Oval Office at 8 p.m."

"May I ask about the reason for this meeting?"

Ms. Halluci paused. "I'll let the president inform you of her reasons."

"Wonderful," said Mr. Knight slowly as he leaned back in his chair. "I'll be there."

James Knight shivered, his heart pounded, and his palms drained sweat as he stood at the door to the Oval Office of the President of the United States. He had traversed many obstacles to try to get this woman fired. He despised every single social and political aim she embraced. He abhorred every special interest cause for which she so bravely stood. He thought she was the personification of wickedness and tyranny, and he was not ashamed to tell her that to her face in front of the entire world. But now, as he prepared to knock on the polished, expertly etched, cherry wood door to the famous American room, he trembled.

Knock, knock, knock.

Almost immediately, the secretary pulled open the tall, heavy wooden door and invited him inside. He felt like a novice congressman as he walked into the foyer that led to the Oval Office. He saw Margaret Brighton sitting behind her broad, well-organized desk. She motioned for him to enter. He carried his briefcase in his left hand and wiped his right on his thigh as he tried to prepare for a handshake with the infamous President Brighton.

She stood and extended a hand, which he grabbed and shook briefly. "Thank you for agreeing to meet on such short notice," she said, her gray-green eyes barely discernible behind her squinty smile. "Would you like a cup of coffee or water?"

"No thank you." They sat down simultaneously.

"How's your family?" Brighton asked.

"They're fine. Have you met my family?"

"Unfortunately not." She shook her head. "Not yet. I hope to someday…"

James Knight was keenly conscious of his pounding pulse in his neck and head as he watched her lips move. He really didn't want to be there. He interrupted her bluntly: "What is it I can do for you, President Brighton?" He wanted to get right to the point of the visit. She took his hint and leaned forward on her elbows to answer his question.

"I know that you've attempted to advance discussion of my impeachment in the House. You've even got some moderates and a leftist Democrat to stand with you. I don't know how you got Theo Jefferson on board with you, but you did."

Mr. Knight shifted in his chair and cleared his throat.

"We are having a serious problem in our nation right now, Mr. Knight."

"I'm aware of that," he responded, confident that they would disagree on exactly what the problem was and that debate was probably futile.

"The people of this nation are divided," she paused, "confused." She tilted her head and turned her gaze out of the room's window. "I'm worried about the direction our nation is headed. There are some violent factions that, I know, both you and I would oppose." He nodded. "They are being stirred to radical lawlessness by the popular political and social division. You can help us keep the peace, Jim."

"James, please," he corrected her. "I don't like the division any more than you do."

"We agree then."

"Tell me this, Madam President. Is it true that the explosion was an accident?"

The president smiled and looked away. "No, I'm afraid that's unfounded. It was terror and I'm afraid the impeachment debates and partisan squabbles contribute to the terrorists' goals. Do you want that?"

"No, but I'm willing to endure it if that is what is necessary to secure the freedoms you threaten."

She did not react kindly to his forthright comment. For a second, he saw her face flinch and a spark of anger burst in her eyes, but she quickly subdued her rage and took a deep breath. She faked a warm smile and said, "I'm humbling myself before you, Jim..."

"James."

"I'm pleading with you, James, to drop this notion of impeachment. If you do, I've obtained promises from the leaders of your party that you'll be in the top three for the run for Republican majority leader next year."

I can't believe this is happening! he thought to himself. Her appeal to his desire to move up the political ladder offended him deeply, as if he were the type that would subject his conscience to selfish ambition. He expected her to try to persuade him to back off his impeachment efforts, but he didn't expect an appeal to his selfishness.

"Not for my sake," the president said, pointing at her chest with her thumb, "but for the sake of our country. Help me put an end to the division and the violence." Her expressions were passionate and heart-felt. "Join me in restoring peace to our country. Together, we can lead in the healing. You must know that this is what America so desperately needs right now. If I may be so bold as to say it, I'm confident that this is the will of God for you."

James Knight took a deep breath. "On one condition."

President Brighton sighed and smiled pleasantly. "Anything!" She leaned back in her chair, reveling in her apparent victory.

"Keep your promise."

After a pause, she said, "What promise?"

"During your inauguration, you put your hand on the Bible and promised to uphold and defend the Constitution. The Constitution guarantees the right to life, free speech, and the people's right to keep and bear arms. Keep your promise. Help me to put an end to the violence against the innocent, the preborn, the elderly—"

"Mr. Knight!" she blurted out. She suddenly put up a palm, looked away, drew in a deep breath, and then put her palm down and spoke more calmly. "Mr. Knight, believe me when I say this. I know we have great disagreements on abortion, euthanasia, and gun control, but please believe me, I sincerely want to do what's right for America. I want abortion to be rare. I want the common man to be able to own guns safely. Can't we agree to disagree peacefully without inadvertently encouraging this contentious division and hateful violence that is spreading across our land?"

"As long as you want abortion to be rare, I want impeachment proceedings to be rare." He paused to let those words sink in. When he could see that she comprehended his point, he grinned. "That I want it rare doesn't comfort you much when you're that rare exception does it? Neither is your desire for rare abortions comforting to the babies slaughtered in the abortions you justify."

"All right then," she nodded, preparing for a concession. "I'll end Title X funding for abortion in my budget if you'll back off your support for statewide abortion bans in the Coalition states. You don't have to condemn the Coalition states, just stop supporting them. How's that?"

Knight was stunned. "What? You'll stop Title X Medicaid funding of abortion?"

The president nodded. "These abortion bans in the Coalition states *will* fail," the president predicted, "but I'll keep my promise and cite your influence as the deciding factor on stopping federal funding of abortion. Now, that's a victory for your cause that will last, one that you can take to the bank. Be a hero on both sides of the aisle, James, and back away from the edge of the cliff for the good of the country."

She paused and let Knight consider the matter. She could see that his wheels were spinning. He weighed the issue carefully. What pro-lifer could deny that it would be good and right to end federal funding of abortion? There had been decades of funding through Title X and every attempt to end it failed. The GOP was too compromised to unite against it. What a victory this would be for the pro-life cause and for his congressional legacy! Sure, the abortion ban in his state of Wyoming would likely fail without his continued support and the bans in the other CFC States would also suffer. But those abortion bans may fail anyway, and at least this way, an important pro-life victory could be assured.

An intense pang stung his conscience and Knight swooned under its heat. Immediately, he knew what was happening. This test had felled many men of God throughout history, and he felt shame for being momentarily seduced under its persuasive spell. It was the same test that made Israel fail to drive out all of the pagans from the Promised Land as God commanded. It was the same test that made the church of Corinth tolerate a little bit of leaven in its fellowship. A little bit of compromise for a little more peace, at the expense of complete obedience to God and His unhindered blessing. Knight closed his eyes and imagined his Savior, nailed to the cross for his sins, and his passion went from lukewarm to white hot once again. *No, it is better to lose a battle that God can bless than to win a battle that stops short of full obedience. It is unbelief that accepts anything less than God's Will, and it is not the will of God that one of these little children should perish.*

Knight opened his eyes, fixed his gaze on President Brighton and shook his head back and forth. He calmly uttered a single syllable - "No" - and the president's hopes were dashed.

Animosity oozed from her grimace, but her cold stare, her clenched fists, and her quivering extremities did not move James Knight in the slightest. "Isn't peace an attainable goal for you?" she said, more calmly than Knight would have predicted from her body language. "Is your ideological purity so precious to you that you couldn't compromise in the slightest to keep the nation at peace?"

He grabbed his briefcase and prepared for his dismissal. "Peace in a slave's cage is a devil's trick and I won't fall for it."

She pointed to the door and ordered him to "Get out!"

"That's what I thought." He hastened from the room. "Stiffen your neck and hasten God's judgment upon you and our country."

"Now! Out!"

When Knight shut the door, she cursed, grabbed her computer mouse, and clicked her pointer over the "Send" box on the open e-mail on her computer.

Chapter 26

The secretary stood as James Knight quickly walked out of the Oval Office.

When the elevators shut, James took a deep breath and tried to assimilate what had just transpired. When he made it to the underground parking lot, his car was one of the last remaining.

He pushed the button on his key ring to unlock his Lincoln Town car. *Hmmm. Doesn't work.*

He inserted the key to unlock the door manually, and his heart dropped when he saw that the interior light didn't come on. "Oh no." He tried to start the car, but it wouldn't crank. He got out of the car, unlocked the trunk, and felt around in the dark for his battery cables. *Where are those cables?*

"No cables. Great!" he complained out loud. He searched the trunk again, blaming his wife under his breath. The lamp overhead wasn't functioning, so he activated the small light on his cell phone to search the trunk more thoroughly. He looked up and saw a man in a suit leave the building and begin to walk towards him. When he got within 50 feet or so, James shouted, "Sir! Do you have any battery cables? My battery's dead."

"Sure!" he responded. "Be right over."

The man arrived a few minutes later and parked his car directly in front of Knight's with the headlights on and the car running. He stepped out and extended a gloved hand.

"Robby," he introduced himself as they shook hands. Robby had a full face with a fair complexion and a dark mustache. He wore a black wool cap, atypical for the warm evening. "I'm an intern," he said, "fortunate enough to get a special pass to park in a congressional lot."

"Whose aid?"

"Oh, I'm here and there."

"I'm James Knight."

"Yes, the Obstructionist," Robby said as he opened the hood and began to connect the battery cables.

"Excuse me?"

"Giving Brighton a run for her money, aren't you?"

Knight didn't respond. Robby got back into his car and cranked it as Knight stood beside his open hood with his hands in his pockets. Robby walked back and spoke firmly to the congressman. "I think you ought to let Brighton be. It's not healthy to try to impeach the President of the United States solo."

"I'm not solo."

"Start your car," said Robby. Knight stepped into his car and cranked it successfully on the first try.

"You know," said Robby as he gathered up the cables, "you could get hurt stretching your neck out like that." He gave Knight a cold stare through his windshield. "Or your family."

Knight rolled down his window and angrily inquired, "What do you mean by that, sir?"

Robby cast the words carelessly over his shoulder as he tossed the cables into the trunk of his car. "Or your little girl."

"My little girl?" Knight jumped out of his car and ran up to the strange fellow as the man slammed his trunk shut and jumped into his driver's seat. Knight stood, fists clenched, at the window of the man's small, two-door, black vehicle. "How dare you! What's your name, sir?"

The man didn't respond, and Knight grew furious. "Are you threatening me? What do you know about my family?"

"I know that they could be in serious danger. You need to think about your family, your cute, sweet, little 7-year-old daughter."

"How do you know about my daughter?!"

"Don't be a sucker, James Knight. Your family is too vulnerable." The stranger rolled up the window and raced across the parking lot in the direction of the exit.

Knight starting walking in the direction of the car, shouting, "Stop! This minute!" His pace progressed until he was running toward the car as fast as he could. Knight was hoping to catch a glimpse of the license plate, but he was unable to see the plate number in the dimly lit lot.

Knight, breathing heavily, dialed home on his cell phone. But he got a message, "Welcome to AT&T. Message 821." He tried again. Same message. He tried to call the number on speed dial for parking lot security, but heard the same message. He ran to his car, jumped in, and skidded off in the direction of home, hoping that he'd discover better phone coverage on the way. When he heard the same message on the highway, he pulled over and looked for a phone booth. He placed the necessary money into the slot and called his wife.

"Hey James. Are you getting my texts?"

"Nancy! Is Bethany okay?" he asked hurriedly, breathing heavily.

"She's fine. What's the matter?"

"Are you sure everything's fine? When was the last time you checked on her?"

"She's right here coloring. What makes you think something could be the matter with Bethany?"

Knight breathed a sigh of relief. "We'll talk about it when I get home."

He drove home quickly, fretting about the troubling conversation with the suspicious character in the congressional parking lot. He wondered about the events of the past two days: the blackmailing of the House speaker, the Bureau leak that threatened the president's agenda, his failed attempts at impeaching the president, the meeting with Margaret Brighton, the dead car battery, the missing cables, the broken lamp in the parking lot, the malfunctioning phone, the strange congressional aid with the black wool cap – it was all too eerie to be believable. He skidded to a stop in his garage and hopped out of his car as the garage door closed noisily behind him.

Nancy met him at the door that led from the garage into the kitchen. She had their daughter Bethany at her side. "What's wrong?" she asked without even greeting him.

He looked at his 7-year-old daughter, picked her up, and looked directly into her eyes. "Are you okay, my little princess?"

"I'm fine," she said in a whiny voice, wondering why Daddy was acting so weird. "Mommy said I could stay up until you got home."

He looked at Nancy with bewilderment in his eyes. "I had an unusual encounter in the parking lot with a suspicious man who helped me recharge my dead battery."

"Your battery died?"

"And I didn't leave any lights on inside. I checked. Did you take my battery cables out of my car?"

"No. Why would I do that?"

"Did you see anything suspicious today?"

"I don't think so."

He hugged and kissed his daughter on the cheek and then turned his gaze to Nancy.

"Daddy, Daddy," his daughter interrupted. "I have something for you."

Nancy added, "She brought something home for you from school today. She's been talking about it all day. She wouldn't tell me what it was. She said it was a surprise."

Mr. Knight put his daughter down and asked, "Have you seen a fellow with a dark mustache and a pale complexion walking around our house or anything like that?" He walked toward the front window and peeked through it into the front yard. The damp side-walk was evidence of a recent drizzle and the reflection of the street lamp overhead sparkled in the sporadic puddles. The dimly lit road was empty.

"No. Who was it?"

"I don't know."

"Here Daddy, here," she tugged at his pants and held her gift into the air with a broad smile on her face.

James looked down and smiled at his precious daughter's gift. She was full of pride at the piece of candy she extended to him.

"A lollipop. Thank you, honey." He took the candy and winked at his wife. "How thoughtful."

Nancy knelt down and asked their girl, "Where did you get that, honey?"

"A teacher at school gave one just to me, plus one for you, Daddy. It's a surprise!"

"A teacher at school?" Mrs. Knight's smile faded to a frown. She found that strange since the teachers at the private Christian school would never single out a student and give them candy.

James Knight bent down to look his daughter in the eye. "Who?" He looked closely at the wrapped cherry lollipop as if he were looking at some kind of poisonous insect or a miniature bomb that would blow up any second.

Her daughter looked puzzled. "Don't you like it?"

"Who gave this to you?" her mother said.

"The nice man with a mustache in front of the school. He said he was a new teacher."

"Oh God!" James picked his daughter up in his arms and his wife looked on in horror. "Did you eat that lollipop he gave you?"

"Yes. It was cherry." Her father felt her pulse and looked into her eyes. "He said that you would be surprised if I gave it to you as a special gift."

He carried her to the car as his wife followed close behind. "Where are you going, James? You're scaring us."

"To the E.R."

Fear filled Nancy's eyes as she watched her husband frantically reach into his pocket for his keys. "James, I'll call the principal and see if there were any new teachers at the school today that fit his description."

"Call on the way," he told her. "Get Derek and follow in the other car."

The physician's wrinkled green surgical scrubs and sweaty brow emanated exhaustion. It was the end of an 18-hour shift, and he was anxious to hit the sack. He studied a clipboard with the lab results affixed. The Knights' daughter slept in a gurney twice as long as she was. James Knight sat in a chair holding his sleeping 6-year-old son as his wife caressed their daughter's cheek with her fingers.

"Well, everything looks fine," the physician informed them halfway through a weary sigh. "We certainly would've picked up on it if she'd ingested anything toxic. She probably would have some symptoms by now."

"You're sure?" Nancy responded in a worrisome tone.

"She's in perfect health, as far as we can see." The physician reached down with a gloved hand and picked the lollipop up off of a napkin on the table. "Since you're a congressman, I suppose the FBI would do a better job of investigating this than the local police." As the physician held the lollipop by the stick, a piece of white paper could be seen protruding from the edge of the wrapper. "What's this?"

He laid it down, pulled out the white piece of paper, and read it, "Don't be a sucker."

"We've got all the Utah and most of the Dakota reps on board," Montana Representative Allen Chandler said with a smile as he plopped into his chair next to Knight. Besides him were three other junior reps. James Knight appeared oblivious to the announcement as he gathered his papers and put them in his briefcase after a committee hearing.

"I expected you to be more enthusiastic than that. James, are you okay?"

"Uh, yeah. Sorry." Knight sighed heavily and didn't make eye contact. "We've had some threats – my family, that is."

"Threats?"

"It's probably nothing. Just someone trying to intimidate me into backing off on the push for investigations into Brighton." Knight shook his head back and forth, and then looked up into the eyes of the men who sat before him. "Please pray for us, especially for my wife. I sent her away with the kids for a while and she's not taking it too well."

"What happened?"

"Oh, it's a long story and I'd rather not talk about it right now." Knight turned to leave and ran right into Representative John Dobson.

"We've got Stevenson and Kingley from Colorado on board," Dobson vigorously announced.

Knight's eyebrows raised and he looked back at Chandler. This was a surprise announcement indeed. Stevenson and Kingley were not known to be authentic conservatives; they voted party line Republican and had no devotion whatsoever to conservative ideals.

"On board with what?" Chandler asked for clarification.

"Our push for impeachment! They're with us."

"That's good news indeed." Knight headed out of the room with the others following close behind. "How'd you manage that?"

"Their governor's been pushing them hard. You know Colorado's a member of the Coalition."

"Barely," Knight commented. "What is the Coalition anyway? I'm not that impressed yet."

"You're not impressed? Why?"

"It's a TEA Party of state leaders. All talk."

"What do you mean?" John Dobson was perplexed. "Some of them have banned abortion already."

"On paper. I've spoken to their leaders, John. They have no intention of enforcing it if the judiciary rules against it. They naively think that their abortion/euthanasia ban will make it to the Supreme Court and that the Court will overrule *Roe* and *A.M.A.*, but that's not going to happen. When they finally arrest an abortionist, then I'll be impressed."

As Knight made his way into a stairwell, Montana Representative Bo Bennett joined their entourage. "Washington State's almost unanimous. Ninety percent of them are with us!"

Knight was taken aback. He never would have guessed that 90% of Washington State's reps would join his call for impeachment. "Wow!"

"Brighton's mistake was arresting Governors Cropp and Adams," Bennett informed them. "That was the last straw for Washington State's leadership. That and Brighton killin' her husband on TV."

Knight turned and smiled. "They can't ignore us now."

"Theo Jefferson." The Speaker of the House, Troy McAvery, invited the elderly senior Democrat to the microphone.

When Jefferson reached the microphone, he said something that no one expected. "I'd like to invite the honorable representative from Wyoming, James Knight, to speak on my clock. James?"

The Democrats gasped in horror as James Knight made his way to the microphone beside Theo Jefferson. A rumble of applause came from the religious conservatives in the room as the progressive Dems recoiled.

"The list of victims in the wake of this administration continues to grow," Knight said as whispers of disapproval rose in the assembly. "Her armed squads assault innocent Americans every single day. It's one thing to disagree with the governors and legislatures of Texas and South Carolina and try to persuade them to change their point of view, but to raid and arrest them, to hold them without a charge, without trial, without bail, and erect a military dictatorship in their stead, that's another thing entirely. FBI SWAT and ATF troopers at this moment raid and pillage from house to house, attempting to deprive citizens of their lawful property, shooting or imprisoning resisters…"

The South Carolina and Texas reps began to cheer wildly as liberals protested. Troy McAvery was stumped. Had Theo Jefferson gone crazy? Was he so far gone that he would sit idly by and let James Knight say such things on his time clock? McAvery didn't know what to do. If he cut Knight off, Knight might carry through on his promise to expose McAvery's infidelities. He didn't figure that Knight had the votes for impeachment, so he thought it safest to let him get it off his chest.

"She murdered her husband on television, for God's sake! A senior FBI agent has testified that she lied about the explosion that killed President Fitzgerald, a fact he retracted only after he was offered a quarter million dollars a year. If he lied from the get-go, tell me, why was he rewarded for it? Where's our sense of justice? States are debating secession at this moment, while we pretend all is well. Our country's on the verge of an armed revolution and this Congress is asleep at the wheel…"

McAvery wasn't prepared for this new level of abrasive, divisive speech to which Knight was resorting. When a few liberals vigorously shouted their disapproval from the floor of the House, McAvery picked up his gavel and prepared to interrupt, but his cell phone vibrated and distracted him. He glanced at the caller identification and answered it hurriedly, turning his back to the assembly to converse with the caller in anxious whispers.

"If the loss of our constitutional freedoms is the cost of bipartisan unity, for God's sake, let's be disunited and let as many as possible get on the right side of this conflict while we still have the opportunity. I implore all lovers of liberty in this assembly, we must impeach this president and work to heal the wounds she's inflicted on our people before we lose our country to violence and strife."

Chattering rose in the assembly like a growing hum of a huge swarm of bees that were rapidly approaching from a distance, preparing to launch an attack upon the uninvited messenger. Some representatives were typing on their laptops and making frantic calls on their cell phones. Millions of Americans tuned into C-Span to watch these events unfold, prompted by the phone calls and text messages of friends and family.

Troy McAvery closed his cell phone with a slap, turned and shouted into the microphone on his podium, "James Knight, you're out of order! Take your seat, now!"

"He's on my clock," Theo Jefferson announced.

"I don't care! He's espousing treason!"

"Mr. McAvery," Knight turned and said calmly, "I think you need to keep your peace, unless you wish this distinguished assembly to know exactly *why* you are refusing to allow discussion of impeachment."

"Enough!" growled McAvery furiously. The assembly curiously grew quiet, craving for more details of Knight's implied allegation.

"I think this country would be very interested in knowing *why* you have so diligently impeded all of the legitimate requests, some bipartisan, for an impeachment discussion and debate. Pastors, sheriffs, statesmen, fathers, and mothers have been terrorized, kidnapped, and forced into the NEA's tolerance classes. Still you won't listen. Barry Friar's wife was shot through the head while carrying her infant and you shut us down. Now, the governors, cabinets, and many legislators of Texas and South Carolina are being held without charge and denied their constitutional right to trial by jury and still you impede the fulfillment of our constitutional duties to investigate—"

"Enough!" McAvery shouted, thumping his gavel against his podium.

"Tell us, Mr. McAvery, why are you so reluctant to—"

"Quiet!" shouted McAvery, now trembling, fearful of Knight's courage. If eyes were lasers, McAvery would have incinerated him. He glared at Knight, his face beet-red, voice shaking, and hands trembling with poorly concealed rage. "Shut your mouth, you! This minute!"

Knight ignored him, turned, and passionately implored the assembly, "I beg of you in the name of Jesus to join me in appointing independent investigators to look into this administration's abuses of executive powers. Join me in condemning these Gestapo tactics on American citizens and let's begin a discussion of Margaret Brighton's impeachment." He had to practically scream to be heard over Troy McAvery's orders from the microphone to return to his seat or be ushered from the assembly in contempt of Congress. The assembly let out repeated gasps as the confrontation unfolded, with McAvery screaming at Knight in the microphone, Jefferson urging the House speaker to settle down, and Knight passionately pleading for Congress to immediately push for investigation and impeachment on the House floor.

"Shut your mouth, you impetuous fool!" shouted McAvery into the microphone, clearly losing control of his emotions. He appeared so distraught that he began to embarrass his Democratic colleagues in the House, as well as those watching the events on national television.

"This is a partisan witch hunt!" the minority leader Ken McGinnis stood and shouted, earning the reproofs of the reps sympathetic with Knight. "This is hate speech! It's illegal!"

"The tyrant's last frontier," said Knight calmly with a pointing finger, "is the mind of a free man." He tapped his forehead. "Man has the natural right to think freely and the constitutional right to speak his mind." Knight unfolded a letter from his top pocket, and said, "According to a Children's Services memo in an internal e-mail in my district, the White House has given explicit instructions to social workers that if parents are against abortion or homosexuality, or if they harbor a strong belief in the Bible, those facts can be grounds to remove children from their homes. Religious home-schooling is a factor that this memo specifically mentions that can be used to remove children." He waved the memo above his head. "I thought Congress shall make no law respecting an establishment of religion, nor prohibiting the free exercise thereof. Nor shall we abridge the freedom of speech and the right of the people to peaceably assemble. And the president shall make no law, period! In our separation of powers, Congress is the law-making body. This is tyranny!" He waved the paper in the air.

A few slurred shouts and murmurings were raised throughout the assembly with some congressmen and women even shouting at each other across the aisles. Knight looked back at the House speaker, who turned his gaze to the floor, fearful to flex his authority further to suppress Knight for fear of Knight's retaliation.

"Why don't you, Mr. McGinnis," - Knight turned to the liberal icon, and then back to the McAvery - "Mr. Speaker, send Brighton and her minions to come and arrest me, right here, right now? Come arrest me! I meet almost every one of her criteria."

The uneasiness in the room increased as Knight glared at McGinnis and dared him, "Have her arrest me for my free speech like she's arrested hundreds of ministers and abortion protesters. Have her troops raid my office like they raided Sheriff Randall Woods and Governor Henry Adams' offices. Have her steal my children"- he paused, his voice choking with emotion - "like she has so many other little boys and girls, removing them from their parents for no other reason than that their parents harbor religious beliefs that the president despises. Have her send the tanks to silence my protest like she silenced the peaceful assembly in Bozeman, where FBI troops killed and maimed peaceful protesters. Have her commit me to a psychiatric institution and to NEA brainwashing like she did Pastor Henderson in Auburn. Have her send the FBI and the ATF to raid my house like she raided Barry Friar's home, slaughtering his family and friends who were guilty of nothing other than defending themselves from a bunch of camouflaged soldiers who charged them with automatic weapons while they were having a barbecue. I have guns, too – lots of them! And I'm not turning mine in!"

Those comments caused a roar of chaotic shouts from the floor of the House.

"Randy Woods was a racist!"

"Barry Friar was a child molester!"

"They were harboring a terrorist!"

"Clinics have been bombed!"

"They were shooting illegal weapons!"

"Governor Adams was conspiring to kill American troops!"

"That's treason!"

The rebuttals were indiscernible when proclaimed all at once. Knight raised his hands as the House speaker slammed his gavel down a few times.

Theo Jefferson, trembling from adrenaline as he faced his own Gethsemane moment, moved close to Knight's microphone. "He's speaking on my clock. I demand respect!" This silenced some of the disorder.

McAvery couldn't make sense of the famed liberal's defense of James Knight's traitorous rhetoric. "Mr. Jefferson, do you agree with Mr. Knight?"

Theo Jefferson's mouth went dry. He certainly wouldn't have been as harsh as James Knight. He could not vouch for all of his accusations. He took a deep breath and closed his eyes, fully aware that his days as a congressman were soon drawing to a close for daring to let Knight issue such rebukes on his time. He imagined his son behind bars, and wondered if he would be proud of him. His tired eyes met Knight's, and Knight nodded confidently at him. Jefferson sighed and turned back to the McAvery and answered his question confidently: "Yes." The whispers in the House rose again to a small roar.

James Knight raised his hands and spoke directly into the microphone to be heard above the tsunami of chatter. "Quiet! I still have the floor…"

"Oh no you don't," McAvery mumbled under his breath. He reached down and pushed a button underneath the podium. "You asked for it, James Knight." Two guards from the foyer came rushing to the front of the House as its members erupted in chaos and accusations.

The guard nearest Knight tapped him on the shoulder. "My admonitions have come to an end," James Knight calmly informed the assembly. He turned to follow the guard down the aisle. "I implore you," he lifted up his voice in earnest as he walked, "let us defend our constitutional republic from this tyranny."

"We'll be voting on your censure long before we vote on the president's impeachment," the House speaker barked.

"Yes!" proclaimed Todd Hamilton as he watched the proceeding on C-span in his office. "Finally!" He knew he could not safely arrest a Congressman for hate speech unless he'd been censured before Congress. Now he could make the president happy and safely remove this thorn from her side under her hate speech EOs.

As Knight was being led down the aisle, hedged in from the front and the rear by congressional guards, the elderly Democrat, Theo Jefferson, returned to the microphone, shouting to be heard over the murmurings and whispers that filled the building. "Call to order! It is inappropriate for the House speaker to make proposals for a censure vote as long as I still have the floor, which I do for another 30 seconds."

"He's right!" some shouted.

"And I'd like to use that time to defend James Knight's proposals. I second Knight's valiant call for impeachment proceedings!"

The assembly erupted in a roar of cheers and jeers. "Todd Hamilton and Victor Meyers have shown themselves suspiciously recalcitrant to Congress' calls to have them provide the details of the Columbus, Ohio, investigation," Jefferson continued, "and I'm suspicious of the president's claim that those records were completely destroyed in the Billings explosion. They must answer for their incompetence." Dozens of sympathetic reps stood up to agree to the call for impeachment hearings and independent investigations as Troy McAvery tried to gain control of the House by slamming his gavel against the podium.

"We will have order in the House! We will vote on no such thing, not as long as I am the Speaker of the House."

A well-composed, tall Republican gentleman in the front stood and waved to gain the attention of the assembly. "As the majority whip, I make a motion to dismiss Troy McAvery as House speaker!" The deep voice and broad, muscular frame of this usually quiet, retired Marine Corps captain from Iowa demanded respect.

The congressmen and women in the House almost unanimously erupted in applause and shouts of affirmations. The minority Democrats would benefit from Republican Speaker McAvery's ousting because McAvery was a top Republican contender for future executive leadership, and toppling him increased the likelihood that the Democrats would keep control of the White House. In addition, the majority whip, Rich Faulkner, was almost as liberal as McAvery. They had little to fear from Faulkner. The Republicans benefited from McAvery's removal because he was showing himself to be vulnerable in the face of Knight's accusations and the religious conservatives' uprising, whose strength was growing in the House.

"Rich?" McAvery was stunned at the proposal of the majority whip, who was also his friend and fellow liberal Republican. "Why?" Rich Faulkner didn't need to answer. McAvery knew. The Republicans were betraying their leader in the House. McAvery had become a liability, and the GOP was throwing him under the bus.

"That's it!" Representative Alan Chandler turned, smiling, to shake one of the applauding hands of Derek Williams.

"I think that Troy McAvery," said Rich Faulkner, "has shown himself to be suspiciously recalcitrant to the pleadings of both the Democratic and Republican calls for investigations and impeachment proceedings."

"You are out of order, Mr. Faulkner!" McAvery aimed an index finger at the GOP's second-in-command in the House.

"Mr. McAvery," Faulkner calmly said, "would you like us to bring James Knight back here and have him testify under oath to the details of his charge of your indiscretion?"

That word *indiscretion* stung him. "No, no," said McAvery, softening his tone and shrinking from the microphone. "That won't be necessary."

A long moment passed, pregnant with mystery and tension, as McAvery tried to regain his composure and formulate a response. McAvery gripped the podium mercilessly and looked down, straining to silence his pained conscience as it flogged his mind and body with adrenaline and fatigue simultaneously.

"Mr. McAvery," Faulkner repeated, "should we call for James Knight?" "Don't bother." McAvery's voice was now resigned and calm. He kept his gaze fixed on the podium. "Don't even bother with voting." After an uneasy moment, he looked up at the majority whip with a downcast, melancholy smirk. "I'll put in my resignation immediately."

He turned to walk off the stage as the assembly watched in silence. His head hung in shame. He walked slowly toward an exit that was already bustling with media personnel shouting out their questions as he approached.

"Mr. Speaker!"

"Mr. McAvery!"

The reporters clamored with their microphones for answers to their spontaneous questions. McAvery tried to dodge the microphones and squinted through the bright camera lights all around him.

One reporter obstructed his path and lifted a microphone to his face. The camera over her shoulder focused his lens on McAvery's gloomy frown. "How do you respond, Mr. Speaker, to James Knight's charges of indiscretion?"

McAvery's only response to the vigorous inquiry was the statement all too common in the District of Columbia when a politician was exposed for sexual infidelity. It was a sad statement that was frequently too little and too late to affect the predictable outcome of the neglected marriage headed for the cliff of divorce, doomed to crash against the rocks of hurtful words and custody disputes.

"I need to spend some time with my family."

"I regret that they never got to the censure vote that Speaker McAvery proposed." Cameron gripped his pulpit in front of a media-pundit-packed audience on the edge of their seats in the White House pressroom. "Mr. Knight has drawn his battle lines so far to the right that no representative in his or her right mind would stand with him for fear of being charged with hate crimes. It's a politically motivated *witch-hunt*. A few anti-choice religious zealots are trying to hold Congress hostage with their threats and name-calling. James Knight has even told some of his esteemed colleagues that they were going to burn in hell," he said amidst disbelieving gasps throughout the building. Cameron snickered. "That's the kind of thing Congress has had to deal with in recent days from the right-wing extremists. They are hysterical in their war against reproductive choice, against reasonable gun control, and against equal rights for our GLBT citizens. I'm confident that the House majority will come to its senses and hold these fanatics accountable. Nothing will come of this impeachment effort. The loss of Troy McAvery to the witch hunters is unfortunate, but they've not found a more sympathetic leader in Rich Faulkner, I'll tell you that." The room full of journalists nodded and grunted in affirmation. "As in all of James Knight's previous impeachment efforts, there's nothing even worthy of investigation. It's a witch hunt and the new Speaker of the House knows it." He pointed to a raised hand on the first row.

"What does the president have to say about the raids and the deaths in Texas, South Carolina, and Montana?" asked the FOX news correspondent. As the question was asked, Cameron reminded himself, *Witch-hunt – say that again with every response. Witch-hunt…*

"She's doing the best she can to peacefully resolve conflicts, but it's very difficult with so many state and national leaders, like Governor Boswell and Congressman Knight, defying federal law and instigating open rebellion. American soldiers and federal agents are being treated with disrespect and even violence in some of these insubordinate states. Their witch hunt is going to backfire on them because most Americans are fed up with their religious extremism." *Oooh, that was good,* Cameron thought with self-adulation, mentally patting himself on the back.

"What are the president's views on China's transformation?" another asked. "China's leadership certainly hasn't been bashful about their negative views of President Brighton's domestic agenda and the deaths and arrests that have resulted from her anti-terrorist proposals."

Cameron laughed, then scratched his brow and sighed through a shiny, practiced grin. "The president is very excited about China's venture into democracy. Our country walked the same road almost 250 years ago and we've been the light of democracy throughout the world ever since. The president's campaigned for maintaining favored trade status with China throughout her career. Of course, she's disappointed with the unprovoked attacks upon her character, as all Americans are offended with some of the statements that Chinese officials have made. What can you say?" He raised his palms toward the ceiling with a curious shrug as if commenting on the incorrigible behavior of an unpredictable 3-year-old. "We're a diverse country that has learned the hard way to be tolerant of others in this grand melting pot. At the beginning of our nation's history, I suppose we were a little cocky and intolerant at times, and so I shouldn't be too critical of the same immaturity found in other nations attempting to imitate our experiment in democracy. The president is sending a special envoy to China this week to discuss our differences and secure trade relations with the new government." His broad smile emanated confidence throughout the room during his well-rehearsed responses.

"Good job, Cameron," the president said as she applauded from the couch where she sat alone in the large, White House living room.

"Your euthanasia executive order is still hurting you badly in the polls." Dena Halluci, as well as everyone else in the room, knew it was the mercy killing of her husband that had damaged her in the polls more so than her euthanasia EO, but Dena thought that this was a more palatable way to break the news. "This morning, the streets of Tallahassee were teeming with 75,000 anti-euthanasia marchers, half of them over the age of 60."

"I heard about that."

"The media's coverage is dismal. Picture gray-haired folks with canes or wheelchairs as far as the eye could see, crying out in unison, 'Thou shalt not kill.' Little kids holding pictures of their grandparents—"

"Any violence?"

Dena shook her head. "This wasn't that kind of crowd. One policeman did accidentally knock over a gray-haired mother of 12 and grandmother of 22, who suffered a broken hip. Imagine a policeman with a helmet and riot stick standing over a sobbing gray-haired lady with glasses taped in the middle, holding a sign that says, 'Euthanasia is elderly abuse.'"

Brighton shook her head in disbelief. "My karma is incredulous," she mumbled.

"These polls are the worst we've seen so far." Dena patted a stack of newspapers beside her. "According to a CNN/Time poll that came out this morning, your approval rating has dropped to 16 percent. It can't all be chalked up to our euthanasia initiatives either. Half of the Americans polled condemn the arrest and incarceration of the governors and cabinets of Texas and South Carolina. One-third thought that states had the right to resist the federal government's attempt to disarm and deprive citizens of their free speech rights."

"We can't give up," the president chirped, trying to remain optimistic. "It's always darkest before the dawn. Most of the rotten apples in Congress are sure to be replaced in this year's election."

"You don't understand, Madam President," Hamilton dared to interject. "Congress' resistance is the direct result of the opposition they're getting from their constituents. Resisters previously at odds with each other are uniting and the cost of our plan is rising."

"Is there anything in my speech or demeanor, Mr. Hamilton," the president responded curtly, "that would lead you to believe that I'm any less willing to pay that cost today than I was yesterday?" She sat erect behind the desk in the Oval Office and paused as if waiting for an answer to her obviously rhetorical question.

Hamilton leaned back in his chair and sighed deeply. He was done with trying to convince this president to slow down the pursuit of her agenda.

It was now the DOJ director's opportunity to step up to the plate and make their case. "Let's look at the landscape, Madam President.

The juries are refusing to convict people of hate speech charges, especially in the Bible Belt and in the Rocky Mountain states. State and local authorities are resisting and are wildly popular for it. It's time to admit that we've over-reached. We thought the terrorist attacks would make it easier for us, but we can't plug all the holes in the dam. Too many Americans prefer their guns and Bibles to tolerance and security. The ATF's attempts at gun confiscation have been an utter disaster."

"Not so fast," ATF Director Bill Erdman interjected.

"I thought you told me that we've had some success," the president said, glancing at Erdman.

"Yes, we have."

"A hundred million dollars for 10,000 guns at the cost of 60 deaths is not success by any standard," the FBI director opined. "Not to mention the cost of incarcerating the thousands we've arrested for gun violations."

"Wait a minute! Most of those deaths are in martial law zones or in the Coalition states," Erdman protested Hamilton's criticism.

"At this rate, we'd have to spend the wealth of the world to get half of the nation's guns," Hamilton rebutted. "Our present dilemma isn't any fault of your own, Bill. Heaven knows you've done the best you could with the hand you were dealt. But we have dozens of sieges all over the south and northwest. Citizens are holed up in their homes, shooting it out with military and police, making more allies of their neighbors every single day they resist."

"What do you propose we do?" the president barked. "Let the traitors out of jail and turn their states back over to them? Let everybody keep their assault rifles? Is that what the United States Armed Forces do when the going gets tough? We give up and turn the helm of the ship back over to the terrorists?"

"No," Dena Halluci responded to the president's rhetorical question. "We get more aggressive with the violators." She flashed up the front page of the Lincoln Herald for all to see. The lead article read, "82 % of Nebraskans Refuse to Turn In Guns." She tapped the photo of a hillbilly holding a military-style assault rifle. "The citizens of Nebraska are buying *more* guns with our confiscation program. If we back down in these troubled areas, we'll have ten times the level of insubordination."

"Sometimes race car drivers have to slow down around the turn as a means to complete the race," Hamilton argued. "We're going too fast and that's just going to launch us into the stands and push us back decades."

"Gentlemen!" the president blurted out. "Our strength has not failed us! We've not even begun to flex our military might. It's our lack of commitment to our agenda that is our biggest problem."

"We're committed," Vic Meyers assured her as the others nodded, "but as Hamilton said, you need to be aware that the cost is rising. If we persist without relenting at all, there will be more blood spilled, Madam President, and many more uprisings. We've got a half a dozen state legislatures hoisting the Texas flag over their own statehouse as they debate secession."

"Some of those states are nuclear-armed, Madam President," Department of Homeland Security Director Tom Davis added. "We are seeing the strongest secession movements since the 1880's."

"I'm aware of that, Tom, but to conquer our crisis like Abraham Lincoln conquered the crisis of secession during his administration, we must be willing to resort to Lincoln's heavy-handed remedies. Rather than retreat when challenged, we must raise the stakes – we have the winning hand. We don't fold with a royal flush. We've got to make resistance more costly. We're going to increase the severity of the disincentive for rebelling."

After an uneasy pause, Hamilton asked, "How?"

"*Overwhelming* force. We're going to more aggressively inter- rogate religiously-motivated enemy combatants."

Chairman of the Joint Chiefs of Staff General Green spoke up to protest the president's aggression. "This is not Israel, Saudi Arabia, or a UN military zone, Madam President. We don't torture reli- giously motivated peaceful protesters. Endorsing secession doesn't make a citizen an enemy combatant."

"Well, maybe it should!" Dena Halluci barked.

General Green ignored the interruption. "Even the military has judicial oversight, Madam President, especially within our borders. Judges have shown themselves willing to apply constitutional restraint to federal overreaches."

"Well, then we'll bring the UN in to do the dirty work, if we must!" The president thumped her fists against her desk. "I know General Urlich won't placate our enemies. We will implement my executive orders and kill anybody who gets in the way. Strategies must be adjusted in times of war, and make no mistake, we are at war! And we *will* win it!"

Chapter 27

Helena, Montana

"Hello, Jeff." David walked up to a scruffy-looking camper sitting outside his RV at the campsite just outside Helena. "Can I borrow your phone again?"

"Sure, Mr. Jameson." The elderly man handed David his bulky cell phone and David thanked him. He felt more comfortable making phone calls from older cell phones, since they were less likely to carry programs and internal software that the FBI could exploit, and the sound quality was often poor, making voice recognition technology useless.

David dialed the memorized numbers as he walked around to the other side of the RV and leaned against it. He tipped his faded green John Deere cap lower over his eyes.

After three rings, an older woman picked up. "Yellow?" came the slurred, toothless greeting from the elderly Mrs. Brawn.

"Hello," David spoke in a deep, gruff voice. "Is Bob there?"

"Just a minute." She laid the phone down and hollered across the house. "Bob, ya got a phone call." David listened intently for any young voices in the background, for any glimmer of hope that his wife and daughters had arrived.

"Hello?"

"Hey, Bob. It's me again. Have they arrived yet?"

"Not yet."

David sighed heavily and his head hung low.

Mr. Brawn sensed his anxiety. "Do you want me to call you when they get here?"

"No, no," David interrupted. "I'll call you in a day or so. Thank you so much for stepping up to the plate for me."

"Don't mention it."

"Please keep this a secret and keep them in your prayers."

"I will."

David slid down the side of the RV and set the phone on the ground. He dropped his head into his hands and the fears began to assault him again, robbing him of peace. He constantly cast his cares upon the Lord, entrusting his wife and daughters to the Father's keeping, but inside his mind the battle was constantly raging. Fret and anxiety constantly lured him from his place of faith and peace and tempted him to despair and doubt God.

"God, I trust you to keep them safe. Save Darlene and my daughters from any suffering that does not glorify Your name."

San Antonio, Texas

"Stay here," the camouflage-clad, African-American soldier coldly ordered the pale woman in a worn-out hospital gown. He turned and left her in a small four by six cell with a chair in one corner and a mirror on the wall. An initial psychological assessment determined Darlene Jameson to be susceptible to panic attacks and they intentionally left her in the extremely small room to try to induce claustrophobia.

She glanced at the mirror, knowing that agents dedicated to intensifying her misery were studying her and intricately conspiring against her on the other side.

In the first few days after her arrest, Darlene Jameson cried out all the tears she had. She thought that being removed from her children would be the hardest cross to carry, but that theory had only begun to be tested. Her head was shaved and her personal items removed. She was placed in a hospital gown that had a missing tie over the lower back, exposing her buttocks to everyone. She'd been treated with the utmost disgust and scorn. As she gazed into the mirror, she was shocked at how thin she'd become. She had tried so hard to lose those 30 pounds that three children packed on her hips. Now she was as skinny as when she was a high school senior.

Having her children taken from her was acutely painful. She had two choices: not trust the Lord with their welfare and live in fear and doubt, or trust the Lord and receive the peace that He promises to those who trust Him. God *always* keeps His promises, so if the promise of peace isn't realized, it's because we haven't met the conditions. She frequently meditated on Scriptures such as "Through faith and patience we inherit the promises." She must not give up. She must embrace her cross, arming herself with a mind to suffer: "Forasmuch as Christ has suffered in the flesh, arm yourselves likewise with the same mind, for he that has suffered in the flesh has ceased from sin." A mind to suffer was her weapon against the enemy. She was confident that the Lord was pleased with her, and that He would never leave her or forsake her. When she totally surrendered the care of her children to the Father of the fatherless and her body to her tormenters, her storm of worry calmed and was replaced with a soothing confidence that all would turn out well.

However, the two weeks she'd been on a starvation diet under intense interrogation with over 15 hours of intermittent sensory deprivation every day was taking its toll. She was growing mentally numb. Under this type of torture, she had both hands cuffed to the arms of a chair, earmuffs were fastened around her head, and she was blindfolded. With the hypnotic medication injections they were giving her, ten minutes seemed like an hour, and an hour of solitary confinement seemed like a week. All she could do was cry and pray, try to settle her pounding heart and keep her thoughts coherent.

Her desire to see her children again kept her sane. She knew that if she told the FBI the truth, she'd never see her children again. The truth is that she shared her husband's moral and political views. The truth is that she knew that her husband had directed her through code words to seek shelter at Bob Brawn's old farmhouse just south of Toledo, and that is probably where he intended to meet her. But she couldn't tell them that.

On the way to Texas, David warned her about the possibility of being arrested and interrogated, but she never thought that the feds would be so cruel. She didn't know how much her mind and body

could take. She was beginning to have visual and auditory hallucinations. She thought that she could feel her children touch her arms
or legs. She wondered if she was going mad. If that happened, she'd
be locked in an institution and *never* get to see her family again.
She had to bring every thought captive to obedience to Christ or the
demons would lure her from her black world of sanity into the vivid
rainbow world of hallucinations and madness. She recited every
Scripture she could recall and sang every song she could remember
thousands of times it seemed. "God has not given us a spirit of fear,"
she reminded herself, "but of love, of power, and a sound mind."
Struggling with the fear of what would come next was now the most
troubling temptation. She constantly threw herself on the Lord for
His mercy and strength, knowing that God in His love would never
give her more than she could bear.

The small cell door opened suddenly and in burst a man in a
suit with a black tie. Darlene jolted and then quickly regained her
composure.

"Can I have something to drink please?"

"Sit down!" he bluntly ordered her without even acknowledging
her question.

Darlene walked over to the chair against the wall and seated
herself as modestly as her short hospital gown allowed her. He stood
across from her.

"How long have you been here, Mrs. Jameson?"

She stuttered the words, "I, I don't know for sure. A month?"

"It's been six days," the agent responded coldly, "and we can
keep going like this for months, for years." It had actually been two
weeks since Darlene Jameson had been brought into his charge, but
he wanted to twist her sense of reality.

At hearing those words, Darlene began to sob, but no tears came
out. The FBI physicians assigned to her made sure that she teetered
on the edge of dehydration in order to weaken her resolve. Dizziness
came upon her, and she tried to subdue her erratic emotions in order
to maintain consciousness. "God will never leave me," she heaved
the words as she tried to fight off the panic attack she felt coming on.
"God will never leave me. God will never leave me..." She repeated
the whisper over and over again between anxious breaths.

"What?" The agent mocked her with a cock-eyed grin.

Darlene took a deep breath and uttered, "Yea, though I walk through the valley of death, I will fear no evil, for Thou art with..."

"What?!" The agent put his head back and laughed as she continued to offer proclamations of faith in the midst of the emotional flogging he was giving her. "You have got to be kidding me!" He dropped to one knee to get eye level with her. "We know you're hiding the truth from us." He searched her eyes. "We'll find the truth inside that brain of yours. How much you have to suffer between now and then is completely up to you. It's your choice."

She stared into his eyes. "I've told you the truth," she said as softly and sincerely as she could, "and I will not lie to ease my suffering. He wasn't involved in any bombing. You told me I could go home and be with my children if I told you the truth."

"Your home," the agent shouted, "will be the dark hell hole in which I can bury you indefinitely if you don't cooperate! You will long for the fiery comforts of hell before I'm done."

She looked in the mirror and thought that she saw two agents in the reflection. She realized that her mind was playing tricks on her. She recalled the encouraging words of Richard Wurmbrand, *Have no fear.*

She took a deep breath and turned her attention to the agent who studied her. "I'm an American citizen and I have rights."

"You have a right to tell me the truth – that's it! If you want to see your children, just tell me the truth. Tell me that your husband planned and blew up the Columbus Civic Center. Tell me that you justify violence against abortionists and gays. Tell me that he's urged the Governor of Texas to secede and kill American soldiers. Tell me where David Jameson is hiding."

"I want to speak to a lawyer."

"I am your lawyer!" He drew near to her and she cowered with his heightened volume. "I am your prosecutor! I am your daddy! I am your rapist! I am your rescuer! I am your king of kings and lord of lords!"

She shivered with every proclamation. He saw her tremble and smiled. He softened his tone and put his hand on her forearm. "I'm also the only friend you have and I stand in front of the painful world that lies ahead of you on the path that you're now walking. Do you want salvation? I offer it to you on the condition that you tell me what I want to hear. Do you want your three daughters to grow up in the homes of foster parents who are church-going Christians or suspected child abusers?"

She placed her head in her hands and began to sob afresh. "Oh, my Jesus, help my girls! Help me, Jesus!"

He smacked the arm of her chair and she jolted. "Tell me what I want to know!"

"It's not working." One of the FBI superiors on the other side of the mirror could not see any change in the suspect's responses. "She's tough as leather."

"It's only been 14 days."

"The president wants results now. We need a conviction for the Columbus bombing. Now this woman's husband is the leading suspect and all of our sensors agree that she knows something. President Brighton's entire agenda, decades of hard work and hundreds of billions of dollars of investment depend on a conviction."

The inferior agent dropped his clipboard on the table and sighed. "It's only been two weeks. Everybody gives after a few weeks."

"No, not everybody. No more blindfolds and earmuffs. We need to step it up. If she's telling the truth, then for her own good we need to get to where we're going quickly and figure it out, don't we?"

"What? So now, compassion for this poor woman is causing you to move to more aggressive interrogation techniques? Oh, please, don't tease yourself."

"I've had enough of your pathetic conscience," the superior agent barked. "She's matter. That's it! Just matter. And all matter can be manipulated." He picked up the phone and tapped a number. "She wants water to drink, we'll give her water."

Darlene's body, arms, and legs were tied to a table and her head placed in a vice grip to keep her from turning her head from side to side. A black towel was placed over her face and running water was poured over the towel through a hose. Over and over they did this for minutes at a time as she coughed, gagged, and swallowed water to allow her a chance to breath, but water gradually entered her lungs. She vomited and heaved coughs as hard as she could to try and clear her lungs, but to no avail.

When her oxygen levels began to drop, as evidenced by the pulse oximetry sensor that was taped to her big toe, she would drift into unconsciousness. Then they would unlatch the table so that it would rotate in the middle; they would lower her head and raise her feet until she was upside down. They would slap her bare chest until the water drained out of her lungs and she revived. The table was then flipped again until she was upright.

"All I want is the truth, Mrs. Jameson. Did your husband blow up the Columbus Civic Center?"

"No!" she screamed between coughs.

"Who's responsible?"

"I don't know!"

"Do you justify violence against abortionists or agents of the government?"

"No! No!"

"You will tell me what I want to hear or I'll do this to your kids in front of you one at a time!"

Darlene began to hyperventilate to overcome the panic that was arresting her senses. "God help me! God help me!" she screamed. "God help me! God help me!"

Calmly, the agent smiled and moved his face to within four inches of hers, until her eyes were glued to his laser-like gaze. "Mrs. Jameson, there is no God. I offer you proof." The agent flipped the table back down till it was level, and covered the towel over her head as she struggled against the wrist ties. "I'll ask again in a couple of minutes."

He nodded at a subordinate in the corner of the room as he headed for the door. "Drown her slowly, and then revive her. I'm going to get some voltage. I'll be right back."

Notes

[1] The document that sets the framework for the secession of South Carolina from the United States of America:

THE STATE OF SOUTH CAROLINA
In the Year of Our Lord Two Thousand Twenty

A RESOLUTION affirming States' rights.

Whereas the Constitution of the State of South Carolina, declares in Article I, Section 1, that all political power is vested in and derived from the people only, therefore, they have the right at all times to modify their form of government;

Whereas Article I, Section 2, declares the citizens of South Carolina to have religious freedom;

Whereas Article I, Section 3, declares the privileges of the citizens of South Carolina shall not be abridged, nor shall any person be deprived of life, liberty, or property without due process of law, nor shall any person be denied the equal protection of the laws;

Whereas, Article I, Section 9, declares that courts shall be public, not secret, and Section 14 declares the right of a trial by jury is inviolable and shall be preserved;

Whereas Article I, Section 20, declares the right of the people to keep and bear arms shall not be infringed, and that the military power shall always be held in subordination to the civil authority;

Whereas South Carolina has asserted its sovereign power to govern itself and whose elected leaders are bound to govern lawfully and independent of any coercive foreign power or central government;

Whereas the legislature of South Carolina has the lawful and natural right to interpose itself between their people, whose freedoms and justice they are obligated to secure, and the offending power;

Whereas South Carolina entered into the contract with the United States voluntarily, and that contract has been manifestly and repeatedly violated contrary to state law and contrary to the contract of the U.S. Constitution that created the central government;

Whereas the ninth and tenth amendments of the Bill of Rights of the U.S. Constitution secures that the rights of the people of South Carolina are supreme and transcend the interests of the central government;

Resolved by the House of Representatives, the Senate concurring:

That the several States composing the United States of America are not obligated to give unlimited submission to their central government. South Carolina retains the right of self-government and whensoever the central government assumes undelegated powers, its acts are void and may be justly opposed.

That since the Constitution of the United States limits the central government to specifically enumerated powers and to prosecute specifically enumerated crimes such as treason, all acts of the central government which assume to create, define, or impose penalties or punishments other than those enumerated in the Constitution are altogether void and of no force. All of the arrests and kidnappings committed against the people of South Carolina by the federal government for reasons that are outside the federal government's lawful jurisdiction, and are inherently unlawful and prosecutable under state law.

That no power over the freedom of religion, freedom of speech, or freedom of the press has been delegated to the United States by the Constitution, therefore these powers were reserved to the States or the people. Therefore, all acts of the central government which do abridge the freedom of religion, the freedom of speech, and the freedom of the press are not law, but are altogether void and of no force, and may be justly resisted.

That any Act by the Congress of the United States, Executive Order of the President of the United States, or Judicial Order of the United States which assumes a power not delegated to the central government by the Constitution and which serves to diminish the liberty of the states or their citizens shall constitute a nullification of the relationship between South Carolina and the central government created by the Constitution of the United States – that contract which covenants the states to the central government and governs our relationship. Acts that would cause such nullification include, but are not limited to:

I. Establishing martial law or a state of emergency within one of the States without the consent of the legislature of that State.

II. Requiring involuntary servitude or governmental service other than a draft during a constitutionally declared war.

III. Surrendering any power over the citizens of South Carolina to any corporation or foreign government, such as the United Nations.

IV. Any act regarding religion or limitations on freedom of political speech, or of the press.

VI. Infringements on the right to keep and bear arms including prohibitions of type or quantity of arms or ammunition; and

That should any such Act of Congress or Executive Order or Judicial Order be put into force, all powers previously delegated to the United States of America by the Constitution for the United States shall revert to the states individually.

That a committee of conference and correspondence be appointed, which shall have as its charge to communicate this resolution to the Legislatures of the States and to the central government. This committee will ascertain whether the central government responds appropriately to these grievances. If usurpations continue contrary to this resolution, contrary to the law of the state of South Carolina or the Constitution of these United States, then the committee will submit to the Legislatures remedy that may include secession from these United States for the preservation of our natural and constitutional liberties, as is our natural, lawful, and historical right.

That we do hereby bind the central government down with the chains of the Constitution, and if the central government will not defer to law and reason, we declare our intention to pursue whatever lawful means is necessary to preserve our inalienable, God-given rights, including armed resistance and divorce.